47

Mike.

I hope you enjoy.

www.connectionsbooks.co.uk

LOMAX AND THE BIKER

THE COMPLETE TRILOGY

By

PAUL STUART

Lomax & The Biker – The Trilogy

Published by Lulu for

www.connectionsbooks.co.uk

This edition first published in July 2014.

Paul Stuart asserts his right to be identified as the author of this work under the Copyright, Designs and Patents Act 1988.

This novel is entirely a work of fiction. The names, characters and incidents portrayed within it are the work of the author's imagination. Any resemblance to actual persons, living or dead, events or localities is purely coincidental.

ISBN: 978-1-291-93539-4

All rights reserved. This book is sold subject to the condition that it shall not be resold, lent, hired out or otherwise circulated without the express prior consent of the author and/or the publisher.

ALSO BY PAUL STUART

Connections – Who Did You Sit Next To Today? (paperback).
Connections 2 – Hell Has No Fury. (paperback).
Connections 3 - That's None of Your Business. (paperback).
The Mobile and the Ring – The John Lomax Story (paperback).
The Mobile and the Ring –The John Lomax Story (hardcover).

FOREWORD

This limited edition volume has been produced by special request. It is the trilogy of John Lomax and the Biker in its entirety.

I may be a writer, but I cannot find words with sufficient meaning to adequately convey my gratitude to family and friends who have supported me throughout the process of writing these first three connections books. You know who you are and I am forever thankful.

Lomax & The Biker – The Trilogy

PART ONE - WHO DID YOU SIT NEXT TO TODAY?

Lomax & The Biker – The Trilogy

Acknowledgements

I have come across some people who don't have anybody special in their lives. They have my utmost admiration because they deal with their loneliness better than I ever could. I therefore count myself very fortunate that I have people who are special to me and I hope they know who they are.

I dedicate this book to my wife Janet, whose patience and love knows no bounds and without whom this book would not have been possible. How she tolerates me I'll never know.

My mother proof read my thesis at college. It concerned Beowulf and Geoffrey Chaucer and the old English was a nightmare for her. She would have found this work easier. My mother has always been in my corner and I am thankful for that. My father has never wavered in his support and tolerance. He has been what a father should be and much more besides.

I cannot express how much all three have done for me and how much they mean.

I also thank friends and family who have supported my writing and bought my earlier books, as well as everybody else whose names I cannot know.

John Lomax discovers that the only way to keep a secret is to never tell a living soul.

It's the only real way to guarantee anything.

But it has a price.

That price is isolation, loneliness and silence.

Isolation is frightening and loneliness is insidious.

But silence is different. It encompasses isolation and loneliness. It is not quiet because it has a shattering noise all of its own and it gets into your very being.

Lomax & The Biker – The Trilogy

– 1 –

The weekend had been a complete failure. She had been tetchy and disagreeable throughout. Whatever he had tried to do or say made no difference; she was, for some reason, disgruntled and he could not change it. Try as he might, and he really had tried very hard, nothing softened her mood. Saturday morning breakfast in bed with the paper, flowers, a good meal and fine wine at their favourite restaurant, a gentle Sunday morning stroll with lunch at the village pub, even a lazy Sunday afternoon by the open fireside. None of these things had brought about one iota of change in her.

Something was bothering Karen and for the life of him he did not know what it could be. When he had left for work on that Friday morning all had been fine; easy and comfortable.

He tried, of course, to find out, but none of his usual methods had proved successful. He had tried wit, cheerful banter, silence, anger, cajoling and everything else the normal male has tried throughout history. You name it, he had tried it. In the end he had given up completely and retreated into the solitude of his study with a bottle of single malt. Karen was unapproachable and untouchable. Out of bounds. Off limits. Verboten. Interdit.

The Monday morning routine was proving equally as difficult. John Lomax sat in his seat (not first class as his employers had yet to sufficiently acknowledge his worth) on the 7.44 to Paddington. He had burst out of the house much as a champagne cork explodes from its bottle: under pressure and glad to be free.

Lomax & The Biker – The Trilogy

Relieved to be going to work, where at least he was appreciated, albeit in a minor and perfunctory way, he hadn't bothered with breakfast yet again and had already burned his lips on the coffee hastily purchased from the station. He had never quite got the hang of dealing with those infernal take away coffee cartons. Should he remove the lid and risk major spillage over his immaculate and expensive suit as the train jolted on its stuttering way, or should the lid remain in place, so that he had to raise the carton to a ridiculous angle to even get a sip out of the improbably tiny hole? Even then the lid was only safely in place in so far as the half asleep shop assistant had pressed it down tightly, and he certainly couldn't trust that particular specimen of today's youth.

Why are even supposedly simple tasks so difficult? He balanced his briefcase on his lap with the carton precariously on top and extricated his mobile from his jacket pocket.

He didn't really like using the mobile in public as he viewed those who did as being vulgar, showy and pretentious. He was most certainly not like that! He didn't want to know somebody else's evening arrangements, what Jenny was having for tea or worse still, what Mary was doing with Frank and how many times she expected to do it. He also hated the tinny noises that emanated from those tiny earphones and those awful bleeps when people texted each other. He loathed the stupid ringtones some people had programmed into their mobiles and insisted on having turned up to ridiculous volumes to show how important they were.

He sympathised with many of the views forwarded so charmingly by The Grumpy Old Men on TV even at his age.

Just as he was lost in thought with these matters his own mobile warbled insistently. The sound made him jump and he spilled a dollop of coffee on his suit trousers in a most embarrassing place.

"Shit," he whispered, flipping open the phone amid a flurry of fumbling fingers and a searing pain in his groin. Sod's Law had struck.

"Hello?"

"John?"

His wife! Considering her mood when he had left she was the last person he expected to be calling. She knew he hated using his mobile in on the train, so something must have happened. He decided to be curt, to show he was irritated specifically by the call, his present situation, the entire weekend and all of life in general.

"What is it?" he growled, rubbing the wet patch in his groin furiously, and drawing a few curious glances. Maybe they thought he was rubbing a little too hard, so he carried on to spite them, but found time to give an embarrassed smile to a particularly inquisitive and good looking woman in the hope of either shaming her into stopping her grinning at him or, hopefully, opening the way to productive conversation later. Who said men can't do two things at once?

"John? Is that you? What are you doing? Sounds like you've run the 100 metres. Either that or you've got a woman with you."

Lomax & The Biker – The Trilogy

He concentrated on his trousers. Did he have another pair at the office? No. But he knew where he could get one. Gradually he realized that Karen was crying.

"Karen, calm down. What is it?" She annoyed him in many ways with her incessant nagging about coming home for dinner, her refusal to recognise when things needed doing around the house, her blind devotion to mindless soaps on the box, her continual worrying about how much things cost. But crying was not one of her faults. She hardly ever cried.

"There's another one!" she snivelled.

His stomach did somersaults as a multitude of his secrets flew across his brain.

"Another what?" he asked, playing for time.

"Another body: a woman this time."

"Is that all, Karen? Is that all you phoned me for?" He twinkled his eyes at the woman opposite and was gratified to get more than a courteous smile in return. Perhaps the day would get better, he mused, and put the briefcase on his lap both to cover the damp patch and hide the evidence of his rising interest in the woman. Karen sniffled in his ear but he hardly heard as his imagination explored the day's possibilities. He allowed it to roam freely and was lost in what it came up with. Suddenly, he realised he was not listening to his wife and, with an effort, snapped back to reality.

There had been several bodies found in the last few years, two of which had been local. They had been stabbed to death and then eviscerated, for no apparent reason. One, following what appeared to be a minor argument about a supermarket parking space, and the second apparently because a shop window had been broken.

The police could find no links with either of the two murders or any of the others, and the cases remained unsolved.

"John," Karen said, catching her breath, "it was in Paddington."

"That's miles from us," he dismissed, but at the exact same time felt a definite chill. He walked through Paddington twice each day, to and from the office. Indeed he was going there now. Perhaps he'd brushed past the killer, shared a carriage or, God forbid, sat close to him on the train.

"But that makes three now!"

"I know, I can count too," he snapped. "Karen, the chances are millions to one he's got you or me in mind for the next one. There's no need to worry." He was placatory now.

"No need to worry!" She exclaimed, "why not? Don't you see?"

He didn't.

"What do you think?" She asked.

"What do I think about what? He asked in return, being deliberately obtuse.

"The victims have all been in their thirties, and they all lived near Paddington."

"I can take care of myself," he said absently, again smiling at the vision opposite.

Lomax & The Biker – The Trilogy

"I'm worried, John. About you, I mean. I've been thinking about this all weekend. You've been getting home so late and you never know who's around or close. And that walk in London. It's dangerous, John."

"Karen, I'm busy." He risked another glance. "Look at it this way: The papers say he picks a victim once a month."

"Mmm."

"So there's no need to worry for a while, is there. I know it's a callous way of looking at it, but it's true. So, we can relax for a while, can't we?" He knew he sounded patronising, but couldn't help it and didn't actually care. He was fed up with the subject and wanted to end the call.

"Are you trying to be funny?" Karen asked.

His voice rose. "Karen, I really have to go. I don't have time for this." The woman opposite gave him an even more meaningful glance and his mind raced to inevitable places.

"Excuse me, sir?" The voice belonged to a sandy haired businessman next to the woman opposite, and, although polite, carried a tangible menace.

"Yes?" John was not in a mood to be intimated, did not appreciate the interruption and he made sure his face showed it.

"I'm sorry," he said, "but you're rather loud and some of us are trying to read."

John took in several of the other commuters and there was irritation on their faces. He was in no mood for lectures. He was committed by now and stood his ground. Everybody used mobiles on the train, he reasoned. If one rang a dozen hands went for their own phones faster than a western gunfight.

"Well," he said, "I was here first. There are always quiet carriages you can use. You saw me on the phone and then sat down, so it's your own fault. Now, if it's all the same to you…"

"Well, I didn't mean anything," the man blustered and blinked, taken aback. "I was only wondering if you could speak more quietly. We don't all want to hear, you know."

"Karen, just don't worry about it. Nothing's going to happen. Now, can you do me a favour? I need my best shirt for tomorrow."

"Tomorrow! What's happening tomorrow?"

John didn't actually need it but he was irritated by his wife's call and the other man, so he said, more loudly than he needed to, "I just need it for tomorrow. Can you get it ready for me?"

"I'm actually quite busy today," she said, "why didn't you say something last night?"

John let silence hang between them.

"OK," she sighed eventually, "but you must promise me you'll be careful today."

"I promise. I have to go now. Bye." He shoved the mobile into his jacket pocket, trying to make sure it couldn't interrupt him any more for a while. The man gave him an annoyed look but seemed sufficiently cowed and sighing loudly and pointedly, gathered his newspaper and briefcase and moved several seats away.

It had been a bad weekend. Karen was grouchy and unapproachable, now his crotch was damp with coffee and he'd been forced to use his mobile on the train. He had defended the indefensible he thought, quite well and he felt his mood lift. He cheered himself with the thought of the woman opposite, who seemed impressed by his feisty defence and had taken the opportunity to move to the empty seat next to him. She sat close enough for him to feel her thigh press against his.

Although a man of experience, the train was a first for him. Despite pretending to be in no hurry, he knew they had limited time as the train rushed towards Paddington. It was bumpy and the jolts quite often arrived at odd and disconcerting moments, but the train had a certain rhythm to it which they quickly adjusted and the woman seemed to have enjoyed herself. She had certainly entered into the spirit of the occasion and had proved amazingly flexible in such a confined space.

Every cloud has a silver lining and Sod's Law had been defeated at least for a while. Great way to start the day, he thought, as the woman left the train at the next station. Back in his seat and feeling enlivened he found his mobile.

"Jayne's Flowers?" he asked. More commuters were getting on the train. John tossed his briefcase onto the seat next to him to discourage anybody else from sitting there.

A moment later the woman's voice answered. "Hello?"

"Hey, sweetheart, it's me."

A moment of silence hung in the air.

"You were going to call me last night," the woman said coolly. He'd known Susan for eight months. She was, he'd heard, an estate agent and was also, he supposed, a wonderful, generous woman in many ways. But what he knew about her-all he really cared to know-was that she had a soft, buoyant body and long, cinnamon-coloured hair that spread out on pillows like warm satin."I'm sorry sweetheart; the meeting went on a lot longer than I thought."

"Your secretary didn't think it went on all that late."

Hell. She'd called his office. Why? She hardly ever did.

"We went out for drinks after we revised the deal contract and then I ended up at the Four Seasons. You know."

"I know," she said sourly.

He asked, "What're you doing for lunch today? Meet me at your place?"

"No. Not today. I'm annoyed with you."

Annoyed? Why? I only missed one phone call?"

"No, because you've missed about three hundred since we've been seeing each other."

Seeing each other! Where did she get that phrase? She was his mistress. They slept together. They didn't see each other, they didn't go out, they didn't court and spark.

"You know how much money I can make on this deal. I couldn't let it go sweetheart."

Shit! What a mistake. Susan knew he called Karen "sweetheart" and didn't like it when he used the endearment with her.

"Well," she said frostily, "I'm busy at lunch. I may be busy for a lot of lunches, maybe all the lunches for the rest of my life."

"Come on, Sue."

Her laugh said: Nice try. But he wasn't pardoned for the "sweetheart" glitch.

"Well, do you mind if I come over and just pick something up?"

"Pick up something?" She asked.

"I need a pair of trousers."

"You mean, you called me just now because you wanted to pick up some laundry?"

"No, no, Sue. I wanted to see you. I really did. I just spilled some coffee on my trousers while we were talking."

"I've got to go, bye, John."

"Susan."

Click.

Shit! Mondays!

He wondered if life was similar for other people, with every day being a mixture of good and bad, either being in control or being buffeted by fate without redress or certainty. He was, he concluded, certain of one thing. He absolutely hated Mondays.

-2-

Much against his deeply held principles he used his mobile again and found the number of a jewellery shop near the florists in which Susan worked. He bought a £300 pair of diamond earrings on his card and arranged to have them delivered to her as soon as possible. The note he dictated read, "To my number one lover, a small token of what I feel about you. John."

The train was by now close to London. The large commuter houses with their fenced and tidy ordered gardens had given way to terraced places and thrusting tower blocks. Blue and red plastic toys and parts of toys sat in backyards. A heavyset woman hanging laundry paused and, frowning, watched the train speed past as if she were watching an unfolding disaster on the news.

He made another call.

"May I speak to Richard Dunne, please?"

A moment later a gruff voice came on the line. "Hello."

"Richard? It's John. John. John Lomax."

"John, how's our project going?"

He wasn't expecting the question quite this soon in the conversation.

"Very well," he said after a moment, "very well indeed."

"I hear a 'but'."

"What do you mean?"

Dunne said, "it sounds like you're trying to tell me something."

Lomax & The Biker – The Trilogy

"No .... It's just things are going a touch more slowly than I thought they would. But it's all fine, really."

"What do you mean, more slowly? Dunne asked.

"They're putting some of the information on a new computer system and it's a little harder to find than it used to be."

"That's not my problem. I need that information and I need it soon."

The morning's irritations caught up with Lomax and he whispered fiercely, "listen, Richard, I've been at Wells & Co. a long time. Nobody's got the insider information I have except Wells himself. So just leave it okay? I'll get you what I promised."

Dunne sighed. After a moment he asked, "You're sure he doesn't have any idea?"

"No, he's completely in the dark."

A fast, irritating image of his boss flickered in John Lomax's thoughts. Frank Wells was a large, quirky man. He'd built a huge insurance agency from a small firm in Soho. Lomax was a senior account executive now, but still didn't warrant first class travel expenses. He'd risen about as far as he could in the company doing account work but Wells had resisted Lomax's repeated suggestions that the company create a special title for him. It irked him and tension sat between the men like a rotting plum. Over the past year Lomax had come to believe that Wells was persecuting him intentionally, continually complaining about his expense account, his sloppy record keeping, and his unexplained absences from the office. Finally, when he'd only been given what he considered a derisory increase in salary after the annual appraisal, Lomax decided to retaliate. He'd gone to Hunter & Dunne and offered to sell them insider client information. The idea had troubled him at first before he calculated it was just another way of collecting the twenty percent rise he thought he was due.

Dunne said, "I can't wait much longer, John, if I don't see something soon, I may have to withdraw."

Crazy wives, rude commuters and now this! Shit, what a morning.

"This will be gold, Richard. Don't worry."

"It better be. It's costing more than gold itself."

"I'll have some good stuff by this weekend. Fancy coming up to my place in the country and you can look it over. It'll be nice and private."

"I didn't know you had a country place."

"I don't broadcast it. The truth is, well, Karen doesn't know. A friend and I go up there sometimes ...."

"You have a friend?"

Lomax ignored the sarcasm.

"Yes, a friend. And she's got a girlfriend or two she could invite up if you wanted to come."

"Two?"

Lomax noted that the sarcasm had been replaced by interest, but let it go.

Lomax & The Biker – The Trilogy

A long silence followed as Dunne digested the suggestion, before he chuckled. "I think one friend would be enough, John, I'm not a young man anymore."

"Where is this place?"

Lomax gave him directions. Then he said, "What about dinner tonight? I'll take you to The Savoy."

Another chuckle came down the line. "I could live with that."

"Good. Let's say eight."

John was tempted to ask Richard to bring Jill, a young assistant account executive who worked at his agency and who also happened to be the woman he'd spent the evening with at a Holiday Inn on more than one occasion when Susan had been trying to track him down. But he thought: Don't push your luck. He and Richard hung up.

John closed his eyes and started to doze off, hoping to snatch a few minutes' sleep, but the train lurched sideways and he was jolted awake. He stared out the window. There were no houses to look at anymore; only brick apartments. Lomax crossed his arms and sat for the rest of the journey, which had at least had some all too brief moments of pleasure, in agitated silence.

His day improved quickly. Susan loved the earrings and she came close to forgiving him, though he knew full restitution would involve an expensive candlelit meal and a night at an hotel in central London, whose prices would be exorbitant.

In the office, Wells was in a surprisingly cheerful mood. John had been worried that the old man was going to grill him about a recent, highly padded expense account. But not only did Wells approve it, he complimented John on a job well done. He even offered him an afternoon of golf at his exclusive country club next weekend. John had contempt for golf and particular contempt for exclusive country clubs. But he liked the idea of taking Richard Dunne golfing at Wells' expense. In the end he dismissed the idea as too risky, even though the thought amused him secretly for much of the afternoon.

He suddenly remembered Karen and phoned home. There was no answer so he dialled the school where she'd been volunteering recently and found that she hadn't come in today. He called home once more. Still she didn't respond. He was troubled for a moment. Not that he was worried about the murderer; he just felt instinctively uneasy when his wife wasn't at home. In truth, he was afraid that she might find him with Susan or whoever. He was also reluctant for her to find out about his deal with Richard. The more money she knew he had the more she would want. He called once more and got their answering machine.

It was time to leave for dinner and, since Wells had left for the night, Lomax ordered a taxi and put the expense down to general office charges. He drifted into The Savoy and enjoyed a good dinner with Richard Dunne. At eleven o'clock he dropped Richard off at Waterloo Station and asked the cabbie to take him to Paddington. He caught the last train home and managed to get to his car, still resting undisturbed in the station car park, and drove home in peace and quiet. Like many people he often felt grateful that cars couldn't speak and spill their well kept secrets. Cars are much like humans he thought. They are only pristine once, immediately after construction or birth, and thereafter they gradually fill up with a multitude of secrets which for the most part are better left untold. Some break down, some need much care and attention, but others seem to soldier on, with normal servicing, forever and a day. In both cases the lifespan is finite and the outcome inevitable.

By the end of the evening Karen had partaken of two glasses of her favourite good quality Shiraz and was fast asleep and John Lomax had watched television for a while before falling asleep on the sofa.

-3-

He awoke late the next morning and made his train with seconds to spare. He wondered whether the woman from the previous day would be on the train, so he made sure he was in the same carriage and as close to the same seat as he could manage. He gave its occupant a filthy look, trying to convey his right to the seat. No luck. She was nowhere to be seen and he resigned himself to letting the journey pass uneventfully, whilst maintaining a hardly hidden disdain for the occupant of his favoured seat.

John Lomax strode purposefully into the office at half past nine, thinking to himself that Monday had gone, was done and dusted, and that a new day with all its possibilities was upon him. He decided to be pro-active and familiarise himself with the new computer system. He promised himself that he would at the very least print a list of prospective clients for Richard Dunne, before lunchtime. He also promised himself that he would phone Tracey and charm her into drinks after work.

He had just stepped into his office when Frank Wells, even more cheerful than the day before, waved at him and wondered if they could "have a chat." His immediate thought was that perhaps Wells had changed his mind and was going to give a good salary increase after all. If that happened, what should he do about selling the confidential information as promised to Richard? His dilemma didn't last long, because he reasoned to himself that he would still do it as it would make up for the last five insulting years.

Lomax & The Biker – The Trilogy

He sat down in Wells' overly cluttered office. It was in fact an accurate reflection of the man himself. He didn't hold conversation. He rambled, digressed, and even made up words. Clients found it charming, but Lomax had no patience for the man's scattered personality. But today he was in a forgiving mood and smiled politely as Wells chattered away and eventually came to the point.

"Here's the thing. Brian and Sam, from our legal department, you know them I think, were at The Savoy having dinner. They worked late and then went there. I sometimes wonder about those two, you know, but it's none of my business really."

Lomax froze as Wells continued.

"Now I've never been there but I believe it's very easy to hear what's being said around you. Anyway, to cut a long story short, they heard every word you and Richard Dunne said. So, there you have it. Security is clearing your desk as we speak and they will be here shortly to escort you off the premises. My advice is to find a good solicitor; one who's familiar with the law concerning theft of trade secrets. I'm just a lowly wordsmith and know little about it, I'm afraid, but I do know it's a serious matter. I won't say good luck to you, but I will say that you should leave now. Oh, and by the way, I'm going to do everything I can to make sure you never work in this industry again. Goodbye."

Five minutes later he was on the street, briefcase in one hand, mobile phone in the other, watching boxes of his personal effects being loaded into a hired van. He couldn't understand how it had happened. Nobody from the agency ever went to The Savoy. It was considered off limits because for one thing expenses didn't normally stretch that far and for another nobody else from within the industry ever went there, so there were no secrets to be purloined. Brian and Sam wouldn't have gone there unless Wells had told them to. Somebody must've blown the whistle. His immediate thought was to blame his secretary. Lomax decided if it was Eileen, he'd get even with her in a big way.

He walked for some time trying to decide what to do and when nothing occurred to him he took a taxi to Paddington.

Bundled in the train as it clacked west, speeding away from the great grey city, Lomax sipped whisky from the tiny bottle he'd bought at the train buffet. Numb, he stared at the grimy apartments then at the pale bungalows and the increasingly large and expensive properties as the train sped onwards. Well, he'd make something happen. If there was one thing he was good at, it was turning adversity into success. He tried to cheer himself with those thoughts as well as recalling other more physical triumphs. He opened a second miniature and then the thought came to him: Karen would have to go back to work. She wouldn't want to, but he'd talk her into it. The more he thought about it the more the idea appealed to him. After all, she had mooched around the house for years. Now it would be his turn. Let her deal with the pressure of a nine-to-five job for a change. Why should he have to put up with all the crap?

Lomax & The Biker – The Trilogy

Lomax parked in his drive, paused, took several deep breaths and walked into the house. His wife was in the lounge, in her favourite chair, holding a cup of tea.

"You're home early."

"Well, I've got something to tell you," he began, leaning against the fireplace. He paused to let her get nervous, to rouse her sympathies.

"Redundancies are in the air at work. Wells wanted me to stay but they just don't have the money. Most of the other senior people are going too. I don't want you to be worried, love. We'll get through this together. It's really a good opportunity for both of us. It'll give you a chance to start teaching again. Just for a little while. I was thinking...."

"Sit down, Jonathan."

Alarm bells began to sound. Jonathan? Only his mother called him Jonathan, and then only when she was annoyed.

"As I was saying, a chance to..."

"Sit down. And be quiet."

He sat and was quiet. She sipped her tea with a steady hand, eyes searching his face like x-ray scanners.

"I had a talk with Susan this morning."

His neck hairs danced, but he forced a smile onto his face.

"Susan?"

"Your girlfriend; she seemed nice. It was a shame to upset her."

Lomax kneaded the arm of his chair.

Karen continued, "I didn't plan to. Upset her, I mean. It's just that she'd somehow got the idea we were in the process of getting divorced." She gave a brief laugh. "Getting divorced because I'd fallen in love with our young gardener; where would she get an idea like that, I wonder?"

"I can explain-"

"We don't employ a gardener, young or otherwise, Jonathan. Didn't it occur to you that it was a pretty stupid lie?"

Lomax's hands slipped together and he began worrying a fingernail. Gardener had been the first thing that had come to mind. And, yes, afterwards he did think it was pretty stupid.

"Oh, if you're wondering," Karen continued, "what happened was someone from the jewellery store phoned, wanting to know whether to send the receipt here or to Susan's apartment. By the way, she said the earrings were really tacky, but she's going to keep them anyway. I told her she ought to."

Why the bloody hell had they done that? When he'd placed the order he'd very explicitly said to send the receipt to the office.

"It's not what you think," he said.

"You're right, Jonathan, I think it's probably a lot worse."

Lomax walked to the drinks cabinet and poured himself another whisky. His head ached and he felt stuffy from too much alcohol. He swallowed a mouthful before setting the glass down. He remembered when they'd bought this set of crystal.

His wife took a deep breath.

Lomax & The Biker – The Trilogy

"I've been on the phone with a solicitor for three hours. He seemed to think it won't take much longer than that to make you a very poor man. Well, Jonathan, we don't have much more to talk about. You should pack a suitcase now and stay somewhere else."

"Karen, this is a really bad time for me."

"No, Jonathan, it will be bad. But it's not bad yet. Good-bye."

Lomax knew that Karen used fewer words the more determined she became. Half an hour later he had finished packing. As he trudged down the stairs with a large suitcase Karen studied him carefully. It was the way she examined aphids when she sprayed them with an aerosol and watched them curl into tiny dead balls.

"I..."

"Good bye, Jonathan."

Lomax & The Biker – The Trilogy

-4-

Lomax was halfway to the front hall when the doorbell rang. He set the suitcase down and opened the door. He found two large policemen standing imposingly in front of him. There were two police cars in the drive and two more coppers on the lawn.

He noticed that their hands were very close to their truncheons or whatever they were called nowadays. Oh God, Wells was pressing charges! Jesus. What a nightmare.

"Mr Lomax?" the largest of the policemen asked, eyeing his suitcase. "John Lomax?"

"Yes. What is it?"

"I wonder if we could talk to you for a moment."

"Certainly, what's the matter?" He had, in fact, never been less certain of anything in his life.

"May we come in?"

"I, well, please."

"Where are you going, sir?"

He suddenly realized that he didn't have a clue.

"I ... I don't know."

"You're leaving but you don't know where you're going?"

"Little domestic problem .... You know how it is."

They stared at him, stone-faced.

Lomax continued. "I suppose I'm going to London." Why not? It was as good a place as any.

The second officer asked, "Is this your MasterCard number, Mr Lomax?"

He looked at the slip the officer was holding out.

"Umm, yes it is. What's this all about?"

"Did you place a mail order yesterday with Northern Outdoor Supplies in Halifax?"

Lomax told the officers that he had never heard of Northern Outdoor Supplies.

"I see," said the large one, not believing him. "You do own a house on Lake Windermere, don't you?"

Again he felt the sizzling chill in his spine. Karen was looking at him with a look that said nothing would surprise her any longer.

"I"

"It's easy enough to check, sir. You may as well be honest."

"Yes, I do."

"When did you get it, Jonathan?" Karen asked in a weary voice.

"It was going to be a surprise.... our anniversary ... I was just about to tell you. Three years ago," he said, searching for something plausible.

The shorter of the policemen persisted, "And you didn't have an order sent by Northern Outdoor Supplies via overnight delivery to that property?"

"No. What order?"

The policeman read from his notebook: "Order number 367457A, for a hunting knife."

"I haven't a clue what you're talking about."

"Mr. Lomax, the knife you ordered-"

"I didn't order any knives."

"The knife ordered by someone claiming to be John Lomax and using your credit card and sent to your property was similar to the knives that have been used in recent murders."

"John!" Karen gasped.

"I don't know anything about any knives!" he cried. "I don't!"

"We had an anonymous tip about some bloody clothes on the shore of Lake Windermere. It turned out to be your property; a T-shirt from the victim two days ago. We also found another knife hidden near the T-shirt. The blood on it matches blood from the victim killed two months ago."

God, what was going on?

"No! This is a mistake! I've never killed anyone."

"Oh, John, how could you?"

"Mr Lomax, you have the right to remain silent." Whilst the large policeman intoned the rest of the caution the other slipped the handcuffs on him. They took his wallet from his pocket and his mobile phone as well.

"No, no, let me have the phone! I'm allowed to make a call."

"Yes, but you have to use our phone, sir. Not yours."

They led him outside, fierce grips on his biceps, as he struggled frantically.

As they approached the police car Lomax happened to look up. Across the street was a slightly built man with sandy hair. A pleasant smile on his face, he leaned against a tree as he watched the excitement. He seemed very familiar.

Lomax & The Biker – The Trilogy

"Wait," Lomax cried, "wait!"

The policemen didn't wait. They firmly shepherded him into the back of their car and drove out of the driveway. It was as they passed the man and Lomax glanced at him from a different angle that he recognized him. It was the same man who had challenged him on the train yesterday. The rude one who'd asked him to be quiet.

Oh, no. No! Lomax began to understand. The man had heard all of his mobile phone calls. With Karen, with Richard Dunn, with Susan, with the jewellery shop. He'd taken down the names of everyone Lomax had been talking to, taken down his MasterCard number, the name and address of his mistress and the details of his meeting with Richard Dunn and the location of his house in the Lakes! He had called Wells, he had called Karen, he'd ordered the hunting knife and he'd called the police too, because he was the killer. He was the man who murders because often the least affront, such as a minor argument about a supermarket parking space, or a shop window being broken, can turn into the most important thing in the world to a person. With a wrenching gesture, Lomax twisted around and saw the man gazing at the receding police car.

"We have to go back!" Lomax shouted. "We have to! He's back there! The killer's back there!"

"Yes sir, now if you'll just shut up, we'd appreciate it. We'll be at the station in no time."

Lomax & The Biker – The Trilogy

"No!" he wailed. "No, no, no!" As he looked back one last time he saw the sandy haired man lift his hand to his head. What was he doing? Waving? Lomax squinted. No, he was ... he was mimicking the gesture of holding a mobile phone to his ear.

"Stop, he's there! He's back there!"

"Sir, that'll be enough," the large one said.

Streets behind them, the commuter finally lowered his hand, turned away from the street and started down the pavement.

Lomax & The Biker – The Trilogy

-5-

John Lomax was taken to Paddington Green police station. It is used to house people who have been arrested for serious crime such as murder and is not a place one would choose to be housed voluntarily. The cell area exudes menace. He was "processed" rapidly and efficiently, stripped of all dignity in an instant. One moment free, albeit with a shattered home life, the next incarcerated, under arrest sitting in a lonely cell accused of murder.

He knew he was innocent but was at a loss as to how to prove it. There was something wrong with the whole situation. He knew he had been set up, but couldn't for the life of him (and that was what was at stake he realised) work out what was amiss. He had to think. He had to concentrate. His head spun and he broke into a cold sweat. His entire future was at stake and he was helpless. He shook and curled up on the cold clammy cell bench with his arms around himself, teeth chattering as darkness fell outside. Inside the cell the light burned relentlessly all night and insinuated itself into his confused brain.

He failed in his quest for sleep. He lay awake, endlessly scrolling through events, searching for the slightest clue that would tell him how to fight. He jolted as his cell door was slung open and smashed against the wall. He blinked and wiped his blurred eyes. The uniformed sergeant place his breakfast on a tray on the floor.

"Eat. You'll be collected in twenty minutes; for questioning."

"Wait!" exclaimed Lomax, "what about my phone call?"

Lomax & The Biker – The Trilogy

"All in good time," responded the officer over his shoulder, without so much as a backward glance, as he pulled the cell door firmly shut behind him.

The door closed with a resounding bang, which emphasised the impenetrable finality of the barrier it represented, and the overwhelming, all consuming silence returned. Without even knowing why, John Lomax dashed to the door and peered intently through its minute peephole opening. A split second before the sergeant swept it closed the image of a sandy haired man was burned into his half awake brain.

Lomax & The Biker – The Trilogy

-6-

Nearly a month later, Detective Inspector Lane sat in his chair in his office and was content. He ran his hand through his hair, the colour of which had been the source of his nickname from his first day at Hendon Police College. It had stuck throughout his career. He hadn't liked it at first but had come to realise that there are some things in life that cannot be changed and being called Sandy wasn't the worst thing in the world to happen to a man.

No, he mused to himself, the worst thing in the world would be to be convicted of a crime you didn't commit, particularly a murder. Or to be a murderer set up by a bent copper. He made those things happen to others and John Lomax was merely the latest and he was looking forward to many more. His thoughts strayed to the eleven people he had already managed to put away in his stead. They were men and women who deserved their fates because they had in some way crossed him or were actually murderers whom he couldn't catch in conventional ways. Usually the reasons were insignificant, as in Lomax's case where he had simply irritated him with his mobile phone and cocksure attitude. He rationalised his crusade because he usually also found out that his victims were in many ways deserving of their fate because they had cheated or deceived or worse. He had to admit that one particular victim, a woman named Anna French, had turned out to be totally innocent of anything, but he dismissed her as collateral damage and besides he had enjoyed her along the way. One out of eleven, now twelve, wasn't bad after all.

Lomax & The Biker – The Trilogy

He walked down the long corridor with its walls of grey and heard a bell somewhere nearby. He hadn't been in this part of the building for some time and the sound, though cheerful enough, was oddly unsettling. arrived at the end of the corridor and faced the last room. It contained John Lomax. The situation made him feel like Clarice Starling outside Hannibal Lecter's cell. The guard unlocked and opened the door.

"Hello, John," Lane said.

"So you're him."

He saw in John Lomax's face what he had seen in the other eleven at times like this: insolence, anger, pride, fear and most of all, resentment. But something was missing, Lane decided. What? Yes, that was it, he concluded. Behind the eyes of most of them had been a pool of bewilderment. In John Lomax this was absent. He dropped his file on the table and then flipped through it quickly.

"You're the one," Lomax muttered.

"Oh, I don't deserve all the credit, John. We had a lot of people looking for you."

"But the word is they wouldn't have kept going if you hadn't been behind them, applying the pressure. No sleep for your men and women is what I heard."

Lane was surprised to see something that had not been there in the interrogation tapes. What was it? Yes, Lomax's eyes had grown enigmatic. Lane opened his notebook, took out a biro and set it far out of the man's reach.

"I've been asking to see you for almost a month, since you've been held waiting for your sentence," Lane said amiably. "You haven't agreed to a meeting until now."

Sentencing was due on Monday and after the judge pronounced the sentence he was deciding upon at this very moment, Lane was sure that John Lomax would be permanently residing at her majesty's pleasure.

"Meeting," Lomax repeated. He seemed amused. "Wouldn't 'interrogation' be more like it? That's what you have in mind, isn't it?"

"You've not confessed, John. So I need to interrogate you, even though you've been found guilty."

"Why did you make, let's see, was it something like a dozen phone calls to my barrister over the past couple of months wanting to 'meet' me?"

"There are just some loose ends on the case; nothing important."

In fact Lane kept his excitement hidden. He had despaired of ever having a chance to talk to Lomax face to face. His requests had gone unanswered and he was beginning to plan his next victim just to keep himself busy. He had only got the call that morning, so he'd left his wife, Judith and the children at home and raced to the remand cells at 90 mph.

"I didn't want to see you before this," Lomax said slowly, "because I was thinking maybe you just wanted to, you know, gloat."

Lomax & The Biker – The Trilogy

Lane shook his head good-naturedly. He could afford that after all. But he also admitted to himself that he certainly had something to gloat about. When there had been no arrests immediately following the murders, investigations had lost momentum and then become personal. Detective Inspector Lane outwardly a career policeman and privately much, much more versus the elusive innocent publically reviled killer. The contest between the two adversaries had raged in the tabloids, but the contest was even more important in Lane's mind. Still taped up behind Lane's desk was the front page of the Post, which showed a picture of sandy-haired Lane glaring at the camera from the right-hand side of the paper and the police artist's composite of Anna French's killer from the left. The two pieces of art were separated by a bold, black line and the detective's was by far the scariest shot.

Lane remembered the press conference in which he promised that although the investigation had bogged down and slowed they weren't giving up hope and that the killer would be caught. Lane had concluded, "that man is not getting away. There is only one way this is going to end. An arrest and conviction." The comment, which a few months later became an embarrassing reminder of his failure, had, at last, been validated. He knew he now had the ideal opportunity sitting in a cell. He would ensure this individual would go down for the murder of Anna French and it would allow him to continue with his mission.

"There are a few questions I would like to ask you, assuming you don't mind," said Lane, his voice dripping with sarcasm.

"I suppose not. We both know I'm innocent but I find it all boring now. I'm here because you put me here. Now you want to talk to me. What have I got to lose? It will pass the time, and I've got plenty of that on my hands."

Lomax slouched in the chair and his shackles clinked softly. It reminded Lane of the bell he'd heard when he entered the interrogation room corridor. He looked down at the open file.

"So what do you want to know?" Lomax asked.

"Only one thing," Lane said, opening the battered manila folder. "Why did you kill her?"

"Why?" Lomax repeated slowly. "Yes, everybody asked me about the motive. Now 'motive' ... that's a big word, but 'why.' That cuts right to the chase."

"And the answer is?"

"Why's it so important?"

"It isn't. Not legally. You only need to establish motive and produce enough convincing evidence and that's been done."

In Lomax's case although there were no fingerprints found at the crime scene and no DNA testing had verified that his skin was the tissue dug from beneath Anna French's perfect dusty-rose-polished fingernails, the judge and jury had accepted the prosecution case. Lomax had remained silent and let the judge read the guilty verdict. He had remained silent about the matter until today.

"We just want to complete the report."

"Complete the report. Well, if that's not bureaucratic crap, I don't know what is."

In fact Lane wanted the answer for a personal, not a professional, reason. So he could get some sleep. He sometimes woke up thinking about it. In the past week alone when it looked like Lomax was going to maximum security without ever agreeing to meet him he would wake up sweating, plagued by terrible haunting thoughts. They had nothing to do with Anna French's murder; they were a series of gut-wrenching scenes in which the prisoner was whispering something to Lane, words that the detective was desperate to hear but could not.

"It makes no difference in the world to us or you at this point, but we just want to know."

"We?" the prisoner asked coyly and Lane felt he'd been caught at something. Lomax continued, "I suppose you people have theories."

"Not really." Lane was uncomfortable under Lomax's gaze, which was even and steady and seemed to mock. There was something there, something behind the eyes.

Lomax kept studying Lane.

"It's a strange sound, isn't it? The chain, I mean. Do you find the past boring? Lomax asked.

Lane became more uncomfortable under the scrutiny of his adversary, and, even though he recognised the need to establish rapport between them, couldn't bring himself to tell the truth.

"No."

Lomax spotted the lie instantly.

"I do," said Lomax. "I find that once something has passed into history it becomes less interesting; less significant for me. I can make things, events, people become history for me. I'm sure you can too. In the end it's almost as if they weren't ever real at all."

"But that means you can rationalise anything, so that for you it never happened. You can deny your past." Lane wanted to explore.

"Have you ever killed anybody?" asked Lomax.

They both knew the answer and suddenly Lane did not want to explore.

"We're here to talk about you."

"I'm here because you put me here. You're here to talk about me."

Lomax slouched in the chair and the shackles clinked softly. Witnesses had reported seeing a man in the company of a biker after the French murder. The man's identity had never come to light. Lane wanted him on aiding and abetting but was too focussed on Lomax himself to spend time on an accessory.

"I know a biker," Lomax admitted, "we used to drink together and spend days talking. He's hurt people in his day. But it was always because they had crossed him. Or for money. Or something like that. He could never understand why I could just have killed her and he still doesn't believe I did. He'll come forward and you'll be where I am now."

"So you like a drink, do you, John?"

"Yes. But I wasn't drinking the day you say I killed her; well, nothing but coffee."

"How well did you know her? Anna French?"

"Know her? I didn't know her."

"I thought you said you did." Lane looked down at the confession.

"I said I'd seen her, just as I saw the Pope on TV once. But I don't know him."

"She had a husband and a child."

"I heard."

He became conscious of the ringing again. It wasn't the chains. The sound came from outside. The bell he'd heard when he first entered. Lane frowned. When he looked Lomax was watching him, a bemused smile on his face.

"It's the coffee break trolley, Mr Lane. It comes around every morning and afternoon."

Lane nodded and looked down at his blank notebook.

"They'd talked about getting divorced; Anna and her husband."

"What's his name?" Lomax asked. "The husband, I mean. Was he that grey-haired man sitting in the back of the courtroom?"

"He's grey-haired, yes. His name's Bob."

The victim's husband was known as Robert to everyone. Lane hoped that Lomax would somehow stumble over the name difference and give something away.

"So you're thinking he hired me to kill her."

"Did he?"

Lomax grunted. "No, he didn't."

Robert French had seemed to the interrogating detectives to be the model of a grieving husband and it didn't seem likely that he'd had his wife murdered. Even the life insurance policy wasn't much of an incentive. Anna was a woman losing the battle to quit smoking.

"I have nothing else to say."

He had seen the scar on her neck from a cut she had suffered when she had been seventeen and knew she wore scarves to conceal it. The day she'd been killed the scarf she'd worn had been a silk Christian Dior, a light shade of blue.

"She was a very good looking woman, wasn't she?" Lane asked.

"I can't remember."

He closed his eyes and saw photos of Anna French which had been shown at the trial. Her eyes were open, frosted and her long-nailed hand was held outward in a plea.

"Nothing happened, if that's what you're getting at. I didn't even want to."

Lomax had had normal heterosexual responses to the Rorschach and free association tests.

"I'm just thinking out loud, John. You were walking through the forest?"

"That day you say I killed her? I got bored with the fair and just started walking. I ended up in the forest. And there she was, just sitting there, smoking."

"What did she say to you?"

"I said, 'hey,' and she said something I couldn't hear."

"What else happened?"

"That was it."

"Maybe you were angry because you didn't like her muttering at you."

"I didn't care. Why would I care about that?"

"I've heard you say a couple times the thing you hate most is being bored."

Lomax looked at the floor. He seemed to be counting.

"Yes, I don't like to be bored."

"How much," Lane asked, "do you hate it? On a scale of one to..."

"But people don't kill because they hate. They think about killing people they hate, they talk about it. But they really only kill people they're scared of. What exactly do you hate, Detective? Ponder it for a minute. Lots of things, I bet. But you wouldn't kill anyone for that reason, would you?"

"She had some jewellery on her."

"Is that a question?"

"Did you rob her? And kill her when she wouldn't give you her wedding and engagement rings?"

"If she was getting divorced why wouldn't she give me her rings?" Lomax meant this only rhetorically, to point out the flaw in Lane's logic. Anna French's purse, eight feet from her body, had contained eleven credit cards and £80 in cash. Lane picked up the folder, read some more and dropped it on the tabletop.

"Why?"

It seemed appropriate that the operative word when it came to John Lomax's life would be a question. Why had he killed Anna French? And who exactly was John Lomax? He'd never talked much about his past. Even though Lane had found out all his extra marital secrets, all his little mysteries, he still didn't understand the man.

"Some of it might have to do with my family."

Lane thought he was making progress, because Lomax mentioning his family history seemed a significant step. After all, hadn't Lomax said that he could block out the past, make it disappear for himself? He decided to probe.

"In what way would it have to with your family?"

"I only said might, not that it definitely has," replied Lomax. "But it was bad enough. My father left when I was nine and my mother had an affair before that."

A lingering and oppressive silence grew and engulfed them in its shroud. The moment seeped into their very bones and both felt it.

"Are you married, Mr Lane?"

Lane glanced at his left hand. There was no ring. He never wore one. As a rule he tried to keep his personal life separate from the office.

"I am, yes."

"How long?"

"Twenty years."

"That's a long time," Lomax laughed. "Are you happy?"

"Yes. As happy as any man, I suppose."

"I can't remember much laughter at home," said Lomax gazing into the distance. "Tell me more. I'm interested."

Lane knew this was the exact opposite of what he had planned, but was determined to delve more deeply and if it meant giving up some of his own history, then so be it. At a more sinister level, he was beginning to feel that Lomax was toying with him; that a superior intellectual force was leading him by the hand, but he could not resist it.

"I met Judith when I was at the College."

"You've been a policeman all your life. I read that profile of you." Lomax laughed again. "In that newspaper issue with the headline after you arrested me." Then the smile faded.

He's opening up, Lane thought excitedly. Keep him going.

"I've lived in the village three miles from here for nearly twenty-one years."

"I've been through there. It's a pretty place."

Lane said, "Yes it is. But there's another problem. As a copper I've got my share of enemies, you can imagine. So we have to keep moving the kids from one school to another."

"Do you send them to private school?"

"We're Catholic. They're in a parochial school; St Mary's."

"Isn't that the one up the road? That place looks like a college campus. It must cost you a packet."

"Yes, I suppose it does."

They were getting close to something, Lane could sense. Encourage him; gently, gently.

The prisoner laughed. "How old are your children?"

"Michael is ten and Alice is nine." Lane resisted a ridiculous urge to fetch their pictures from his wallet.

Lomax suddenly grew sombre. The chains clinked. Lane was stung by the sudden coldness in the prisoner.

"Do you wish you could spend more time with your wife and children?"

"Oh yes" Lane replied with sincerity. "Judith works a lot. At times I get left with the children but it gets tiring as well as this job."

Lomax drifted away for a moment. His eyes became as glazed as those of Anna French.

"What does your wife do? Lomax asked.

"She's a teacher at St. Mary's."

"That's a good job," Lomax said.

He looked up at the ceiling and seemed to be counting tiles. He began to say something else but fell silent and Lane didn't dare interrupt his train of thought. When the prisoner spoke again he was more cheerful.

"We have all this knowledge in our heads. Everything people ever knew. Or will know in the future. Like how to kill a mastodon or how to make a nuclear spaceship or how to talk in a different language. It's all there in everybody's mind. Only they have to find it."

"What's he saying?" Lane wondered. "That he knows I did it?"

"And how you find all this stuff is you sit very quietly and then the thought comes into your head. Just bang, there it is. Does that ever happen to you?"

Lane didn't know what to say. But Lomax didn't seem to expect an answer.

Outside, in the corridor, footsteps approached then receded.

"Anyway, I didn't kill her. There's nothing else I have to say."

There was no point in continuing. Lane had come for an absolute confession from Lomax, with no obfuscation or doubt, but had failed.

"He won't budge!" Lane announced into the pay phone. He stood in the dimly lit corridor. His voice was filled with anger and frustration. He phoned his wife and his children's school, loudly reciting the number as he dialled and then, as calmly as humanly possible, made his arrangements for the evening to come. He was desperate in two ways. Firstly, he had to make sure they were safe. Secondly, he had to make sure they were not provoked into worrying about anything. He rarely called the school, but it had been known, so they shouldn't, he reasoned, be unduly worried. He settled for finding out that they were still there and leaving a message that he would be late home. He wanted them to act normally until he arrived.

Lomax listened intently from within the room. He didn't have to strain to hear, and smiled as he dialled a number himself. He made the phone call he had asked for earlier.

Sandy Lane stared at the wall in front of him and suddenly realised the enormity of what he had done. Lomax had planned it. It was why he'd held out saying anything. He had drawn Lane in, made him desperate to talk; made him unwittingly give information. When he thought about it he realised that Lomax had actually given him nothing of substance, except denial. Wait, calm down. He's locked up. He can't do anything to anybody. He's not getting out-oh, no ...Lane's stomach churned.

Lomax's friend, the biker! Assuming he lived nearby, he could be at the school within minutes. Lane dropped the phone and raced up the hall to the prisoner cells.

"Where's Lomax?" Lane screamed.

The guard blinked at the frantic detective.

"He's right there in the cell. You can see him."

Lane glanced through the double glass at the prisoner sitting calmly on a bench.

"What's he been doing since I left?"

"Reading. That's all. Oh, and he made one phone call."

Lane lunged across the desk and grabbed the guard's phone.

"Hey!"

He punched in the number of the children's school. It began to ring. As Lane waited desperately for an answer, he saw Lomax look at him, smile and mime the act of phoning with a mobile.

Lomax & The Biker – The Trilogy

-7-

He cut off the phone call, smiled and, putting the mobile inside his leather jacket, rested for a few moments collecting his thoughts, pondering his next move. The chains on his jacket jingled, much like John Lomax's shackles and he knew what had to be done. He knew he would not, could not let Lomax down. It was a matter of honour. If a man had saved you or your loved ones, then you owed him. In some cultures it went further, so that owning became involved. What a difference a little letter can make. Ray Quinn, also known as The Biker to all who knew him, understood. It went back to the 7/7 bombings in London. Quinn had taken the tube that day as normal and had been caught in the carnage and mayhem. His life had been saved by a stranger who happened to be sitting near him. That man was John Lomax. Without his presence and quick thinking Quinn knew he would not have survived. As it was he had been left with physical problems and mental scars and never viewed life in the same way again.

Although they met only occasionally for a pub lunch to ponder the meaning of life and other issues they had become friends and theirs was a bond that was special. It would not be broken and they had helped each other cope with the aftermath of the atrocity.

He hadn't been a biker then, just a typical faceless city worker much like anybody else. He took up biking to get away from the grime of the city and its haunting memories. He had given up his job and now made a living doing "this and that" as the need arose. He wasn't well off by any means but he got by and he certainly

Lomax & The Biker – The Trilogy

wasn't down at heel. He wasn't averse to sailing close to the wind and he now found that nothing seemed to frighten him. Before "That Day", as he called it, he had been a shy person who found threat in many things, but it had changed him. He now faced life with a quiet confidence and a steady gaze that others found intimidating.

Now, his friend John Lomax was in trouble and needed his help and was most definitely going to get it. He had decided how to do it and it would surprise the offensive Mr Lane.

-8-

Sandy Lane totally ignored any speed limits as he pressed his right foot hard down and the unmarked police car gobbled up the short distance between the station and the school. He arrived in a cloud of brake dust and almost fell flat on his face as he sprinted towards the school entrance. He had, of course, phoned ahead and his wife and children had been alerted to the crisis. They were waiting and he almost broke down with relief when he saw them standing there. He gathered them up and they drove home in silence as each of them was lost in their individual thoughts about the events of the day.

The silence in the car was different for each of them. Lane himself was so relieved that silence was as much as he could muster. The children were so overawed that they were too scared to speak and knew that a family crisis was happening. Their imaginations ran riot and theirs was a mixture of fear and adrenaline fuelled excitement. Judith Lane was beside herself with anger. Her fury was ice cold. Her husband's job had just threatened her family and nothing was worth that. What was worse in her eyes was that she knew he had brought this upon them. There were going to be words that night, without question. His rotten police career had brought nothing but trouble in so many ways.

The silence continued all evening and the tension was palpable. The children were in bed although not asleep. Judith had disappeared to the bedroom and was reading. Sandy Lane sought solace and relief in a bottle and retired to the bedroom which doubled as his study. He took several slugs of his whisky and began to calm down. He looked around the room and settled deep into his chair. He stretched to ease out the kinks of the day and it was then that he noticed it. Poking out from under his computer keyboard was an envelope. It was not sealed and bore no name. He gazed at it, uncomprehending. He knew it hadn't been there that morning when he had left for work, so it was either from one of the children or Judith. He didn't immediately understand, but his training kicked in and he used his handkerchief to cover his fingers as he removed the contents from the envelope. It was a single sheet of A4 and what he saw hit him like a hammer.

"I could have. I didn't. You will ensure Lomax is released without charge within 24 hours. There must be no excuses and no delays. Do it and you will not hear from me again. I know all about you. Judith will be next if you ignore me....I am watching."

Detective Inspector Lane pulled the curtains closed and rushed round the house closing curtains and blinds and making sure doors were locked and the movement sensor outside was set. His last act of the evening was to close the front door, and as he was doing so he could have sworn he glimpsed a single headlight swinging away in the lane outside. What struck him in that instant was the complete lack of noise.

Silence has a noise of its own he thought. It's not quiet, it's shattering.

Lomax & The Biker – The Trilogy

-9-

John Lomax was released exactly twelve hours later. All charges had been dropped. Lane had declared that he had personally reviewed all the evidence and decided that it wouldn't sustain a prosecution in the heat of battle in court in a trial for murder. The purchase of items on Lomax's credit card was circumstantial at best. No real physical evidence had been brought forward and the CPS had warned him behind the scenes that he risked making himself a laughing stock if he carried on as things were. He needed more concrete evidence against Lomax and he reasoned to himself that his release might prove beneficial in the long run. Give him enough rope. Nobody else knew the real reason. He was bent and Lomax had somehow managed to find out about his murky secrets.

He was under pressure. He reasoned that by letting Lomax go he could have him under constant surveillance and he would make a mistake. The mistake that he could use, turn against him and set himself free to continue with his mission. There was so much more to be done, after all. And so little time. He would let the dust settle for a while he reasoned, before he begun again. Lomax would be so pleased to be free that he would return to his miserable, insignificant life. He would need to sort out his own affairs; his wife, Karen and his job that he had just lost. Lane just did not care what happened to Lomax as long as he was long gone from his life, and he had heard no more from the mysterious envelope man. The real problem, though, was that it all left so many loose ends.

John Lomax and The Biker met soon after his release. Both were very careful and made sure they had not been followed. They sat side by side in The Blind Beggar, scene of famous violence in Ronnie and Reggie's day, with their back to the wall facing the entrance. They were not there long, but it was plenty long enough to set their plan for the demise of Sandy Lane

Now that Lomax had time to think he could be quite creative. He hadn't realised just how much creative talent lay just beneath the surface. He now knew it had been wasted working for Wells. He had been right to set up a deal with Richard Dunne, but that would have to wait. He would get round to it, he told himself, as he was a man of honour. He had verbally contracted to deliver and he would. He had already contacted his friend and persuaded him to be patient. Dunne had no love for Wells and accepted the need for patience and had even offered to help if he could. He knew Lomax of old, and was confident that he would deliver better and more exciting things, especially now that his friend was free of the confining influence of Karen. Everything comes to he who waits.

Lomax & The Biker – The Trilogy

-10-

"We have reason to believe there's a man who wants to cause you some harm, sir."

Standing on the hot pavement outside Lane's house, the muscular man rocked back and forth on his designer shoes. He wore a designer leather jacket, designer jeans and expensive footwear. He put his bag down and his companion, not quite as expensively dressed, stood beside him looking for any reaction from Lane. They both produced authentic ID's that showed them as belonging to a little known security agency that looked after the security of government employees and their families. Lane recognised the badges and relaxed a little.

"Who would that be?" Lane asked.

"His name is Raymond Quinn."

Lane thought about it and shook his head. "I've never heard of him." He peered at the picture being held in front of his face.

"No, I'm sorry. He doesn't seem familiar. Who is he?"

"He works at a company called Hunter & Dunne in the city. They deal with Life insurance, that sort of thing."

"Why does he want to cause me harm? I don't even know him."

"We don't know."

"Well, what do you know?"

"We arrested somebody for a drugs offence. An illegal immigrant called Tareeq. He wanted to make a deal and told us he had some information about a possible crime. Apparently he's worked for this Quinn occasionally. A few days ago Quinn offered him a thousand pounds to call at your house and see if you needed any odd jobs doing. While he was there he was supposed to check out your alarm system."

"You're kidding."

"No."

What was all this about? Despite the intense heat of the hottest day of the year Lane felt a chill run through him.

"What would he want with my alarms system?"

"All we've been told is that it's in return for something you've done."

"I'm sorry, payback?" Lane shook his head in frustration: "Jesus, you knock on my door and tell me that somebody's going to 'cause me some harm' and you don't have any idea what it's about?"

"We were hoping you could tell us."

"Well I can't."

"We'll investigate this Quinn character. But we'd recommend you keep an eye out for anything odd."

"Why don't you arrest him?"

"Sir, as a fellow copper you know we can't. As far as we know at the moment he hasn't committed a crime. I'm afraid that without evidence of an overt act, there's nothing we can do."

Trying to put the encounter out of his thoughts Lane drove to the health club. He needed some time on his own to think. He had a heavy case load and the Lomax business had disturbed him. More importantly he was feeling the need to find another one.

He drove into the health club car park, parked and walked through the fierce sun to the front door.

"Hello, Mr Lane. You're early today."

He nodded to the daytime desk manager, Gavin.

"Yes. I snuck out when nobody was looking."

He changed clothes and headed for the aerobics room, empty at the moment. He flopped down on the mats to stretch. After ten minutes of limbering up, he headed off to the machines, pushing hard, doing his regular circuit of twenty reps on each before moving on and finishing with stomach crunches. He felt he had to keep in trim as part of the job, but he was intent on keeping powerful for his more sinister reason. His stomach had been testing the waistband of his trousers lately. He didn't like to look flabby and he knew women didn't either, whatever his wife Judith told him. After the crunches he hopped on the treadmill for his run, trying to push his problems out of his mind.

No matter how hard he ran he couldn't get Raymond Quinn out of his mind. He scanned his memory again but came up with nothing. He fell into the rhythm of his pounding feet and ran for longer than intended. At five miles slowed to a walk, cooled off and shut the treadmill down. Lane pulled a towel over his neck and, ignoring a flirtatious glance from a woman who was pretty but a few years past being worth the risk, returned to the changing room. There he stripped, grabbed a clean towel and headed for the sauna. Lane liked this part of the club because it was out of the way and very few members came here at this time of day. Now it was totally deserted.

Lane wandered down the tile corridor. He heard a noise from around the corner. A click, then what sounded footsteps, though he couldn't tell for sure. Was somebody there? He got to the junction and looked. No, the hallway was empty. But he paused. Something was different. What? He realised the place was unusually dark. Glancing up at the lights he saw that several bulbs were missing. Seven hundred pounds a year for membership and they couldn't replace the bulbs? The murkiness, along with a hiss from the air conditioning made the place eerie. He continued to the door of the redwood sauna, hanging his towel on a hook and turned the temperature selector to high.

It started inside when a sharp pain shot through into his foot.

"Aargh!" he shouted and danced back, lifting his sole to see what had stabbed him. A wooden splinter was sticking out of the soft pink fleshy underside of his foot. He pulled it out and pressed his hand against the bleeding wound. He squinted at the floor where he'd stood and noted several other splinters.

Gavin was going to get an earful today. But Lane's anger abated when he glanced down and found what he supposed were the splinters. He picked up two slim wooden wedges, hand carved, lying on the floor near the doorway. They were like door stops, except that the only door here (to the sauna) was at the top of a two step stairway. The door couldn't be wedged open. But the wedges could be used to wedge the door closed if somebody pounded them into the jamb when the door was shut. They'd fit perfectly. But it'd be crazy to do that. Somebody trapped inside would have no way of turning down the temperature or calling for help; there were no controls inside the unit. And heat in a sauna could kill. Lane and his wife had just seen a TV story about a woman who'd died in a sauna after she'd fainted in hers.

Holding the wedges, staring down at them, a sudden click from nearby made him jump. Lane turned and saw a shadow against the wall, like that of a person pausing. Then it vanished.

"Hello?" Lane called.

The silence was unnatural and deafening. Lane walked into the hallway. He could see nobody. Then he glanced at the emergency exit door, which didn't seem to be closed all the way. He looked out. The alley was empty. Turning back he noticed something on the edge of the door. Somebody had taped the latch down so he could get inside without being seen by anyone in the lobby. Five minutes later Lane was hurrying out of the club, not bothering to give Gavin the lecture he deserved. He was carrying the wedges and tape wrapped in paper towels. He was careful to try and preserve any evidence.

"They're in here." Sandy Lane handed the paper towels to Bill Clough.

"At your health club, you said?" asked his fellow detective, looking over the wedges and the tape.

"That's right." Lane couldn't resist adding the name of the exclusive place. Clough didn't seem impressed. He stepped to the doorway and handed the evidence to another colleague.

"Fingerprints, DNA, tool marks. Everything you can as quickly as you can, please." The young officer vanished.

He turned back to Lane. "But nobody actually tried to detain you in the sauna?"

Detain? Lane asked himself wryly. You mean: Lock me inside to roast me to death?

"No."

"The way I see it, Quinn found out your routine. He got into the club and taped the back door open so he could get in without anybody seeing him from the entrance."

"How could he do that? Is he a member?"

"I don't know." Clough held up a finger and called the club. He had a brief conversation.

"No record of him as a member or a guest."

"How easy would it be get a member's ID?"

"That's probably very easy. I think I surprised him. He was going to use those wedges to trap me but he had to get rid of them quickly."

A young officer entered the room and announced that they had found no fingerprints, DNA or tool marks.

Clough lifted a piece of paper from his desk and read it.

"Well, we've looked into this Quinn. He seems like any normal bloke. No police record except for a speeding offence a few years ago. But there is something. He has a service record. He was in Iraq until he was medically discharged. He spent a year in counselling. Apparently he does some security work and is readily available for personal protection and similar more pro-active work.

"Christ, so somebody could have hired him?"

"Who've you upset, recently or in the past? Is there anybody who would have reason to bear a grudge badly enough to try something like this?"

"I don't know. I'd have to think about it."

Clough said, "you know that expression 'revenge is a dish best served cold?"

"Of course."

"You need to think. As a copper there could be plenty of people who'd want to harm you, but kill you? That's a serious step. In the meantime I think we need a little chat with this Mr Quinn, see what he's got to say for himself."

-11-

Sandy Lane pulled up in his driveway. He climbed out of the car, locked the doors and looked around to make sure he hadn't been followed. There was no sign of anyone, but he still double locked the door behind him as he would only normally do last thing at night.

Judith joined him in the hall. She glanced at the door.

"What's with that?"

They never used the deadlock during the day. He realised that he would have to explain things to her, but he had to be sure that he didn't arouse her suspicions about himself or make her hysterical. After all, she'd had a nasty shock and was obviously still coldly angry.

"It's just a precaution, love. After what's just happened its best that we're careful. There's somebody out there who bears a grudge and I want to make sure you and the children are safe. Not that we're in any danger," he hurriedly put in. "There've also been some burglaries around here and we've told everybody to make doubly sure that their places are secure. No worries, just sensible precautions. Oh and there'll be more patrols at random times until they've been caught."

Judith digested the information for a few moments.

"Can we still go to the club for dinner? You remember the children are with friends for the night?"

"I'm knackered, love. Let's do it another night."

Lomax & The Biker – The Trilogy

He couldn't tell whether she was disappointed or just testing him, but Lane knew how to bail out sinking ships. He mixed her favourite drink, poured a large malt whisky for himself and selected her favourite CD. In twenty minutes the drinks and music had dulled her disappointment and she was talking about wanting to go to their favourite hideaway on Exmoor. They'd come across a small hotel/inn called The White Horse at Exford which had a great atmosphere, served wonderful food and made them personally welcome every time they went.

He gave it a minute and then, sounding casual, said, "I've been thinking that we need to look at life insurance. Perhaps increase it. We've never done anything about it since I became a DCI, so we could afford to have better cover. I've been doing some looking around at various companies and agencies. You know Clough at work? He's recommended an agency called Hunter & Dunne. I might give them a call, see what they can do for us."

Judith felt a shiver of unease at his announcement, particularly after recent events. She thought it too coincidental, but as she had always left that side of the marriage to Lane, she didn't question him about it.

Dinner was eaten largely in silence, but Judith made it subtly clear that she wanted an early night for them both as the kids were away.

"You go on, love. I've got a few things to look at. I won't be long."

"Oh, okay." She sighed, picked up a book and drifted upstairs.

Lomax & The Biker – The Trilogy

When he heard the door click shut he walked into his study, turned off the lights and peered out at the dark sweep of moonlit grass behind the house. Shadows, bushes, flowers, stars ... he always loved to look out in this way. It changed constantly with the clouds and seasons, but remained the same in a strange way as well. He stayed like that for five minutes, then, pouring another large scotch, he stretched out on the couch. A sip of smoky liquor. Another.

Sandy Lane began a trip through his past, looking for some reason that Quinn, or anyone, would want him dead.

Because he had Judith on his mind, he thought first of women who'd been in his life. He was a logical man and went all the way back to the beginning. He wandered down memory lane as far back as his first experience. It was in the last year at junior school and Toni gave him his first kiss. Actually, he remembered, it wasn't so much a kiss as a desperate lunge followed by a bite of sorts. Nevertheless he had returned for more, but so unfortunately had most of the other boys and Toni denied nobody.

He hadn't had any other dabbling until he was sixteen and a girl at the local youth club, Alison, had become his first real firm girlfriend. Well, he mused with a smile to himself, firm and soft at the same time. Happy days, but she fell by the wayside when he went away for police training. There had been a woman at Hendon Police College, but she turned out to be most uncooperative and was only really interested in her career and chasing her superiors. He had later learned that this tactic had succeeded as she had climbed the ladder to lofty heights in the Met. There had been a woman named Leanne, but he tried not to think about her. Then he had met Judith and that was that. He therefore couldn't think of any woman who would want him dead. No, there had to be another answer. Certainly there must be many a villain who wanted revenge of some sort, but to go as far as to kill a policeman would be suicidal.

And then there were the eleven who he had killed. Nobody knew of his involvement in their deaths, of course, or he would have been behind bars by now. Certainly, nobody could possibly connect him to any of them.

A dozen other incidents flooded into his thoughts, two dozen, people ignored and insulted, lies told, associates slighted. His memory spat out not only the serious offences, but the petty ones too: rudeness to waitresses, hitting an elderly salesman who'd sold him a duff car, laughing when a man's toupee blew off in a heavy wind.

And most recently there had been the Lomax affair. He had done what he'd been instructed by Lomax and made sure he was released with no charge, but he didn't think Lomax would end the matter there. The phone call and the panic stricken rush to his wife and children were all too fresh in his mind, so he came to the conclusion that the sauna incident could be traced back to Lomax.

Maybe Quinn was his best friend, brother or been hired. It was exhausting. He took another scotch ... then another...and another; and the next thing he knew the sun was streaming through the window.

He squinted in pain from the hangover and groggily looked at his watch. Nine! Why hadn't she wakened him? She knew he had things to do this morning. He staggered into the kitchen, and Judith looked up from her toast.

She smiled. "Breakfast's ready."

"You let me sleep. Why didn't you wake me?"

"You looked so peaceful and I though you needed the rest."

Lane winced in pain. His neck was sore from sleeping in an awkward position.

"I haven't got time for breakfast," he grumbled.

"Mother always said breakfast is the most important meal of the day. So you've told me many times."

Lane was silent. He rose and walked into the living room. He sighed. It was like walking on eggshells sometimes. He retreated to the bedroom. He was fishing for aspirin in the medicine cabinet when the phone rang.

"For you," was his wife's cool announcement.

It was Clough. "We've found Quinn. Pick you up in twenty minutes."

-12-

"Yes, can I help you?"

"Raymond Quinn?" Clough asked.

"That's right."

Quinn exuded confidence. His brown hair, flecked with grey, was short. His square-jawed face shaved perfectly. Although it had not been long since that he had stood on Lane's front doorstep, his appearance had been transformed and Lane showed no sign of recognition. For his part, Quinn's eyes betrayed no surprise at seeing Sandy Lane in front of him.

"Sir, we understand you were seeking some personal information about Mr. Lane here."

"Mr Lane; who's he?"

"This gentleman here," he said, indicating his colleague.

Quinn frowned.

"You're mistaken, I'm afraid. I don't know him."

"You're sure?"

"Yes."

"Do you know a man named Tareeq? Perhaps you've hired him to do a specific job at some time."

"Is this an immigration issue? My people are supposed to check documentation."

"No, sir, it's not. This Tareeq claimed you asked him about Mr. Lane's security."

"What?" Then Quinn squinted knowingly. "How'd this all come about? By any chance, has Tareeq been arrested for something?"

"That's right."

"So he made up something about a former employer to get a lighter sentence. Doesn't that happen?"

"Sometimes, yes that happens."

"Well, I didn't do what this Tareeq said I did."

"Were you in the local health and country club yesterday?"

"The fancy one? No, that's not how I spend my spare time. Besides I was in Hertford."

"Perhaps before you left for Hertford?"

"I have no idea what you're getting at but I don't know this man and I don't have any interest in his alarm systems."

Clough felt Lane touch his shoulder, who pointed at a pile of wooden boards, about the same thickness of the wedges.

"Do you mind if we take a couple of those with us?"

"Please do, but I'll need to see your warrant first."

"Are you worried about what we might find?" Clough asked.

Lane sighed loudly. Quinn looked him over coolly.

Lane said, "if you have nothing to hide then there'll be no problem."

"If you have a real reason then there'll be no problem getting a warrant."

"So you're telling us you have no intent to endanger Mr. Lane."

Quinn laughed. "That's ridiculous."

Then his face grew icy. "What you're suggesting is pretty serious. You start spreading rumours like this, it could get embarrassing, for me and for you. I hope you realize that."

"Assault and breaking and entering are very serious crimes," Clough said.

"If there's nothing else …"

"No, there's nothing else. Thanks for your time." Clough and Lane started back to the car.

When they were in the car park Clough said, "he's up to something."

Lane nodded. "I know what you mean. That look he gave me. It was like he was saying, 'I'm going to get you. I swear'."

"Look? That's not what I'm talking about. Didn't you hear him? He said he wasn't interested in your alarms. I never told him that's what Tareeq said. I only mentioned security. That could mean anything. Makes me believe Tareeq was telling the truth."

Lane was impressed. "I never noticed it. Good catch. So what do you think we should do now?"

"Have you got that list of anybody who might have a grudge against you?"

He handed over a sheet of paper.

"Anything else I should do?"

Lane was deliberately making Clough believe he was leading this investigation. In reality, he was making sure it didn't take any unwanted twists and turns.

Looking at the list Clough said, "One thing. You might want to think about a bodyguard."

-13-

Detective Inspector Lane had not gone to the lengths of employing a bodyguard. He had, however, called in a favour from an old friend; a retired colleague named Mike Baxter, and set up a very thorough and extremely deniable investigation into Mr Raymond Quinn. Lane and Baxter sat in the kitchen.

The man unbuttoned his jacket. He always wore a suit and tie, whatever the temperature.

"First off, let me tell you what I've found out about Quinn. He was born in Lincoln, got a degree in engineering at Nottingham. He got married and went into the army. After he was discharged he came back here. Then his wife died."

"Died? Maybe that's the thing. He blames me for it. What happened?"

Baxter was shaking his head. "She had cancer. And you don't have any connection with the doctors that treated her or the hospital."

"You checked that?"

"Now about his family: He's got three kids. Philip, Celeste and Cindy, ages fourteen, seventeen and eighteen. They're all in local public schools. Good kids, no trouble with the law."

He showed candid pictures that looked like they were from school yearbooks: a skinny, good-looking boy and two daughters: one round and pretty, the other lean and athletic.

"Do you know the girls?"

Lomax & The Biker – The Trilogy

"God no!" Lane was offended. Whatever else he was or had done in his life, he had some standards. Baxter didn't ask if Lane had ever made a move on the son. If he had, Lane would have kicked him out there and then.

"Quinn was single for a while and then last year he remarried, Nancy Stockton, an estate agent, thirty-nine. She got divorced about five years ago, has a ten-year-old son." Another picture emerged. "You recognize her?"

Lane looked at the picture. Now, she was somebody he could definitely go for. Pretty in a girl next door sort of way, she was probably great for a one night stand or even two. But, he reflected, no such luck. He would've remembered. But he stored the image in the murky recesses of his mind, to be recalled whenever needed.

Baxter continued, "Now, Quinn seems like a reasonable man, loves his children, drives them to football, swimming and their after school jobs. Model parent, model husband and good businessman. Made a ton of money last year. Pays his taxes, even goes to church sometimes. Now, let me show you what I've come up with for your security plan. The plan provided for two teams of security specialists, one to conduct surveillance on Quinn and the other to serve as bodyguards. It will be expensive, but because of our history I'll do it for nothing for two weeks and then it will have to be at cost price. But frankly I don't think this'll go on for too long, sir."

The "sir" had been automatic, but Lane thought he detected a hint of contempt there.

Baxter explained that all seven people he had in mind for the security detail were former policemen and knew how to run crime scenes and interview witnesses and, critically, would keep their mouths shut.

"With all of us on it, we'll build a solid case, enough to put him away for a long time."

Lane gave the man his and Judith's general daily routine, the shops they used and so on. He added that he wanted the guards to keep their distance; he still hadn't shared all details with Judith.

"She doesn't know?"

"No. Probably wouldn't take it too well. You know women."

Baxter didn't seem to know what Lane meant exactly, but he said, "we'll do the best we can, sir."

Lane saw him to the door and thanked him. The man pointed out the first team, in a black Ford, parked two doors down. Lane hadn't even noticed them when he'd answered the door, which meant they knew what they were doing. As Baxter drove off, Lane's eyes again looked into the garden. He returned inside and pulled the curtains closed on every window.

As the days went by there were no further incidents and Lane began to relax. The guard details watching Lane and Judith remained largely invisible, and his wife had no clue that she was being guarded when she went on her vital daily missions. The surveillance team kept a close watch on Quinn, who seemed oblivious to the tail. He went about his life. A few times the man fell off the surveillance radar but only for short periods and it didn't seem that he'd been trying to lose the security detail.

When he disappeared the teams on Lane and Judith stepped up protection and there were no incidents. Meanwhile, Clough and Baxter continued to look into the list of people with grudges from Lane's past. Some seemed likely, some improbable, but in any event none of the leads panned out.

-14-

Lane decided to get away for a long weekend. The children were staying with friends, so it was an ideal opportunity. Baxter made sure the children were covered. Lane chose to leave the bodyguards behind, because they'd be too hard to hide from Judith. Baxter thought this was okay; they'd keep a close eye on Quinn and if necessary a team would hurry to cover Lane immediately.

The couple set out early. Baxter had told Lane to take a complicated route out of town, and then pause at a particular point where he could make certain they weren't being followed, which he did. No one was following.

Once away from the city Lane pointed the car into the dawn sun and eased back in the Mercedes' leather seat, as the slipstream poured into the convertible and tousled their hair.

"Want to put on some music?" He called to Judith.

"OK. What do you fancy?"

"Whatever you want love."

Sitting in his white surveillance van, near Ray Quinn's, Baxter heard his phone chirp.

"Yes?"

"Mike, we've got a problem."

"Go on."

"Has he left yet?"

"Lane? Yes, an hour ago."

"Oh."

"What's the matter?"

"I'm at a Halfords near their house."

"And...?"

"Two days ago a man who looked like Quinn ordered a copy of a technical manual for Mercedes sports cars. It came in yesterday and he picked it up. At the same time, he bought a set of metric spanners, wrenches and battery acid. Mike, the book was about brakes. And that was just around the time we lost Quinn for a couple of hours."

"You think he could've got to Lane's Mercedes?"

"Not likely but possible. I think we have to assume he did."

"I'll get back to you." Baxter hung up and immediately called Lane. A distracted voice answered.

"Hello."

"Sandy, it's..."

"I'm not available at the moment. Please leave a message and I'll get back to you as soon as possible."

Baxter hit disconnect and tried again. Each of the five times he called, the only response was the pre-occupied voice on the voicemail.

Lane was nudging the Mercedes up to seventy.

"Isn't this great?" he called, laughing. "Whoa!" It's great!"

But she didn't answer. She was frowning, looking ahead.

"There's, like, a turn up there."

She added something else he couldn't hear.

"What?"

"Umm, maybe you'd better slow down."

"I'm fine."

"Love, please! Slow down!"

"I know how to drive."

They were on a long straight road, which was about to drop down a steep hill. At the bottom the road curved sharply and fed onto a bridge above a deep valley.

"Slow down! Love please! Look at the turn!"

Christ, sometimes it just wasn't worth the battle.

"OK."

He lifted his foot off the accelerator.

And then it happened. He had no clue exactly what was going on as they were caught in a huge swirl of grit and dust, spinning around and around, as if the car had been caught in the middle of a tornado. They lost sight of the sky. Judith was screaming and grabbed the dashboard. Lane, gripping the wheel with cramping hands, tried desperately to find the road. All he could see was dust whipping into his face, stinging like barbed wire.

"We're going to die; we're going to die," Judith was wailing.

Then from somewhere above them, a tinny voice crackled.

"Lane, stop your car immediately. Stop your car!"

He looked up to see the police helicopter thirty feet over his head, the downdraft of its rotors the source of the dust storm.

"Who's that?" Judith screamed. "Who's that?"

The voice continued, "Your brakes are going to fail! Don't start down that hill!"

"Shit!" He cried. "He tampered with the brakes."

"Who? What's going on?"

The helicopter sped forward toward the bridge and landed presumably so the rescue workers could try to save them if the car crashed or plummeted over the edge. Save them, or collect the bodies.

He was doing ninety as they started over the crest of the hill. The nose of the Mercedes dropped and they began to accelerate. He pressed the brake pedal and the brakes seemed to grip. But if he got any farther and the brakes failed he'd have nowhere to go but into rock or over the edge; there was no way they could make the turn doing more than thirty-five. At least there was gravel just past the shoulder.

Sandy Lane gripped the wheel firmly and took a deep breath.

"Hold on!"

"What do you mean?"

He swerved off the road. Suitcases, bags and coats flew from the backseat. Judith screamed and Lane fought with all his strength to keep the car on course, but it was useless. The tyres skewed, out of control, through the gravel. He just missed a large boulder and ploughed into the countryside. Rocks and gravel spattered the body, spidering the windscreen and peppering the bumper and bonnet like gunshots. Weeds and bushes pelted their faces. The car bounced and shook and pitched. Twice it nearly flipped over. They were slowing but they were still speeding at forty miles an hour straight for a large boulder. Now, though, the gravel was so deep that he couldn't steer at all.

"Jesus, Jesus, Jesus." Judith was sobbing, lowering her head to her hands.

Lane jammed his foot onto the brake pedal with his left foot, shoved the gearstick into reverse and then floored the accelerator with his right. The engine screamed, gravel cascaded into the air above them. The car came to a stop five feet from the face of the rock. Lane sat forward, head against the wheel, his heart pounding, drenched in sweat. He was furious. Why hadn't they called him? Then he noticed his phone. The screen read, 7 missed calls 5 messages marked urgent. He hadn't heard the ring. The wind, the engine and the music had blocked out all other sound.

Sobbing and wiping at the mud and dust that covered her white trouser suit, Judith snapped at him, "What is going on? I want to know. NOW!"

As Baxter walked toward them from the helicopter, he told her the whole story.

"I didn't want to worry you."

"You mean you didn't want me to ask what you did to somebody to make them want to get even with you. Take me home; now!"

They drove back in silence, driving in a rented car; the Mercedes had been towed away by the police to look for evidence of tampering and repairs. An hour after walking through their front door Judith left again, suitcase in hand saying she was going to pick up the children.

Lane was secretly relieved she was going. He couldn't deal both with Quinn and his wife's moods. He returned inside, checked the lock on every door and window and spent the night with a bottle of malt whisky.

-15-

Ten days later at about five p.m. Lane was working out in the "gym" he'd set up in a bedroom as he was avoiding the health club and its deadly sauna. He heard the doorbell. It was Baxter. Three locks and a deadbolt later, he gestured his friend inside.

"Got something you should know about. I had two teams on Quinn yesterday. He went to a cinema for a matinee. There's a rule: if anybody under surveillance goes to a film by himself ... that's suspicious. So the teams compared notes. It seems that fifteen minutes later a bloke in overalls left with a couple of rubbish bags. Then about an hour later, a delivery man in a uniform turned up at the cinema, carrying a big box. But my man talked to the manager. The workers there don't usually take the first rubbish out to the bins until five or six at night, and there weren't any deliveries planned that day."

Lane grimaced. "So, he dodged you for an hour. He could get anywhere in that time."

"He didn't take his car. We had it covered. And we checked cab companies. Nobody called for one in that area."

"So he walked somewhere?"

"Yes, and we're pretty sure where. Hansford Chemicals. He looked at his notebook. "They make acrylonitrile, methyl methacrylate and adiponitrile."

"What the hell are those?"

"They're industrial chemicals, which by themselves are not any big deal. But what is important is that they're used to make hydrogen cyanide."

"Jesus. Like the poison?"

"Like the poison. And one of my men said there's no security. Cans of the chemicals were sitting right out in the yard by the loading dock. Quinn could've walked up, taken enough to make a batch of poison that'd kill a dozen people and nobody would've seen him."

"Could anybody make it? The cyanide, I mean."

"Apparently it's not that hard. And with Quinn having been in the army, you'd have to think he knows about chemicals and fertilizers."

Lane slammed his hand down on the counter.

"Christ, so he's got this poison and I'll never know if he's slipped it into what I'm eating. Jesus."

"Well, that's not exactly true," Baxter said reasonably. "Your house is secure. If you buy packaged food and keep an eye on things at restaurants you can control the risk."

"Control the risk!" Lane shouted with disgust. "I can't even go outside to buy my own food. I'm a prisoner. That's what I am."

He walked into his hallway to pick up his unopened post from the floor. Just at that moment a voice yelled, "No!"

Startled, Lane reached for his truncheon. But before he could reach it, he was tackled from behind and tumbled hard to the floor, the breath knocked from his lungs. Gasping, in agony, he scrambled back in panic. He stared around him and saw no threat.

He then shouted at Baxter, "what're you doing?"

Breathing heavily, Baxter rose and pulled Lane to his feet.

"Sorry ... I had to stop you .... The post."

"The-?"

"Post. Don't touch it."

Baxter grabbed a jiffy bag and put the post into it.

"When I was asking you about the shops you go to for the security plan, I forgot about your post. This was sent from Paddington."

Lane knew it was not far away.

"Uh-uh." Baxter sniffed the bag carefully. "Cyanide smells like almonds." He shook his head. "I can't tell."

"Almonds," Lane whispered, "almonds."

He smelled his fingers and began washing his hands frantically. There was a long silence. Rubbing his skin with paper towels, Lane glanced at Baxter, who was lost in thought.

"I think it's time for a change of plans."

The next day, Sandy Lane parked his leased Mercedes in the hot, dusty car park of the police station. He looked around uneasily for Quinn's car, but didn't see it. Lane climbed out, carrying jiffy bags containing his post and food from his kitchen. He carried them into the building. In a ground-floor conference room he found Clough and Baxter, and a man who was wearing exactly the same clothes as Lane himself. The man introduced himself as Peter Billings, an undercover officer.

Lane muttered something nobody could hear and turned to Baxter.

"Here they are."

The detective took the bags and tossed them absently on an empty chair. None of the envelopes or food contained poison, according to a test Baxter conducted at Lane's. But bringing them here was an important part of their plan. They needed to make Quinn believe for the next hour or so that they were convinced he was going to poison Lane.

After the tests turned out negative Baxter had concluded that Quinn was faking the whole cyanide thing; he only wanted the police to think he intended to poison Lane. Why? A diversion, of course. If the police were confident they knew the intended method of attack, they'd prepare for that and not the real one. But what was the real one? How was Quinn actually going to get at Lane?

Baxter had taken an extreme step to find out: breaking into Quinn's house. He had disabled the alarm and surveillance cameras, then examined the man's office carefully. Hidden in the desk were books on sabotage and surveillance. Two pages were annotated with Post-its, marking chapters on turning propane tanks into bombs and on making remote detonators. He found another note as well "Trotter Garden Supplies." That was where Sandy Lane went every Saturday afternoon to refill his barbecue's gas tanks. Baxter believed that Quinn's plan was to keep the police focused on a poison attack when he was in fact going to arrange an "accidental" explosion after Lane picked up his new propane tank.

Baxter couldn't go to the police with this information as he'd committed trespass. He's heard from some sources that Quinn was asking about propane tanks and where Lane shopped. There was no evidence to justify a search warrant but Clough had reluctantly agreed to Baxter's plan to catch Quinn in the act. First, they'd make it seem they believed the cyanide threat. Since Quinn probably knew Lane went to the propane shop every Saturday around lunchtime, and that he would take his post and food to the police, apparently for testing, which would occupy them for several hours. Quinn would be following. Lane would then leave and run some errands, among them picking up a new gas canister. Only it wouldn't be Sandy Lane in the car, but Detective Peter Billings, the look-alike. Billings would collect a new gas tank from Trotters, though it would be empty, for safety's sake and then stash it in his car. He'd then return to the Garden Centre to browse and Clough and his men would wait for Quinn to make his move.

"So where's our man?" Clough asked his partner.

Quinn had left his house at about the same time as Lane and headed in the same direction. They'd lost him in traffic for a time but then picked him up at a Tesco's supermarket. One officer saw him inside. Doing his impersonation of Lane, Billings walked outside, got into the car and headed into traffic. Baxter and Lane climbed into one of the other cars and eased after him, though well behind so they wouldn't get spotted by Quinn if he was, in fact, trailing Billings. Twenty minutes later the undercover officer pulled up in front of Trotter Garden Supplies and Baxter and Lane parked a discreet distance away.

"Okay," Billings radioed through his hidden microphone, "I'm getting the tank and going inside."

Lane and Baxter leaned forward to watch what was happening. Lane could just make out his Mercedes up the street. Billings came on a moment later.

"I've loaded the fake tank in the car on the back seat. I'm going back inside."

Fifteen minutes later Lane heard an officer's voice urgently saying, "I have something .... There's a man in a hat and sunglasses, could be Quinn approaching the Mercedes. He's got a shopping bag in one hand and something in the other. Looks like a small computer. It might be a detonator, or the device itself."

Baxter nodded at Sandy Lane, sitting beside him, and said, "here we go."

"I can see him," another voice said. The surveillance officer continued. "He's looking around. Hold on ....OK, the suspect just walked by Lane's car. Couldn't see for sure, but", he paused, "I think he might've dropped something underneath it. Now he's crossing the street and into The Red Lion. That'll be where he'll detonate the device from. OK everybody, let's seal off the street and get an undercover officer inside the pub to keep an eye on him."

Baxter lifted an eyebrow to Lane and smiled.

"This is it."

"I hope so," was the uneasy response.

Now officers were moving in slowly, sticking close to the pub where Quinn was waiting for "Lane" to return to the car, detonate the device and send him to his death.

A new voice came on the radio. "'I'm inside the pub; I can see the subject by a window on a stool, looking out. No weapons in sight. He's opened up what he was carrying before, a small computer or something with an antenna on it. He's just typed something. Assume that the device is armed."

Baxter said, "we're in position. The street's been blocked off and the back door's covered. We're ready. What's that?"

Lane turned. On the boot of the car was a small shopping bag. While they'd been staring at Lane's somebody had put it there.

"This is Baxter. Stand by. Oh hell, he saw us! He didn't plant anything under the Mercedes. Or if he did there's another device on the car. It's in a Tesco bag, a little one. We're getting out!"

"No, no," another voice called over the radio. It could have a pressure or rocker switch. Any movement could set it off. Stay put, we'll get an officer there."

Baxter muttered, "it's a double feint. He leads us off with the poison and then a fake bomb at the Mercedes. He's been watching us all along and he's planning to get us here. Jesus! Everybody, get into the pub. Don't let him hit the detonator."

Baxter covered his face with his jacket. Sandy Lane had his doubts that that would provide much protection from an exploding gas tank, but he did exactly the same.

They crashed through the door and froze as they saw Quinn, who merely turned, alarmed and frowning in curiosity like the other patrons, at the sound of the officers.

"Hands up; you!"

Quinn stumbled back off the stool, eyes wide in shock. He lifted his hands. An officer from the bomb squad stepped between Quinn and the detonator and looked it over carefully, as an officer threw him to the floor and handcuffed him.

"I didn't do anything! What's this all about?"

The detective called into his microphone, "we've got him. Bomb Units One and Two, proceed to make safe."

In the car there was complete silence. Baxter and Lane struggled to remain motionless but Lane felt as if his pounding heart was going to joggle the bomb enough so that it would detonate. They learned that Quinn was in custody and couldn't push the detonator button, but that didn't mean that the device wasn't fitted with a hair trigger. Baxter had spent the last five minutes telling Lane how sensitive some bomb detonators could be, until Lane had told him to shut the hell up. Wrapped in his jacket, Lane, the bent copper, peeked out and, in the wing mirror watched the policeman in a green bomb jacket approach the car slowly.

Through the radio's tinny speaker a voice commanded "Baxter, Lane stay completely still."

"Absolutely," Baxter said in a throaty whisper, his lips barely moving.

Lane could see the policeman step closer and peer into the shopping bag. He took out a flashlight and pointed it downward, examining the contents. With a wooden probe, like a chopstick, he carefully searched the bag. Through the speaker they heard what sounded like a gasp. Lane cringed. It wasn't a gasp; it was a laugh, followed by: "Rubbish."

"It's what?"

The officer pulled his hood off and walked to the front of the car. With a shaking hand, Lane opened the window. "Rubbish," the man repeated, somebody's lunch. They had prawn sandwich, crisps and an apple. Not a meal I myself would've chosen."

The first bomb unit called in; a search of the area beneath Lane's Mercedes had revealed nothing but a crumpled Coke can, which Quinn might or might not have thrown there. Baxter and Lane walked angrily into The Red Lion. The patrons had resumed eating and drinking and were clearly enjoying the show. The uniformed officer who'd just searched Quinn recited: "wallet, keys, money, nothing else." Another detective from the bomb squad had carefully examined the "detonator" and reported that they'd been wrong; it was only a small laptop computer.

Lomax & The Biker – The Trilogy

As Lane was mulling this over, a plain-clothed officer appeared at the door and said, "We searched Quinn's car. No explosives."

"Explosives?" Quinn asked, frowning deeply.

"But there was an empty gas tank," the policeman added. "From Trotters."

Quinn added, "I needed a refill. That's where I always go. I was going there after lunch." He nodded at the bar menu. "You ever try the steak pie here? It's the best in town."

Lane muttered, "You played us like a fish, goddamn it. Making us think your rubbish was a bomb."

Another cold smile crossed Quinn's face. "Why exactly did you think I'd have a bomb?" There was silence for a moment. Quinn nodded at the computer.

"Press the play button." It's not a bomb. And even if it was, would I blow myself up as well?"

The detective hit the button. "Oh, Christ," muttered Baxter as a video came on the small screen. It showed the security man prowling through an office.

Quinn said, "he's in my office at home. I was going to stop by the police station after lunch and drop off the copy. But since you're here ... it's all yours."

The officers watched Baxter ransacking Quinn's desk.

"I think that's breaking and entering and trespass too. And, if you were going to ask, yes I want to press charges."

"But I'm sure I ..." the security man stammered.

"You did what?" Quinn interrupted and then completed the sentence for him. "You shut the power off; and the backup too? But I've been a little paranoid lately, thanks to Mr Lane. So I have two battery backups."

"You broke into his house?" Sandy Lane asked Baxter, looking shocked. "You never told me that."

"Don't be such a hypocrite!" Baxter exploded. "You knew exactly what I was doing. You agreed to it! You wanted me to!"

"I swear," Lane said, "this is the first I've heard about it."

Quinn called after him, "if you're interested, those books about bombs and things? I got them for research. I'm trying my hand at a murder mystery. Everybody seems to be doing it nowadays. I've got a couple of chapters on that computer. Why don't you check it out, if you don't believe me?"

"You're lying!"

Then Lane turned to Clough, who had remained in the background until then. "You know why he did this, don't you? It's all part of his plan. Think about it. He sets up a sting to get rid of my security man and leave me unprotected. And then he does all this, with the fake bomb, to find out about your procedures, the bomb squad, how many officers you have, who your undercover officers are."

"Did you leave a Tesco bag on the boot of Mr. Baxter's car?" Clough asked.

Quinn replied, "no. If you think I did, why don't you check for fingerprints? I have to say, I'm getting pretty tired of this whole thing. I'm sick of my house being broken into, sick of being watched all the time. I think it's time to call my solicitor."

Lane stepped forward angrily. "You're lying! Tell me why you're doing this! Tell me, goddamn it! I've looked at every bad thing I've ever done in my whole life. I mean everything. The homeless guy I told to get a job when he asked me for a quid, the waitress I called a stupid cow because she gave me the wrong order, the valet I didn't tip because he couldn't speak English. Every little goddamn thing! I've been going over my life with a microscope. I don't know what I did to you. Tell me! Tell me!"

His face was red and the veins jutted out on his neck. His fists were clenched.

"I don't know what you're talking about, so I think it's time you removed these handcuffs, before I think of another charge to bring."

Clough took a decision and unlocked them.

"I'm inclined to believe him. I think Tareeq was making the whole thing up."

"But the sauna..." Lane began.

"Think about it, though. Nothing happened. And there was nothing wrong with the brakes on your Mercedes. We just got the report."

Lane snapped. "But the repair guide. He bought one!"

"Brakes?" Quinn asked.

Lane said, "you bought a book on Mercedes brakes. Don't deny it."

"Why would I deny it? Call the DVLA. I bought an old Mercedes and it needs new brakes. I'm going to do the work myself. Sorry, Lane, but I think you need professional help."

"No, he just bought the car as a cover," Lane raged. "Look at him. Look at his eyes! He's just waiting for a chance to kill me."

Baxter said, "Sandy, if you're so sure that somebody is trying to kill you, then I think you'd better find another babysitter. I've done all I can and you've tested our friendship enough. I frankly don't have time for any more of these games." He turned to his team. "Come on, let's pack up. We've got some real cases to get back to."

The detective noticed the bartender hovering nearby, holding Quinn's steak pie. Quinn sat back down, unfolded a napkin and smoothed it on his lap.

"Good, huh?" he asked Quinn.

"The best."

Clough needed to save face and limit damage. "I'm sorry, Mr Quinn. We'll leave now. I hope you enjoy your meal."

Quinn shrugged. Suddenly his mood seemed to change. Smiling, he turned to Lane, who was heading out the front door, and called, "Hey."

Lane stopped and stared back.

"Good luck to you," Quinn said, and before starting on his lunch, pretended to make a call on a mobile phone. Lane saw the gesture and went ghostly white before rushing out to get fresh air into his lungs.

-16-

At ten that night Ray Quinn made the rounds of his house, saying good night to his children and stepson, as he always did. Then he showered and climbed into bed, waiting for his wife, who was finishing the dishes. A moment later the lights in the kitchen went out and she passed the doorway. His wife smiled at him and continued into the bathroom. A moment later he heard the shower. He enjoyed the hiss of falling water. Lying back against a half dozen thick pillows, he reflected on the day's events, particularly the incident at The Red Lion. Sandy Lane, face red, eyes frightened. He was out of control. He was as crazed as a lunatic. Of course, he also happened to be 100 percent right. Ray Quinn had in fact done everything that Lane had accused him of, from approaching Tareeq about the alarms to planting the rubbish on the boot of Baxter's car. Yes, he'd done it all. But he'd never had any intention of hurting one hair on Lane's head. He'd asked Tareeq about Lane's security system but the next day had anonymously turned him in for drugs (Quinn had seen him dealing crack on the street). He knew he'd be desperate enough to attempt to make a deal and give enough information to set the whole thing up.

The payback wasn't exacting physical revenge; it was simply making the man believe that Quinn was going to kill him, guaranteeing that Lane would spend a long, long time wallowing in paranoia and misery, waiting; just waiting. Was that just a stomach cramp? Or was it the first symptom of arsenic poisoning?

Lomax & The Biker – The Trilogy

He grinned inwardly as he recalled that Lane had asked desperately what he had done to upset him and had actually mentioned the very transgression that afternoon at The Red Lion. Quinn thought back to it now, an autumn day two years ago. His daughter Celeste had returned home from her after school job, a troubled look on her face.

"What's the matter?" he'd asked.

The sixteen-year-old hadn't answered but had walked immediately to her room and closed the door. These were the days not long after her mother had passed away and occasional moods were not unusual, but he had persisted in drawing her out and that night he'd learned the reason she was upset. There had been an incident during her shift at McDonald's. Celeste confessed that she'd accidentally mixed up two orders and given a man a chicken sandwich when he'd asked for a Big Mac. He'd left, not realizing the mistake, but had returned five minutes later, walked up to the counter and looked over at the heavyset girl. He had curled his lip and snapped, "So you're not only a fat cow, you are stupid too. I want to see the manager; now!"

Celeste had tried to be stoic about the incident but as she related it to her father a single tear ran down her cheek. Quinn was heartbroken at the sight. The next day he'd learned the identity of the customer from the manager. A single tear for some people, perhaps, not even worth a second thought, but because it was his daughter's tear, it meant everything to Ray Quinn. He decided it was payback time.

Lomax & The Biker – The Trilogy

He now heard the water stop running, and detected a fragrant smell of perfume wafting from the bathroom. His wife came to bed, laying her head on his chest.

"You seem happy tonight," she said.

"Do I?"

"When I walked past before and saw you staring at the ceiling you looked ... what's the word; content?"

He thought about the word. "That describes it."

Quinn turned out the light and, putting his arm around his wife, pulled her closer to him. "I'm glad you're in my life," she whispered.

"Me too," he replied.

Stretching out, Ray considered his next steps. He'd probably let him have a month or two of peace. Then, just when the bent copper was feeling comfortable, he'd start up again. He knew all about Lane and his terrible history, but felt that between himself and Lomax they could extract more appropriate and dreadful revenge than the system.

What would he do? Maybe an empty medicine vial next to his car, along with a bit of harmless Botox on the door handle. That had some appeal to it. He'd have to check if there was a trace of anything sinister like botulism bacteria.

Now that he'd convinced the police that he was innocent and Lane was paranoid, the copper could cry wolf as often as he liked and he would not be believed. The playing field was wide open.

Lomax & The Biker – The Trilogy

Perhaps he could enlist Lane's wife. She'd be a willing ally, he thought. In his surveillance Quinn had seen how badly the man treated her. He'd overheard Lane lose his temper at her once when she kept pressuring him to let her apply to a local college for promotion. He'd yelled as if she were a teenager. He had followed Judith Lane to a solicitor's and had found out that she was preparing for divorce. Perhaps she'd be willing to give him some information that he could use.

Another idea occurred to him. He could send Lane an anonymous letter, possibly with a cryptic message on it. The words wouldn't be important. The point would be the smell; he'd sprinkle the paper with almond extract which gave off the tell tale aroma of cyanide. After all, nobody knew that he hadn't made a batch of poison. Oh, the possibilities were endless....

He rolled onto his side, whispered to his wife that he loved her and in sixty seconds was sound asleep.

-17-

Ray Quinn and his good friend John Lomax were very pleased with the outcome. In fact Lomax had been most impressed by the subtlety of it all. They decided that it was not going to stop. Lane was alive, he was free. Certainly he was frightened, but they knew he would not stop and decided that they were the most appropriate people to pursue him and all he held dear. He was that most loathsome of creatures: a bent copper who thought and acted as though he was above the law. Worse than that in their view, if not controlled, he would continue to use his position for his evil ends. He had to be made to pay but not, maybe, solely in monetary terms. Oh no, they had something far more satisfying in mind. They could use the situation to their own advantage and gradually destroy Lane at the same time.

As for Detective Inspector Lane, his life had changed irrevocably and he knew there was no turning back. He also realised that he could be vulnerable. Perhaps to blackmail, perhaps to coercion, perhaps, he thought, to anything at all. Was his family safe? Was he safe himself? Would his colleagues find out his awful secrets?

Sandy Lane constructed a plan. He would make sure John Lomax would be out of his way for many years.

Lomax & The Biker – The Trilogy

-18-

Exactly twelve months later to the day of Lane's "embarrassment" the knocking on the door not only woke John Lomax from an afternoon nap, but it told him immediately who his visitor was. It was not a polite single rap, not a friendly Morse code but a repeated slamming of the brass knocker. Three times; four; six.

Lomax was dreamily and wistfully recalling the unexpected and surprisingly pneumatic encounter on the train with the mysterious woman. It seemed a lifetime ago now. So much had happened; his life had changed so much. He was so much more content these days. Lomax was even tempted to catch that particular train again just to see whether the lady would appear and be equally as willing. He was, after all, on his own now.

He did not appreciate the disturbance and he took a moment to slip into a slightly higher level of wakefulness. It was five p.m. and he'd been gardening all day, until about an hour ago when a beer and the warmth of a May afternoon had lulled him to sleep. He flicked on the light and, walking unsteadily to the door, pulled it open.

He recognised the sandy haired man immediately and his hackles rose. He was instantly alert and on his guard. Without waiting to be invited Lane brushed past Lomax and strode into the living room. Behind him was an older, burlier man dressed in a tweedy brown.

Lomax & The Biker – The Trilogy

Once more not waiting for an invitation, Lane sat on the couch as if he'd just stepped away from it for a trip to the bathroom.

"Who're you?" Lomax asked the other one bluntly.

"Detective Sergeant Hathaway."

"You don't need to see his Warrant Card, John, do you?" Lane said. It was not a question.

Lomax affected a yawn to show both that they had interrupted his slumber and, more to the point, that he was already irritated and bored with the presence of the despicable Lane. He'd wanted the couch but the uninvited visitor was sitting stiffly in the middle of it so he took the uncomfortable chair instead. Hathaway didn't sit down. He crossed his arms and looked around the dim room, then let his vision settle on Lomax's faded blue jeans, dusty socks and grubby T-shirt. They were his gardening clothes.

Yawning again and brushing his hair into place, Lomax asked "you're not here to arrest me because you would've done that already. So, what do you want?"

Lane's hand disappeared into his suit jacket and returned with a notebook, which he consulted. "Just wanted to let you know, John, we found out about your bank accounts at Barclays in Paddington."

"You'd need a court order to do that and I would have known."

"You don't need a court order for some things, and you would most certainly not have known."

Leaning back in the chair Lomax wondered if they'd put some kind of trace on his computer. He'd only set up the accounts last week and had been very careful to install all the recommended security measures, but was nevertheless not surprised by what Lane had just said.

He noticed that the tweedy detective was surveying the inside of his modest bungalow.

"No, Sergeant Hathaway, I don't look like I'm living in luxury, if that's what you were observing, because I'm not. Tell me; did you work on the Anvex case?"

The sergeant didn't need the glance from his boss to know that he should say nothing.

Lomax continued, "but you do know that the burglar netted about five hundred thousand. Now if, like Mr Lane (the name was almost spat out contemptuously) you think I was the one who stole the money, wouldn't I be living in something a little nicer than this?"

"Not if you were smart," the sergeant muttered and decided to sit down.

"Not if I were smart," Lomax repeated and laughed.

Hathaway looked around the dim living room and added, "we think this is sort of a safe house. You probably have some better places overseas."

"I wish."

"Well, don't we all agree that you're not a typical resident for this area?"

In fact John Lomax was a bit of an oddball in the neighbourhood. He'd suddenly appeared there about six months ago and everybody around thought he had some businesses deals in the area. He was single, travelled a lot, had a vague career (he owned companies that bought and sold other companies was how he explained it). He made good money but had picked for his residence this modest bungalow, which, as they'd just established, was nowhere close to luxurious. So when Sandy Lane's clever police computer compiled a list of everyone who'd moved to the town not long before the Anvex robbery four months ago, Lomax had earned suspect status, and Lane was delighted by the convenient opportunity. He saw the chance to make Lomax go away for good. Also, as the policeman began to look more closely at Lomax, the evidence got better and better. He had no alibi for the hours of the robbery. The tyre tracks left by the getaway car were similar to those on Lomax's new Lexus. Lane had also discovered the previously overlooked fact that Lomax had a degree in electrical engineering. The burglar in the Anvex case had dismantled a sophisticated alarm system to get into the strong room. Even better, though, from Lane's point of view, was the history between the two of them.

Oh, he knew in his heart that Lomax was behind the Anvex theft and he went after him zealously. He'd already arrested Lomax once, a month ago, and the case was looking watertight until a witness had come forward and said the man seen leaving the Anvex grounds just after the robbery didn't look at all like Lomax. Lane was still not aware that the mysterious witness was one of Ray Quinn's many girlfriends. The CPS had decided there was no case against him and ordered Lomax to be released. This had turned the screw even more for Lane and, apoplectic with rage, he vowed on his mother's life that Lomax would go down for the robbery. Lane still fumed at the embarrassment whilst Lomax savoured the sweetness of it all. Lane had found no other leads so he returned to Lomax with renewed vigour. He kept digging and where necessary inventing and slowly began shoring up the case with circumstantial evidence. Lomax frequently played golf on a course next to Anvex, the perfect place for staking out the company, and he owned an acetylene torch that was powerful enough to cut through the loading bay door at Anvex. Lane used this information to ensure surveillance on Lomax and this had led to the interrupted nap today.

"So what about the Anvex money, John?"

"What about it?" John Lomax now entered into the spirit and decided to be clever.

"Where'd the money come from?"

"I stole the crown jewels. No, it was the Great Train Robbery. Sorry, I lied. I knocked over a casino in Mayfair."

Sandy Lane sighed and momentarily lowered his lids, which ended with perfect, delicate lashes.

Lomax asked, "what about that other suspect, the BT worker in his van down a hole in the ground. You were going to check him out."

Around the time of the robbery a man in a BT jacket had been seen pulling a suitcase from some bushes near the Anvex main gate. A passing driver thought this looked suspicious and noted the registration number of the van. He had phoned the police on his mobile and the van, which had been stolen a week earlier in Manchester, was later found abandoned at Gatwick Airport's North car park.

"Didn't have any luck finding him," Lane lied.

"I mean," Lomax grumbled, "that it was a long shot, he's out of the picture and it's much easier to chase me than it is to find the real thief." He snapped. "Shit, you people really are useless. Mr Lane," he continued, his voice dripping with sarcasm and contempt, "the only thing I've ever done wrong in my life was listening to a couple of friends I shouldn't have when I was seventeen." He decided not to tell that particular story. "You and I have history, as you know, but I don't bear grudges and would much prefer to live and let live."

That was also a lie. Lomax definitely did not intend to live and let live as far as Lane was concerned. He knew about Lane. He was his enemy, and Lomax had already promised himself the excitement to be derived from destroying him. The game was already proving more interesting than Lane could ever appreciate.

"Can you prove the funds came from a legitimate source?" the sergeant asked formally.

Lomax ignored Hathaway disdainfully. "What happened to your other assistant, Detective? I liked him. He didn't last too long. Perhaps working with you is the problem."

Lane had gone through two assistants in the time he'd been after John Lomax. He supposed that though the public and media were impressed with the obsessive policeman he'd make his colleagues' lives miserable.

"Okay," the detective said. "If you're not going to talk that's just the way it is. Oh, but I should let you know, we've got some information we're looking at right now. It's very interesting."

"Ah, more of your surveillance?"

"Maybe."

"And what exactly did you find?"

"Let's just call it interesting."

Lomax said, "interesting. You said that twice. Do either of you want a drink?"

Lane answered for both of them. "No."

Lomax fetched a Heineken from the kitchen. He continued, "so what you're saying is that after you've gone over this interesting information you'll have enough evidence to arrest me for real this time. But if I confess it'll go a lot easier. Correct?"

"Come on, John. Nobody was hurt at Anvex. You'll do, what, five years. It'd be a church social for you."

Lomax nodded for a moment, drank a good bit of lager, then said seriously, "But if I confessed, then I'd have to give the money back, right?"

Lane froze for a moment. Then he smiled. "'I'm not going to stop until I nail you, John. You know that." He said to the sergeant, "Let's go. This is a waste of time."

"At last there's something we agree on," John Lomax offered and closed the door after them.

The next day, Sandy Lane, wearing a perfectly pressed grey suit, white shirt and striped red tie, strode into the police station nearest to the Anvex site with Hathaway behind him. He nodded at the eight people sitting down. The men and women fell silent as the detective surveyed his officers. Coffee was sipped, pencils tapped, pads doodled upon, watches glanced at.

"We're going to make a push on the case. I went to see Lomax yesterday. I lit a fire under him and it had an effect: Last night he transferred fifty thousand pounds from a bank in Paddington to a bank in Lyon, France. I'm convinced he's getting ready to flee the country."

Lane had managed to get increased surveillance on Lomax. This high-tech approach to investigations involved establishing real-time links to his online service provider and the computers at Lomax's credit card companies, banks, mobile phone service and the like. Anytime that Lomax made a purchase, went online, made a call, withdrew cash and so on, the officers on the Anvex investigation team would know almost instantly.

"Big Brother's going to be watching everything our boy's doing."

"Who?" asked one of the younger men.

"1984?" Lane responded, astonished that the man hadn't heard of the novel. "The book?" he asked sarcastically. When the officer continued to stare blankly he added, "Big Brother was the government. It watched everything the citizens did." He nodded at a nearby dusty computer terminal and then turned back to the officers. "You, me, and Big Brother, -we're closing the net on Lomax." Noting the stifled grins, he wished he'd been a bit less dramatic. But, sod it, didn't they realize that they had become the laughing stock of The Met for not solving this case?

Lane divided the group into three teams and assigned them to shifts at the computer workstations, with orders to relay to him instantly everything that Lomax did. As he was walking back to his office to look further at Lomax's transfer to France he heard, a voice.

"Dad?"

He turned to see his son striding down the corridor in his direction, dressed in the typical uniform of a seventeen year old: shabby T-shirt and jeans so baggy they looked like they'd fall off at any moment. He hadn't seen Billy in quite some time. He kept in touch and paid maintenance of course (he convinced himself he had some integrity) but rarely spent any time with his son. Billy was an intelligent youth despite the first impressions created by his appearance, nothing like the troublemakers that Lane dealt with in an official capacity.

"What're you doing here?" he asked.

"It's evening night tonight. I just wondered if you would come for once."

Lane felt the sharp sting of the verbal rebuke and realised that Billy must have a reason for asking. He was supposed to be having a conference call with French officers about Lomax's transfer of funds, so he would probably be late, but decided not to favour Billy with the information.

"I'd be glad to come."

"Good, Dad, it's important," Billy said.

"Billy, are you still taking French?"

His son blinked. "Yeah, I don't like it though." He grunted with typical teenage moodiness.

"Who's your teacher?"

"Mrs. Vandell."

"Is she at school now?"

"Yes," Billy replied regarding his father with suspicion. "Why?"

"I need her to help me with a conference call. Tell your mother I'll be at the meeting as soon as I can."

Lane left the boy standing in the middle of the hallway and jogged to his office, so excited about the brainstorm of using the French teacher to help him translate that he nearly collided with a workman hunched over one of the potted plants in the corridor, trimming leaves.

"Sorry," he called and hurried into his office. He phoned Billy's French teacher and when he told her how important the case was she reluctantly agreed to help him translate. The conference call went off as scheduled and the woman's translation efforts were a huge help; without his brainstorm to use the woman he couldn't have communicated with the two officers at all. Still, the investigators in France reported that they'd found no impropriety in Lomax's investments or financial dealings. He paid taxes and had never run into any trouble with the gendarmes. Lane asked if they had tapped his phone and were monitoring his online and banking activities. There was a pause and then one of the officers responded. Billy's French teacher translated, "They say, 'We are not as high tech as you. We prefer to catch criminals the old-fashioned way." They did agree to alert their customs agents to check Lomax's luggage carefully the next time he was in the country. Lane thanked the two men and the teacher then hung up.

"We prefer to catch criminals the old-fashioned way"....which is why we'll get him and you won't, thought the detective, as he spun around in his chair and began staring intently at Big Brother's computer monitor once again.

-19-

John Lomax stepped out of the department store, following the young man he'd noticed in the jewellery department. The boy kept his head down and walked quickly away from the store. When they were passing an alleyway Lomax suddenly jogged forward, grabbed the skinny kid by the arm and pulled him into the shadows.

"Jesus," he whispered in shock.

Lomax pinned him up against the wall.

"Don't think about running." He took a glance toward the boy's pockets. "And don't think about anything else."

"I don't-" the boy said with a quivering voice, "I don't have a knife or anything."

"What's your name?" Lomax barked.

"Sam. Sam Phillips. Like, what do you want?"

"Give me the watch."

The boy sighed and rolled his eyes.

"Give it to me. You don't want me to have to take it off you." Lomax outweighed the boy by fifty pounds and the boy reached into his pocket and handed him the Seiko that Lomax had seen him lift off the counter at the store. Lomax took it.

"Who're you? Security? Police?"

Lomax eyed him carefully and then pocketed the watch.

"You were clumsy. If the guard hadn't been taking a leak he would've caught you."

"What guard?"

Lomax & The Biker – The Trilogy

"That's my point; the little bloke in the tatty jacket and dirty jeans."

"He was a security guard?"

"Yes."

"How'd you spot him?"

Lomax said grimly, "Let's say I've had my share of run ins with people like that."

The boy looked up for a moment, examined his assailant and resumed his study of the tarmac in the alley. "How'd you spot me?"

"It wasn't hard. You were skulking around the store like you'd already been spotted."

Lomax looked up and down the street cautiously, and then said, "I need somebody to help me with this thing I've got going tomorrow."

"Why me?" the boy asked.

"There're some people who'd like to set me up."

"Police?"

"Just some people." Lomax nodded at the watch. "But since I spotted you pinch that, I know you're not working for anybody."

"What do I have to do?"

"It's easy. I need a driver for half an hour's easy work."

Billy was suddenly afraid and excited in equal measure. "Like, how much?"

"'I'll pay you five hundred."

Billy undertook another examination of the scenery as he struggled with the events. "Five hundred for half an hour?"

Lomax nodded.

"Shit, five hundred?"

"That's right."

"What're we doing?" he asked, a little cautious now. "I mean, exactly."

"'I've got to ... pick up a few things at this place, a house. I need you to park in the alley behind the house while I go inside for a few minutes."

The boy grinned. "So, you're going to get some stuff?"

Lomax shushed him. "Even if I am, you think I'd shout about it?"

"Sorry I wasn't thinking." The boy squinted then said, "Hey, there's this friend of mine? And we've got a connection. He's getting us some good stuff. We can turn it around in a week. You come in with a thousand or two and he'll give us a better discount. You can double your money. You interested?"

"Drugs?"

"Yeah."

"I don't ever go near them, and you shouldn't either. They screw up your life. Remember that. Meet me tomorrow, okay?"

"When?"

"Midday. Over there in Starbucks." Lomax started to walk away.

"If this works out you think maybe there'd be some more work for me?"

"I might be away for a while, but yes, possibly; if you handle it right."

"I do a good job, mister. Hey, what's your name?"

"You don't need to know that."

The boy nodded. "That's cool. Sure, but there's one other thing. What about the watch?"

"I'll dispose of the evidence for you."

After the kid had gone Lomax walked slowly to the mouth of the alley and peered out. There was no sign of Lane's surveillance team. He'd been careful to lose them but they had this almost magical ability to appear from nowhere and nail him with their Big Ear mikes and telephoto lenses. Pulling on his baseball cap and lowering his head, he stepped out of the alley and walked down the pavement quickly, as if satellites were tracking his position from ten thousand miles in space.

The next morning Sandy Lane was late coming into the office. He'd screwed up by missing the parent's evening yesterday, so he had made an attempt to apologise to Billy.

When he walked into the police station at nine-thirty Sergeant Hathaway told him, "Lomax has been doing some shopping you ought to know about."

"What?"

"He left his house an hour ago. Our boys followed him. They lost him but then we got a payment notice from one of his credit card companies. He bought six books at Waterstones. We don't know exactly what they were but the product code from the store listed them as travel books. Then he left and spent thirty-eight pounds at Tyler's Shop."

"What do they sell?"

"Don't know, but we soon will. We lost him after that so the team went back to his house to wait."

"Got something else," called a young policewoman nearby. "He bought some tools for forty quid as well."

Lane pondered. "So, it sounds like he's planning another robbery. Then he's going to flee the country." Gazing at one of the computer screens, he asked absently, "What're you going after this time, John Lomax? A business, a house?"

Hathaway's phone rang. He answered and listened. "That was the babysitter in front of the house. Lomax is back home, but something's not right. He was on foot. He must've parked up the street somewhere." He listened some more. "They say there's a painting truck in his driveway. Maybe that's why."

"No. He's up to something. I don't trust anything that man does."

"Got another notice!" one officer called. "He just went online."

The police had no court order allowing them to view the content of what Lomax downloaded, though they could observe the sites he was connected to. "Okay. He's on the Anderson & Cross website."

"The burglar alarm company?" Lane asked, his heart pounding with excitement.

"Yes."

A few minutes later the officer called, "now he's checking out Travel Central dot com. It's a service that lets you make airline reservations online."

"Tell the surveillance team we'll let them know as soon as he goes offline." They should be ready to move. I've got a feeling this is going to happen fast."

We've got you now, Lane thought. Then he laughed and looked at the computers affectionately. Big Brother Is Watching You....

Lomax & The Biker – The Trilogy

-20-

In the passenger seat of his car John Lomax nodded toward a high fence in an alleyway behind Tremont Street. "Sam, pull over there."

The car braked slowly to a stop.

"That's it?" The nervous kid asked, nodding toward a white house on the other side of the fence.

"Yes. Now, listen. If you see the Old Bill just drive off slowly. Go around the block but turn left at the street. Got that? Stay off Tremont Drive, whatever you do."

The boy asked uneasily, "You think somebody could come by?"

"Let's hope not." Lomax looked up and down the alley, took the tools he'd just bought that morning out of the boot and walked through the gate in the fence. He disappeared around the side of the house and returned ten minutes later. Hurrying through the gate he carried a heavy box and a small shopping bag. He disappeared again and returned with several more boxes. He loaded everything in the back of the car and wiped sweat from his forehead. He dropped hard into the passenger's seat. "Let's go."

"Where're the tools?"

"I left them back there. What're you waiting for? Go."

The boy accelerated hard and the car jumped into the middle of the alley. Soon they were on the main road and Lomax gave directions to a Holiday Inn. There he climbed out, walked into the reception and registered for two nights. He returned to the car.

Lomax & The Biker – The Trilogy

"Room 129. He said it's round the side in the back."

They found the spot, parked and climbed out. Lomax handed the boy the room key. He opened the door and together they carried the boxes and the shopping bag inside.

"Don't like this room," the boy said, looking around.

"I won't be here that long."

Lomax turned his back and opened the grocery bag. He extracted ten fifty pound notes and handed them over. He added another twenty.

"You'll have to take a cab back to town."

"Shit." He said, nodding at the bag of money.

Lomax said nothing. He stuffed the bag into a suitcase, locked it and slipped it under the bed. The kid pocketed his money.

"You did a good job today, Sam. Thanks."

"How'll I find you, mister? I mean, if you want to hire me again?"

"I'll leave a message at the Starbucks."

"OK. That's good."

Lomax glanced at his watch. He emptied his pockets on the dresser. "Now I need a shower and then I've got to see some people."

They shook hands. The boy left and Lomax swung the door shut after him. In the bathroom he turned the shower on full, the water hot. He leaned against the wobbly basin and watched the steam roll out of the cubicle like stormy clouds and considered what was about to happen.

-21-

"There's something wrong!" Hathaway called out.

"What?"

"I don't know; a glitch of some kind." He nodded at one computer. "Lomax is still online at his house. Look. The trouble is we've just been told by Barclays' credit card computer that somebody using Lomax's card booked a room at the Holiday Inn about forty five minutes ago. There's got to be a mistake. He-"

"Oh, Christ," Lane spat out. "There's no mistake. Lomax left his computer on so we'd think he was home. That's why he parked the car around the corner. So our men wouldn't see him leave. He snuck through the side or out the back."

Lane grabbed the phone and raged at the surveillance team that their subject had got away from him. He ordered them to check to make sure. He slammed the receiver down and a moment later a sheepish officer called back to confirm that the painters said Lomax had left over an hour ago.

The detective sighed. "So while we were napping he knocked over the next target. I don't believe it. I just-"

"He just made another payment, sir. Petrol at BP; filled it up."

Lane nodded, considering this. "Maybe he's going to drive somewhere to catch a flight."

Walking to the wall map, the detective stuck pins in the locations. He was calmer now. Lomax may have guessed they'd be monitoring his online activity but obviously didn't know the extent of their surveillance.

"Get an unmarked car to follow him."

"We've just had a report from the speed camera main computer," one of the officers across the room called. He turned off the M1 at Brent Cross four minutes ago."

Another pin was stabbed into the map. Hathaway directed the pursuing officers. Fifteen minutes later, the officer monitoring the speed camera computer called out once again, "he just turned off and stopped."

Eastbound? Lane reflected. He was heading for a tough area, populated by bikers. If Lomax had an accomplice that place would be as good as any. And nearby there were plenty of derelict sites with many places to hide the Anvex haul.

"Still no sighting yet," Hathaway said, listening on his phone to the pursuing officers. "Damn. We're going to lose him."

But then another officer called, "I just got a ping from Lomax's mobile phone company, he's turned it on and he's making a call. They're tracing it." A moment later he called out, "Okay. He's moving again."

Another blue tipped pin in the map. Hathaway relayed this information to the vehicles pursuing Lomax. Then he listened and gave a laugh.

"They've got the car. He's pulling into an estate. Okay.... He's parking near a block of flats. He's getting out. He's talking to a white male, thirties, shaved head, tattoos. The male's nodding toward a shed at the back. They're walking back there together ...."

They're getting a package out of a shed .... Now they're going inside."

"That's good enough for me," Lane announced. "Tell them to stay out of sight. We'll be there in twenty minutes. Advise us if the suspect starts to leave."

As he started for the door, he said a silent prayer, thanking both the Lord and Big Brother for their help.

The drive took closer to forty minutes but John Lomax's car was still parked in front of the flats. The officers on the scene reported that the robber and his bald accomplice were still inside, presumably planning their escape. The four police cars from headquarters were parked some distance and nine Met officers, three armed with shotguns, were crouching behind sheds and weeds and rusty cars.

Everybody kept low, believing that Lomax might be armed. Lane and Hathaway eased forward toward the flats. They had to handle the situation carefully. Unless they could catch a glimpse of the Anvex payroll money through a door or window, or unless Lomax carried it outside in plain view, they had no cause to arrest him. They circled the place but couldn't see in; the door was closed and the curtains were drawn. Hell, Lane thought, discouraged. Maybe they could... But then he had a thought.

"Smell that?" Lane asked in a whisper.

Hathaway frowned. "What?"

"Coming from inside."

The sergeant inhaled deeply. "Cannabis or something," he said, nodding. This would give them all they needed to enter.

"Let's do it," Hathaway whispered."

"No. He's mine."

He took off his suit jacket and strapped on a bulletproof vest, then drew his automatic pistol. Gazing at the other officers, he mouthed, "Ready?"

They nodded. The detective held up three fingers, then bent them down one at a time. One ... two ..."GO!"

He shouldered open the door and rushed into the flat, the other officers right behind him.

"Police, police, stay still!" he shouted, looking around, squinting to see better in the dim light. The first thing he noticed was a large plastic bag sitting by the doorway. The second thing was that the tattooed man's visitor wasn't John Lomax at all; it was his own son, Billy.

-22-

Sandy Lane stormed into the police station, flanked by Sergeant Hathaway. Behind them was another officer, escorting the sullen, handcuffed boy. The owner of the flat, a biker, had been taken down the hall and the weed booked into evidence.

Lane had ordered Billy to tell them what was going on but he'd clammed up and refused to say a word. A search of the property and of Lomax's car had yielded no evidence of the Anvex money. The officers who'd been following Lomax's car when Lane had raged at them about misidentifying his son as the businessman had given Lane a very frosty reception.

"I don't remember you ever bothered to put his picture out," one of them said.

Lane now barked to one of the officers sitting at a computer screen, "Get me John Lomax."

"You don't have to," an officer said. "He's right over there."

Lomax was sitting across from the desk sergeant. He rose and looked in astonishment at Lane and his son. He pointed to the boy and said sourly, "So they got you already; Sam. That was fast. I just filled out the complaint five minutes ago."

"Sam?" Lane asked.

"Yes, Sam Phillips," Lomax said.

"His name's Billy, he's my son," Lane muttered. The boy's middle name was Samuel, and Phillips was the maiden name of the boy's mother.

Lomax & The Biker – The Trilogy

"Your son?" John Lomax asked, his eyes wide in disbelief. He then glanced at what one officer was carrying; an evidence box containing the suitcase, wallet, keys and cell phone that had been found in Lomax's s car.

"You recovered everything," he said. "How's my car? Did he wreck it?"

Hathaway started to tell him that his car was fine but Sandy Lane waved his hand to silence the big policeman.

"Okay, what the hell is going on?" he asked Lomax. "What did you have to do with my boy?"

Angry, Lomax said, "Hey, this kid robbed me, I was just trying to do him a favour. I had no idea he was your son."

"Favour?"

Lomax eyed the boy up and down.

"Yesterday I saw him steal a watch from Maxwell's, over on Harrison Street."

Lane turned a cold eye on his son, who continued to keep his head down.

"I followed him and made him give me the watch. I felt bad for him. He seemed like he was having a tough time of it. I hired him to help me out for an hour or so. I just wanted to show him there were people out there who'd pay good money for legitimate work."

"What'd you do with the watch?" Lane asked.

Lomax looked indignant.

"I returned it to the shop. What did you think? I'd keep stolen merchandise?"

Lomax & The Biker – The Trilogy

The detective glanced at his son and demanded, "What did he hire you to do?"

When the boy said nothing Lomax explained.

"I paid him to watch my car while I moved a few things out of my house."

"Your house?" the boy asked in shock. "On Tremont Drive?"

To his father Lomax said, "That's right. I moved into a motel for a few days. I'm having my house painted and I can't sleep with the paint fumes."

Lane remembered the van in Lomax's driveway.

"I couldn't use the front door," Lomax added angrily, "because I'm sick of those goons of yours tailing me every time I leave the house. I hired your son to stay with the car in the alley; it's a clamping area back there. You can't leave your car unattended even for five minutes. I dropped off some tools I bought this morning and picked up a few things I needed and we drove to the motel." Lomax shook his head. "I gave him the key to open the door and I forgot to get it when he left. He came back when I was in the shower and ripped me off. He took my car, my cell phone, money, wallet, the suitcase." In disgust he added, "To think I gave him all that money. And practically begged him to get his act together and stay clear of drugs."

"He told you that?" Lane asked.

The boy nodded reluctantly. His father sighed and nodded at the suitcase.

"What's in there?"

Lomax & The Biker – The Trilogy

Lomax shrugged, picked up his keys and unlocked and opened the case. Lane assumed that he wouldn't be so cooperative if it contained the Anvex money but he still felt a burst of delight when he noticed that the paper bag inside was filled with cash. His excitement faded, though, when he saw it held only about three or four hundred pounds, mostly rolled up five and ten pound notes.

"Household money," Lomax explained. "I didn't want to leave it in the house. Not with the painters there."

Lane contemptuously tossed the bag into the case and angrily slammed the lid. "Jesus."

"You thought it was the Anvex money?"

Lane looked at the computer terminals around them, cursors blinking passively. To hell with Big Brother! The best surveillance money can buy and look what had happened.

The detective's voice cracked with emotion as he said, "You followed my son! You hired the painters so you could get away without being seen, you bought the tools ....and what the hell were you doing looking at burglar alarm websites?"

"Comparative shopping," Lomax answered reasonably. "I'm buying an alarm system for the house."

"This is all a setup! You-"

John Lomax silenced him by glancing at Lane's fellow officers, who were looking at their boss with mixed expressions of concern and distaste over his paranoid ranting. Lomax nodded toward Lane's office.

"Would you prefer to talk in there?"

Inside, Lomax swung the door shut and turned to face the glowering detective.

"Here's the situation, Detective. I'm the only prosecuting witness in the car theft case against your son. If I decide to press charges he'll do some serious time, particularly since I suspect you found him in the company of some not so savoury friends when he was arrested. Then there's also the little matter of Dad's career path after his son's arrest hits the papers."

"You want a deal?"

"Yes. I want a deal. I'm sick of this delusional crap of yours, Lane. I'm a legitimate businessman. I didn't steal the Anvex payroll. I'm not a thief and never have been."

He eyed the detective carefully then reached into his pocket and handed Lane a slip of paper.

"What's this?"

"The number of a BA flight six months ago, the afternoon of the Anvex robbery."

"How did you get this?"

"My companies do some business with the airlines. I pulled a few strings and a contact at BA got me that. One of the passengers in first class on that flight paid cash for a one way ticket from Gatwick to Toronto four hours after the Anvex robbery. He had no luggage to check into the hold. Only hand luggage. They wouldn't give me the passenger's name but that shouldn't be too tough for a hardworking officer like you to track down."

Lane stared at the paper.

"Of course," he said as the penny dropped, "the bloke from BT? The one the witness saw with that suitcase near Anvex?"

"Maybe it's a coincidence, but I know I didn't steal the money. Maybe he did."

The paper disappeared into Lane's pocket. "What do you want?"

"Drop me as a suspect. Cut out all the surveillance. I want my life back. And I want a letter signed by you stating that the evidence proves I'm not guilty."

"That won't mean anything in court."

"But it'll look pretty bad if anybody decides to come after me again."

"Bad for my job, you mean."

"That's exactly what I mean."

After a moment Lane muttered, "How long have you been planning this?"

Lomax said nothing. But he reflected: Not that long, actually. He'd started thinking about it just after the two policemen had interrupted his nap the other day. He'd wire transferred some money to one of his banks in France from an investment account to convince the police that he was getting ready to flee the country (the French accounts were completely legitimate; only a fool would hide money in Europe). Then he'd done some surveillance of his own, low-tech though it was. He'd pulled on overalls, glasses and a hat and snuck into police headquarters, armed with a watering can and clippers to tend to the plants he'd noticed inside the station the first time he was arrested. He'd spent a half hour on his knees, his head down, clipping and watering, in the hallway outside the watch room, where he'd learned the extent of the police's electronic invasion of his life. He'd heard too the exchange between Billy Lane and the detective, a classic example of an uninvolved father and a troubled, angry son.

Lomax smiled to himself now, recalling that after the meeting Lane had been so focussed on the case that, when he nearly tripped over Lomax in the corridor, the policeman had never noticed who the gardener was. He'd then followed Billy for a few hours until he caught him palming the watch. Then he tricked the boy into helping him. He'd hired the painters to do some interior touch up to give him the excuse to park his car elsewhere and to check into the motel. Then, using their surveillance against them, he'd fooled the police into believing he was indeed the Anvex burglar and was getting ready to do one last robbery and flee the country, by buying the travel books and the tools and logging on to the alarm and travel agency websites. At the motel he'd tempted Billy Lane into stealing the suitcase, credit cards, phone and car, everything that would let the police trace track the boy and catch him red handed.

He now said to Lane, "I'm sorry, Detective. But you didn't leave me any choice. You just weren't ever going to believe that I'm innocent."

"You used my son."

Lomax & The Biker – The Trilogy

Lomax shrugged. "No harm done. Look on the bright side. This is his first arrest and he's picked a victim who is willing to drop the charges. If it had been anybody else he wouldn't' have been so lucky."

Lane glanced through the blinds at his son, standing forlorn beside Hathaway's desk.

"He's saveable, you know." Lomax said. "If you want to save him .... So, do we have a deal?"

A disgusted sigh was followed by a disgusted nod.

Outside the police station, Lomax tossed the suitcase into the back of his car, which had been towed to the station by a police lorry. He drove back to his house and walked inside. The workmen had apparently just finished and the smell of paint was strong. He went through the ground floor, opening windows to air the place out. Strolling into his garden, he surveyed the huge pile of mulch, whose spreading had been postponed because of his interrupted nap.

The businessman glanced at his watch. He had some phone calls to make but decided to put them off for another day; he was in the mood to garden. He changed clothes, went into the garage and picked up a glistening new shovel, part of his purchases that morning. He began meticulously spreading the black and brown mulch throughout the large garden.

After an hour of work he paused for a beer. Sitting under a apple tree, sipping the Heineken, he surveyed the empty street in front of his bungalow, where Lane had positioned the surveillance team.

It felt good not to be spied on any longer. His eyes then slid to a small rock sitting halfway between a row of rose bushes and a hydrangea. Three feet beneath it was a bag containing the £543,300 from Anvex Security, which he'd buried there on the afternoon of the robbery, just before he'd got rid of the BT jacket and driven the stolen van to Gatwick Airport North car park.

John Lomax had planned the robbery in meticulous detail. After all, this was his new life. He had to find income somehow, and commuting to London every day was, with the exception of the occasional friendly female traveller, sheer drudgery.

Should he dig it up now? No, he decided; it was best to wait till dark. Besides, the weather was warm, the sky was clear and there was nothing like gardening on a beautiful spring day. Lomax fetched his mobile phone from his pocket and almost rang The Biker, to let him know the outcome and thank him for providing a biker friend as part of the meticulous detail. He was also very tempted to phone Sandy Lane, just to turn the screw a little bit more, but he resisted for the moment. There would be time enough. Just imagining his present discomfort was sufficient for now, but he knew that feeling wouldn't last; wouldn't be enough. In addition he knew a mobile phone call could be traced. He smiled. Lane would have to be sharper than that. Lomax finished his beer, picked up the shovel and returned to the pile of pungent mulch.

-23-

John Lomax sipped his malt whisky and reflected how much his life had changed. No more trudging up to London on a daily basis. No more bowing and scraping to an employer who didn't value his real worth. No more money worries whatsoever. He considered his secret stash to be no more than he deserved. It wasn't a fortune, but with careful handling he could live very comfortably thank you very much and not have to worry where the next penny was coming from. He knew he would have to be careful, of course, because he was in no doubt that the despicable Detective Inspector Sandy Lane would not rest until he had exacted his revenge. Perhaps Lane would ensure HM Revenue & Customs would investigate his affairs. Well, he thought, I've covered that base with my legitimate business interests and he had already engaged an accountant of impeccable reputation and completed self assessment tax forms in the appropriate way. No, Lane would have to try other, more underhand and devious ways of bringing him down.

The only thing missing now was something that he had taken for granted for a long period of his life. He did not have the love of a good woman. Nor, indeed, did he have the lust of a bad one, and he missed both.

Sometimes such opportunities came along unannounced and you had to grab them with both hands, so to speak, as he had done on that morning on the train to Paddington. He was, however, wise enough to know that this couldn't be guaranteed, so he reasoned that he would have to put himself in situations which would increase the chances of meeting someone. He did not want to lower himself to haunting pubs and clubs that he knew existed in which the clientele were of the desperate variety. That would never do. It would be below his station and erode his self esteem.

Then he had a bright idea. He had always been interested in the theatre, and had been something of a keen actor in his school days, so why not join an amateur dramatic society? It would occupy him during the evenings and he knew of the reputation such groups had when it came to fatal attractions. He realised that he had often considered this in the past, but his wife had put her foot down. Now that he no longer had the imprint of her shoe upon his head, he would indulge himself in that direction he decided.

He joined an "amdram" group and went along to his first session. There were fifteen people there, ranging in age from eighteen to over seventy. The group actually had more than forty members, but for some reason only fifteen turned up to the session. John Lomax was the only new recruit and initially felt a little isolated as the others mingled and chatted comfortably with each other, safe in their familiarity.

The next project was to be entitled "How to Maintain a Healthy Level of Insanity." It was to be scripted by the group members themselves, so much intensive work needed to be done and they used that night's session as an ice breaker. John was told that it was traditional at the first meeting of a new project for each

Lomax & The Biker – The Trilogy

member to contribute a "one liner" as an idea for the theme to fit the proposed project.

The ideas began in sober fashion and nobody was much enthused by what they were hearing. Everybody seemed to be a little too reserved in John's view, so when his turn came he determined to shake them up with some risqué and amusing thoughts.

"My turn then," he said quietly as all eyes turned in his direction.

"I've got a few thoughts, but some may raise a few eyebrows. Please don't be offended, but I'm new to this, so here goes. My suggestions for ways to maintain a healthy level of insanity:

1/. At lunch time, sit in your parked car with sunglasses on and point a hair dryer at passing cars. See if they slow down.

2/. On all your cheque stubs, write ' For Marijuana.'

3/. Skip down the street rather than walk and see how many looks you get.

4/. Order diet water in restaurants and keep a straight face.

5/. Sing along at the opera.

6/. When the money comes out of the ATM, scream 'I Won! I Won!'

7/. When leaving the zoo, start running towards the car park, yelling "run for your lives, they're loose, they're loose."

8/. Tell your children over dinner, 'due to the cutbacks, we are going to have to let one of you go.'

9/.And the final way to keep a healthy level of insanity is pick up a box of condoms at the chemist, go to the counter and ask where the fitting room is."

For an awful moment John thought he had gone too far. There was a mixture of shuffling feet and embarrassed faces. However, a few were obviously struggling to conceal smiles and giggles. A pretty woman with bobbed brunette hair and tight jeans eventually gave up the unequal fight.

"Oh for God's sake," she cried, "don't be such a bunch of tight arsed prudes. I seem to remember all of you at the party last summer. What you've just heard is positively innocent compared to how all of us behaved then. And I include myself." She turned her attention to a middle aged, grey haired man, dressed in sober fashion. He paled at what was about to become public.

"Harry, would you like to tell us what you were doing with Lucy in the props cupboard? I don't think it was research for costumes for the next production and her knickers seemed to suddenly appear in your jacket pocket."

Harry declined the invitation to answer and said he would prefer to pick up on one or two of "our new friend's ideas."

Lomax sympathised with his predicament and came to his rescue. "I really didn't mean to cause any difficulty for anybody," he said. "I only meant to bring a little humour in order to ease the tension for myself. Selfish of me, I know, but I'm normally quite shy and I find it difficult to meet people for the first time."

Lomax & The Biker – The Trilogy

This wasn't true, of course, but Lomax thought it a good ploy that would ensure the attention paid to him was sympathetic and may even elicit a more tender response from some of the women in the group. He wanted to come across as a successful businessman, who was comfortable and confident in his own world, but was less so when outside his comfort zone. He wanted to appear unprepossessing and genuine; in short a "really nice man, who had a sense of humour." The ladies liked that and the men would not, he hoped, feel threatened.

Harry, the man he had rescued from embarrassment, was very grateful and made a point of seeking John Lomax out after the session and thanking him. Lucy, the props cupboard partner, was also very grateful and went out of her way to make him welcome. There was no doubt she was attractive, thought John, but she still seemed intent on flirting with Harry, so Lomax shelved that line of progress.

He couldn't have known, however, that he had inadvertently upset one of the other men in the group. Lucy's ex husband still harboured ambitions of winning her back and hadn't known about the assignation. The revelation shocked him and he blamed Lomax for it becoming public knowledge. He made it his business over the following few weeks to get to know Lomax and he set himself the task of finding out as much as possible about the newcomer's background.

Everybody usually went to the nearest pub after rehearsals and the combination of the atmosphere, alcohol and the artistic temperament combined with every passing week to allow people to explore whatever relationships they preferred. These ranged from the obvious long standing "pairings", of all varieties, through small group "arrangements" to new, exciting and developing affairs. John quickly identified who moved in which circles, even discovering that a few individuals wandered from one situation to another with apparent ease and acceptance by all concerned.

Lucy's ex, Brian, was one of these. As far as John knew Brian was between assignations and had latched onto him somewhat. This was fine at first as it helped him get to know people, but after a while Lomax found it irksome and limiting.

Things came to a head when Brian introduced him to a woman named Leanne, who joined the group some six weeks after John. She was quite simply stunning in every way. John suddenly understood what Mario Puzo had meant in "The Godfather" when Michael Corleone had first set eyes on his Mediterranean bride to be and been struck by "the thunderbolt."

John Lomax, who had considered himself to be in control of all aspects of his new and very rewarding life, was now blown sideways. Leanne became the focus of all his waking moments and the subject of his increasingly imaginative dreams.

He found himself unable to concentrate on any routine whatsoever. His entire being had been hijacked by this beauty, and he forgot about everything else, with the exception that he was sharp enough to keep up his guard for any sign of Lane re-entering his world. That was one guiding principle that he would never let go.

Rehearsals became increasingly significant each week as John and Leanne got to know each other. She, for her part, definitely preferred his company to anybody else's. For her, he was intriguing and attractive in a manly way. He seemed a man in control of his life, who knew what he wanted and usually got it. He was a passably good actor at the amateur level and she enjoyed playing opposite him. One particular scene called for them to embrace and kiss at the end of a particularly emotional moment as the curtain descended at the end of Act One. Both knew it was scripted, of course, and both prepared for it. John knew he would let it linger for more than was necessary and Leanne knew the same. When it came it confirmed all his hopes. The world stood still for them both for what seemed an eternity as their lips met and their arms enfolded each other. They were the only two on stage, but it wouldn't have mattered to either of them if nuclear war had been declared at that very moment. In fact the meeting was nuclear in its own way. Both felt a deep, stirring, rising passion and totally forgot their surroundings. They didn't even know that the curtain had fallen and the stage hands needed to change the set. It was only the need to breathe that finally ended the moment.

Slightly embarrassed by the public display, John sheepishly led Leanne off the stage, but did not let go of her hand. He knew he had to say something, and could not let the moment pass.

"Forgive me, Leanne. I don't know what came over me," he said.

He realised this was the whole truth. He didn't know what had come over him. He knew it had happened, he knew he would not be the same again, but he was at a loss to explain it. He had been reduced almost to a quivering adolescent, fumbling for the right words and a way forward.

"I...."

"Don't say anything, please John. Words would be pointless. I know how I feel and I think you do too. Take me home. Not to mine, to yours. I want to wake up with you in the morning."

John didn't need to awake in the morning because he hadn't slept at all. He had experienced the most amazing night of his life. The morning came with a shaft of sunlight. It washed the sleeping Leanne with a blaze of glorious colour and moved the watching Lomax immensely. He stayed there just dreamily watching the rise and fall of her breasts, her completely relaxed body bathed in the sunlight, which was splintered into the colours of the rainbow by the prism effect of the vase on the window ledge. How beautiful she looked. He traced a feather-light fingertip across her flat stomach and wondered at her beauty and serenity. He determined in that moment never to let another living being take her from him.

"Penny for your thoughts," she whispered, her eyes staying closed.

"No need," he replied, "you read me well enough. My soul is completely exposed to you."

Lomax & The Biker – The Trilogy

He had never felt anything like it in his life, and he just knew it was right. But what to do from here; how to proceed? He had never been at such a loss before, so he let his instincts guide him.

"How do you fancy breakfast in bed?" he asked.

"I'd prefer to have it in the kitchen," she replied, "I can't stand crumbs in the bed."

She half closed her eyelids and looked demurely away towards the window.

"I'll make sure I get rid of them," he responded.

"No need," she answered. "We'll have breakfast in the kitchen and then I have plans for you back in here, and they do not include crumbs!"

She stayed for a week; a whole idyllic week. At the end of it he was exhausted and more blissfully happy than he'd ever been. They had talked, made love, talked some more and made love some more for each of seven days and nights. At the end of the week she said that she needed to go home and sort a few things out. He offered to take her, but she insisted he stayed at home and rested.

A car arrived to pick her up, driven by a man whose identity was obscured by the reflected glare of the sun off the windscreen, but whose outline seemed familiar.

As she walked out of his front door, she turned and said "Mr Wells will take me home. He would like you to return the paperwork you stole while working for him. In return he says he will return the information about your bank accounts that I e-mailed to him from your computer in your study while you slept, and will take no other action. If you don't he calculates it to be worth £543,300. He'll be in touch. Oh, and I'm sure you know enough not to involve the police. By the way, for what it's worth, I really did enjoy the week. Such a shame circumstances aren't different. You never asked my name, John. Call me," she said, as she put an imaginary mobile phone to her ear. "It's Leanne Lane."

-24-

Leanne Lane's maiden name was Leanne Phillips. She was the mother of Billy Lane and was Sandy Lane's first wife. They had parted reasonably amicably, largely due to the pressures of his training at Hendon and his job, but Billy had grown up in a household devoid of a father figure, which explained his teenage activities. Leanne Phillips was the daughter of the woman who had married Frank Wells, for whom Lomax had worked before all his troubles began.

The link between Frank Wells and Sandy Lane, though reasonably tenuous, was nevertheless very much alive and both had taken the opportunity of using it against John Lomax. Both had good reason to seek revenge and were very pleased with the subtlety of the plot. They looked forward to the outcome.

Wells hoped Lomax would not return the stolen company information. He preferred the thought of blackmailing Lomax into submission for the entire sum, which he had agreed to split with Sandy Lane. Of course, if Lomax did capitulate in this way, then there would be no reason for Wells and Lane to stop. They could apply pressure for as long as they so wished. Leanne had already been recompensed handsomely for her role in the intrigue and would certainly help again if necessary. She had even said that she had enjoyed it.

For his part, Lomax was still at a loss to explain what had happened. He realised that Leanne had quoted the exact sum that had been taken from Anvex and was now resting peacefully in his garden. That just could not be coincidence.

-25-

Leanne Lane had not wanted to be part of their plan. She had argued against it, telling Frank Wells and Sandy Lane that it was fraught with danger and couldn't possibly succeed. She had at first refused to go along with them, but she owed them both, individually and collectively, too much to hold out for long. Her mother had married Frank Wells at a time when both she and her mother were almost homeless and penniless. He had given their lives stability and made sure that Leanne had been given every opportunity to succeed in her life. He had also looked after her mother and Leanne knew what that meant to her.

Frank Wells had become embroiled in a friendship of sorts with Sandy Lane. The detective had solved a fraud and burglary at Wells' company and during the investigation had become besotted with Leanne. She had married Lane, not through love she later realised, and had borne him a son, Billy. The marriage had fallen apart over a period of time. That process had begun when Lane had decided to become a policeman and gone to the police training college at Hendon. He met a woman called Judith, who later became his wife, but that didn't stop him enjoying flings with several female officers and numerous women he had met in the course of his duties. Leanne did not, however, know about his other life as a bent policeman and all its gory details.

Leanne luxuriated in her bath, bubbles up to her neck, and dreamily reflected on the past week. She sponged herself all over, and could still feel John's touch. She slowly spent extra time on the places which still tingled from John's attention. Such a shame she thought, for she had really liked John Lomax and she felt sure that given different circumstances they could have spent much more time together. He had actually been very good in certain areas, and she would have liked to have explored them more.

She had just got to that stage of a bath when fingertips and toes begin to wrinkle when her mobile interrupted her.

"Hello, Leanne. Thanks for the week. I hope you enjoyed yourself as much as me. I think it's a pity that we had to meet in such circumstances and I really shouldn't leave myself open by calling you, but I can't get you out of my head. I'd like to see you again. There's a lot I need to ask you. You said your name is Leanne Lane, so I assume you're related to Sandy Lane, the policeman. Please don't insult me by trying to deny it. I think we need to talk. There's a lot I need to know and there's a great deal I want to tell you about Mr Lane, that I think will interest you."

"You sound different," she said. "Are you alright?"

"No, I'm not alright."

"I really didn't want to do it you know, but they made me. They told me things about you. About what you did to Frank Wells. He's my step-father you know. Also they said things about you and Sandy Lane. I was his first wife and Billy is my son. I think you must remember him."

"I remember," replied John.

Leanne allowed a lengthy pause to develop and decided to wait for him to speak next.

Lomax & The Biker – The Trilogy

"I've decided I have no choice. I'll have to give Mr Wells what he wants. You need to tell him, though, that I haven't got it all. If he'll accept £400,000 I'll consider the matter closed. If not, then he needs to know that I will not rest until both he and Lane are brought down. They know me well enough to know that I will pursue them and they really don't want to be looking over their shoulders for the rest of their lives. I'm sorry to talk in this way to you, really I am. I care for you and would like to think we can pick it up again when this business is over."

Leanne realised he had not threatened her at all. Perhaps there was a chance for them.

"I'll tell Frank Wells what you've said. Can I get back to you on the number that's come up on my screen?"

"Yes. But don't take long. I'll give it an hour and then I'll be making other arrangements."

John Lomax ended the call. He noticed that Leanne had made no comment about his wanting to pick things up with her and was disappointed. On the other hand, he told himself, she hadn't dismissed the idea either. Perhaps things might work out after all. He walked quickly away from the park bench he had been sitting on. Nobody else had been close to him when he had made the call, and he strolled across the green spaces of the park looking to all intents and purposes like a man without a care in the world.

He had already made his arrangements, so he could only wait. He killed time by lingering over coffee at Starbucks, before deciding to buy a newspaper and sit in the sunshine. He had reached page 7 of The Guardian when the mobile chirped.

"Hello, Leanne. You cut it fine. Five more minutes and the trouble would've started. What news?"

"Hello John. I'm OK, thanks for asking."

Sarcasm wasn't her strong suit but she couldn't resist. The problem was that it showed him she actually cared and she preferred him to pursue her.

He decided to let the silence and space between them hang. It lingered and ate away at them like so much corrosive acid. She broke first and that told him everything. She was interested in him, despite recent events, or perhaps due to some of them. Time would tell.

"I've spoken to Frank Wells. He isn't happy that you've only got £400,000. He wants to meet and collect the money though. Oh, and he wants Sandy Lane to be there as well."

"Has he promised that will be the end of things?"

"Yes, he has. He told me to tell you that he isn't a greedy man, he just wants decent recompense for the disrespectful way you treated him and his company before you were sacked."

"So why does he want Lane there?"

"I don't know, he didn't say."

"I think I'd like to make the arrangements with Wells direct. No offence, but it would be better for you if you weren't part of it. I've still got his mobile number, so I'll phone him now. I'll call you when it's done."

Lomax & The Biker – The Trilogy

"Wells wanted me to be the go-between, you know. I'm supposed to let Lane know the arrangements and he will contact Wells."

"Well I don't. To misquote a phrase of yours, 'I've got other plans for you'."

"Now that sounds interesting. I'll wait for your call."

"It will be," Lomax muttered to himself as he ended the conversation. She was easily persuaded he noticed, but put that to one side for the time being.

He wondered why Lane wanted to play such an important role. He decided it was too good an opportunity to miss, so he changed his own plans. "Two birds with one stone," he told himself and chuckled inwardly.

John Lomax retrieved another mobile phone from his pocket. It was a cheap, very disposable model. He inserted a SIM card. It was a copy of one he had stolen from Sandy Lane. He didn't, however, make a phone call because voices were identifiable. He sent a text message to Frank Wells giving explicit details and instructions for the drop and pick up. It read:

"Bag arrives 2U @ 4 2day. Meet Britannia after."

It was not long before the reply came.

"OK."

John Lomax was very pleased. He now had a text record, which could be traced, of a brief but meaningful exchange between Wells and Lane. He swapped the SIM card back again.

Lomax & The Biker – The Trilogy

The biker, complete with courier's uniform, made very certain he was not being followed or watched and entered Wells' offices. A pretty receptionist signed for the bag, which was labelled as being for Mr Wells himself, and the biker left without ceremony. The receptionist had not been told to expect a delivery. Wells was nothing if not careful. The bag was taken to Wells by another lackey.

Wells waited until he was alone in his office before opening the bag. It contained £100,000 in used notes of different denominations and a copy of The Godfather, with the corners of several pages turned down. They were the parts where Khartoum's severed and bloody head is found in the bed and the extract where a wrapped fish is delivered to show that Luca Brasi sleeps with the fishes. The message was crystal clear in both cases. However influential, powerful and indestructible you may think you are, think again. Back off. Walk away now while you still have your health.

The Britannia was a popular pub and was already filling with workers noisily ending their working day, trying to unwind, finishing some office business or simply putting off going home. Nobody took any notice of those they were not immediately involved with, which was precisely why it had been chosen. Lane was lucky to get a table. He put his mobile phone and his briefcase on the table in front of him, spreading out as much as he could to discourage others from sitting with him. He sipped his pint and waited for Wells. He had been phoned by Leanne and given the arrangements. That was John Lomax's way of making her feel involved. It also ensured she was implicated if things went pear shaped.

The scruffy student stumbled into Lane's table and knocked everything flying.

"Oh I'm sorry," he slurred, and bent down to pick up whatever he had sent clattering to the floor.

"Idiot!" shouted Lane, as his shirt was liberally splashed with best bitter and he struggled to wipe himself down. He had just about settled down again when Wells appeared at his side.

"Is this yours?" Wells asked him, as he picked a mobile off the floor and put the bag in its place.

Lane grunted, still damp and distracted, as he took the phone and put it in his pocket. He looked questioningly at Wells, waiting impatiently to be told how successful they had been.

"£100,000 and a warning," Wells said softly. He said nothing else and waited for Lane to react.

Amongst his police colleagues Lane's temper was legendary and Wells was now witnessing his internal struggle to control it. It was obvious to Lane that Wells had double crossed him and kept the rest of the money and that the warning was a product of Wells' imagination.

Lane's phone buzzed insistently gradually insinuating itself into the tension that crackled between them. He fished it from his pocket.

Lomax & The Biker – The Trilogy

"Listen very carefully. I will not repeat myself. What's in the bag is all you two are getting. Share it, live with it, whatever. You don't deserve it. Also, take heed of the book. Don't ever interfere in my life again. Oh, and by the way, the texts between you are on a SIM card in my possession."

Neither of them recognised the voice, but both knew with the utmost certainty on whose behalf it was being said. They also knew that there would be no point in trying to trace it.

John Lomax smiled inwardly. He was satisfied with the execution of his plan. He had now set Lane and Wells against each other to the extent that they would be pre-occupied for a very long time and he would be free to pursue Leanne at his leisure. He settled into his favourite chair. The malt whisky in his favourite tumbler was definitely not a normal pub measure and he savoured the gathering warmth that only self-satisfaction and fine scotch could bring.

He pondered on the situation. The £100,000 he had given away in the bag had been made up of used notes and was of different denominations. He inched down more deeply into the leather chair and reflected upon the knowledge that the money he had given away had been that which he knew had numbers the police could trace. Those numbers had been publicised in the press. He had therefore only given away those notes. If either Frank Wells or Detective Inspector Lane used them they would be caught very quickly. Would they be sharp enough to spot it? For both it would mean arrest, a trial, prison and ignominy. The rest of the money was untraceable, but he would not use it foolishly. He had planned what to do with it and how to use it wisely so that he would never be implicated. The SIM card was now safely stowed with the money.

All in all it had not been a bad day's work. His nest egg was intact. Admittedly his lump sum was somewhat depleted, but he knew it would have become a millstone around his neck and may have eventually caused his downfall, so it was a small price to have paid. He had offloaded the only evidence that could trap him; he had untraceably passed it on to his two most hated enemies; he had set them against each other and they could settle it between themselves or fight over it. He didn't care, but he knew he would be interested in how they resolved the problem. Lastly, he had the incriminating SIM card safely hidden with the money and the card that had been used had been replaced in Lane's phone. It was therefore a ticking time bomb for Lane.

There was a bonus of course. It needn't be just the two birds with one stone as had been planned. He could now look forward to the very pleasant prospect of a long, physically demanding and most satisfying relationship with Leanne.

He allowed himself another glass of malt, and closed his eyes, deep in thought. What would they do? Perhaps they'd share the money and let it all go. That seemed very doubtful. Perhaps they'd dream up a plan for revenge. That was quite possible, but risky. Perhaps they would each suspect the other and fall out. That was much more likely. Lomax hoped that would happen and savoured the prospect. In a battle of wits Lomax wondered which of the two would prevail. He knew Lane to be the more sinister, but Wells had surprised him before, so anything could happen. Either way, he would be left with only one man to deal with.

He could have mused endlessly on these and other possibilities, but he preferred to slip gradually into much dreamier waters. He brought back vivid memories and images of his week with Leanne and let his mind wander.

Lomax & The Biker – The Trilogy

-26-

John Lomax would have given a great deal to have been a fly on the wall as Frank Wells and Detective Inspector Sandy Lane sat in The Britannia and glared at each other. They both realised that they had been duped and neither could think of an immediate response.

Wells knew he had not crossed Lane but was very fearful that he might look at it that way. He knew what Lane had done to various people in his varied and murky past and had witnessed at first hand one or two examples of his brutality and temper.

Lane for his part assessed the situation. He thought Wells had kept the rest of their money. He had at first thought Wells had invented the extra detail of the book, but the phone call had specifically said "what's in the bag is all you two are getting." He had not specified how much was in the bag and that made Lane believe Wells was double crossing him.

Still struggling to control his temper, he set his jaw and whispered, "where's the rest? You've kept it, haven't you? You get this one chance to set this straight right now. We'll leave together and you can take me to it. No messing about or you're a dead man."

Wells caught his breath. "I swear there's no more. It's all there. That's all he sent. He's playing us off against each other. He knows what you're like."

The words came out in short bursts, exposing his fear and Lane saw it. He stared menacingly at Wells, took hold of the bag and, lifting it from the floor, set it down on the table on top of his own briefcase. He unzipped it and found the book. It proved nothing because he was convinced Wells had put the book there, with the pages turned down, in an attempt to persuade him to just accept the situation and let it go.

"I think I'll just take this lot. You have my word that'll be the end of it," Lane whispered, his mouth so close to Wells' ear that he could feel his hot breath.

Lane closed the bag and grabbed his briefcase as well. He turned away and walked slowly out of the pub. He didn't look back.

Frank Wells was stunned. It had happened so fast. He had been intimidated by Lane and didn't know what to do next. He had been left just sitting in The Britannia feeling foolish and, for the first time since he was a young boy, alone and vulnerable. He got up from his seat, attempting to retain what little dignity he felt he had left and walked to the entrance. He looked left and right but there was no sign of Lane. Deep in thought he hailed a passing taxi and set off for home.

Sandy Lane hadn't turned right or left when he left the pub, he had simply crossed the road and got into a car which he had parked earlier just down the road. He watched as Wells left the pub, searched in vain for him and then got into the taxi. He followed at a distance, driving carefully so as not to arouse suspicion but having to hurry occasionally to keep up.

Lomax & The Biker – The Trilogy

Wells paid his fare and watched as the taxi left the unlit station car park. The night was velvet black, but the force with which he was struck was anything but a velvet touch. Lane's stolen car was black, large and unyielding. It struck Wells squarely from behind at about 50mph and simply ran straight over him. He had no time to react. He was mown down, dragged under the car and spat out the back like a chewed piece of meat. He actually resembled meat quite closely. His head had been split wide and his brain squashed. His right leg lay shattered at a very odd angle and his torso was scraped so severely that his jacket had been torn off. It attached itself to the underside of Lane's vehicle and became entangled in the rear axle. It still contained what remained of Wells' left arm.

Lane rid himself of the car by covering it in petrol and setting it ablaze. This he did in a deserted quarry far from any sign of human habitation. He knew nobody would find it for years, if ever. He had also been very careful not to leave any evidence, covered as he was from head to foot, including hood, in a police crime scene officer's protective suit. He later soaked that in acid, burned the remains and scattered the ashes in several rubbish bins across London.

Lomax & The Biker – The Trilogy

-27-

Lane slept like an innocent baby that night, just as he had whenever he had rid himself of an "issue". As a police officer he had witnessed violence and its aftermath at first hand and it never got to him. Indeed, over the years he had become inured to it and he had become a cold, calculating man. He like to believe he possessed the normal emotions of any human being, including the ability to love, but the truth was that such trivial inconveniences had long since disappeared.

He turned his mind now to the remaining problem of John Lomax. He realised that Lomax was the only person left alive who could pose a threat and he had to be dealt with.

Lomax found out about the disappearance of Wells when his absence from his home and work became too lengthy to be explained by a sudden holiday or anything else. The papers told of an ongoing investigation but Lomax knew that Lane was the cause. He decided against volunteering helpful information to the police, preferring instead to follow events watchfully from a safe distance. He knew that Lane's phone could always be used to focus damning publicity in the appropriate direction and he would not hesitate to use it whenever it became necessary.

Other loose ends had still to be tied up. Did he need to take any action about Richard Dunne? He knew things about Lomax that he would rather remained between the two of them, but was he an actual threat? Would removing him cause more problems than it would solve? Judith Lane? She now had no reason to be loyal to Sandy Lane, but would that ensure she faded away quietly and got on with her own life? Billy Lane? What familial bonds remained between father and son? What was the long term effect of the jewellery incident? Could he be absolutely certain of Ray Quinn's loyalty and silence? They went back a long way and had survived a great deal together, but how much did Quinn feel he owed to Lomax and would he remain loyal.

Lomax couldn't bring himself to doubt Quinn. He was after all a friend who had proved himself honourable and loyal, so he spent no time at all on that issue. After all, there has to be somebody in life whom you can trust. Was it inevitable that Lane himself would have to be dealt with in the end?

Who can you really trust?

And what was he to do about Leanne? He had a hold over her because she was party to blackmail, but was it enough?

For the time being he was content to turn over in bed and take in the rather pleasant sight of the naked Leanne beside him. She felt his gaze, stirred and gently guided his hand.

Lomax & The Biker – The Trilogy

-28-

John Lomax took his seat on the London bound train. It was the same seat and very pleasant memories came flooding back. He looked out at the scenery and buildings and noticed again how the character of the architecture changed as the train bumped and jolted closer to Paddington.

When the train arrived at Paddington he had his return ticket ready to show. He was immersed in a tide of humanity as it disgorged from the crowded train and flowed towards the barrier. The uniformed man with a company cap pulled low over his face and eyes, looked at it, punched a hole in it and returned it. Lomax walked across the concourse, and made his way to the taxi rank. He queued with his fellow travellers until it was his turn and a taxi appeared. He gave the driver the address of Hunter & Dunne.

He arrived at Richard Dunne's plush new offices and took out his wallet to pay the taxi. As he pulled out a £10 note his train ticket fell at his feet. He bent to retrieve it and noticed that it had a piece of paper attached. He opened it and read.

"You won't find Dunne at work, or at home. In fact you will not find him at all. I will come for you when I'm ready."

The note was typed and unsigned but he knew its origin. Shaken, he struggled for composure, whilst the driver looked at him waiting for payment. Lomax gave him the £10 note and whispered "keep the change". He looked up and down the pavement, half expecting to see a recognisable figure, but there was nobody.

Lomax & The Biker – The Trilogy

He took a decision and walked hurriedly away from Hunter & Dunne. He ended up in Hyde Park, but couldn't remember how he had got there. He sat on a bench, trying to clear his head. A pretty woman passed in front of him and never gave him a glance. He followed her progress with unseeing eyes.

He gradually came to the realisation that the ticket collector at the barrier must have passed him the note. He tried hard to recall anything about the man, but all he could focus on was the cap. Why was he wearing a cap? He struggled with this for some time, before it hit him. Other collectors had not been wearing caps. It must have been to hide something. Was it his face or his hair, or both? Then Lomax realised that a wisp of sandy coloured hair had been showing from beneath the cap.

-29-

When John Lomax reached home that night the first thing he did was to check on his money hidden beneath the small rock in the garden. It was still there and had not been disturbed. He went inside and methodically checked the house thoroughly and painstakingly, trying to satisfy himself that no unwanted visitors had called. Eventually satisfied, he poured himself a large, steadying whisky and sat to collect his thoughts.

He came to no conclusions or decisions that night, but his last thoughts as he dozed in the chair were that he would have to take some action before long.

When he awoke at 6am he was still in the chair. His empty whisky glass had slipped from his fingers and landed softly on the carpet next to the empty bottle. Sunlight was filtering through the blinds in narrow parallel shafts that carried particles of dust in suspension. His mouth was dry cardboard and behind his eyes sat an all encompassing headache. The eyes themselves felt as though they had rolled upwards and were trying to escape through the top of his head and his vision was blurred. His eyelids were sticky and heavy, his hair was all over the place and his clothes were crumpled. His shoulders ached and his back creaked, complaining at the abuse visited upon it. His right leg was bent underneath the left and cramped painfully when he tried to straighten it. The tops of his feet hurt because his shoes were still tightly laced. It took a massive effort to lever himself up and stumble into the shower. The hot, stinging water took a long time to do its work. He stayed there reviving and punishing himself, until he was satisfied that he could function properly and think with clarity. He could only face coffee and toast.

By 10am he was ready to face the world again. The morning paper had arrived. He watched as the postman passed by without delivering, so at least there were no bills to be dealt with.

At 11.30am a courier knocked on the front door holding a small parcel. Having signed for it, Lomax took it into the kitchen. He poured himself another coffee and opened it. It was a small cardboard box which contained a package wrapped in tissue paper. Inside the tissue Lomax saw a ring. He recognised it immediately as belonging to Richard Dunne. He also realised in the same instant that the perfectly severed finger it encircled had belonged to Richard Dunne.

Sickened and feeling dizzy, Lomax searched the box for a note or message. There was nothing. It must have come from Sandy Lane, he reasoned. Who else would do such a thing? Who else would send it to him? There were no clues to be gained from the box or tissue and the signed paperwork had been cleverly spirited away by the courier.

He understood then that the package, though small in size, was a significant message in itself. It was a warning that Lane was keeping his promise. He was coming and was dealing with loose ends as he did so.

Lomax slowly sipped his coffee while formulating his next move. The last vestiges of his night's whisky induced coma disappeared quickly now, forced away by what had just happened. His eyes were clear and his mind was sharp, jolted into focus.

He wrapped the grizzly present in its tissue and placed it carefully in the box. He carried it into the garden and dug for a while before putting it beside his bag of money. It would have to suffice as a resting place for time being, whilst he decided what should be done with it. He very carefully replaced the soil and made sure it looked as though it had not been disturbed.

He prepared lunch for himself. He had come to enjoy being in the kitchen and was extending his range and skill quickly. Today he did not want to be complicated, so he prepared tuna salad sprinkled with his own dressing and ground black pepper. He cut some crusty bread and poured an orange juice. Such healthy lunches had become the norm for him, and made him feel virtuous.

He sat browsing through the paper, eating his food. His mind wandered and, without knowing why, he realised that his would be nemesis was actually dealing with the loose ends that Lomax had identified for himself earlier. Richard Dunne had been the first person he had himself identified as being a potential problem. It was the reason he had travelled to talk to him. It was uncanny that Lane had got to Dunne first, but how had he known he was first on his list? Was that just a lucky guess? If Lane followed the order that Lomax had identified for himself then Judith Lane would be next. Surely Lane wouldn't harm his own wife, even though she had walked out on him. Surely he would allow her to fade away and get on with her own life. Lomax pondered for a long time and came to the conclusion that Lane was now so committed, had gone so far, that he wouldn't stop. He couldn't leave any loose ends.

Both were in a similar position. The two of them were on a collision course and anybody connected with either or both would not be safe.

Lomax determined there and then that he would prevail, but he would need to be very clever and careful because Lane was still a policeman and had very useful resources and contacts at his disposal.

Lomax & The Biker – The Trilogy

-30-

Ray Quinn, The Biker, found Judith Lane first. She had gone to a hotel for a few nights when she had first left Lane, and then arranged to rent a small bungalow in Hertfordshire. Quinn had begun his search by recalling that Lane was a member of a club near Hertford. It transpired that it was a family membership, so Judith's details were registered. Quinn had managed a look at the records when the young girl on duty at reception had slipped outside for fresh air and a cigarette. He always thought it laughable that smokers went outside into the fresh air and then polluted themselves with cigarette smoke.

Quinn had obtained Judith's mobile number and car registration. He gambled that she wouldn't go too far away to begin with, so did a sweep of local hotels within a 20 mile radius. She was, he knew, quite particular in her desire to be of a certain social standing, so would only have gone to an expensive hotel. He found her at the second one he tried. Her car was parked in the hotel car park under a tree, which served to hide it well. Many people would not have seen it, but Quinn was thorough.

Quinn did nothing. He watched Judith for some days, making sure neither Lane nor anybody else were close. He followed her when she moved out of the hotel to the bungalow. He kept vigil for many days and nights without himself arousing suspicion. He treated it like a military operation, which indeed to him it was. He took note of her movements, her contacts, her routine. He was thorough and was able to identify when and how she could be taken. He also knew that the longer he stayed around the more likely it became that somebody would remember him afterwards.

He knew what he was going to do. He had already discussed it with Lomax and the decision had been made.

Judith woke up with John Lomax looking down at her intently. She was bound tightly and gagged. She did not recognise her captor. As Lomax saw her awake and knew she could understand her situation, he did a strange thing. He walked over to her, gently removed the gag from her mouth and carefully untied all her bindings.

"I'm sorry you have been inconvenienced," he said, "but it was necessary to talk to you without anybody knowing. I sincerely hope you haven't been hurt. I would ask only that you listen to what I have to say. When that's done you are free to leave. I'll take you anywhere you wish and you will not be harmed. Would you like a drink?"

Judith Lane stared at him with unbelieving eyes. She asked herself why would this man kidnap her, bind and gag her, then set her free to scream and shout. Why was he talking so reasonably? Why was he so courteous? What was he about to say?

"Mrs Lane, again I must apologise for this. I'll come straight to the point. I have a problem. I know you also have a problem. Our problem is mutual. Your husband has become intent on doing me harm. He has already harmed a friend of mine. I'm not sure whether or not my friend is still alive, but your husband cut off his finger and sent it to me. I have it and will show you if necessary. I am sure he intends to make an attempt on my life. I also feel you may be in danger. I am aware that you have moved out and are living separately and would think that you would like him to leave you alone to get on with your own life. I believe you know deep down that he is capable of all sorts of things. You may even know some of the things he has done..."

"But"

"Please Judith, let me finish. I do not propose to stand by and let him make an attempt to harm me or any more of my friends. Nor would I wish any harm to come to you. I think we can make an arrangement that will both ensure our safety and bring your husband's activities to a halt. To do this we will need to trust each other. I have begun by being frank with you and will keep my promise that you are free to leave or I'll take you anywhere you wish. My plan is as follows."

John Lomax told Judith Lane his plan in great detail during the next half an hour. When he had finished she readily, and unreservedly, agreed to his scheme. She accepted a gin and tonic and they sealed their compact.

Lomax drove Judith to her bungalow and she left him feeling better than she had for many years. She had a purpose now. She knew that her decision to leave her husband had been the right one and now she had proof and the means to ensure he would never again bother her or anybody else. She opened her handbag and took out the £50,000 she had been given. Her life could begin again.

Lomax & The Biker – The Trilogy

With a huge sigh of relief she flopped into a chair and closed her eyes, imagining a changed lifestyle of designer clothes and easy living.

John Lomax also breathed a sigh of relief when he dropped Judith Lane at her bungalow. He drove away intent on fulfilling his part of the bargain. He called Ray Quinn to confirm the arrangements, confident that by nightfall Detective Inspector Lane would not want to be an irritation again.

The very next day Lane received a courier delivered letter. Inside was a photograph of his son Billy with his right hand swathed in bandages and Judith similarly strapped. Both held their injured arms across their chests in slings. On the reverse of the photo were the words "as ye sew so shall ye reap."

Judith's silence was assured by the simple device of not letting her know whether Billy had been injured or not. When the photo had been taken she had been brought into the room separately and only saw him with his bandages covering his right hand. The sight had numbed her even though Billy was not her own son. Similarly, Billy had no idea whether or not Judith had lost a finger and he felt equal revulsion. The photo therefore portrayed genuine dreadful shock and pleading in the eyes of both and it was this that Lane saw and took for real.

Billy Lane flew out of Heathrow bound for his new job in Australia exactly an hour before the courier delivered the letter. Like Judith, he had no injuries and was in perfect health. He had left no forwarding details with anybody. John Lomax had found him a new life and provided the funding. Billy had been only too willing to go along with the plan. After all, he reasoned, his life hadn't amounted to much up to now and a clean start with sufficient money and a new job would be an exciting venture. He promised himself that he would keep his side of the bargain as it had been made crystal clear to him by Ray Quinn that it would be very much in his interests to do so. The sight of the severed finger of Richard Dunne together with heavy duty pliers held against his fingers had helped him make up his mind quite quickly.

Lomax was pleased that he had taken control of his "loose ends" list. Lane had removed Dunne, but Lomax himself had taken care of Billy and Judith without bloodshed and ensured the lifelong silence and co-operation of both.

All of which left only Leanne. She had been party to blackmail so Lomax felt confident about her. Besides they had become an item and their relationship was flourishing on all levels. She had moved in with him. He had plenty of money, but had not told her where it was, of course.

He had solved all of his problems but one. However, he felt sure Lane would take heed of the warning and fade from his life. He had no wish to pursue him, even though he knew he remained a very bent policeman and murderer. But he remained afraid of what the loose cannon might do.

He wrestled with the problem for weeks in his mind. The very fact that nothing untoward had happened during that time began to convince him that his life had settled into an easy and very acceptable pattern.

John and Leanne spent the next year or so settling in together. They had many gentle Sunday pub lunches, (invariably followed by not so gentle bedroom exercise) took several peaceful weekends away and gradually became comfortable and worry free.

The only problem for Lomax was how to increase his income. He had already used a good proportion of his lump sum and needed to somehow increase the pot to fund their future. It wasn't yet a pressing issue, but it would need addressing before long. He had been wrestling with it for some days.

-31-

Leanne's mobile was set to vibrate. She didn't notice it at first, but its non- stop insistence became gradually more intrusive. She rolled over onto her side and quietly picked up her phone from the bedside table. She tried to move slowly and gently in an effort not to wake John.

She was very pleased that she had taken such care when she read the text message.

"Must meet. No choice. Tell nobody. White Hart. Midday. Come alone."

She didn't recognise the number and there was no clue as to who had sent it. She slipped out from under the duvet, looked back to make sure John was still asleep, and closed the bedroom door behind her. She took a quick shower, dressed and moved on to the kitchen to make coffee and toast. She hoped Lomax would sleep on because she needed time to think and try to find out what was going on.

The phone buzzed again and the same message arrived, with an addition that warned "if you don't come, you'll regret it."

Lomax appeared in the kitchen later that morning. Leanne said that she needed to go into town to do some shopping and convinced him that he would be bored, so she set out on her own.

She chose a seat at a corner table in the pub which allowed her to face the entrance. The pub was not crowded and she scrutinised everybody almost to the point of rudeness, but she didn't recognise anybody. She sipped a chilled white wine and nervously looked at her mobile which lay inert, silent and threatening on the table.

She realised gradually that her nervousness had produced a need to go to the toilet. When she returned there was a woman sat at her table smiling at her and beckoning.

"Hello, Leanne."

"I'm sorry. Do I know you?"

"No. We haven't met, but we have a mutual interest."

"How do you know my name? Who are you?" Leanne's defences were on alert and she sensed danger.

"My name is Susan Lomax. I am John Lomax's wife. The man you are living with, I believe. It's a long story so I won't bore you with the details, but I've come to warn you that you should be very careful about trusting him. He cannot be trusted for one moment. He can be loving and kind and treat you well, but once he gets an idea in his head nothing gets in his way. That can be a good trait in a man, but in him it's not. I'm not speaking as the woman scorned. I'm simply letting you know that you must never let your guard down."

The pub had become more crowded and noisy with lunchtime trade, so nobody paid any attention to Leanne and Susan at their corner table.

"I've learned that you really should be very careful," she continued. "Watch your back and make sure you have a way out."

PART TWO - HELL HAS NO FURY

"Heaven has no rage like love to hatred turned,
    Nor hell a fury like a woman scorned."
From The Mourning Bride, by William Congreve, (1670-1729).

Lomax & The Biker – The Trilogy

-1-

The realisation that the woman had called herself Susan Lomax gradually formed in Leanne's brain. John's wife was named Karen. So was this woman really her, using another name, or was it somebody else? If so what was her agenda?

She had warned that he was not to be trusted, but could Leanne trust this woman? Had John sent her as a test? What did this woman know? Who else would appear out of the woodwork? What else would come to light? Could she trust John?

Leanne was now utterly confused. She just didn't know what to think. They had been through a great deal and each had been devious with the other along the way, but surely things had settled down and they would be able to get on with their lives without constant crises.

"I'm sorry if what I've said has worried you," continued the woman, "but I know him inside out and, believe me when I tell you, he just cannot be trusted. When we split it was because I found out he had been seeing another woman. There may have been more than one. I asked him to leave and he was just about to go when the police arrived and arrested him on suspicion of murder. I know he got off that and I know some of the things that have happened to him since. You may have real feelings for him, I have to admit I did once, but you must realise that not only is he devious, he is also weak when it comes to being tempted by a woman, as well as having a very determined and hard streak. The only person he really looks after, when push comes to shove, is himself."

Leanne stared intently at the woman as she spoke and began going through things in her own mind. She was trying to argue inwardly against what the woman was telling her, but couldn't help recalling issues and events that told her she was right. Little things, small pointers, which on their own were insignificant, now became crucial. She was so deeply lost in thought she didn't realise that the woman had stopped talking and was staring fixedly at her, awaiting a response.

"Why are you taking this trouble?" Leanne asked.

"Before I tell you I need your promise that it will remain between the two of us."

"I don't know. I realise things may have happened between you that you resent and that you may want revenge for the way you have been treated and even deceived, but I don't know how I can help."

"I'm not asking for your help," answered Mrs Lomax, "I'm trying to help you. It's just that you should take great care and don't put yourself in situations where you can be exploited. He really is not to be trusted."

"I'm perfectly capable of looking after myself," said Leanne, "and I'm quite offended that you see me as a weak and vulnerable woman. I won't make promises I can't keep."

"OK, fine, but please remember you have been warned. I won't contact you again. If you need me at any time, my number is on your mobile."

With those words Mrs Lomax took her leave. Leanne stayed put and, with the help of a second chilled white wine, concentrated on recalling the details of her relationship with John Lomax. Half an hour later she shook herself from her reverie. She had concluded that she should dismiss most of what she had been told as it could only be based on the woman's hurt feelings and an obvious desire for revenge. Besides, she thought John Lomax loved her deeply. He had said as much many times. She did, however, think that perhaps there may have been some kernel of truth in what she had just heard, so she decided to be more wary all round, especially where John Lomax was concerned. The problem was that by becoming more careful, she knew she may just be doing what Mrs Lomax wanted by spoiling her own relationship with John. She was left with the nagging feeling that this was what was intended all along. The woman had subtly planted a seed of doubt in her mind and it would be difficult to ignore, despite the fact that the woman had deliberately used the wrong name.

-2-

Susan Lomax tapped out the number she had been given and waited. She did not have to wait long before the expected voice answered.

"How did it go?"

"Well, I told her, and she listened. I think she was confused by the name. She didn't want to accept what I said, but I think she will have the message in her brain now and it will come back to her at various times."

"Good. That's all I wanted. Thank you. I'll be in touch."

Sandy Lane smiled to himself as he disconnected. He inwardly congratulated himself on using Karen Lomax to warn Leanne. Leanne might suspect that the woman she had met who had called herself Susan Lomax, was, in fact, Karen Lomax, John's wife. It was she who Lomax had called from his mobile phone on the train on that fateful day when DCI Sandy Lane had overheard their conversation and put the information to good use.

Having finished her brief phone call she was overcome by a feeling of emptiness. She sat down and began to recall the events that had preceded it.

Her husband, John Lomax, had been acting strangely even before that fateful day when the police had arrived to arrest him just as he was about to leave her, suitcase in hand. She had followed subsequent events, of course, and had become increasingly inured to their twists and turns. She knew he was clever but had never realised just how ingenious he really was. His affair had irretrievably changed her feelings towards him and had helped ease her heartache. His arrest and then his release, however, had the opposite effect. It angered her. That emotion became fury when she discovered that he was living with another woman. Karen realised that it was more than coincidence that the latest woman was Leanne Lane.

She had not told Sandy Lane her reasons for agreeing to meet Leanne because she wanted him to believe that good old fashioned revenge was her motive. If DCI Lane thought he was using her, then let him. She would make her own move when she was ready.

Her life had been so completely shattered that her motivation was much, much more deeply rooted than mere revenge. She wanted, actually needed, John Lomax to be totally destroyed and stop at nothing and use anybody to that end. If both Lane and Lomax could be devious, then she could be more so. Hell hath no fury....

Karen Lomax made two phone calls. When they had been completed she walked to her kitchen, opened a bottle of red wine and poured herself a glass. The sunlight caught the crystal and its contents and sprayed blood red reflections, surrounding her where she stood. She raised the glass and drank deeply.

-3-

Although not in financial difficulty, John Lomax was acutely aware that he needed to make better provision for his future. Quite a large chunk had been taken from the proceeds of the Anvex robbery and the residue, although a significant sum, would not last forever. This would soon be particularly true as he and Leanne were leaving the next day on a cruise. He had booked it because he wanted to rekindle the ease of their relationship and because it would give him time to think. He had needed to think of something that would see him through the rest of his days without attracting the unwanted attention of DCI Lane or any of his colleagues. All the money in the world would be no use to him rotting at Her Majesty's Pleasure. He had also needed to get the odious Mr Lane off his back once and for all.

He sat in his garden chair, in the cooling shade of a weeping willow, not far from his buried secret. It amazed him that the police had not literally dug around in his garden. If they had only bothered to do so, they would have found the remaining Anvex money, a ring and a SIM card which contained a text message exchange that incriminated DCI Sandy Lane in murder. He had resolved to move these, but was at a loss as to where to put them. Certainly depositing money in any bank would be as good as advertising it to the police, even if he split it between several banks and used different accounts and false names. These were devices well known to the law and he knew Lane was monitoring his every move.

Lomax & The Biker – The Trilogy

Lomax had thought it all through thoroughly and eventually constructed a plan. It involved trusting his good friend Ray Quinn, the biker. Although experience had taught him harsh lessons about trust, Lomax was as sure as he could be that Quinn was his man. He had outlined it all to him and Quinn had agreed for two reasons. Firstly, he wanted DCI Lane to suffer more ignominy and secondly because he could think of nothing better to do for the foreseeable future. Also, it would be entertaining and he liked the idea of going into business with Lomax. Now Lomax could enjoy the cruise while his friend looked after the business.

Lomax used some of the remaining Anvex money to rent shop premises in London, and set up a jewellery business. He avoided items that were very expensive because he wanted rapid turnover. This meant that the Anvex proceeds were quickly laundered and distributed in small amounts, which were untraceable. Another part of the business was devoted to pawn. This allowed him to deal with people who avoided authority as much as possible. He kept the ring that up until then had been in the burial place in his garden, in the shop safe along with other pawned items. It was therefore hidden in plain sight.

Lomax was sitting in his shop with Quinn that morning listening to a customer. He was a regular and had become a familiar face over the last couple of years. Quinn had, however, become suspicious of him for that very reason. He was too regular. There are not many people who use the same jewellers at least every month for two years. The man had just tried too hard and both Lomax and Quinn were on full alert. Nevertheless what he had to say was of very great interest to them.

"Do you remember the Anvex robbery?" he asked. "Nearly half a million they reckon, and as far as I know it's never been found. Rumour has it that a Detective Chief Inspector Lane took it as a personal insult that he never caught the villain, and was even humiliated by the robber in some way."

"You seem well informed," commented Quinn.

"I even heard the owner of Anvex has contacts in very high places."

"Go on," said Lomax, trying not to appear too interested.

"Apparently, it wasn't the money that bothered him. He must have more money than sense. It was that a ring was stolen during the robbery. He had bought it for his wife's birthday and he was going to get it sized the next day. It's worth an awful lot of money, they say."

"Who are they? Quinn asked.

"What does it look like?" Lomax enquired. "If we see it we'll report it. There might even be a reward."

"I doubt that," said the customer, "they want it kept quiet but I understand this Lane has some leads. Something about a photo, I believe."

Lomax caught his breath as he linked the item in question to that now sitting a few feet away in his safe. He covered his unease well, but Quinn saw it and jumped in.

"Pardon me for asking, but how do you know so much about it? Especially as all the reports I remember concentrated on the money. In fact, I can't recall a ring being mentioned at all."

"It wasn't," the customer, who was obviously well informed, whispered in reply. He looked out of the window and up at the London sky. "What's more," he lowered his voice even further, as if he was afraid of being overheard even though he was the only customer in the shop, "I've heard that the police have reason to believe that the thief has a connection to the jewellery trade."

Alarmed, Lomax whispered "why on earth would they believe that? Have they got a grass?"

"No, they discovered certain clues that led them to that conclusion."

"Clues; what clues?"

Lomax knew he had been especially meticulous not to leave anything of his own behind. He'd taken everything he had needed with him and disposed of them immediately afterwards. He had worn gloves and a forensic suit, including a hood. He had got rid of his shoes, had a shower and scrubbed himself clean diligently. He had then run the water for ages so that nothing would remain in the plughole or drain.

But this customer now chilled his blood further.

"Apparently they found traces of some particular substances at the scene. You know how good forensic science is now. It's almost impossible not to leave a trace of being somewhere no matter how hard you try. I'm told they identified some cleaning stuff that's only used in the jewellery business to make things sparkle and look tempting in the window and under the glass counter. They're trying to find who supplies it and then who they supplied it to. They also found traces of some sort of wax."

The man glanced at the counter and seemed to study the sparkling gems beneath the glass.

Lomax sighed inwardly at his own foolishness. He'd polished the ring only that morning, but if most jewellers used it, then they could not possibly connect him to its theft. The police must have something else.

"Do you know anything more?" he asked his informant.

"No, what I know about this case is only what I've overheard in random conversation."

"Of course, I understand. Thank you for this."

"What are you going to do?" the customer asked.

The question took Lomax and Quinn by surprise.

"Why should I need to do anything?" asked Lomax. "It's nothing to do with me. It's just interesting when something like this happens so close to home."

"Perhaps we'll have to leave the country!" Quinn joked. "Take a long holiday. From what you've told us, the police might even be on their way here now."

He looked the customer up and down and frowned.

"Perhaps you should go. You don't want to be caught up in anything, do you?"

"Yes, I think you're right. It's an odd business, this."

Lomax & The Biker – The Trilogy

The man half turned towards the door, but stopped before asking "what will happen to you if they do come here?"

"I'll be arrested and imprisoned, of course," Lomax said. He hoped it sounded as though he was joking. "I'll hope for the best, but there's nothing to worry about. We'll still be here when you come next. Now, perhaps you should go before they get here. They'll probably arrest you as well!"

The customer suddenly became nervous and hustled towards the door. He still made the effort to shake Lomax by the hand, which the latter thought very strange.

"If you do leave the country, I wish you the best of luck," said the customer returning the joke.

Lomax was lost in thought, busy remembering how he had come to possess the ring.

At 11.30 one morning about two years before this conversation, a courier had knocked on his front door holding a small parcel. Having signed for it, he had taken it into the kitchen. It was a small wooden presentation box which contained a package wrapped in tissue paper. Inside the tissue he saw a ring. He had recognised it as belonging to Richard Dunne, a former friend who was now longer alive. He had also realised in the same instant that the perfectly severed finger it encircled had also belonged to Richard Dunne. There had been no note, no explanation, but Lomax had known it had come from DCI Lane. He had understood it was a significant message in itself. It said that he was dealing with loose ends. Lomax had wrapped the grizzly present in its tissue, placed it carefully in its box, and buried it with his money and the SIM card in the garden. It was now sitting in its cleaned and newly waxed box in his safe in the shop, having been relieved of its decomposed finger and polished.

Lomax realised with a jolt that he had been set up. Lane had sent the ring, knowing where it had come from and knowing that he could use it as a reason for further investigation whenever he chose. He was letting Lomax know that the real value of Dunne's ring lay in its link to Dunne's murder and his killer. Also, it showed that this very valuable ring stolen during the Anvex robbery was now in the possession of the killer and that he intended to frame Lomax both for Dunne's murder, the Anvex robbery and the theft of that ring. Lomax understood with sudden clarity that it meant that Lane had stolen the ring because he knew he had only taken the money. Lane must have made sure the ring was polished before sending it to Lomax. It also meant that Dunne had somehow got hold of the ring from Lane, but had lost his finger because of it. In addition, he knew that Lane did not now care that Lomax would know he had stolen the ring. He obviously felt safe enough to take this step. Finally, the customer obviously knew a great deal about the matter and could only have been sent by Lane to throw a pebble in the pond.

Lomax was deep in thought as Quinn ushered the customer out.

"He didn't buy anything," said Quinn, "in fact he didn't even look at anything. He's been getting on my nerves lately."

"Mine too," said Lomax, "but he obviously knows something. We need to keep an eye on him."

"I think I need to have a word," said Quinn.

He ghosted from the shop and caught a fleeting glimpse of the customer just as he turned the corner at the end of the road. Without appearing to hurry and with no discernible sound he closed the gap rapidly.

-4-

The shop was now deserted. Lomax slipped into his office and opened the safe hidden behind a Turkish rug he'd mounted on the wall and further concealed behind a panel of oak constructed to resemble part of the wall.

He extracted a cloth bag, containing the ring in a box and several other gems that people had pawned and failed to collect.

The other items paled in comparison. The light from his table lamp hit the gems and fired a fusillade of white and blue beams into the room.

Since beginning in the jewellery business he had built up a network of people who would be interested in buying these pieces. He could, of course, place them for sale in his window as is the normal practice with uncollected items, but he thought that might bring unwanted attention, so he was undecided.

He knew he could sell the ring to a jeweller in Hatton Garden for a large sum, but again that may bring its own problems. He wanted his business to be openly legitimate and untainted, even though it was in reality a means, a front, for laundering his Anvex money. So the disposal of a ring that was known to have been stolen was a difficulty.

Lomax replaced the ring and the other items in the safe and counted the cash inside. The money had been safely transferred from its muddy hole in his garden and gradually exchanged for honest cash through the business. Mental arithmetic told him that there was now over £500,000 at his disposal, though not all kept on the premises. At his home in London he had another three thousand pounds, which he thought to be not an unreasonable amount to keep as ready cash.

He had jokingly said to the customer that he might leave the country, but he knew that would be seen as proof of guilt. He had also said that he may take a holiday and he now began to warm to that idea.

He swung the safe door shut and closed the secret panel, letting the tapestry fall back over it. An hour later he had decided that a holiday would be an excellent idea. He would take Leanne on a cruise and Ray Quinn could look after things. He would discuss it when Quinn returned.

It was then that a new customer walked into the shop and began to browse. Lomax smiled a greeting and asked the man if there was anything in particular that he was looking for. The man said that he merely wanted to browse if that was OK. Lomax kept an eye on him. He was a tall, slim man in a black overcoat with a similarly shaded suit beneath and a white shirt.

He was carefully examining items with the eye of someone intent on buying something and getting good value for his money. Lomax had long since learned to be observant of detail and as a shopkeeper he had come to know the behaviour of customers. He was now struck by the curious fact that the man was only looking at the wooden jewellery boxes that were on one of the counters. Lomax stocked these because he had found that people liked them as a means of keeping their jewellery at home.

Lomax & The Biker – The Trilogy

He had a range of such boxes and cases which consisted of porcelain, mother of pearl, pewter, brass, silver and gold. Lomax had noticed that customers usually looked at most of them in order to assess their value and quality in general, even if they really only intended to buy a wooden one.

Lomax then noted something else. The man was subtly running his finger along a crevice in the seam of a box. So, his interest wasn't in the wood itself but in the wax covering it, a sample of which he captured under his nail.

The "customer" was not that at all, Lomax understood with dismay; he was police collecting "evidence."

As with the cleaning spray for his jewellery, Lomax knew he was not the only user. The wax he used, although somewhat rare, due to its price and availability only in commercial quantities, was hardly unique; many furniture and antique dealers bought the same substance. This was not by any means conclusive evidence of his guilt. But he was feeling increasingly uneasy, because the discovery of both substances at the scene of the robbery and at his shop was beginning to stretch credulity.

The man rose and prowled up and down the shop for some moments longer. Finally he glanced toward the counter.

"Are you John Lomax?"

John's neck hairs pricked up. He thought for a moment and decided that being cagey would not be wise.

"I am," he said, for to deny it would merely arouse suspicion at a later time. He wondered if he was about to be arrested on the spot. His heart beat fiercely as he had no desire to repeat that particular experience.

"Nice shop," the man said, attempting and failing to appear friendly.

Lomax detected the coldness of an inquisitor in the eyes and he felt his palms begin to sweat and his stomach turning somersaults.

"Is there anything that takes your interest?" he asked.

"No, thank you. In fact, I must be going."

"Have a nice day, do come back," John said without sincerity.

"I shall," replied the man and walked outside into the London air.

Lomax stepped back into the depths of his shops and breathed out. He watched as the man appeared to be leaving the area. Just as John was about to turn his attention to something else, the man stopped and dived into an alleyway opposite the shop. He was now lost in its shadows, but Lomax knew he could easily be keeping watch from there.

He could not wait for Quinn to return. He didn't know how long he would be or how far away he had gone. He thought for a moment and decided to activate a plan he had concocted a little while earlier.

Lomax & The Biker – The Trilogy

-5-

Bill Butler was hunched over his cluttered, beer stained table at the Green Man Pub, surrounded by a half dozen of his cronies, all of them dirty and dim. They were half-baked Falstaffs, whose only earthly reason for being there was to do Butler's bidding as quickly and as ruthlessly as he ordered.

The thug, dressed in unwashed, fashionably torn jeans, designer hoody and trainers, looked up as John Lomax approached. He attended to his teeth with a gold pick and the light caught his imitation Rolex. He didn't know much about Lomax except that he was one of the few shopkeepers on his patch who coughed up his weekly "business fee", and didn't need a good slap or a slash with a razor to be reminded of it.

The arrangement also suited Lomax. It meant he didn't have to deal with nasty situations and so draw attention to himself. He remembered a recent shoplifter. It was known in London, and probably elsewhere, as "boosting" or "the five finger discount" or "shrinkage". Bill Butler's business fee had been earned that day. He had shown the shoplifter the error of his ways. He was still in hospital many weeks later and would never talk about the incident.

Lomax stopped at the table and nodded at Butler.

"What's brought you 'ere, your lordship?"

Although he knew the man, Lomax could never quite get used to his turn of phrase. It was as if Butler had been stuck in time and place. The title was ironic, of course. Lomax didn't have a drop of noble blood in his veins, but in a city where class was the main yardstick by which to measure a man, more so even than money, Lomax swam in a very different stream than Butler.

The thug's East End upbringing had been grim and he'd never had any helping hand along the way, unlike Lomax, whose parents had come from a pleasant part of Surrey. That was reason enough for Butler to dislike him, despite the fact he coughed up his fee on time.

"I need to speak to you."

"Do you, now? Speak away, mate. Me ear's all yours."

"Alone."

Butler continued to dig at his teeth.

"Leave us, boys," he grunted towards the others around the table, and, tutting or grumbling, they moved away with their pints.

He looked Lomax over carefully. The man was trying his hardest to be carefree but he clearly had a desperate air about him. Ah, this was tidy! Desperation and its cousin fear were far better motivators than greed for getting men to do what you wanted. Butler pointed toward Lomax with a blunt finger that ended in a nail blackened from a collision with something unyielding.

"I ope you aven't come to tell me there's no fee this week."

"No, no, no. I'll have your money. It's not that."

Lomax lowered his voice to a whisper and the silent listener in the corner had to strain to hear.

"Hear me out, Butler. I'm in trouble. I need to get out of the country quickly, without anybody knowing. I'll pay you handsomely if you can arrange it."

"Oh, whatever I do for you you'll pay 'andsomely," he said, laughing. "Rest assured of that. What'd you do, mate, to need an 'oliday so quick?"

"I can't tell you."

"Ooh, too shy to share the story with your friend Bill? You shagged some woman and her ol man arter yer? You owe money to a bookie?

Then Butler squinted and laughed harshly.

"But no, you're too much past it to pull a married bird. An yor too tight to bet more an a fiver, so, who's after you, mate?"

"I can't say," he whispered.

Butler sipped more of his beer.

"No matter; get on with it, it's me dinnertime and I'm ungry."

Lomax looked around and his voice lowered yet further.

"I need to get into France. Nobody can know. And I need to leave tonight."

"Tonight?" The thug shook his head.

"I heard you have connections all over the docks."

"Can't say."

"Can you get me onto a cargo ship? Anywhere in France will do. I need to get to Lyons a s a p."

Lomax had set up a bank account in Lyon some time ago, and had on one occasion transferred enough funds to alert DCI Lane that he may be about to flee. Although it was a ruse at the time, the money was still there.

"That's a bleedin' tall order, mate."

"I don't have any choice."

"Well, now, I might be able to." He thought for a moment. "It'll cost you twenty thousand."

"What?"

"It's bloody twelve o'clock, mate. Look at the clock. It ain't easy, what you're asking, you know. I'll 'ave to run around all day like a blue arsed whatsit. Blimey. Not to mention the risk. The docks're lousy with security 'n customs. Thick as flies they are .... So there you 'ave it, mate. Twenty K."

He resumed the excavation of his teeth, found something and chewed it.

"All right," Lomax said, scowling and the men shook hands.

"I need something up front. 'Ave to paint some palms, understand."

Lomax pulled notes from his wallet and counted.

"Christ!" Bill Butler laughed as his hand reached out and snatched the wallet. He emptied it, threw it down on the table, but then picked it up again and put in his own pocket.

"Ta. Now, when do I get the rest?"

Lomax glanced at his watch.

"I can have it by four. Can you make the arrangements by then?"

"Rest assured I can, Butler promised, waving for the barmaid.

"Come by the shop."

Bill Butler squinted and looked the man over warily.

Lomax & The Biker – The Trilogy

"Maybe you won't own up to what you done, but tell me, mate, just ow safe is all this? For me, I mean."

Lomax gave a grim laugh. "You've heard the expression 'giving somebody a taste of their own medicine'?"

"I ave."

"Well, that's what I'm going to do. Don't worry. I know how to make sure we're alone."

Lomax sighed once more and then left the Green Man. Butler watched him leave, thinking "twenty thousand quid for a few hours' work. Desperation is just plain bloody beautiful." He failed to notice that Lomax was being silently followed out by a shadowy figure who had seen and heard it all. Lomax, however, knew he had been followed because he had seen the man glide from the shadows of the alleyway and slip silently into a seat in the pub close enough to hear everything.

At five minutes to four that afternoon, John Lomax awaited Bill Butler's arrival. He had kept up the appearance of going through his business as usual. But he'd continued to observe the street outside. Sure enough, he'd noted several plain-clothed detectives standing well back in the shadows. They pretended to be watching the construction work on the site opposite but in fact it was obvious that their attention was mostly on Lomax and the store.

John Lomax now put his plan into action. He called a courier company that he used regularly. He acted furtively on purpose, like a ham actor in a downbeat melodrama. He slipped the young deliveryman a paper-wrapped package, which contained a box. He gave him instructions to take it to his own house as quickly as possible. Witnessing the apparently suspicious mission, and probably assuming that the box contained money or other damning evidence, one of the detectives started after the young man as soon as he left the shop.

Lomax then used a craftsman that he had earlier briefed and gave him a similar package, with instructions to take it home with him and make sure the box mechanism was dependable. The remaining detective observed the craftsman leave the shop clutching the parcel and, after a moment of debate, appeared to decide that it was better to pursue this potential source of evidence rather than remain at his station.

Lomax carefully scoured the street and saw no more detectives. The workers had left and everywhere was deserted except for a married couple, who paused at the front window, then stepped inside. As they looked over his shop, Lomax told them he would return in a moment and, with another glance outside into the empty street, stole into the office, closing the door behind him.

-6-

He sat at his desk, lifted aside the Turkish rug and opened the secret panel, and then the safe. He was just reaching inside when he became aware of a breeze wafting on his face, and he knew the door to the office had been opened.

Lomax leapt up, crying, "No!"

He was staring at the husband of the couple who'd just walked into the shop who was holding a menacing looking hand gun. Lomax gasped.

"What do you want?"

"We're not here to rob you Lomax, we're here to arrest you," he said calmly. "Please don't move. I don't want to harm you. But I will if you give me no choice."

He then spoke into his radio, and a moment later, beyond him, Lomax could see the door burst open, and in ran two Met officers in plain clothes, as well as two uniformed constables. The woman who had obviously been posing as the first detective's wife waved them toward the office.

"The safe is back there," she called.

"Good," shouted one detective, who was the lean, dark man who'd been in the store earlier; masquerading as a customer. His fellow officer was dressed similarly, with an overcoat over a suit, though this man differed in physique, being taller and quite pale, with a shock of flaxen hair. Lomax immediately recognised DCI Sandy Lane. Both policemen took the shopkeeper by the arms and led him out into the shop.

Lomax & The Biker – The Trilogy

"What's going on?" Lomax blustered.

Lane was enjoying himself and chuckled. "I think you know well enough."

They searched him and, finding no weapons, released his arms. The detective who'd entered with the woman on his arm replaced his gun with a notebook, in which he began taking down evidence. They dismissed the woman and she explained that she'd be back at the station if they needed her for anything else.

"What is this about?" Lomax demanded.

The lean officer deferred to Lane, who looked Lomax over carefully.

"So we meet again, Mr Lomax. Do you mind if I call you John? We have known each other a long time, after all. One of my officers visited your shop recently. And during that visit he managed to collect a sample of wax from a wooden box. The substance is identical to the wax we found traces of on a jewellery box which used to contain a certain ring, stolen during the Anvex robbery some time ago. We have also found traces of a cleaning spray which is used by professionals to make their goods sparkle. Both these traces were present at the Anvex site which, as you know, was relieved of a large sum of money some time ago. Our investigations have now taken us to the point where we need to ask for your co-operation in resolving the matter."

He was enjoying himself, deliberately taunting him with the use of flowery and officious language in order to emphasise his power, authority and control.

"I don't see how I can help you, Mr Lane."

John Lomax deliberately did not refer to the hated policeman by his nickname. Recognising the need not to react, he kept proceedings on a proper footing.

"Don't you, John?" Lane sneered.

True to type, thought Lomax.

"I would prefer it if you showed some respect, Mr Lane, and used a proper title and a civil tone, as you are supposed to do and as you notice I am doing for you."

DCI Lane flushed crimson with anger. Lomax was deliberately needling him and had succeeded in embarrassing him in front of junior officers, seemingly without having tried.

"Mr Lomax," continued the policeman, only just maintaining an even temper, despite an overwhelming urge to knock the man to the floor, "it really would be better if you just admitted your part in the Anvex robbery. We know you have the money from the robbery as well as the ring. We have the evidence we need. You are going to jail. A guilty plea would obviously be better for you in front of a judge."

"This is absurd," stated Lomax, calmly looking his adversary in the eye, "we have been through all this before. Do you not remember having to release me before because the evidence you had was, as the CPS said at the time 'insufficient to lead to a reasonable chance of a successful prosecution.' That's a direct quote by the way in case you memory is failing you. Also, would you like me to remind you of the arrangement we have about this matter in front of your colleagues here? I bet you haven't told them have you? Perhaps I ought to tell the court when the time comes as well. That should cause a nice stir, don't you think?"

Again, Lomax was succeeding in making Sandy Lane tremble with rage. His colleagues recognised the signs of his inner struggle to maintain an even temper, and privately looked forward to the next few minutes.

"Go search the safe", Lane barked to a constable, nodding toward the back office.

He then explained, "My officers have been trying to ascertain where you might have a hiding place for your ill-gotten gains. But your shop has far too much stock and too many nooks and crannies to locate what we are looking for without searching for a week. So we stationed those two detectives outside on the street to make you believe we were about to arrest you. As we had anticipated, you led them by the hand far too obviously in pursuit of two parcels. We now know both were a trick."

"What, those deliveries a moment ago?" Lomax asked his eyes wide in mocking innocence. "I sent one box home for myself to work on tonight. The other was taken by a craftsman colleague to do the same."

Lomax was really beginning to enjoy himself now, and it was starting to show.

"So you say. But I suspect you're stalling."

"This is most uncalled for. I-"

"Please, allow me to finish. When you sent our men on a wild goose chase it told us that you were planning to leave, so my colleague here and a typist from the station came in posing as customers, as they'd been waiting to do for several hours." He turned to the policeman who'd played the husband and added, "good job, by the way."

"Thank you, Sir."

The DCI turned back to Lomax.

"You were fooled by the married couple and, because you knew the net was closing around you, you were kind enough to lead us directly to the safe."

"Mr Lane, I really must protest again. I am merely an honest jeweller trying to make an honest living in these difficult times."

DCI Lane said nothing, while the "husband" continued to take everything down in his notebook.

"Sir," the constable said as he stepped from the office. "Could I have a quiet word?"

"Is there a problem? Is the safe locked?"

"No, sir, the door was open. The trouble is that ring is not inside."

"What ring?" Lomax asked, continuing with his innocent air.

"What is inside?" Detective Chief Inspector Lane asked, trying to ignore the increasingly irritating act.

"Only money, sir, that's all. There's about five hundred pounds, in various notes. The serial numbers don't follow each other either."

Lomax & The Biker – The Trilogy

"There's bound to be money in there," Lomax contributed helpfully, "I'd be stupid to have that much out in the front of the shop. That would be asking for trouble, don't you think?"

Lane frowned, looked into the office beyond them and was about to speak when at the same moment the door opened again and in strode Bill Butler. The thug took one look at the gathering and started to flee. He was seized just as he thought he had escaped and dragged back inside.

"Well now, look who we have here. Billy Butler as I live and breathe," said Lane, lifting an eyebrow in his pale forehead. "We know about you, oh, yes. So you're in this with Lomax are you? I always knew he couldn't have done it without help. Mind you, I didn't for a minute think he'd stoop so low as getting webbed up with this low life."

"Let me go!" protested Butler. I don't know what you're yacking abart, you bastard. I don't know nuffin."

"If you swear again I'll arrest you," said Lane. "Now shut up and let's see what we have here."

Lomax, who was really enjoying himself by this time, seized the opportunity.

"He's done nothing wrong. He comes in sometimes to look at my jewels. I'm sure that's all he's doing here today."

The DCI turned to him. "There's something going on here, I know it. Don't be stupid Lomax. You can make this easy or hard. I'd prefer hard, but I'm giving you the chance because I'm a fair man."

Lomax & The Biker – The Trilogy

Lomax swallowed the urge to snigger with contempt at the thought of Lane being a fair man. He knew it was better to remain calm in the situation. He knew he would not be arrested because it would have happened already.

"Keep your flamin' mouth shut," Butler warned through gritted teeth.

"Quiet, you," a constable growled.

"Go on, Lomax, tell us. It will be better for you in the long run."

John Lomax appeared to be wrestling with himself inside. Everybody in the shop saw his inner turmoil and took it as he intended. He wanted all to see that what he was about to say was only being said because he had no choice. He swallowed and looked away from Bill Butler.

"That man has been extorting money from me and others in return for protection. He extorts money and goods, and threatens us with violence. He has a gang and they drink at The Green Man. He comes in every Saturday and demands his 'business fee'. I know of at least one person who has ended up in hospital after a session with him and his friends."

"We've heard rumours about this," put in one of the officers.

Sandy Lane looked closely at Lomax.

"Today's Monday, not Saturday. Why is he here now?"

Butler could see his situation was worsening by the second and shouted at the Lomax, "I'm warning you…"

"One more word and you're down the nick." Lane was fast losing what little control he had left.

Lomax took a breath and continued. "Last Thursday he surprised me in my shop at eight a.m. I hadn't opened the doors by then, because I'd come in early as I had finished work on several pieces late the night before and I wanted to wax and polish them before I opened up. It's an old fashioned practice, but it works."

DCI Lane nodded, considering this information.

"He made me open the door. He browsed among the boxes and looked them over carefully. He selected that one right there." He pointed to a rosewood box sitting on the counter. "And he said that he was taking that box as well as his fee this week. He then told me to build a false compartment in the bottom. It had to be so clever that no one examining the box, however carefully, could find what he'd hidden, in there."

He showed them the box and the compartment which he'd just finished making a half hour before.

"Did he say what he intended to hide?" Lane asked.

"He said some items of jewellery and money."

Billy Butler roared, "E's a flamin' liar! E's a dead man when I get my hands on 'im."

"Shut up," one of the officers said and pushed the big man down roughly into a chair.

"Did he say where he'd got them?"

"No," replied Lomax.

The detectives eyed one another.

"So Butler came here," the senior man offered, "selected the box and got wax on his fingers."

"Looks like it," Lomax helpfully put in. "We were all too scared to report him. He hurts people for fun. I know I sent the police across the street on a wild goose chase, but I had no idea why they were here. I had to get rid of them. I knew Butler would be here soon, and that he would spot the law. They do stand out, you know. I knew if that happened he would think he was being set up and I would be in for a real hiding or worse."

"Search him," Lane ordered, nodding towards Butler.

They found some coins, a gold tooth pick, a wallet containing a good deal of money, a Stanley knife and a cosh. Lane looked inside the wallet.

"Well, well, well. Oh dear. My, my. Will you look at this? Twenty pound notes with consecutive numbers. I'd bet my police pension they're on the Anvex list."

"That wallet is not mine!" Butler raged. "It's 'is!"

"That's a lie!" John Lomax cried. "Why, if it were mine, would you have it? I have mine right here."

He pulled a cheap leather wallet from a pocket and flourished it for all to see. It contained only a few pounds, some cards and a driving licence. The serial numbers on the notes were not consecutive. He had been very careful on that point.

"It's a fit up! 'E come to me wiv a story of avin to get 'is arse to France tonight."

"Now why would he do that?" asked Lane.

"'E didn't say," Butler admitted.

"Convenient," muttered another detective wryly. It was clear that they didn't believe Butler.

Lomax kept a curious and cautious expression on his face. He was still not totally certain that this theatre would work. He'd had to act fast to save himself. He'd told Butler that he was going to treat the police to a taste of their own medicine, but he hadn't said he was not going to France. No, he'd used evidence to connect Butler to the Anvex robbery by using a fabricated story about the box with the hidden compartment on the one hand and, on the other, making certain Butler took the incriminating wallet from him at the Green Man.

But would the police accept the theory? It seemed for a moment that they would. But just as Lomax began to breathe somewhat more easily, DCI Sandy Lane turned quickly to him.

"Show me your hands, Lomax."

"I beg your pardon?"

"I want to see your hands. I am not yet completely convinced the facts are as they seem."

Lane knew, of course, that this was nothing but a display, a show put on for the benefit of his colleagues. He was trying to have the last word over Lomax and be seen to be in control of the whole affair. He was trying to recover lost respect.

"Well, yes, of course."

Lomax held his palms out, apparently struggling to keep them steady. The detective looked them over. Then he looked up, frowning. After a moment he lowered his head again and smelled Lomax's palm. He said to Butler, "now yours."

"Listen 'ere, filth, you bloody well aint-"

But two officers grabbed the man's beefy hands and lifted them for the Detective Chief Inspector, who again examined and sniffed.

He nodded and then turned slowly to Lomax.

"You see, the ring is an unusual design, being silver and gold, which is not all that common. Gold, as you know, needs no polishing to prevent tarnish. But silver does. Mr Dunne, may he rest in peace, told us that the ring had been recently cleaned with a particular type of polish that is scented with perfume derived from the lily flower and is sprayed on. It is quite expensive but Dunne had bought it as a present for his wife, so he thought the expense worth it. Unfortunately, he has since died, but you know that already don't you?"

This was a reference to the fact that Lane had sent Lomax the ring, still encircling Dunne's finger and was also a warning to Lomax that he was in control and could have him arrested at any moment. Nobody else in the room understood the true meaning of Lane's words. Lomax also realised that Lane was letting him know that Butler would be charged and convicted of the Anvex robbery, but that he knew Lomax was the real villain. On this occasion it suited Lane to have Lomax in a position of debt. He was telling Lomax that this was another loose end being tidied up and the number of those was decreasing. His turn would surely come before long.

Lomax, for his part, knew he still had the ring. He also now knew it was almost certainly more valuable than he had imagined. He had managed to get Butler off his back, with the likelihood of a long sentence, and had apparently convinced Lane that Butler had the ring.

Lane turned to Butler as Lomax was having these thoughts.

"Your hands have a marked scent of lily, while Mr. Lomax's do not. There's no doubt in my mind that you are the Anvex robber and that forensics will prove me correct."

The sudden politeness and correctness was not lost on Lomax or Butler.

"No, no. This is wrong. I'm being fitted up 'ere!"

"Read him his rights, constable. You'll have your chance to make a statement at the station."

Lomax's heart pounded fiercely from this final matter about the spray polish. He'd nearly overlooked it but had realised that as forensics were now so good that people could be linked to the scenes of crimes, then he also needed to be just as conscientious. If a burglar could leave evidence during the commission of a crime, he might also pick something up there that might prove equally damning. He thought back to the ring and the Anvex site. He recalled that he'd recognized the scent of the tarnish-preventing spray and on the way to the Green Man, he'd bought some. He had sprayed it liberally on his palm and, shaking Butler's hand to seal their agreement, had transferred some to the thug's skin.

Before returning to his shop, Lomax had scrubbed his own hands clean with disinfectant soap and discarded the remaining spray.

"I think it would be a good idea for you to co-operate. It will go easier on you," the constable said to Butler.

"Piss off! I'm sayin nuffin. I've been 'ad."

"Where is the ring? Lane asked quietly.

"What ring? I don't know nuffin abaht any ring."

"Perhaps we'll find it when we search your house."

No, Lomax thought, they wouldn't find the ring. But they would find a half dozen other pieces stolen by Lomax in various burglaries over the past year. Just as they'd find a crude diagram of the Anvex building, drawn with Butler's own pencil on a sheet of Butler's own paper. He had planted them there this afternoon after he'd met with Butler at the Green Man and had taken exemplary care this time to leave no traces that would link him to that incursion.

As he was having these thoughts he noticed a priest pass the shop, look intently through the window and hurry on his way.

John Lomax could not resist it. He just had to turn the screw.

"I hope you find the ring at Butler's place."

Lane considered him carefully and finally whispered, "perhaps we will, but I very much doubt it, don't you?"

Lomax & The Biker – The Trilogy

DCI Lane glanced around the shop and turned back to Lomax, his eyebrow cocked quizzically.

"Perhaps you can help me in another matter, since you deal in boxes."

Lomax was immediately on his guard. What is Lane up to now? Why would he ask him for help?

"I've been on the lookout for a particular box for a friend of mine."

Lomax very much doubted that Lane had any friends at all, let alone particular ones, but resisted the urge to comment.

"It is in the shape of an octagon on a gold base. The box is rosewood and is inlaid with ivory. As you know, international trade in ivory was finally banned in January 1990, but under English law, only ivory carvings dated before 1947 can be sold, and they must be sold with proof of age documents. As the box I'm looking for is dated before 1947 it will be quite valuable and would be a fitting gift."

Lomax thought for a moment.

"I'm sorry to say that I'm not familiar with that particular piece, but if I come across it, I'll be sure to get in touch. Have you still got the same mobile number?"

Lomax knew this question would alert Lane to the fact that getting to him would present no problems whatsoever. He thought it a clever, subtle and very appropriate warning.

After the shop had been emptied, Lomax went to the cupboard and poured himself a glass of whisky. He paused at one of the jewellery cases in the front of the store and glanced at a bowl containing cheap cuff links. Beside it was a sign that said, 'Any Two Items for £1.'

He checked to make certain the ring was discreetly hidden beneath the tin and copper jewellery, where it would remain until he met with his French buyer tomorrow. Lomax then counted his daily takings and, as he did every night, carefully ordered and dusted the counter so that it was ready for his customers in the morning.

-7-

Everyman has his own breaking point and the customer was a particularly brave man. Very few could have held out for as long as he did. Eventually he gave up the battle and told Ray Quinn what he wanted to know. By that time he had lost four fingers, an ear, most of his teeth and all toes on his right foot. It had been when Quinn leaned in close to his remaining ear and whispered, very politely and reasonably, that he saw no reason to continue with the unpleasantness. He quietly reasoned that as the man seemed determined not to use his tongue and to prefer silence, he might as well forego the aforesaid organ and be done with it. Perhaps he would prefer the silence of his own thoughts for the rest of his life. Silence is not quiet, he warned, it has a unique shattering noise, sharper and more piercing than broken glass, and it seeps inevitably and unnoticed into your very soul. Besides, on a far more practical level, it just wouldn't do for anybody to think that Quinn was losing his touch as he had a reputation to uphold. These thoughts were imparted in an understated, hushed tone that was terrifyingly menacing and grew infinitely more full of meaning as they insinuated themselves into the brain and were gradually understood.

The customer finally exhaled heavily, broke down and told his tale. Quinn considered removing his tongue anyway and sending it to Lane as a warning. He thought better of it, firstly because he couldn't decide whether to do so post mortem or not, but mainly because it would be a sign to Lane that his man had talked. Better to keep Lane guessing on that point.

Ray Quinn pondered his next move. He had promised Lomax that he would look after the shop while he was away, and the cruise was full so he couldn't join in the fun. Besides, how would he explain to his wife that he was going on a cruise without her? He couldn't take her because he didn't want her involved. Also, closing the shop would appear suspicious to any observers that Lane had placed in the vicinity. He needed to have everything as normal and routine as possible, but he needed to let Lomax know what the customer had told him before he had slipped gratefully into the oblivion of death, where there could be no more pain.

He pulled on a pair of surgeon's gloves and used the customer's mobile phone to call his friend.

"Hello John. Our inquisitive customer has decided to take no further part in proceedings, but he was very keen to tell me that he was working for your old friend Mr Lane. He was instructed to gather information about anything to do with you, and if possible pave the way for, or plant, enough evidence for you to be arrested. He started by taking a particular interest in a ring that he knows you have and was then going to progress from there. Also, Lane has placed at least two of his people on your ship. They may have been late arriving, so it could have been delayed. I can't be with you for obvious reasons. Good luck. Enjoy yourself but be careful. I'll look after the shop."

Still using the customer's phone he then sent a text to DCI Lane.

"All OK. Will have what you want in next few days. Lomax has ring and is going on cruise soon. Sure you can get details. Do not contact me; I'll be in touch."

Ray Quinn slipped the phone into a plastic bag and put it into his pocket. He had deliberately made no mention of his own presence in the shop.

The shop maintained its normal opening and closing times for the entire time that John Lomax was away. This was just as well because it was under continual surveillance. Quinn knew that of course, but made no sign to the watchers of his knowledge. He wanted them to believe they were good enough at their job not to have been discovered.

Lomax & The Biker – The Trilogy

-8-

Unknown to them, Sandy Lane had been informed about John Lomax's large deposit in Oxford about an hour after it had been made. He reacted by placing an all ports alert and instructing a team of detectives to ascertain whether any airline, cruise and ferry company or Eurostar had received a booking for John Lomax and Leanne Lane or any couple who could possibly bear resemblance. He took the precaution of widening the search for all couples of their age and individuals who may have been booked to the same destination or on the same holiday.

Twenty four hours before the ship was due to sail, he had located his quarry. He had moved quickly and managed to arrange for two ex policemen to travel on the ship in the guise of being on holiday together. The ship's departure was only delayed by an hour because they had rushed from the Isle of Man to Southampton. As the cruise was full, an elderly couple had been taken off the cruise after being offered an alternative, with an upgrade, as well as the incentive of a large sum of money. It was sold to them as being in the national interest, so they couldn't believe their luck and duly accepted. They did not know that their luggage had already been removed from the ship before they had even been approached.

Lomax & The Biker – The Trilogy

-9-

Both John and Leanne had waited for the first day of their holiday with impatience. They were like little children, excited and bubbling. It had been John who suggested it first, and it took Leanne all of two seconds to agree. They needed, deserved, a really relaxing break away from it all, John had reasoned. Something just for the two of them, so they could rediscover the ease in their relationship after the traumas they had both suffered.

John was surprised by her quick reaction, but hid his suspicion. He had come to the conclusion that he must not allow himself to trust anybody. He knew others did not trust him, and perhaps with good reason, but he could not help that. The clock could not be turned back.

The morning was clear and bright as they set off. The car was warm, the music carefully chosen and the roads not too crowded. They stopped for an early light lunch and arrived in Southampton at about 2pm. John joined the queue of cars as it snaked its way forward whilst Leanne craned her neck to gaze in awe at the overwhelming size and majesty of the cruise ship. She was pure white and gleamed in the sunshine.

Their luggage was unloaded onto a trolley, and taken away not to be seen again until they opened their cabin door. Even their suits and dresses on hangers inside their carriers were labelled with name, deck letter and cabin number. John wondered whether they would see those items again.

Lomax & The Biker – The Trilogy

Passports were checked, Boarding Cards issued and they were shown to a comfortable waiting lounge. Deck letters and cabin numbers were gradually called and passengers embarked without rush. Porters and officials were extremely polite and very efficient. It was all very civilised and pleasant. John noted how much better these arrangements were as a start to a holiday than the crush, stress, exhaustion and interminable waiting at an airport.

Their cabin was actually what the cruise line termed a "stateroom." This meant that it was an exterior room with its own balcony. They unpacked in haste as they did not want to miss the ship leaving port. To his pleasant surprise, their suits and dresses were already neatly hanging inside the wardrobes. John put their passports, money and cards in the safe within the wardrobe. He set its code, but omitted to tell Leanne what it was. He was determined to show her that he was in control and she need not worry about anything at all. She wouldn't need money as it did not change hands on the ship. Passengers simply signed for whatever they purchased and it was charged to their cabin. John had registered his card details with the Purser's office, so the bill would be taken from his card on the last night of the cruise. He had made sure two days earlier that there were more than enough funds on the card to cover everything. This had meant taking a large amount of cash and physically depositing it in his account. He knew it was a risk, but he had no choice. He couldn't really take such a sum onto the ship and deposit it with the Purser because that would be even more suspicious. He took the precaution of travelling to Oxford rather than using his own local bank. Just a precaution, and not really very effective he knew, but it might buy time in an emergency.

So it was that John and Leanne stood on deck in the warm afternoon sunshine, sipping champagne, holding hands, watching as the ship made its final preparations to be released from the quayside and gently nudge its way out into Southampton Water.

He had already set his mobile to vibrate before coming out on deck and he felt its buzz in his trouser pocket as he gazed down at the final few passengers hurriedly boarding. He decided not to even look at the phone until he was alone. Whatever it was would have to wait.

For some unknown reason his attention was drawn to an elderly couple who seemed to be having their luggage taken away from the ship rather than it being loaded. They appeared a little confused and were driven away in the back of a large and shiny car.

"Ladies and gentlemen we are sorry but we have had to postpone our departure for an hour. We shall now be leaving at 6 o'clock. All onboard facilities are now open, so please feel free to take the time to explore the ship and settle in. Your cabin steward will be happy to deal with anything you may want. This slightly later departure will not affect our arrival time at our first port of call, Lisbon, in Portugal. This evening's dining arrangements are unchanged."

Lomax & The Biker – The Trilogy

John and Leanne decided to remain on deck and soak up the late afternoon warmth. Leanne was dozing when, just before 6pm, John strolled to the side and looked down at the quayside. A moment later two men rushed into sight, followed by their luggage on a trolley. They were hurriedly ushered aboard and their cases quickly stowed. He remembered that his phone probably had a voice or text message, so he fished it from his pocket. He listened to Quinn's message and wished he had taken more notice of what the two men had looked like.

-10-

The cruise was a thirteen night luxury trip. Leaving Southampton, the journey would take them past The Isle of Wight, and find them following the line of the southern English coast, passing Plymouth, Falmouth, Penzance and the Isles of Scilly and out in a mainly southerly direction to cross The Bay of Biscay.

John Lomax looked forward with ill disguised anticipation to long sunny lazy days, fine food and excellent wine, as well as relaxed and entertaining evenings. Most of all he anticipated endless lovemaking with Leanne. He remembered the week she had spent with him. How could he forget? He had never been so happy or exhausted in his life and he wanted more; much, much more.

He intended this to be the new beginning he felt he deserved and had been promising himself. He felt he could now move on with his life, away from the horrors provided by Sandy Lane. He felt he could move on from what he now realised had been a tedious and restrictive marriage, which had been coupled with a tedious and restrictive working life. No longer would he be answerable to anybody else. He had moved on. He had sufficient funds to be going on with and he had, in the jewellery business, the means to generate more as well as to launder the dirty Anvex money. Only his close ally, Ray Quinn, The Biker, knew anything that could prove threatening and he was so inextricably linked with the whole saga that Lomax knew he could be trusted. He had proved himself many times and was even now doing so again.

He desperately wanted Leanne. He wanted her in his life forever and he had never felt like that in his entire existence. He knew her history, and he knew he was taking a risk, but he reasoned that it was utterly worth it. For her part, she was also taking a risk.

He turned to look at her beauty. She recognised the longing in his eyes, smiled knowingly and they moved towards each other without breaking eye contact. Dinner was at 8pm, so there was time, and they made use of it. They were both at ease and did not hurry. Already the relaxed power of the cruise was having its effect.

Lomax rose from the bed and gently nudged the dozing Leanne. Her eyes lazily opened and he was lost in their pools.

"I hate to break this up," he whispered, "but we need to get ready for dinner."

She rose on one elbow, deliberately exposing one breast to him.

"Mmmm. All this has made me hungry. Why don't you get ready and find a bar for a drink? You don't want to have to wait and watch me."

"Oh, don't I?"

"Take your mobile and let me know where you are. I'll be with you in half an hour or so, in time to have a drink before dinner. Don't drink too much, though. I expect we'll have wine with our meal and I want you fully functioning later."

"If you insist," he said and gently took her breast to kiss it before walking to the shower.

He stood under the hot water, still partially aroused, and contemplated. Eventually he turned off the water, stepped out and dried himself. It did not take him long to dress for dinner. The first night had been designated as "smart", which meant a lounge suit. He took particular care over his appearance for the first night. He wanted to make an impression on his table companions, but also for Leanne. He prided himself on his ability to tie a perfect Windsor knot, which he thought a dying art. Not for him the careless wrap around and tuck it in. He carefully lined up his expensive silk tie, which had been especially purchased for the occasion, and performed his wizardry. Pleased with the result, he donned his jacket.

He turned towards Leanne and was greeted with the stunning sight of her exquisite form confronting him with stockings and lacy underwear.

"Are you sure you don't want any help?" He managed to gasp.

"You were not meant to see this until later!" she lied, "now go and have a drink before I change my mind and find my baggy pants."

Lomax did as he was told. He sat at a stool in front of the first bar he came across and listened intently once more to Ray Quinn's voice. He also studied the text message he had received earlier. He knew it would not have been safe to reply, but he needed more detail. He was wrestling with this dilemma when another text arrived.

"Butler is ready to strike a deal and will give evidence. I am sorting it out now."

Lomax realised this had been sent by Ray Quinn using the mobile phone he had taken from the customer. He also realised there was nothing he could, or should do. Ray Quinn was perfectly capable of dealing with the situation effectively. That did not, however, stop him worrying.

-11-

John and Leanne had opted for the second sitting, so they were due to begin the evening meal at 8pm. They had elected to sit on a table for six, and although it could be a recipe for disaster, they liked the idea of meeting new people.

At about the same time as Lomax and Leanne were sitting down for their first night's dinner, a man in clergyman's attire was seated behind a table which was bolted to the floor in a hastily arranged interview room within the confines of The Central Criminal Court in London. He was not handcuffed or shackled in any way and sat quietly awaiting the arrival of DCI Sandy Lane, who had asked for the meeting. There was a pot of freshly made coffee and a plate of biscuits on the table, with one spare cup. The clergyman recognised good coffee when he tasted it and sipped appreciatively. He wondered why he had been asked to meet Mr Lane here at such short notice. He had in fact been chauffeur driven to the meeting. It had been explained to him that there was no compulsion to even agree to the meeting.

Whilst he sat patiently waiting he tried to recall what he knew from school about the place in which he now found himself. He was pleasantly surprised by how much he could remember.

The Central Criminal Court, more usually known as The Old Bailey, stands on the site of Newgate Prison at the corner of Newgate Street and Old Bailey, just inside the City of London. It was originally located at the site of Newgate, in the Roman London Wall. The gate/prison was built in 1188 and significantly enlarged in 1236, and the executors of Lord Mayor Dick Whittington were granted a licence to renovate the prison. It was destroyed by the Great Fire of London in 1666, and rebuilt in 1672.

According to medieval statute the prison was to be managed by two annually elected Sheriffs, who in turn would sublet the administration to private "gaolers" or "keepers", for a price. These keepers in turn were permitted to exact payment directly from the inmates, making the prison one of the most profitable in London. Inevitably, the system offered incentives for the Keepers to exhibit cruelty to the prisoners, charging them for everything from entering the jail to having their chains put on and taken off. The clergyman muttered a prayer of thanks that he was not in such a position in that same place.

Among the most notorious Keepers in the Middle Ages were Edmond Lorimer, who was famous for charging inmates four times the legal limit for the removal of irons, and Hugh DeCroydon, who was eventually convicted of blackmailing prisoners in his care.

Over the centuries, Newgate was used for a variety of purposes including imprisoning those awaiting execution but it was not always secure. Burglar Jack Sheppard, for example, escaped twice before he went to the gallows at Tyburn in 1724. In 1783 the site of London's gallows was moved from Tyburn to Newgate and public executions outside the prison drew large crowds enjoying a day out. Again the clergyman silently prayed, but this time for the souls of the departed, hanged in that place.

Lomax & The Biker – The Trilogy

Until the twentieth century future British executioners were trained at Newgate. From 1868 public executions were discontinued and executions were carried out inside Newgate. Michael Barrett was the last man to be hanged in public outside the prison in May 1868. He was in fact the last person to be publicly executed in Great Britain. The prison closed in 1902.

The clergyman was pleased with his mental effort and congratulated himself on his detailed recall. There being still no sign of DCI Lane he continued with his musings and turned to trying to conjure up names of notable Newgate prisoners.

He remembered John Bradford, a religious reformer in the sixteenth century. He went on to remember Giacomo Casanova the bigamist; William Cobbett, parliamentary reformer and John Frith, priest and martyr. He also recalled Thomas Cream, the doctor who poisoned many of his patients and who claimed to be Jack the Ripper while on the gallows. Daniel Defoe and Ben Jonson also languished at Newgate as did William (Captain) Kidd, Titus Oates and William Penn, the Quaker who founded the state of Pennsylvania. Women were not spared the delights of Newgate either. Jane Voss, highwaywoman and thief and Mary Wade were there. The latter became the youngest female convict transported to Australia. Catherine Wilson, a nurse and suspected serial killer, was incarcerated in Newgate before becoming the last woman hanged publicly in London.

His thoughts were interrupted as DCI Lane swept into the room.

Lomax & The Biker – The Trilogy

"My name is Detective Chief Inspector Lane and I have asked you here today because I would like your help."

The clergyman quietly noted the fact that Lane had announced his job title as if it were part of his actual name. Such pomposity was intended to reinforce his importance to his guest and stress his seniority. The clergyman thought it vain and was not impressed, so he said nothing and awaited developments. He also noticed that the man had not even bothered to ask his name. He decided that he would not offer that information. After all, there was no point in giving anything unnecessarily. He stroked his beard patiently.

Lane suddenly became quiet and gazed intently at the clergyman. This went on for quite some time until, realising it had become embarrassing he said, "I'm sorry. Forgive me, but you remind me of somebody else. I see you've already got coffee."

He poured himself a cup and offered the Reverend a refill.

"I must say this is much better than we are forced to put up with at the station. How the other half live, eh?"

"Yes", said the clergyman, trying to quicken the pace of the meeting.

"I have a problem," said Lane, "and I hope you may be able to help."

"So you've already said," responded the clergyman, willing the irksome detective to get on with it.

"I have a prisoner in the cells who is shortly to stand trial. He has committed grave offences, including murder, extortion and assault. Before I go into any more detail I must have your assurance that this conversation is strictly in confidence and will go no further."

The clergyman had already noted the lack of any recording device as well as the fact that there had been only one spare cup before Lane had entered the room.

"Detective Chief Inspector," said the clergyman, deliberately flattering him, "it goes without saying that whatever you say to me is confidential. I would never betray the trust of my calling."

"Good," said DCI Lane. "As I was saying I have a man in custody. His name is William Butler, but he is known throughout London as Billy. He was arrested at a jeweller's shop recently for a previous burglary at an Anvex Security warehouse. Over £500,000 was stolen as well as valuable jewellery. The jewellery is the link to the shop in which he was arrested. It belongs to a Mr John Lomax, who we believe to also be involved in the Anvex theft. Our problem is that we have not yet been able to conclusively link Lomax with the Anvex burglary. We thought we had done so at one point, but the CPS believed the evidence as not sufficiently conclusive as to stand a realistic chance of a successful prosecution."

"I don't see how I can help," put in the clergyman, hoping his interruption would bring the sententious detective to the point he was trying to make.

"I'll get to that. This Billy Butler is now telling us that he will give evidence against Lomax, not only for the Anvex burglary but also for other crimes as well, but he says he will only do so in front of a priest. I have no idea why, as he is definitely not religious and is a really rough character."

"Perhaps he wants forgiveness," responded the clergyman.

"Perhaps," replied Lane doubtfully.

"I still don't understand why you have asked me," said the clergyman. "There must be hundreds of others who would be equally as useful."

"I saw you pass the jeweller's shop window when we were inside making the arrest. You looked in and seemed interested. I had you followed to the church round the corner."

"I hadn't realised I was followed, but the scene inside the shop did catch my eye. It's not every day you see police in a jewellery shop and a man in handcuffs. I take it that was Billy Butler."

"Yes," continued Lane. Now I need a religious expert."

"I wouldn't claim to be an expert," laughed the clergyman.

"More of an expert than the ordinary man in the street," said Lane, returning the laugh. "So, my query has to do with the New Testament. Before I get to that, however, I must tell you that Butler has been promised a new beginning in return for the evidence he gives. He will escape prosecution. Normally he would expect a life sentence for the crimes he has committed, but I have been authorised to offer him a completely anonymous fresh start. We are worried, however, that certain criminal elements in London, including John Lomax, will attempt to silence him permanently."

"I still don't see how I can help," said the clergyman.

"It's my job to make sure Butler stays safe and gets to give his evidence. Personally, I don't really care what happens to him after that."

"How Christian," observed the clergyman.

"To continue, we have had a tip off that a professional has been contracted to ensure Butler's silence."

The clergyman appeared uncomfortable, and ran his finger inside his stiff white clerical collar.

"Now I can tell you how you may help. Our informant who gave us the tip off has been killed for his trouble. It seems they will stop at nothing to ensure Butler's silence. Before this man died, he was stabbed by the way, he wrote a note about a Bible passage. We think he was trying to tell us how Butler will be silenced."

The clergyman appeared intrigued.

"Something from the New Testament?" he asked.

"Yes," replied Lane and, referring to his notebook, said 'he's on his way. Look out.' Then he wrote a chapter and verse. We think he would have written more but he didn't get the chance."

Lane proffered a Bible, which he had brought in with him.

"Luke, Chapter twelve, verse fifteen," he said.

The clergyman read: "Then to the people he said 'beware! Be on your guard against greed of every kind for even when someone has more than enough, his possessions do not give him life."

Lane asked "is there anything there to suggest how they might try to kill Butler?"

The clergyman read some more, turning the tissue thin pages.

"In chapter twelve of Luke's Gospel Jesus is warning the people about the Pharisees, urging them not to live a sinful life."

Lane was lost.

"Who were the Pharisees?" He asked.

"They were a religious sect. They believed that God existed to serve them rather than the other way round. They felt they were better than everybody else and put people down."

The clergyman read the passage a few more times seemingly lost in deep concentration.

"I really don't know," he said. "I need more time to think about this. Leave it with me and I'll get back to you if I come up with anything. Have you a number I can contact you on?"

Lane gave him a card with his mobile number printed boldly underneath his title and name. The clergyman was again reminded of the vanity of the man.

"I'll have you driven back," said Lane.

"No need," replied the clergyman, "I could do with the fresh air."

Lane escorted him to the steps outside the Old Bailey and shook his hand.

"Thanks for the coffee, I'll be in touch," said the clergyman, before strolling away. He now fully understood why Lane had arranged for the meeting to take place there. It had to be secret and safe and where better than an isolated room deep in the bowels of the Old Bailey.

Lomax & The Biker – The Trilogy

DCI Lane watched as the clergyman gradually faded into the distance, his clerical robes being caught by the breeze. He pushed his hands deep into his pockets and was still troubled by the uneasy feeling that he had met the man before. He would be grateful if the clergyman came up with anything but he was discouraged that he had provided no quick answers.

He walked down the steps of the Old Bailey, got into his waiting car and drove back to the police station in which Billy Butler was currently being held.

Butler was being his usual obnoxious self, complaining constantly. There were two officers outside his cell and they reported that there had been no sign of any threats to their charge. They, in their turn, complained about Butler's noise and offensive language.

He had a sudden thought and decided to have the prisoner moved. He had realised there were too many people who knew exactly where Butler was being held and it would be safer to move him. He made a phone call to a contact in the security services and made arrangements for Butler to be moved to one of their safe houses.

The prisoner was put into the back of an unmarked police car, wedged between two burly officers. The driver and front seat officer were armed. Lane was relying on the fact that it had been done at such short notice and very few people knew about it. When the car had left the station Lane breathed a sigh of relief. There was surely nothing else he could have done.

Lomax & The Biker – The Trilogy

He returned to his office and made a few phone calls to his secret list of underworld contacts, but nobody had heard anything more about a hired professional killer. He was left with no alternative but to go back to studying the biblical text, but the more he did so, the more his eyes glazed over. He sighed and looked out of the window. The sun had gone down and the evening was damp and gloomy to match his mood.

He discovered a message from forensics. The scientist had tested the murdered informant's note about the Bible passage and found no significant evidence on the sheet and, neither the ink nor the paper, were traceable. A handwriting analysis suggested that it had been written by the informant, but there could be no certainty. And as the hours passed there was still no word from the clergyman.

Lane re-read the passage and grew angry. A man had died leaving these words to warn them. What was he trying to say?

He was exhausted but as a last resort used the internet. He found a website about word games and puzzles. He wrote down the first letters of each of the words from Luke 12. 15 and began rearranging them. He got several names: Bob, Tom, Don, but he could find no clear meaning. He tried the obvious code of assigning numbers to the letters, A equals 1 and so on, but when he applied it he ended up with pages and pages of random digits. He tried everything his sharp and devious mind could think of. He was about to give up when his tired and fuzzy eyes settled upon an anagram sequence he had tried earlier. It had given him *spies, session, nose, sepsis.* A bell rang in his tired and befuddled brain. Sepsis meant a blood infection. He became alert and found another sequence that produced the word *drug*.

In the end, exhaustion got the better of him so he crossed his arms on the desk and laid his head upon them. He was asleep almost instantly.

He was eventually awoken by his own snoring. He sat up, closed his dry mouth, winced at the pain in his back and stood up. Massaging his stiff neck he staggered out of his office. He showered in the station and put on a fresh shirt which he kept in his office. He went through his discovery again and convinced himself that it was to be a doctor who would attempt to kill Billy Butler.

He called his small, elite team together.

"I think he's going to use a doctor to try to kill Butler," he announced to a sceptical audience.

He went on to tell them about his painstaking night's work. He speculated that the killer would buy or steal a doctor's white jacket and get fake identification and a stethoscope for a touch of authenticity. A half-hearted attempt would be made on Butler's life, which would be enough to get him taken to a doctor, who would kill him. Lane then instructed the room to make sure that if anybody didn't show up for work for any reason, or if they saw somebody in the station they did not recognise, he was to be told immediately.

Lane had convinced himself that he was correct. It was to be a doctor who would make the attempt. The deciding fact was that he had discovered, by judicious use of the internet and cross reference to the Bible, that Luke was a doctor. That could not be coincidence. How could he be wrong? Something in the recesses of his mind niggled at him. If only the clergyman would contact him. He spent the morning making sure his team had checked hospitals and surgeries for doctors who had not come in to work. The only effect that had was to produce masses of names of people who, for whatever reason, had not reported in for work that day. He was amazed by the sheer numbers involved. He had neither the time nor the resources to check each and every one in the time frame that he thought he had. It may prove to be a useful line of enquiry after the event, but that is all it would be.

His phone rang. He jumped with an involuntary movement and it was in his hand next to his ear before he even realised it. His heart thudded and he sat forward. His face drained of all colour as he listened to the voice at the other end.

"Is he OK?" He asked fearfully.

"Yes, the car is badly damaged, but he's alright. Screaming blue murder and swearing like a trooper, but not badly hurt."

"What do you mean, 'not badly hurt?' He's either injured or he isn't. Don't bandy words with me, just tell me exactly."

"Butler and one of the officers have been hit with some metal splinters, but it's nothing serious. We would have sent them to the hospital, but we remembered what you said about the attempt being made by a doctor, so we thought it better to take him here to the nearest police station. He's in a cell now, still shouting. I'll get the duty doctor to look at him."

"Good," said Lane, breathing a sigh of relief. At least one of his officers had shown good judgement.

He sat down, his arms resting on his desk with his hands held together by his interlocking fingers in a praying pose. He was not a religious man. How could he be with his history? But he closed his eyes at that moment and thanked whoever was out there that nothing had happened to Butler. Being thankful for the safety of his officers never even entered his head.

His theory was being borne out. The attempt to silence Butler was designed to kill him. It was meant to get him taken to A&E at the nearest hospital, where a bogus doctor would be waiting. Lane scanned the list of people who had not shown up for work at that hospital and narrowed the search. He shouted for one of team and barked his instructions for the names to be visited immediately.

He then phoned the police station holding Butler and asked to speak to the duty sergeant. While waiting to be connected he glanced at the clock on his office wall. It was midday. He realised that was the time that shifts changed in some stations. He was eventually connected to the duty desk officer and introduced himself.

"Has the new shift been told about my prisoner?" he barked.

"No. I'll do it now."

"No. I want him brought back here," he shouted, "now. Immediately! And I want proper officers guarding him and decent security. It's more secure here. Get it done."

Lane slammed the phone down. Upon such incompetence life or death may hang he knew. Feeling let down, he slumped in his chair and, almost in a trance, wondered what to do next. He didn't know how long he had been there like that when the phone rang again. He was told he had a visitor.

"It's a clergyman. He says it's important that he sees you immediately. He said to tell you that he's worked it out."

"I'm on my way," shouted Lane, throwing the phone down.

DCI Lane met the clergyman at the front desk. He saw that he looked exhausted.

"Have you been working on this all night?" he asked.

"Yes. I couldn't sleep. Looks like the same happened to you," the clergyman said, smiling.

"Let's go to my office, you can tell me what you have there."

Even though Lane was confident in his own analysis and convinced the clergyman could add nothing to what he already knew, he began to take him to his office and listened.

The clergyman couldn't wait.

"I was thinking," said the clergyman, as they walked down a corridor, "that we shouldn't limit our thoughts to the passage your informant noted down. That brought me to what I think is the answer. You see, the actual passage he quoted is just a sort of introduction to something that follows. Do you know the parable of the rich farmer who has a good harvest and therefore has too much grain. He intends to build bigger barns and spend the rest of his life living from his good fortune. However, God strikes him down because of his greed. You see he is rich in a material way, but he's spiritually poor."

"Mmmm," was all Lane could manage. He couldn't see the relevance of the clergyman's little speech.

"The point is," continued the clergyman, "greed. I think it's the key to what he was trying to tell you."

They had arrived at a security door. There was an armed officer standing there. Lane was pleased to note that his orders to increase security had been acted upon.

The clergyman continued his diatribe.

"So, I began to wonder what greed is all about."

Lane didn't think he could stand a sermon and was about to tell him so when the security van carrying Butler arrived. He watched as it slowly backed in. An officer knocked on the back door and Butler and his bodyguard hurried out.

Butler started complaining immediately. He had a cut on his forehead and a bruised cheek, but he moaned as though he had been brutally attacked with a baseball bat.

"I want a doctor. Look at me. Look at me!" he shouted, appealing to anyone who may be within earshot. "You bleeders won't get away with this. I've been stuffed. I were goin' to 'elp, but I might change me mind nah!"

Lomax & The Biker – The Trilogy

Butler began to fight against his handcuffs and his escorts. He was a strong man and one of the officers was forced to use a taser to subdue him. He shook violently on the floor.

The clergyman witnessed the whole episode and was shocked at its violence. He stepped forward and intervened with a ministerial authority that brooked no argument.

"Get this man water, now," he ordered. The surprise of a clergyman issuing orders to every officer present, without regard to their rank or importance, stunned them into inactivity. A plastic cup of water appeared from somewhere, and the clergyman bent over the prone Butler.

"Don't struggle, my son. "Nobody can harm you now. Drink this, it will help. You are in God's loving care."

He said this quietly, but with a firm conviction that reached into the prone man's very core and Billy Butler was calmed by the clergyman's words. He drank the entire beaker of water and then lay back down as if drifting off to sleep. Two officers lifted him and dragged him to a cell, where they lay him on the unyielding bed.

The clergyman rose from his kneeling position and told Lane that he saw no point in continuing with his explanation as matters had obviously resolved themselves. He walked with Lane beside him to the front entrance of the police station. Lane did not notice him slip the plastic cup in to his pocket.

"Thank you for your efforts," said Lane. "I'm sorry. I've been rude. I have never even asked your name. I need to put a name in my report."

The clergyman appeared to be lost in thought.

"Luke," he replied and walked through the exit door. As he did so, he glanced up at a clock on a wall. It said 12.15.

DCI Lane watched the clergyman disappear into the distance with the breeze picking at his clerical attire.

-12-

Ray Quinn strode purposefully towards the nearest public toilet. He found a cubicle, took off the clerical robe and collar and stuffed them into a plastic bag. He then leant over a sink and gently soaked his face until the beard could be peeled off. He stuffed that into the bag as well. He looked at his watch. It had been almost ten minutes since he had given Butler the poison. He would not wake up again and the poison could not be traced. Butler had died in police custody after having been shot with a taser.

"Tidy, very tidy," The Biker whispered to himself, mimicking Butler's own idiom.

He returned to the jewellery shop and, again using the stolen mobile phone, left a message for his friend John Lomax.

-13-

Leanne waited until she heard the water from his shower. She then picked up Lomax's mobile phone, studied the text messages and listened to the voice mails. She quickly sent them to her own phone and deleted all traces of having done so. They remained on his phone, so he would never know. She had placed her mobile in her handbag and was adjusting her underwear just as he emerged from the shower.

-14-

She found him in the first bar she came across, sitting on a stool at the bar chatting to the barman. She tapped him on the shoulder and he turned. He got down from the stool and looked at Leanne.

"You look lovely," he said and he meant it, although it helped to already know what was underneath her dress.

"You don't look so bad yourself, for an old man," she teased.

"What would you like?" He asked.

"Gin and tonic please," she replied.

He ordered her drink and a single malt whisky for himself and signed the payment slip, which was swiftly removed by the barman and put into the till. The bar was gradually filling with people, eagerly gathering for the first night's evening meal. They found a table and sipped their drinks, talking about nothing in particular as the noise level rose. They looked around and took in the scene. Women were dressed in a variety of colours and styles and John noted that there was plenty of expensive jewellery on display. The men were smartly dressed in lounge suits and were gallantly paying attention to their ladies. It was all most pleasant and sophisticated.

Lomax was about to order more drinks when people began to drift towards the dining room. There were many places in which to dine on the ship, but they had chosen to take their meals in the main formal dining room. They wanted a relaxed and unhurried experience, with first class food and excellent service.

Lomax & The Biker – The Trilogy

They found their table, which was agreeably situated to one side of the room so that waiters would not be brushing past all evening. John held Leanne's chair as she sat and he moved round the table to sit opposite. Before long they were joined by two women. John rose as they took their seats and he introduced Leanne and himself. The women said their names were Barbara and Margaret. John thought their ages to be around fifty or so, although he was particularly bad at guessing the age of women. All four had just begun to study their menus when two men approached and took the remaining seats. They too introduced themselves as David and Tim. They too appeared to be in their fifties. Somebody, somewhere, had done their homework about matching dining companions.

After some discussion it was agreed that each "couple" would deal with their own drinks, so John ordered what he hoped would be a particularly noteworthy bottle of red wine and returned to his study of the menu. He had already decided that he would let others take the lead in conversation until he was sure who he was dealing with. Leanne was already deep in conversation with the woman called Barbara and seemed at ease. Margaret was looking at her menu. The two men, despite being the last to arrive at the table, appeared in no hurry to view the menu, and were looking at John. He felt their gaze resting on him.

He felt the mobile phone vibrate in his pocket, but decided not to look at it. He knew the only person it could be was Ray Quinn, and he would look at the message or listen to the voice mail when he could be alone.

"Sorry to hold you up," said David. "It's been a bit of a rush. We booked late and were only told that two places had become available this morning. Apparently an elderly couple have had to leave the ship because their daughter has been taken ill. I hope things are Ok for them. We've had a hell of a rush to get from the Isle Of Man all the way down here in just a few hours. Luckily we just about caught a ferry and then a friend drove us down. He must have been breaking the speed limit most of the way. Anyway we're here now and it's nice to meet you."

"I saw you arrive," said John Lomax. "You were lucky they held the ship for you. I gather they don't usually do that."

"Yes we were," said Tim. "They said they would wait one hour and then the ship would have to leave, so we only made it by the skin of our teeth."

"Well, now you can relax and enjoy the holiday," said Leanne. "My name's Leanne," she continued. "I'm John's better half for my sins. I was sitting here wondering how we were all matched up to sit together."

"Without wishing to upset anybody, our ages seem similar," volunteered Margaret.

"Perhaps they also looked at our interests that we had to put on the booking form," put in Barbara.

"Or our occupations," said John, fishing.

"Well, we're both retired," continued Barbara. "We've been friends since schooldays. I lost my husband last year, but Margaret has managed to hang on to hers."

"Yes, "said Margaret. "He's wonderful. He was originally supposed to be on this trip, but dropped out because he's had to look after his business. He gave his place to Barbara here."

"That's lucky for you," said Tim. David and I used to be policeman, but we took early retirement rather than put up with the homophobic attitudes and treatment. I don't think that is limited to the police force though. Thankfully we negotiated a reasonable package. This is our first holiday together since."

Leanne kicked John under table. She knew his personal feelings about "that sort of thing," as he called it, and was warning him not to get the evening off on the wrong foot.

"What about you, John?" asked David as his eyes searched for reaction. "What's your line of work? You haven't taken early retirement as well, have you?"

"No," replied Lomax, staying calm and smiling at Leanne to show that he understood her under the table message. "I have several interests. I have a company that buys and sells other companies, and I own a jewellery business. Not large, but it gets by. We have been working very hard lately and decided to treat ourselves to this trip."

"Is this your first cruise?" asked Margaret to the table in general.

Lomax & The Biker – The Trilogy

It is a question asked countless times on every cruise throughout the world. On the face of it designed to break the ice and covered in a veneer of politeness, it is actually a form of one-upmanship and is laced with implicit snobbery. Of the six at the table, only Margaret had been on a cruise before and she seemed to John to be too polite to boast about it. In fact, John Lomax took to Margaret and Barbara quickly. They seemed genuinely nice people. He was, however, not so sure of Tim and David, even setting aside his old fashioned prejudices.

"Yes it's our first time," replied John. "You could say we are cruise virgins. What about you, David, Tim?"

"Like you, this is our first cruise. We've been away on holiday before as I said earlier, but this table now has four virgins," said David, making an attempt at humour and utterly failing. "I'm afraid police pay didn't stretch to this sort of thing. To tell you the truth, we've blown a large hole in our retirement packages to do this."

The truth would have been more acceptable thought Lomax to himself. He doubted very much whether these two were footing the bill for this adventure. Nice work if you can get it. He made a mental note to ensure he was on his guard around them. He used his right foot to press on Leanne's leg and gave a warning glance as he sipped his wine. He hoped she would understand his meaning.

"I very much doubt there are any virgins at this table!" exclaimed Barbara, suddenly coming out of her shell. "In fact I think there must be some exciting stories to tell."

Lomax & The Biker – The Trilogy

"Ladies first," said John Lomax, putting on his most charming and gallant smile. "Why don't you start?" This could get very interesting, he mused, when it came to the Manxmen's turn.

Barbara flushed and regretted her witticism. The others looked at her expectantly. She sought solace in her glass whilst thinking about what to say.

"Well, as I've already told you, I lost my husband last year. We had been together for 31 years and I miss him terribly."

Margaret put a consoling hand on her arm and squeezed gently.

"How did you meet him, if you don't mind me asking?" said Leanne, trying to be sympathetic and encouraging.

"I was working in a small garage doing their accounts part time," said Barbara, having summoned the courage to continue. "I have to admit I was a bit of a looker in the early days and all the mechanics wanted to date me. I also have to admit to having gone out with just about all of them. I can't say any of them met my expectations, but it was fun while it lasted. One of them in particular, called Brian, was especially persistent and asked me out many more times than anybody else. I didn't think he was anything special. Besides I thought I could do better for myself than a garage mechanic. How wrong I was. He went on to own a Formula 1 racing team! It all turned out well in the end though. I met my husband soon after and the rest is history. And before anybody says it, I am not on the lookout for anybody else."

Cruises are notorious for being populated with women of a certain age searching for a partner, or at the very least an on board adventure.

"I'm sorry for your loss," said Lomax. "You've been very lucky to have such a loyal and faithful friend as Margaret."

"I suppose I have," Barbara said quietly turning her head to her right and looking intently at her.

Barbara obviously felt she had contributed enough and didn't offer anything further on the subject. She sipped her wine, delicately dabbed her lips with her napkin, lowered her head and returned to her main course. John felt she was being too particular and precise in these movements, and then in cutting up her main course, as a means of ensuring no further eye contact with anybody and therefore no follow up discussion. He thought she was definitely holding something back. He was intrigued and resolved to tease more from her another evening.

"You've been a good friend to her," said Lomax to Margaret, "and now you're on a cruise together. It's a shame your husband couldn't be with you."

"He's had to stay behind to deal with business matters, as I've said," responded Margaret, snatching a fleeting glance at her friend. She hoped nobody had noticed the look, but John Lomax had and was even more intrigued.

John Lomax began to softly caress Leanne's calf with the top of his foot under the table. He was beginning to enjoy himself as the evening became more and more interesting. Leanne returned his soft touch with her toes. John thought it quite extraordinary that there could be as many secret messages passed by feet under a table as there had already been that evening. He liked the last one best as it held promise.

"What about you then, Margaret?" Tim had taken an interest. Have you anything to entertain us with?"

"Oh, my story is quite unremarkable," she replied. "I met my husband at about the same time as Barbara met hers. We all used to go everywhere together. Quite inseparable we were. Then we had to move away for my husband's work, and we only kept in touch by phone and Christmas and birthday cards. As my husband's business grew and became more successful we moved around a lot. Some would say I've been lucky. I've been to most of the glamorous places that you could think of. I would say the high life is all very well and good, but you miss the stability and reliability of having established friends around. I have certainly missed Barbara these last few years. It's strange. There was a short time when we lost contact, just after her husband died. I think she needed to be alone to recover."

Barbara stopped teasing her food and looked her friend straight in the eye.

"Yes, I wanted to be alone. I've not told you this before, but I went away to Portugal. In fact it was Lisbon, or close to it. That's why I was so excited to be coming on this trip with you. Our first port of call is Lisbon. I'm going to show you where I went. It will mean a lot to me to be able to take you there."

Barbara then did a strange thing and asked whether anybody at the table could speak Portuguese. David said he could.

"In that case perhaps our two gentlemen friends here would like to come along. It would certainly help with finding our way around. I know the way quite well, but it would be good to have somebody who spoke the language", she said.

David and Tim exchanged looks. Their policemen's instincts were alert. Both thought there could be something afoot, and both were aware that they did not need any distraction from the job in hand concerning John Lomax and Leanne. But they couldn't refuse and remain polite.

"How intriguing," said Margaret, "I can't wait."

"We'd be glad to accompany you, if that's OK with Margaret," said Tim. She nodded her reluctant assent.

There was a prolonged silence amongst the six diners, each wrestling with their own thoughts. The reverie was broken by John Lomax.

"I don't think we ought to pry any further, do you?" He said to all around the table. "Let's just enjoy the rest of the meal. Perhaps you can tell us about your Lisbon secret after you've been there. How about we leave the rest of us until tomorrow? We've almost finished dinner and we're going to see the show."

"Look," said David, aware of the undertones, "we shouldn't finish the meal like this. We have twelve more dinners together. Why don't we lighten the mood? I know, let's go round the table and each tell a funny story, a joke or even an amazing fact. Whoever we agree is the best gets free wine tomorrow night."

Sceptical looks were exchanged. Tim volunteered to go first, if only to support his partner and lessen his embarrassment.

"Ok," said Tim, "I challenge all of you lick your own elbow. I'll buy a drink for anybody who can do it."

The table became a shambles as they each contorted themselves, in increasingly unsuccessful attempts to complete the task. Other diners stopped their own conversations and joined in. Soon almost the entire dining room was at it and bodies were all over the place, in varying degrees of discomfort and laughter. There were some who cringed with embarrassment, but even they succumbed in the end. The waiters looked at the scene in amazement, but some couldn't resist and joined in.

The scene was brought to the Captain's attention at his table. He had never witnessed anything like it, especially on the first night of a cruise. People were normally reserved, at least until later in the trip, but he didn't disapprove and even tried the feat himself. He failed as completely as everyone else, and ripped his pristine white jacket in the process. Waiters tried valiantly and for the most part in vain to conceal their enjoyment at his predicament. Tim called a waiter over and told him that if they spotted anybody actually licking their own elbow, he would buy them a drink. Nobody did and people gradually realised it was an impossible task and the dining room settled down. By the end of it all the sum total of the chaos was 7 torn dresses and 5 ripped jackets. Also, the following morning the ship's doctor had to deal with a steady stream of pulls and strains in different places which severely tested his stock of painkillers and he ended up having to ration them in order to make them last until he could re-supply in Lisbon.

Tim ordered a drink for all six of them and told a waiter to provide the Captain with his favourite tipple for being such a good sport. He would claim it on expenses he told himself; might as well live a little on this job.

"I can't follow that," said John and they all nodded agreement. "So it's free wine for Tim tomorrow evening."

Dinner ended and they agreed to meet in the bar at 7.30 the following evening for drinks before dinner.

John and Leanne gave the show a miss and returned to their stateroom. Both were tired after a long and eventful day. Neither had wasted much energy on the elbow exercise, but both were satisfyingly exhausted by the following morning.

Lomax & The Biker – The Trilogy

-15-

John Lomax woke early and, seeing Leanne fast asleep beside him, slipped noiselessly out from under the Egyptian cotton sheets. He took his mobile phone into the bathroom, locked the door behind him and read Ray Quinn's message.

Doctor confirmed that Butler has found peace. He became interested in religion.

He put the phone in his dressing gown pocket and re-entered the bedroom. Lomax slipped back between the sheets beside Leanne and contentedly dozed with his hand resting on her thigh.

Lomax & The Biker – The Trilogy

-16-

The gleaming white ship glided serenely along the river Tagus past Magellan's statue and eventually, by skilful and well practised manoeuvre, came to a graceful halt alongside the quay. Passengers leaned over railings to witness the sight, before disembarking to enjoy a slice of city life exploring Lisbon's busy streets, restaurants, bars and cafes. Some boarded coaches to be taken on prearranged trips. Lomax and Leanne preferred to take a taxi from the quayside into the city and explore by themselves, hand in hand strolling without a care in the world.

Ray Quinn's text message had settled Lomax and he began to relax as the effect of the lessened stress took hold. For her part, Leanne was completely at ease as they gradually rediscovered the spark that had originally attracted one to the other. The holiday was weaving its magic, she thought. Besides, she knew what was happening and she knew what the outcome should be.

She had read Quinn's earlier messages and heard his voice-mail that morning while John was in the bathroom on her own mobile. She had not, of course, seen his latest text, but she was sure Ray Quinn could handle anything that may arise. In fact she had received a message from him herself.

Lisbon excursion arranged for 2 gentlemen. Let it happen.

Lomax & The Biker – The Trilogy

-17-

"Where are we going?" Margaret asked Barbara as the hire car pulled away from the quayside in Lisbon harbour.

"It's a surprise," answered Barbara as she changed gears smoothly.

Margaret clicked on her seat belt. She had been to Lisbon before with her husband Brian, but was soon lost as Barbara drove through the city and out along country roads. Tim and David, sitting in the back, were on edge and exchanged meaningful glances.

"A surprise?" Margaret mused just loudly enough for the men to hear, "how nice. May as well sit back and enjoy the ride boys."

Tim and David had already belted up and were quietly seated, holding hands, which were resting between them on the back seat. Both were impressed by Barbara's skilled driving.

"You drive very well," said David.

"Thank you," said Barbara, pleased with the compliment. Garage mechanics have their uses you know. I didn't tell you, Margaret, that I dated several of the mechanics from that garage of yours. They taught me quite a lot."

For a moment she was taken back to summer night drives with some of them and the inevitable and mutually enjoyed moonlight stops in tree covered field entrances and farmers' lanes.

"Well, you're a dark horse," said Margaret, smiling at the thought of her prissy friend coming of age in such ways, but then realising that some of those concerned may well have also 'taught her how to drive.'

Barbara skilfully negotiated another set of sharp turns and ignored a meaningful look from Margaret. There was another sharp turn and a fast change of gears. The sun in her eyes gave Margaret a clue of the direction in which they were travelling. Tim and David in the back had given up trying to follow where they were going and were content to admire the scenery as it flew past.

A little later Barbara made yet another sharp turn, this time down a dim residential street in a rundown neighbourhood, taking a short cut and suddenly skidding to a stop at a kerb.

"What's going on?" asked David.

Barbara climbed out. "I've just got to do something," she replied. "You might want to lock the doors."

She went up to a decrepit house, looked around and entered without knocking. David noticed that she'd taken the car keys which made him feel trapped. He didn't like being a passenger and he hated even more being in the back. It made him feel out of control. Margaret reached across and pressed the button that locked all the doors.

Tim looked out of his window and saw two boys aged about ten, standing motionless, side by side, across the street. They stared at him, unsmiling. One whispered something and the other nodded gravely. He felt a shiver at the unnerving sight. Then, turning to look the other way, he gasped in shock. An old woman's skull-like face stared at him; merely a foot away on the passenger side of the car. The woman must have been sick and near death.

Through the half open window Tim stammered, "can I help you?"

Wearing dirty, torn clothing, the scrawny woman rocked unsteadily on her feet. Her yellow eyes glanced over her shoulder quickly, as if she did not want to be seen. She then looked at the car and frowned.

"I have come to offer my sympathies."

"About what?" Margaret asked.

"The death of your friend's husband."

Margaret and the two men gasped in harmony.

"Forgive me," the old woman continued. "I have troubled you unnecessarily." She then turned and hobbled away.

Barbara returned a moment later, carrying a paper bag, which she set down at Margaret's feet. She said nothing about taking longer than planned. She looked towards the opposite side of the street. The two boys had gone. She selected gear and they were away. She asked about the old woman, but Margaret replied only that she was crazy, not right in the head, but had seemed to recognise the car.

They all fell silent as the car wound its way out of town and gained speed as it found its way out into the countryside again.

"I'm taking us to an old mill. It belongs to a family friend. My husband and I had it renovated. It's a special place and I want to share with you."

Barbara lowered her window and breathed in the fragrant air. "It's lovely out here, nobody around for miles."

She drove for several more minutes and drew to a stop. She picked up the paper bag which sat at her friend's feet.

"Come on everybody," she chirped.

They walked for about fifty yards along a path through an overgrown and thorny olive grove. She then nodded towards a small footbridge which spanned a fast moving stream.

"There it is," she said, pointing to an ancient stone mill which had its windows barred with heavy duty metal rods. Barbara fished in her pocket for the key. Both Tim and David looked down at the black and fast moving stream, which also appeared quite deep. Only a low railing separated them from a sheer, twenty foot drop into the water.

Her voice, close to Tim's ear, made him jump. She had come up behind her. "I know what you're thinking."

"What?" he asked, his heart beating fast in his tightening chest.

"You're thinking about that urge."

"Urge?" he whispered.

"Yes, to throw yourself in. It's the same thing people feel when they stand on the edge of a cliff; that strange desire to step off into space. There's no reason or logic, but it's there, as if there's nothing to stop you from jumping in. Do you know what I mean?"

Lomax & The Biker – The Trilogy

Tim shivered because he knew exactly what she meant, but said nothing. To change the conversation David pointed into the distance to a white cross, surrounded by flowers.

"What's that?"

Barbara gazed into the distance. "Oh, people still leave flowers there, it gets on my nerves."

"Why?"

"A man died here," said Barbara. She looked at her friend Margaret. "He fell in trying to rescue a ball for a couple of young boys. The water is very fast and he was sucked into the sluice there. He was wedged face down and drowned."

Her eyes were locked on the dark, narrow intake where the man had died.

David and Tim exchanged glances. Despite being ex policemen and having seen many disturbing things, both were now unsettled and nervous as they entered the mill. Inside it was actually well decorated, obviously recently refurbished and quite cosy.

"I brought you here because I wanted you to see our place. My husband's and mine, I mean." She said.

David thought it odd that Barbara had not given the name of her husband. He knew that Margaret's husband was a successful businessman named Brian, but there had been no mention of Barbara's husband's name.

"We have a wonderful wine cellar here," said Barbara. "I bought some lovely local bread and cheese for lunch when I stopped earlier. We must make sure we leave enough time to get back to the ship, though. We sail at 5.30 I believe."

Margaret set the table while Barbara went downstairs to the wine cellar and returned with her favourite rioja. They began to eat a leisurely lunch and the wine began to settle nerves. The bottle of wine did not last long, even though Barbara said she wouldn't drink as she was driving.

"I'll fetch another bottle," she said, "same again?"

"Certainly," said Tim, who was gradually overcoming his initial forebodings. "You must have a wonderful wine cellar. May I see it?"

"It's a real mess down there," replied Barbara. "We never got round to tidying it up. It was the last place on our list of jobs."

"Why don't we all muck in and get it done this afternoon?" offered David.

"We haven't got time to do it all," replied Barbara. "Besides, I didn't bring you here to make you work. We're on holiday. I would be embarrassed to show you the mess down there."

"We'll have a look after lunch," said Tim. "We can't let you bring us out to this lovely place and not help you; especially now that you don't have anybody else."

He saw the look of deep loss etched on her face and regretted it as soon as he had finished saying it.

"I am sorry," he said, I didn't mean to...."

"Don't worry," said Barbara. "It's difficult for people to know what to say to me. I often think it's harder for those trying to give solace than for those receiving it; especially if they've never been through it themselves."

"It's strange," Margaret put in, "everybody has to experience grief in their lives at some time or other; it's part of the human condition. We learn about it from an early age when a pet dies or an elderly relative and we see it on television all the time, but none of us are much good at coping with it. We may put on a brave face for the world, we may show others how strong we are, but inside, deep inside, we all hurt."

"Let's not be maudlin," said David. "Tim's right, you must let us help you at least make some progress down there. I'm sure your husband wouldn't have wanted you to struggle when there is help to hand."

Barbara made no response, except to hand the men their refilled glasses. She offered Margaret hers, but her friend declined.

"If I drink any more I shall sleep all afternoon and I'll be no use to anybody," she winked at Barbara. "Why don't you finish the bottle between you two men while I help Barbara with the washing up."

David and Tim looked at each other.

"Well," Said Tim, "it would be impolite to waste such good wine, especially as we have been so expertly driven and well fed in this beautiful place. I can see why you love it, Barbara."

"Yes, it is special, isn't it? I think it's magical really. We always felt we belonged here, as if we had found the place to finish our days."

David and Tim did not take long to empty the bottle. Tim was sure it tasted slightly different from the first one, but as he was no expert he assumed that no two bottles could taste exactly the same.

"OK," said David, "show us what you want us to do, before we fall asleep!" He felt strangely giddy and attributed it to wine.

Barbara opened the door to the wine cellar and stood aside. Margaret remained seated.

"Oh, I'm sorry," she said," I turned off the light. It's on the right hand wall by the bottom step. Be careful, it's quite dark."

The two men felt a distinct unease as they put their feet down gingerly. They held hands to steady themselves and, though they would never admit it, for comfort.

"I can hear water," called Tim.

"Yes," said Barbara. The cellar is built over the stream that goes to the mill. It's useful because it keeps it cool, which is good for wine."

She smiled at her friend, Margaret, who was by now standing alongside her peering into the gloom below.

"Have you found the light switch?" called Barbara.

"Yes," David replied.

"Then I'll shut this door," she said.

"There's no need to do that!" shouted Tim, "we need all the light we can get down here."

The two women did not hear his words because they had closed the door at the top of the cellar steps. At exactly the same moment as the door slammed shut, David flicked the light switch. No light illuminated his world or that of Tim. Instead there was a loud crack and the steps disappeared from beneath them. Hand in hand they plunged into the icy water and were swept helplessly toward the mill. David felt something brush against his cheek and caught a flashing glimpse of a football as it bobbed along beside him. They thrashed in vain to hold their heads above water, but the current was far too strong. They were swept helplessly into the mill and jammed face down in the water. It took them about half an hour to die, as they struggled in vain to free themselves.

Margaret and Barbara sat at the kitchen table.

"Men are so predictable," said Barbara. "All I said was that I had lost my husband and the cellar was a bit of a mess. They couldn't help themselves. They had to come to the aid of a damsel in distress, show off their machismo. Well, I'd better let Ray know."

Barbara extracted a mobile phone from her pocket. It had been Tim's but he had no further use for it. She punched in the letters, which gave the message:

Two less for dinner tonight.

She put the phone back into her pocket, thinking to herself that it might come in handy later.

The women drove in silence. A little later Barbara made yet another sharp turn, down the same dim residential street in the same rundown neighbourhood, taking a short cut and suddenly skidding to a stop at the same kerb.

"You won't need to lock the car," she said. She picked up the paper bag from beside her friend's feet and went into the shop.

When she emerged she had a new paper bag in her hand.

On one side of the car two young boys looked on and one nudged the other, whispering something with a smile on his face. On the other side an old woman's skull-like face stared at the car; merely a foot away on the passenger side of the car. The woman still looked sick and near death. Still wearing dirty, torn clothing, the scrawny woman rocked unsteadily on her feet. Her yellow eyes glanced over her shoulder quickly, as if she did not want to be seen. Barbara handed her the new paper bag. The old woman opened it and peered inside to discover a bottle of barbiturates and a bottle of rioja. The top of the barbiturates bottle showed a dusting of powder, the same colour as the pills inside, which were as yellow as the jaundiced eyes of the old woman. She then looked at the car and smiled, just as the boys had done.

They drove in silence through the countryside towards Lisbon.

"What was in the paper bag?" Margaret asked.

"Pills," replied Barbara. "I crushed some up and put it in their wine. I was glad you didn't want any of the second bottle."

-18-

Each was lost in her own thoughts as they drove back into Lisbon. Margaret couldn't understand what had come over her lifelong friend. Surely she would not have allowed her to drink the poisoned wine. She could easily have forewarned her and yet she had opted to leave it to chance. She had never acted in such strange ways before. What on earth was Barbara up to?

Barbara was glad her friend had not accepted any of the second bottle of wine. She only offered it to her so that the men would not be suspicious and it had worked. It troubled her that she wasn't actually sure that she would have prevented her from drinking it, but she was nevertheless pleased with the day's results. Her knuckles tightened white on the steering wheel as she imagined Detective Chief Inspector Lane's reaction when he learned of the demise of his insurgents. She had good reason to hate Lane, because she was certain he was the reason her husband was dead and she had recognised the Manxmen instantly. Thankfully, they had not recognised her.

Margaret sat bolt upright in the passenger seat.

"Your husband died at the mill, didn't he? Those flowers back at the mill were for him."

"I was wondering how long that would take you," said Barbara. "Detective Chief Inspector Sandy Lane was the man responsible. The details are irrelevant now, except to say that I recognised the two ex policemen as soon as they introduced themselves at dinner last night. They were still in the force a year ago, attached to Lane in London. My husband's company, Anvex, had been broken into and the thieves got away with over £500,000 and some other items. One of those things was a valuable ring that had been bought for a woman. It was in the safe as he was going to have it sized for her the next day. DCI Lane was the investigating officer and those two were in his team. They didn't have any contact with me because it was Lane himself who interviewed me, but they were at the police station. I knew them as soon as I saw them yesterday. I took a dislike to Lane immediately. In fact he struck me as very nasty. I met his first wife as well. Her name was Leanne. We only met because she came to the police station while I was there and our paths crossed. She was obviously upset about something and told me not to trust him. She gave me her number and told me to get in touch if necessary. As it turned out I didn't need to phone her at all. She sat at our table last night! When we had a moment to talk in the loo, she said she knew all about the two ex policemen and then told me how to deal with them. She also gave me a number to text when it was over. Hell has no fury they say and they might be right. I think this holiday is going to be very interesting indeed."

-19-

"Perhaps our two new friends have decided to eat elsewhere tonight," said Leanne.

"In that case Tim will have to wait for his bottle of wine," put in John.

"Wine?" queried Leanne.

"Yes; his prize for reducing the dining room to a shambles last night, with his elbow trick."

"Oh, I remember," said Margaret. "It was quite clever, wasn't it?"

"They came with us on a trip out into the countryside today," said Barbara. "They were quite helpful with translation, actually. We had a very enjoyable day. They seemed to fall in love with the place. We dropped them off on the edge of town on the way back, they wanted to mooch round the shops and cafes. I was too worried about getting back to the ship in time, so we came straight back. The last I saw of them they were hand in hand by some water."

"I hope they got back in time," joked Margaret, "I doubt the Captain would hold the ship for a couple of late passengers. In fact the brochure tells people to make sure they are back in time after a shore trip, because the Captain has to keep to his schedule, and it's people's own responsibility to make sure they are back. If they miss the sailing, they have to make their own way to the next port of call and catch up."

"Actually, I could have sworn they were the reason we were about an hour late leaving Southampton," said John. "I was looking over the side down at the dock and I think I saw them hurrying to get on board, with their luggage being almost thrown in as well. If it was them, perhaps the Captain got fed up with a second time and decided not to wait."

"Well, there's nothing we can do now," said Barbara. "I expect they forgot the time and just got carried away."

Nobody noticed that it would have been more usual for her to have said 'perhaps they got carried away and forgot the time,' except Margaret, who smiled inwardly and looked down at her plate with unnaturally fierce concentration.

The dining room buzzed with the sound of conversation. Waiters moved around as if gliding on air, noiseless and skilful, responding to every raised finger, arched eyebrow and attention seeking glance with well practiced efficiency. Each course was dealt with apparently without effort and certainly without fuss, and was obviously the result of hours and hours of training and management.

As the evening wore on, and more alcohol was consumed, the noise level increased, but never got out of hand.

"That's a lovely ring," said Barbara, looking at Leanne's left hand.

"Thank you," replied Leanne, "it's the first time I've worn it tonight. I think John has been overcome by being on a cruise. He got all romantic and presented me with it just before we came to dinner. In fact, he insisted I wore it."

John Lomax reddened with embarrassment. He was now the only man on the table and the ladies thought he must have felt a little lost.

In fact the cause of his change in colour was a day spent in the sunshine of Lisbon and the effect of the sea breeze, which is all too often underestimated. There was also much more to it. John had intended to give the ring to Leanne on the final night of the cruise, but had decided to do so that night, because he had been overcome by an uneasy feeling about it. Something was pulling insistently within his brain, telling him that it held the key to his future. Something was telling him that he needed to test Leanne and that the ring was at the centre of it. He knew he loved Leanne, had done so ever since he had first set eyes on her, but he also knew that he needed to be very careful. His trusted friend Ray Quinn had told him as much by text and voicemail, and he needed to be certain that she had severed her tie with DCI Lane. Giving her the ring would bring things to a head.

Lomax remembered his own reasoning upon receiving the ring. He realised that he had been sent it in order to tell him that he knew about the Anvex robbery. Lomax knew that he had been set up. Lane had sent the ring, knowing where it had come from and knowing that he could use it as a reason for further investigation whenever he chose. He was letting Lomax know that the real value of Dunne's ring lay in its link to Dunne's murder and his killer. Also, it showed that this very valuable ring stolen during the Anvex robbery was now in the possession of the killer and that he intended to frame Lomax both for Dunne's murder, the Anvex robbery and the theft of that ring. Lomax had understood with absolute certainty that it meant that Lane had stolen the ring because he knew he had only taken the money. Lane must have made sure the ring was polished before sending it to Lomax. It also meant that Dunne had somehow got hold of the ring from Lane, but had lost his finger because of it. In addition, he knew that Lane did not now care that Lomax would know he had stolen the ring. So, giving the ring to Leanne was a clever move and would surely bring matters to a head.

He was not to know that not only did Barbara mean what she had said when admiring the ring, she had also recognised it immediately. It was the ring that her late husband had bought for her and had placed in the company safe until he could get it sized for her the next day. It was the ring that had disappeared on the night of the robbery and had supposedly not been traced by the police. She was devastated to see it catching the chandelier lights and flash brilliant reflections across the table, each point a stinging dagger to her broken heart. Each point was a poignant reminder of the loss of her beloved husband a year earlier.

For her part, Leanne did not notice any change in Barbara's demeanour, so skilfully did she hide her emotions. Leanne knew from having received Ray Quinn's text which had said, rather cryptically, '*Lisbon excursion arranged for 2 gentlemen. Let it happen'*, and having secretly looked at John's phone messages and listened to his voicemail, that the two men who were now absent were not there for their own health. She knew there was a far more sinister explanation, and she realised that John Lomax probably already knew the details, but had, thus far, chosen not to share his thoughts.

Leanne was also delighted with her new ring. She thought it proved John's commitment and the beginning of permanence in their relationship. She now had a choice. Either commit to John totally, rid herself of all scepticism, as she believed he wanted her to do and had signalled as much by giving her the ring, or keep the ring but remain on her guard. The drawback to that was that he would undoubtedly notice and who knew where that would lead? Her heart was telling her one thing and her head was saying something else. She decided to suspend her disbelief and pin her colours to his mast. He had, after all, come up with this fabulous holiday, given her a beautiful and obviously expensive ring and, despite being secretive about his contacts with Ray Quinn since they had been away, he was obviously in control of whatever was happening. Also, he had come through difficult situations before, she knew, and she thought he could manage whatever life threw at them both.

She caressed his calf under the table with her foot, to show him how pleased and happy she was feeling, and to indicate pleasures to come that night.

Barbara covered her inner pain and seemed fascinated by the ring.

"It really is beautiful," she said, "it must have cost a fortune. Where did you get such a gem," she asked looking at John Lomax without blinking.

"As I said last night I am in the trade and I came across it that way. I knew as soon as I saw it that it would be right for Leanne. I've just been waiting for an appropriate moment to give it to her and I decided tonight was that moment."

"Well, she is a very lucky woman," said Barbara, only just managing to hide her gritted teeth.

Her mind then moved to the missing men. She had done all Ray Quinn had asked of her by making sure they were removed as a danger to John Lomax, whilst at the same time taking some measure of revenge for her husband's killing at the hands of the man who had sent them. What she really craved, however, was far more deeply embedded in her psyche. She would not rest until DCI Lane had drawn his last breath and until her so called best friend, Margaret, had seen the error of her ways, for it was she who had stolen the heart of her intended all those years ago. It was she who was still married to him. She thought it ironic and just that he had paid for this trip for both of them. She planned that it would not be long before both were gone. She had got to the point where her own fate had become unimportant, inconsequential. What really mattered was to correct the injustices that had been visited upon her by Lane and Margaret. Ideally she would also have liked to have rid the world of Leanne, who now wore the ring that was rightfully hers, and Lomax, for the simple reason that he had given it to her and must have known its history.

She felt herself to have been wronged on all these counts and so it was that she recited to herself "hell has no fury," raised her wine glass and promised herself success.

-20-

The next port of call was Lanzarote, where beautiful beaches awaited or, for the more adventurous of the passengers, the "valley of a thousand palms" and the Jameos el Agua cave overlooking a saltwater lagoon. Then came volcanic Gran Canaria with its rolling sand dunes and the cosmopolitan and prosperous port of Las Palmas. Tenerife, the largest of the Canary Islands, dominated by the giant Mount Teide was visited, followed by La Palma, the "Fair Isle", with its beautiful scenery and one of the prettiest harbours among all the islands, Santa Cruz.

John and Leanne viewed the holiday as a honeymoon. It certainly marked a fresh start for both of them, individually and together. Neither had known such happiness, such joy, in their lives. They revelled in the wonderful scenery, the spellbinding starlit nights, the amazing sail-away fireworks display from the mountains in the distance and the sumptuous life of luxury on board. They also marvelled at the endless inventiveness of their lovemaking and became enchanted with each other. Nothing else seemed to matter to them and time stood still.

Evening meals with their new friends, Margaret and Barbara, had settled into a steady and relaxed routine, unhurried and untroubled. The Chief Steward had visited the table on one of the nights and asked a few question about their erstwhile companions, but none of them could or would give any helpful information to explain their absence.

Lomax & The Biker – The Trilogy

Barbara said that she wondered if they just wanted to be alone together, and the other three readily concurred that this was probably the case, even though they had not even caught sight of them during the day.

The final port of call was the beautiful "garden island" of Madeira, famed for its scenic splendours, stunning cliff top waterfalls and flora-covered mountains. That day was absolutely magical for John and Leanne as they lost themselves in each other and the incredible island. Neither wanted to return to the ship as each felt it signified an unwanted beginning of the return to reality. Both fell quiet as they clambered up the walkway into the bowels of the great liner. John reflected that he had noticed that each of the islands they had visited had been oddly shaped, but inextricably connected. It was very much like the people they had met on the cruise; each different, each an individual, but each inevitably and deeply connected one with the other. It was quite some time later in his life that he came to fully understand those connections.

-21-

There were still several days at sea before they were due to arrive back in Southampton. Throughout the trip the sea had been calm and compliant, allowing the ship to cut through the surface without resistance, ensuring that even those passengers in possession of the most delicate of constitutions could relax completely. "Virgin" cruisers were smugly content that they had gained their sea legs and talked amongst themselves, congratulating each other, wondering why they had ever worried about the capriciousness of the ocean.

With just two days and two nights left, the sea came alive. The North Atlantic bared its teeth and the ship had to battle its way through a storm. Passengers were warned to remain inboard and not venture out onto the open deck, and restaurants emptied as people retreated to their cabins, there to nurse rumbling stomachs and hold on to whatever came to hand.

Margaret was one of the few passengers who had experienced storms at sea before, as she had travelled extensively when accompanying her husband on trips all over the world. She therefore took a couple of pills and announced herself untroubled by the pitching and yawing of the ship. She was fascinated by the fact that even a liner weighing almost 100,000 tonnes could be moved in such ways.

Barbara was also unaffected. She too had travelled with her late husband, though not to the same extent as her friend, she reflected acidly.

John had religiously taken seasickness pills each and every day of the trip, so the cumulative effect was now bearing fruit. He found himself able to cope and ventured forth for breakfast and then to slowly take a look at the entire ship.

Leanne, on the other hand, despite belatedly swallowing some pills, decided to remain on her bed and ride out the storm. That meant staying there all day and not risking an appearance for dinner that night. The forecast was that the storm would be gone by the following lunchtime, so the ship would have a smooth last afternoon and evening, with arrival in Southampton due at 5am the following morning. That meant that the final evening's Celebration Dinner could be enjoyed by passengers free from, or recovering from, the effects of the storm.

On the first morning of the storm John was feeling fine, so he risked breakfast. In fact, he felt so good that he consumed a full breakfast of bacon, eggs, fried bread, tomatoes, baked beans, and mushrooms, followed by toast, all accompanied by a very fine pot of tea. There was nobody else at his table that morning. Suitably fuelled he set out on his tour of the ship. There were very few people who had ventured out of their cabins, so he was largely left to wander without hindrance.

He, quite literally, bumped into Margaret and Barbara, who were also determined not to allow the storm to dictate their schedule. They chatted briefly, during which time the two women pronounced themselves determined to go out into the fresh air, at least some time during the day. John protectively advised against it, but knew they were both determined ladies who would probably not take any notice.

After a couple of hours, John checked on Leanne and found her sleeping peacefully, curled up on the bed. He was struck by how innocent and childlike she looked, and knew again why he loved her. She had been through so much in her life, and he would be the person to protect and look after her from now on. He kissed her gently and noiselessly on her cheek and retreated through the door into the corridor. He did not notice the faint fluttering of her eyelids as she registered his presence and pretended to be asleep.

He decided to find himself some coffee, before continuing his expedition. He was attracted by the inviting aroma that insinuated itself into his senses, but was distracted by the sight of Margaret and Barbara fighting their way through a door which was doing its best to prevent them from having access to the open deck. They overcame its objections and it slammed shut behind them with indignation.

He decided to keep an eye on them. Coffee could wait.

He lost sight of them for a few moments, but when he saw them again he was dumbstruck. Barbara was holding out her right hand towards Margaret, who was bent backwards at an awkward angle over the railing. Lomax couldn't move. He realised that the women were shouting at each other but couldn't hear anything as the wind and spray carried their voices away out to sea. He realised with fascinated horror that Barbara was gripping a knife in her hand and making thrusting gestures towards

Margaret. The latter was trapped by the rail behind her, and a lifeboat on either side. There appeared to be no escape for her and she looked terrified. Lomax also spotted that nobody else could possibly have seen the women, as the place was probably the only blind spot on the entire ship. He was therefore the only witness to Barbara's final lunge and shove, which saw Margaret fall helplessly and plunge downwards out of sight. His final sight of her were arms and legs flailing uselessly as the storm plucked her up and out, away from the ship. He knew she would probably never be found.

He saw Barbara peer down into the heaving ocean as if to satisfy herself that Margaret had actually gone. With a grim smile she threw the knife as far as her strength would allow into the depths of the North Atlantic.

As she turned away from the rail, Barbara caught a glimpse of John Lomax watching her with a horrified expression on his face and she slowly smiled and mouthed the words "hell has no fury...."

John Lomax curled his hands around his coffee cup and blew away the steam. He thought for a long time about the scene he had just witnessed and came to the conclusion that he should tell nobody, not even Leanne. He knew that Barbara had seen him watching, but she could not be sure whether he would say anything to anybody. That made him a marked man and it could also put Leanne in danger. On the other hand, it could make him an asset to her.

He was onto his second coffee, and about to start nibbling on a pastry, when his mobile vibrated in his pocket.

Barbara is on our side. She has her own agenda, but you are not in danger. All well here.

Ray Quinn had yet again provided him with the answer he needed and he tucked into the pastry with renewed enthusiasm.

-22-

The End of Cruise Celebration Dinner was a grand affair, and most tables were filled with laughter and laden with food and wine. Their table, meant for six, now only had half that number, and looked sparse. He caught people looking with questioning eyes, but did not respond. He decided to make the best of it. After all, it wasn't his fault they had decided to get themselves stuck face down in a mill or thrown overboard.

Leanne seemed to have recovered her equilibrium and now had colour in her cheeks again. Margaret's absence was never mentioned between the three "survivors" and there weren't even any questions from the waiting staff either. John found that odd because he would have thought they would have at least asked whether anybody else would be joining the table that evening. He then spotted that the table had only been laid with three place settings. This puzzled him, but he said nothing and gave no outward display that he had even noticed.

With only the three of them at a table large enough for six people, there was plenty of room for each. Indeed, there was so much space between them, literally and figuratively, that conversation became difficult and long silences developed.

John decided that he needed time to think, excused himself, and headed for the bathroom in their stateroom. He checked his mobile phone as soon as he had shut the door behind him, but there were no further messages or voice mails. He cast around the room, trying to fathom the cause of the suspicious feeling that had overcome him. His eyes methodically searched for anything, but found nothing. He would have given a great deal to have heard the conversation between Barbara and Leanne at the table in his absence.

"Leanne," Barbara began, "I have a great deal to tell you and not much time, so please listen without interrupting. I know all about John's life. His sad marriage, his boring and ill-rewarded job, his friendship with Ray Quinn, his problems with the police and in particular DCI Lane, You need not be afraid. Ray Quinn is the one true friend John has. I am his sister. I know I am somewhat older than him, but that isn't my fault. I also know of your connection with Sandy Lane. Life gets complicated sometimes and we cannot see the wood from the trees, but I'd like you to know that I'm on your side. Well, yours and John's. I have made sure our two new friends from the Isle of Man will not trouble anybody again. They were sent here by DCI Lane specifically to kill both of you. Ray discovered it and sent me to assist. That difficulty is no more, but I won't bore you with the details. However, the cruise also gave me the opportunity to set right something from my own past.

You see, Margaret, who is not with us tonight, was the woman who stole the only love of my life when were supposed to be true friends. I was in love with the man she married. I could have had such a different life. She has now paid the price and will not be troubling anybody again. I am telling you all this, because I know we can trust each other. Each of us has so much to lose if the truth comes out and so much to gain if it does not. You may notice that when I leave the ship, a man will meet me. He is the man I have been missing all these years. So you see, we have much in common. You have found happiness with John and so have I.

It would be nice if we could stay in touch and become friends, but I don't think that would be wise, do you? You go your way and I'll go mine. Hell has no fury, they say, and I suppose we are proof of that. I hope our troubles are over, but I somehow doubt it. I'll give you my mobile number just in case you ever need anything. Please don't let John know you have it. Ray knows everything as well and you must have absolute trust in him. He will help no matter what difficulties may be round the corner."

Leanne was dumbfounded. A million questions need answers, but she couldn't speak. Barbara recognised her difficulty and continued.

"Karen Lomax, John's ex, planned it all. She wanted revenge for the way John had treated her and she was enraged at his lifestyle without her. She had also become insanely jealous of you. Your meeting in the pub had only served to add to these feelings. She couldn't wait for the subtlety of Sandy Lane's approach to work its magic. She wanted dramatic intervention. She contacted Lane and they came up with a plan to ensure that only John Lomax himself went overboard as she reasoned that he would not agree to a plan that involved killing you. I think she was wrong, because it would tidy up a loose end for Lane, but she wasn't to know that. You need to be careful of that in future. The two Manxmen were hired to get rid of John overboard on the last night of the cruise, tonight in fact. Ray found out through a contact in the Met and sent me to solve the problem. We came up with a plan that also solved my difficulty. He's actually quite clever, my brother. All that time in the forces I expect. All in all, it's wonderful symmetry. For Sandy Lane the outcome should have been perfect, but events have not panned out as expected. John still lives and appears to lead a charmed life. Both his hired hit-men have gone and you are still alive. He wanted you dead as well, you know. They were hired to kill you as well. Sandy Lane is now solely responsible for the deaths of 12 people and jointly party to the demise of 2 more. He feels no compunction about planning death, including yours, and no remorse about making it happen. He views such emotions as weakness and a source of vulnerability. He considers the two hired killers to be expendable, no more than collateral damage. They knew the risks. In fact in his eyes there was to be a certain order, even tidiness, to the outcome of the episode as there is no trace back to him at all.

Also, Karen Lomax is now in it up to her neck. She is now jointly responsible for the deaths of two people, and you were also to be a victim. Sandy Lane will always have that hold over her and he won't hesitate to follow that path if necessary.

It's strange, Leanne, how both John Lomax and Sandy Lane have always thought they controlled their own destinies, whereas the truth is that it's the women in their lives who have their hands on the rudder. As I said earlier, Hell as no fury, they say and I suppose there's some truth in that."

Before Leanne could respond John returned to the table. Barbara smiled at him, but there was no life behind the eyes. The grin exposed teeth, framed by red lipstick, that reminded him of a death rictus.

Seafarers are notoriously superstitious and the moment the cruise ended and the ship had docked at Southampton, their dining table, along with its chairs, was removed, chopped up and burned. The ashes were scattered at sea at the beginning of the ship's next voyage. No table was ever positioned in the same place again.

-23-

DCI Lane was not a happy man and paced round his office in London, considering the situation. His hired killers had failed him and had themselves been outwitted by two women. With his sexist outlook, that doubled their failure in his eyes. Leanne had survived as well and, worst of all, John Lomax was still alive. The number of people who knew his secrets had increased to an intolerable level. If his line of work as a high ranking police officer had taught him anything, it was that the only way to keep a secret is to tell nobody else at all. His activities on the darker side of life could be exposed at any moment and he needed to deal with matters.

He could be in danger of exposure from Karen Lomax, Barbara, Ray Quinn, John Lomax and Leanne. Any one of them could bring him down. Then a bombshell thought struck him. What if they got together and pooled their talents and knowledge? That would be catastrophic. Also, he realised that there could well be fellow officers who were compromised and would betray him. At that point in time, he didn't know that had already happened, although if he had considered the possibility carefully enough he would have realised it was the only way that his plans could have been thwarted on the ship.

He sat down behind his desk with a heavy heart, put his head in his hands and closed his eyes. He needed time to think; to gain some clarity, but he didn't know how much time he really had. Would anybody make a quick move? Would he be left alone with the slow and agonising certainty that plots against him were in hand? The one thing he could be sure of was that each of the people concerned was clever and resourceful, with an individual agenda of their own. But if they were to get together for a carefully planned and co-ordinated attack against him, then his chances of survival were very much reduced.

The obvious move would be to get rid of each of them. He knew he could physically do it, but he questioned whether he needed to see them dead. He knew that alive they were a danger, but could they be more dangerous in death? He wanted to remain in his job. It did, after all, provide a good living, but best of all it gave him opportunities others didn't have. He had already taken those chances with the 14 deaths he was responsible for and he wanted to continue with his work.

He decided to make use of his police training and do a thorough appraisal of his work. He took a fresh pad of paper and began to write a list of people who had died either at his own hands, by his instruction or as a result of his actions.

1/. Anna French. Attractive wife and mother. Trying to give up smoking. Lomax accused but never convicted

2/. Georgina Leonard. Lane's first effort. Very messy.

3/. Daphne Woodward. Strangled.

4/. June Washington. Drowned.

5/. Lisa Raymond. Throat cut.

6/. Tracey Smith. Strangled.

7/. Alison Goodey. Broken neck.

Lomax & The Biker – The Trilogy

8/. Alice Richards. Poisoned.

9/. Frank Wells. Former employer of John Lomax. Leanne's father. Scattered in various parts of London.

10/. Richard Dunne. Former friend of John Lomax. Owner of severed finger and ring. Cremated in police drugs incineration exercise.

11/. Ian Honeycombe (ex Isle of Man detective). Drowned in mill accident.

12/. Frank Isley (ex Isle of Man detective). Ditto.

There was also Margaret, who had unfortunately fallen overboard at Barbara's hand. He knew he was implicated in her death, but did not consider himself primarily responsible as Barbara had decided upon that course of action for her own ends. He remembered Barbara's husband, who expired abroad. He smiled inwardly at the memory of that victim giving his life to save his wife from Lane's attentions. He ought to count him, he supposed.

There were no outstanding issues that could come back to trap him from any of them, he decided, so he needed now to move on to dealing with matters that should and, hopefully, could be resolved.

Again he wrote a list.

1/. Find John Lomax's money. Perhaps use Karen Lomax for this.

2/. Find a way to ensure Karen's silence. Permanently. Not such a shrinking violet.

3/. Find his fugitive wife, Judith. And then?
4/. Find his son, Billy. And then?
5/. Decide what to do about Leanne.
6/. Deal with Barbara.
7/. Conclude matters with Lomax.
8/. Settle Ray Quinn.

    He examined the list and was struck by just how lengthy it was. Just the act of putting pen to paper had focussed his mind and he knew that his feud with Lomax had become intensely personal and he could not rest until it was over. He knew, however, that dealing with Ray Quinn was going to be the most difficult item.

    Could he simply ignore any of these matters, in the hope or possibility that they would go away? Probably not, he told himself, but was there any way he could tie up more than one at a time? He yelled for coffee to anybody who would listen and returned to his lists. Coffee was delivered by a pretty young constable, who was in her first day in plain clothes and keen to make an impression. He didn't even look up as the cup and saucer landed respectfully on the desk, but he sneaked a glance at her retreating figure and filed the image.

-24-

Billy Lane opened the front door to his apartment in Brisbane just as his mobile vibrated in his pocket. He hurried to the kitchen to put his groceries down on the worktop and fished the phone from his shirt pocket. He saw that the number had been withheld.

"Hello," he said. "If you are selling anything give up now before I get annoyed. I'm fed up with these calls and you really don't want to annoy me."

"Calm down, Billy. It's me, your Mum." Leanne anxiously drew breath and held it waiting for his reply.

"Oh. What's wrong?" he asked, his senses suddenly on full alert.

"Nothing; I just need to talk to you and it really needs to be face to face."

"If there's nothing wrong, why can't you tell me on the phone? I can hardly just drop in can I?"

"Actually, I was thinking of dropping in on you. I haven't seen you in such a long time and there's something I want to ask you."

"Oh."

"You've already said that," continued Leanne.

"I don't know," he said. "Things are really settled for me here and I don't want anything spoiling my life. I've had a fresh start and things are working out fine for me. I'd rather just be left alone."

"I'm afraid that's not possible, Billy," said Leanne, adopting a sterner tone. "There is something that needs to be done and only you can take care of it."

Billy knew that when his mother spoke in that way, there was no point in arguing. Sons the world over have learned that mothers have that annoying way with their sons. The apron strings are never really cut.

He surrendered. "When will you be here? I'll have to make arrangements. How long will you be staying?"

"I'll be there in twenty minutes," Leanne said, and we'll talk about your other questions when I get there."

The connection was cut and Billy was left staring at his kitchen wall, with a stupid lopsided look of amazement on his face.

"Shit!" was all he could muster. He felt a cramp in his right arm and realised that he still had the phone clamped rigidly to his ear. He was stunned by the news that his mother, whom he hadn't seen in over three years, had come all the way from England and would descend upon him very soon without any warning. Billy eventually put his phone down and felt blood return with a rush to his arm. He sat down on a stool by the worktop and massaged his throbbing arm. He felt light-headed as if the call had not been real or was part of a dream. He hoped it wouldn't turn into a nightmare. It wasn't either, of course, because he wasn't asleep and she was on her way. Less than half an hour!

Outside, rain fell steadily, pattering onto the back yard of the apartment block. He'd lived there for nearly a year, having moved from the Sydney shared house that he had used upon arrival in Australia. He liked it because it was not as noisy or busy and was harder for anybody to find him. He needed distance from his previous life and the location provided that sanctuary. Except his mother had found him, even though he had not told her where he was. The whole of Australia and she had found him! Remarkable.

Billy had settled easily into his life down under. He liked the outdoors and connected with the straightforward ways of the people. He liked his apartment. He could keep it clean and tidy without much effort and his job as a reporter was at least interesting and allowed him to meet all sorts of people. Indeed, he had met a 19 year old girl who worked at the local radio station and held certain hopes in that direction. He certainly didn't want his mother ruining that part of his life before it had properly taken shape.

His thoughts drifted to his mother. He had been angered by her lack of contact over the years and that had been one factor in his decision to try Australia. Of course, another influence had been his father's behaviour, which had stung sharply, as well as John Lomax's financial help. All in all, he pondered to himself, it had been a good move and one which he certainly did not wish to have derailed. He pushed these thoughts aside, reminding himself that whatever the purpose of tonight's visit he welcomed being able to see her again. Also, he knew there would not be enough time to exhume even a fraction of the painful memories that lay between them like so much shattered stone.

Lomax & The Biker – The Trilogy

He glanced at the kitchen clock. Nearly ten minutes had flashed past. He dashed to his bedroom, rummaged through his drawers with an increasing sense of panic until he found what he sought. He grabbed the object, walked to the living room and placed the framed photo of Leanne on his coffee table. He had another which featured Lomax as well, but he preferred the one with his mother on her own. Memories flooded back as he stroked the glass with his thumb and a tear formed in the corner of his eye. He was lost for a while as sorrow rose in his heart like the water level of a rain swollen stream and he found himself having to sit down. He had been lonely many times in his young life and there were far more painful memories than joyous ones. The sad feelings of his childhood rushed back to the forefront of his mind and he struggled to outweigh them with thoughts of happy times. He had many times asked himself why people chose to have children and then subjected them to family upset, misery and heartache. He had been homesick too since coming to Australia and had cried himself to sleep, just as he had done as a child for different reasons. He concluded that age didn't matter when it came to human emotion.

Well, he told himself firmly, don't just sit here, do something. He had found himself having to be firm in this way more often lately. He washed the dishes that had been left in the sink since that morning's rush to work, and gave a cursory glance over the place. He realised it would have to do. He sat and waited for the ring at the door. His mind was wandering back to the shoplifting incident with the watch and Lomax's part in it and the subsequent events that had led to him coming to Australia, when IT RANG!

Leanne stood in front of the door and thought that we all have so many hopes and dreams for our children and they never turn out as we hope. Life is so unfair. Just at that moment he opened the door and Leanne stood there with tears in her eyes. She couldn't move. What she saw was a grown man, not the gawky youth of three years ago. She remembered the teenage tantrums, the slammed doors, the sulking, the sudden mood swings, the unsavoury company he kept, but these were swept away by the young man who stood in front of her.

They stood at the threshold just taking each other in, not moving, until it became uncomfortable.

"Well, don't just stand there, come in," said Billy. "I don't know why you're here but it's good to see you."

Leanne moved towards her son and enveloped him with a hug that she wished could go on forever. To Billy, it felt like it did, so he eventually freed himself and invited her to sit down.

"I see you've got my picture here," she said. She made no comment that it wasn't the photo that showed John Lomax as well.

"Yes, it's been there since I moved in and there it will stay," he lied. "So, what's this surprise visit all about?

Leanne looked away from the picture and directed her gaze at her son. She had planned this moment in her mind many times during the long plane journey from England, but knew in that instant that the only way was to just be straight with him. He had obviously grown up, not just physically but also in all the other necessary ways, so he could cope, she judged.

"Billy, I want you to listen carefully to what I am about to say. Don't interrupt or I shall lose my train of thought."

He shifted his weight back in his seat and waited. Whatever it was, he knew it must be important for her to have come all that way and tracked him down. He hoped it wasn't something that would yet again turn his world upside down, but he had a horrible feeling that he was about to change direction again.

"We have a problem at home, she stated, "and we need you to help us solve it. You will remember that your father and John have never, how can I put it, seen eye to eye. That's an understatement obviously, but things have got worse. It's now at a stage where John and I need to rid ourselves of your father's attentions for good. It's not something that we can do ourselves, out in the open so to speak because we would both be under immediate suspicion. You may remember Ray Quinn. He could do it, and will if we ask him, but that would be too obvious as well. There is one other person who could also help, but she has recently had difficulties of her own. No, the obvious person from our point of view is you. Nobody will suspect you because you are here in Australia and the authorities won't even know you've had a little holiday in England. Ray will arrange for you to be away from here for no more than 48 hours and nobody will even know. Afterwards you can continue your new life here without interruption or interference from us. Before I say any more, I need to know whether you will at least consider what I've said."

Billy gazed at his mother, trying to read her eyes. Surely she wasn't asking him to kill his own father, was she? That would make him exactly the monster he had come here to avoid. It was, however, obvious to him that she was serious.

"I promise to think about it," he replied, "and nobody will learn about what you've already said or are about to say from me."

"That's good," she said, and drawing a deep breath, plunged in. "Now, your father has been responsible for quite a few deaths as well as being involved in other illegal things. The police don't know anything about any of his evil, and he is still trying to pin all sorts of things on John. He even got me to help at one time, but I've moved on and John and I are very happy and only want a quiet life. We want you to come to England and kill him. We have come to the conclusion that he won't stop what he's doing, not even if we give him a really nasty shock. Ray has everything prepared; all I need to do is let him know you are ready. I hate having to say these things to you, but we cannot think of any other way."

"When would I have to leave?"

"As soon as possible."

"I'll need to throw a 'sickie' for work, a bug or something that lasts for 2 or 3 days, perhaps."

"Exactly; but make sure it's nothing that will have people coming here to find out whether you are OK. It needs to be something that people will not want to catch themselves. How about a bout of Norovirus? People are running scared of that. Nobody will visit for fear of catching it and you would be too weak to bother with the phone."

"That could run," he said, "but apart from phoning work, I'll have to phone my girlfriend. Well, she's not my girlfriend exactly but we've been seeing each other a bit and she might drop in anytime."

"That's fine, but don't tell her any more than you have to. Nobody must ever know that you left the country."

"Mum, it's great to see you and I can see that you need my help, but are you sure there is no other way?"

"Absolutely certain," she replied very firmly. "I hate to say it to your face, but your father is an evil monster. Normal rules of behaviour just don't seem to apply to him. He does what he wants when he wants and to hell with anybody else. It's a miracle he hasn't been caught, but he's very clever and I don't trust him at all. No, he won't stop unless we stop him. There's no other way."

Billy looked at the determined woman sitting opposite him and weighed it all up. He let the silence linger, even though he had decided what to say from the moment she asked for his help.

"Of course I'll do it. How could I refuse? I've never forgotten how John Lomax helped me with that watch shoplifting thing. I actually had fun helping him, in a strange sort of way, and he did set me up out here in a way that got Dad off my back."

"Oh, that's wonderful!" Leanne exclaimed and leapt from her seat to hug him once more. He saw her coming and moved swiftly aside.

"Woah!" he said, more loudly than intended. "Hold on. I've only just got my circulation back from the first one."

She looked abashed and returned to her seat.

"There is one small problem, though," he said as she got herself comfortable. My honourable, esteemed evil father, Mr DCI Sandy Lane, has contacted me and asked me to do exactly the same for him. To kill John Lomax, I mean. He did also mention that it would help if you were included as well. So it seems I have a choice and it's not one any son wants to make."

"Oh hell," she said and folded her arms indignantly in an accurate representation of a petulant teenager. "So, what are you going to do now?"

"Well, obviously I don't want to do anything at all. I'm happy here and things are good for me right now."

"The past has a way of catching up, Billy. You can't run away from it forever. I found you easily enough, and your father obviously had no trouble either. I know it's difficult, but nobody would ever know you even left this apartment."

Billy did not say any more and a brief moment of thought became a lingering quiet. The silence was like fire; it seemed to burn into their skin and hearts. Billy was the first to break the moment as he took a mobile phone number from his mother and put it in his pocket.

"That's not my number," she said, "but please call it when you've decided what to do. A man will answer. You remember Ray Quinn. He'll make all the arrangements with you."

'The arrangements' had, in fact, already been made but Leanne didn't tell Billy that. She did not want him to feel under any more pressure than necessary. Leanne's attention was suddenly caught by a flash of light coming through the window, as headlights turned towards them.

"My girlfriend," said Billy, "she often drops in after work."

He rose and moved towards the front door. Leanne moved out of the line of site of the door and the window. She knew it would be better if nobody knew of her visit. She was close enough, however, to hear Billy's response when the doorbell rang.

"Hi," he called. "I can't open the door, I've got a bug and I don't want you to catch it. It's Norovirus I think. I can't stand here for long. I have to be near the toilet and a basin, it gets you both ways!"

Leanne couldn't hear the reply from outside the door.

"You'll have to stay clear for a few days. Tell you what; I'll call you when I'm better. I really don't want you to catch it, it's horrible. Best instant diet ever. We'll spend some time together soon, I promise."

More muffled response from outside.

"Ok. No, don't worry. I can't eat anything at the moment. I'm just sipping water all the time. Don't worry, I'll be alright. They say it only lasts for a few days."

Lomax & The Biker – The Trilogy

Leanne heard more muffled voice, but could just make out the words "love you."

She saw her son redden as he offered "me too."

A car door clunked shut and Billy's new love was gone.

"I suppose you heard that," he said to Leanne, without looking her in the eye.

"Yes. She sounds nice. Thanks for not letting her know I'm here. Does it mean you've made your decision?"

Billy responded by rummaging in a pocket, and tapping out the numbers on his phone. He listened intently for what to Leanne seemed an eternity, before disconnecting. He turned to his mother.

"It's been good to see you, but you need to go now. I haven't much time and you don't need to know the details. What you don't know can't hurt you. Please thank Ray and John for me."

Leanne suppressed the urge to weep, but couldn't help the tear that escaped from the corner of an eye and tracked its way down her cheek. She hugged him tightly.

"Mum, don't please. I've got Norovirus, remember," he said, trying to lighten the moment. "I'll call you when it's all over and we can spend more time together."

He held her hand for a moment and his fingers rested upon the ring given to her by John. He looked down and noticed how unusual it was. She gently withdrew her hand as she slipped through the door and away from him. He gave her a reassuring, firm smile and then she was gone.

-25-

DCI Sandy Lane picked up the phone, even though the number was withheld. He usually ignored such calls, but this one caught him in an unguarded moment.

"Hello," he said rubbing sleep weary eyes with his other hand. He heard Billy's voice and was instantly awake. "Where are you?" he said, asking the question that everybody asks when answering a mobile phone.

"I'm outside your front door!" Replied Billy and waited for the shocked response.

"What on earth are you doing here? I thought we agreed that you wouldn't contact me until it's all over."

"I know, but I need to see you."

Lane managed to sneak a look out of a window and saw nothing untoward, apart from his eldest son standing with a phone to his ear.

"Does anybody know you're here?"

"No, I've been very careful. Please open the door and let me in. I need to talk to you."

Lane let him in. Billy stretched out his hand indicating he expected a handshake, wanting to display a calm and firm assurance. Lane looked at his son's hand and noticed a ring. The unusual design took his breath away.

"Where do you get that?" He croaked in astonishment.

"Mum gave it to me," said Billy. She said she wanted me to have it. I don't know why, but I couldn't refuse and anyway I've got quite attached to it."

Lane spotted the irony. The last time he saw the ring, it was on a severed finger and he had sent it to John Lomax. Now it had reappeared on Billy's finger as if it was coming back to haunt him.

"I've done as you wanted," whispered Billy to his father.

Lane took a moment to digest the information. If true, it signalled the end of the feud and would allow him to carry on with his evil habits. Billy walked past his father and asked him to close the door. He turned round only when he heard it click shut.

"You don't really understand, do you?" All these years, all that's happened and you still don't understand."

The words and their cold tone told Lane something. Billy had changed. He'd grown up and become a man, but why had he come?

"Why are you here? What's point are you trying to make?"

"I think you know," said Billy.

"No, son, I don't know. Some sort of ending, a closure?"

"You could say that, I guess." He looked around the room again. "Let's go."

Lane's breath was by now coming fast.

"Go? Go where?"

"I'm settling things," said Billy as a gun appeared in his hand, its black muzzle pointing in Lane's direction.

"Why this? Everything I ever did was for you."

"I'd say you did things to me, not for me. I need to make sure I have a chance in life. I'm dealing with the past that's caught up with me and now it's caught up with you. "Outside," he ordered.

"What are you going to do?" Lane asked desperately.

"What I should have done long ago. Come with me."

"Now? It's raining."

Billy nodded. "Let's go." He shoved the pistol into the waistband of his jeans and gripped his father firmly by the arm. Billy was struck by the odd thought that he couldn't remember when he had last had any physical contact with him.

"If you do this, you'll regret it for the rest of your life," pleaded Lane.

"No," replied Billy, "I'd regret not doing it."

DCI Sandy Lane, a man who prided himself on being immune to emotion, felt the spatter of rain on his cheeks and couldn't be sure if it was joining tears that he knew were welling in his eyes. He glanced at his son. His face was wet and red too, but this was purely from the rain as his eyes were tearless. Lane was about to ask Billy another question when the cars began to arrive, blue lights flashing, igniting the raindrops around them like sparks at a November 5th fireworks party and cutting through the rain into Lane's consciousness.

A man wearing a dark raincoat climbed out of the first car and walked towards them. He flicked open a leather holder and showed his badge. Two uniformed officers appeared behind him. Billy took a step backwards away from the group and lowered the gun to his side as the raincoat stepped forward and shook his hand. He took the unloaded gun from Billy and pocketed it.

"We'll take over now, son. You've been most helpful. Thank you. If you would like to get into the third car over there, we'll make sure you get back safely."

Billy looked into his father's eyes, trying to detect any sign of regret or remorse. Finding only defiance and contempt, he averted his gaze, turned his back and walked towards the car. As he did so, he heard the words "Detective Chief Inspector Lane, I am arresting you for the murder of Anna French. There will be more charges of murder and other offences but we'll deal with those at the station." Handcuffs appeared and were firmly clamped around Lane's wrists.

As the officer continued with the litany of reading Lane his rights, Billy stopped in his tracks, turned and spoke to the rain-coated officer.

"I think you should search him before you get to the station. Now would be good. I'd like to see what's in his pockets; it will help me with closure."

Lane was taken to the first car and bundled in to the back. A thorough search rewarded the officer with a fruitful harvest of damning evidence. Firstly, a crumpled sheet of paper was found which, when smoothed out, revealed a list of 12 names, some notes about other individuals and a list of what appeared to be items in a plan of action. Another pocket was emptied and an unusual looking ring was discovered. Lane looked out of the window of the first car and Billy smiled at his father. He held up both hands and there was no sign of a ring on any of his fingers.

-26-

Billy Lane opened the car door and, shaking off as much rainwater as possible, settled into the back seat next to Leanne. She put her hand on his leg and applied gentle, reassuring pressure.

"I don't know what to say," she whispered. "We've just condemned him to the rest of his life behind bars. He'll have to be in isolation. Ex policemen are not liked in there and he'll be in constant danger. He might have been better off dead."

"I know," said Billy, "but at least he'll be alive and so will many others he might have had lined up. I just couldn't take his life, you know. I couldn't. It would have made me just like him and I couldn't stand that. I had to break the line of evil. Besides, he doesn't deserve to die. He deserves to live a long time with his demons and have nightmares about all the things he's done. I know he'll suffer in prison, but he surely deserves it. Anyway, who knows, there may be a chance of redemption, even for him."

Billy looked at his mother and put her ring into the palm of her hand.

"How....I don't understand," she said.

"It was Ray's idea," said Billy. "If we weren't going to kill him, then we had to make sure there was enough evidence to condemn him. He had a perfect replica of your ring made. It's amazing what you can get done in a jeweller's shop, these days. You'll remember that John took it for a day to clean it at the shop. Well apart from cleaning it, John had a perfect replica made. We made sure there was no forensic possibility of it being linked to you or any of us. I simply wore your real one when I met Lane, and slipped the fake into his pocket. Now he's inextricably linked to it in forensic terms, by it being in his pocket. You must admit, the symmetry of it is perfect. After all, he did steal it in the first place and then sent it to John to try to frame him. Well, now it's back with him and good riddance, I say, and you've got the original back. Perfect. I think you'd better take good care of it, though. John gave it to you and he really wants you to keep it."

Billy omitted to point out that by making sure Leanne kept the ring, John Lomax was guaranteeing her loyalty, whether it was in doubt or not. She was now permanently committed to him. Billy also realised that he had taken a grave risk by being in danger of being arrested himself, if he had been found in possession of either ring, let alone both. Finally, he recalled that his mother had brazenly turned up at his apartment unannounced and calmly asked him to kill his father. Well he had dealt with that situation creatively and effectively, but what was he to do about her? How far would she go, to achieve what she wanted? Hell has no fury indeed, he mused to himself.

-27-

Sandy Lane's trial took place at The Central Criminal Court, otherwise known as The Old Bailey, in London and lasted many weeks. Despite the best efforts of one of the best barristers in the country, he was found guilty on twelve counts of murder, one of being an accessory to murder, perverting the course of justice and other, more minor, charges. He was sentenced to life for each count of murder, with no possibility of parole for 40 years. In other words, he would die behind bars.

Leanne shed a few private tears whilst Billy wondered if it would have been kinder to have killed him and John Lomax breathed a sigh of relief that his adversary would not be a danger any more. The media was inundated with strident calls for the reinstatement of the death penalty, but there was never any chance of that happening. Great Britain had moved on from those dark days and preferred to incarcerate people.

The prison population across the country followed the trial and sentencing with great interest and many of them yearned for him to be placed in their particular jail. The prison authorities knew, of course, that he would be in danger wherever they placed him and tried to take the appropriate precautions. For his part, he kept to himself as much as possible, but there was inevitable contact with other prisoners at times, although these events were infrequent.

One such occasion happened four years into his sentence. He had been a model prisoner up until then and, although reviled by the guards, he had been treated properly. One particular prisoner was allowed to spend some time with Lane, because he was also considered to be in danger from others and it was easier to keep the two them together from a logistical point of view. One prison officer questioned the wisdom of this arrangement on the grounds that either might pose a threat to the other. That objection was ignored because nobody actually really cared about the welfare of either of them anyway. Indeed, many of the guards secretly longed for some sort of hiatus. Lane and the fellow prisoner had fallen into the habit of playing cards to try and combat the slow passage of time that is the enemy of prisoners everywhere. Prison officers were ever-present, but gradually became more and more lax in their supervision as the perceived danger lessened.

No money changed hands, of course, but that didn't diminish the competitiveness of the players. Lane had not recognised his opponent when they began their run of games, but he recognised the way he spoke. His cocksure attitude and use of language made Lane dismiss him as just another "cockney wide boy" and he felt under no threat from him.

During one of their sessions the library trolley trundled along. It stopped at various times and prisoners returned books and took others. One book, which had always been popular was on the trolley, and was asked for by the man in the cell next to Lane's. The trustee told him firmly that it was not available, and put his hand on it to emphasise the point. He stared meaningfully and the would-be borrower backed down after a few moments impasse.

Lomax & The Biker – The Trilogy

The trolley was pushed along and stopped outside Lane's cell. He declined the offer of any reading as he had not yet finished a rather lengthy novel, which he was trying to make last as long as possible. His card partner, however, indicated that he wanted the book that the trustee's hand was still face down upon. The trustee glanced at the prisoner, who returned his gaze, and handed the book to him. Lane noticed that he took particular care to hold the book in a flat position rather than passing it over upright. He noticed it, but didn't make anything of it. His fellow card player placed the book on the table that was between them and opened it so that it was face down. This action ensured the spine was opened just far enough for him to insert his forefinger. He calmly withdrew the finger and a thin stiletto blade with it. Lane watched unmoving and stunned. He recognised the danger too late because his next moment of recognition was when, with both hands, he gripped the wrist of the hand that was holding the blade firmly in Lane's stomach and moving it up and down. The man calmly withdrew the blade and Lane looked down to see blossoming red on his shirt and ropes of entrails beginning to appear. He fell to his knees as his life ebbed away before his eyes.

His card playing opponent leaned over to whisper in his ear.

"You remember Bill Butler, from the jeweller's shop? You fitted 'im up; 'e sends 'is regards."

He died in a folded, kneeling position with his forehead to the floor and his arms wrapped tightly around his seeping stomach. His card playing opponent gathered up the cards and slowly walked out of the cell, pushing the door closed behind him. The prison officer on the landing turned his back and strolled away to get a cup of tea. It was, after all, time for his break.

That afternoon the card player sat opposite a woman at visiting time. He confirmed Lane's demise and the visitor smiled. She rose from her seat, confirmed the reward that had been arranged and left.

Leanne Lane did not shed any tears as she drove away. If you want a job doing properly, she mused, it's better to do it yourself.

-28-

John Lomax and Ray Quinn greeted each other warmly. There was years of mutual respect and liking between the two men and they expressed it with a firm handshake. No hugging for these two.

"I don't think words can express how much you have done for us," said Lomax.

"It's not necessary," replied Quinn. "We did what had to be done. Don't forget Barbara played her part as well."

"I know," said Lomax, "nevertheless without your planning and contacts we would be in a real mess. I won't ask how you managed to get Billy over here and back to Australia in such a short time. Best I don't know."

"I agree," said Quinn. "There is something that's worrying me, though."

"What's that?"

"You know me well enough by now, so please don't take this the wrong way. Lane's death in prison was nothing to do with me. I was satisfied to help Billy's plan to get him arrested and rot in jail and am sure that would have been enough for you as well. Certainly, Billy didn't want to kill his own father, and I can understand that. It was Leanne's idea and her plan to have him expire in jail. To all intents and purposes, it's a case of revenge by somebody he upset in his work. Nobody is going to spend too much time investigating it, so I think she's safe. I'm told there will be a cursory investigation and then the file will be closed, buried somewhere and lost in the mists of time. There's no good publicity to be had for the police to open it up at any time, either. What worries me, John, is that Leanne felt able to do it at all.

"What do you mean?" asked Lomax, who was listening intently to his old friend.

"Well, John, let's me put it this way. How safe do you feel? How far do you trust her? Is she on a revenge mission to deal with men who she thinks have wronged her? I know you are in love with her, but that can be very dangerous."

"What wrong could she possibly believe of me?" said Lomax in disbelief.

"I don't know," replied his friend. "You may not have caused her any harm at all, but it's what people believe for themselves that counts in life. Take a look at this," he said handing over a piece of paper.

"What's this?"

"It's a copy of a list, written by Lane. It's his checklist of unfinished business. Leanne gave it to me, and I know she has her own copy. Why would she want to keep it, if not to see whether there is anything that needs doing that she hadn't already thought of for herself?"

John Lomax read the list in silence.

1/. Find John Lomax's money. Perhaps use Karen Lomax for this.

2/. Find a way to ensure Karen's silence permanently. Not such a shrinking violet.

3/. *Find his fugitive wife, Judith. And then?*

4/. *Find his son, Billy. And then?*

5/. *Decide what to do about Leanne.*

6/. *Deal with Barbara.*

7/. *Conclude matters with Lomax.*

8/. *Settle Ray Quinn.*

John Lomax maintained the silence as he went through the list again. He looked at his friend with worried eyes.

"I see what you mean," he said. "Let's go through this. The first one talks about finding my money and using Karen to do so. Why would Leanne want to find my money, when she is well looked after anyway?"

"She might be better off financially if she had it all to herself, though."

"I suppose," Lomax said, "but I can't see how she could get at it without getting rid of me....." He stopped when he realised what he was saying, before continuing, "and how could she use Karen to help her? The second item mentions finding a way to ensure Karen's silence. Obviously, if she's used Karen then she would have to ensure her silence. Next, why would she need to find Judith?"

"Hold on a minute!" exclaimed Lomax. Leanne has already seen Judith. She told me she visited her when she was in Australia to talk to Billy. Two birds with one stone, she said."

"Oh shit," said Quinn.

"Then the list mentions finding Billy. We'll she's already found him."

"Actually, I helped her with that," admitted Ray Quinn. "It wasn't difficult."

"We can leave out number 5, which is about dealing with herself."

"No," said Quinn. "That's perhaps the most important one. Sure it was written by Sandy Lane, for his own use, but she might apply it to herself. I think it may prompt her to think deeply about what she does with her own future for herself."

"OK, point taken," replied Lomax. "The next one is about dealing with Barbara. What connection could there be there?"

"I don't know," said Quinn, "but Leanne could no doubt come up with something. Leave that for a moment. It's the last two that worry me more. They concern dealing with you and I."

"Hmm," was all Lomax could manage as he wrestled with his thoughts.

The two friends continued their deliberations for almost two more hours. By the time they had finished they had settled on an overall plan, which was flexible enough to react to any situation they could predict.

The first part of their grand plan was for Ray Quinn, the Biker, to take a holiday. Lomax had argued that he certainly deserved a break, having dealt with the annoying customer by "having a quiet word", then making sure it was business at the shop during John and Leanne's cruise and there had been many other behind the scenes activities as well.

Ray Quinn and his wife decided to take the opportunity of staying at The White Horse Inn at Exford in the heart of Exmoor. Ray and John had recognised the connection, because it was where Lane and Judith had once stayed. It wouldn't hurt to go there, relax, and at the same time dig up any information that they could.

They used their bikes and travelled in brilliant sunshine. One behind the other the A358 from Taunton took them towards Minehead for a few miles before turning onto a minor road. This wound its meandering way through the countryside for over ten miles and Quinn and his wife were in their element. They eventually passed through Wheddon Cross and five miles later caught their first sight of their destination at about 3pm. The White Horse Inn, covered in Virginia Creeper, is a 16th century building which nestles by a bridge over the river Exe. Ray Quinn was impressed and understood why Lane had been so attracted to it. They booked in and were shown to their room, which was in The Lodge. Their room was large and had patio doors to its own private garden.

"I'll unpack," said his wife.

"Ok," said Ray, "I'll be back soon."

Five minutes later he re-entered the room, walked through to the garden and placed a bottle of good red wine with two glasses on the table. The unpacking was left for later as they settled down in the sunshine and listened to the babbling river Exe wending its way close by. Bliss!

After relaxing for the rest of the afternoon, Ray showered, changed and wandered towards the bar. His wife would join him about an hour later for dinner. It was an arrangement that suited them both. Ray was particularly taken by the vast choice of over 150 malt whiskies. More bliss. He tasted several during his stay and vowed to return to continue his research. Evening meals were taken in the restaurant and were a five course affair. They never failed to live up to their billing and were served by warm hearted, attentive staff. All in all, Ray decided that he was rather taken by the place and would definitely return as soon as possible. Every other guest in the inn said the same, and many had been returning for a good number of years.

During their stay Ray and his wife treated themselves to a guided morning's "safari", which involved being bounced around in an old Land Rover for the best part of three hours and proved to be great fun as well as interesting. They were taken to places on Exmoor that people normally don't get to see, but Ray longed for the comfort of his own bike's saddle, as his rear end became increasingly numb as the morning progressed. The painful side of the experience was soon forgotten, however, as they tucked into a sumptuous a delicious cream tea, taken in the sunshine by the river at the front of the inn. The pace was slow and lazy and just what Ray Quinn needed. They explored the coastline for themselves and even ventured out on horseback. Although a

Lomax & The Biker – The Trilogy

seasoned biker and therefore accustomed to being in the saddle, Ray found this experience unsettling, not only because he was still sore from the safari, but also because he much preferred being in control of his own destiny as opposed to his fate being left to the mood or whim of a powerful animal. His wife, however, loved it and so he bore it with quiet fortitude for her sake. He was, however, horrified when she declared that she might like to have a horse of her own. They spent an afternoon at Dunster Country Fair, which began as a Donkey Derby and has grown ever since. Ray was quite gratified when some people showed interest in their bikes, believing them to be part of the items on display. He could have made a small fortune giving rides that day.

All good things must end, so Ray and his wife found themselves lingering over yet another magnificent breakfast, putting off their inevitable departure. They vowed to return, and reluctantly pointed their bikes in the direction of home.

The all too short break had breathed life and energy back into a tired man. He had not discovered anything he hadn't known previously about Lane but had decided against being too open in his digging around because it was obviously a small community there, and his interest may well have been viewed as suspicious. Best left alone he told himself.

Lomax & The Biker – The Trilogy

-29-

Virtually as soon as they arrived home, John Lomax phoned and said he had managed to get tickets to a show in London, for the four of them. Quinn knew from the tone in his friend's voice that something important had come up. Lomax indicated that he needed to talk to Quinn alone, and be seen to be doing so. They arranged that they would have the conversation during the show's interval, whilst Leanne and Ray's wife chatted together. The show was actually quite good. Stand up comedy is a difficult and some say disappearing art. Feedback from the audience is instant and crucial and audiences expect a stand-up comic to provide a steady stream of laughs, and the performer is under pressure to deliver. For the comedian it can be both thrilling and threatening at the same time. Will Ferrell called it "hard, lonely, and vicious." Most people find it difficult to remember jokes, but Lomax and Quinn remembered some during the first break and all four of them were lost in their own world for fifteen minutes or so. Leanne and Quinn's wife decided to return to their seats early. Lomax and Quinn stayed where they were and Lomax ended the cheery banter immediately.

"Ray, I wanted to talk to you before we're disturbed. I have some information we need to discuss. While I tell you, take a look round and make sure the young woman in the corner behind me is listening. She is acting for my ex, Karen, I think. I believe Karen was helping Lane and now that he's dead I'm just not sure what she might do. She could be dangerous."

"Ok," replied Quinn, quickly locating the woman in question. She met his eye, so he favoured her with an appreciative smile before returning his attention to his friend. "She's there; very pretty actually."

"I know," said Lomax. "If you could behave yourself for a moment it might help."

"Just making sure she's paying attention," replied Quinn, enjoying himself now.

The next section of the show wasn't as entertaining, so Lomax and Quinn decided to go to the bar, to be joined by the ladies later. They failed to notice another woman sat in the shadows watching them, also trying to listen to their conversation. Her name was Judith Lane. She had come back from Australia after having been visited by Leanne. Although set up with a new and comfortable life there, she had been persuaded to return to England to help Leanne. Gradually Leanne was organising her forces and they were formidable. Apart from herself, she had recruited Judith Lane, Karen Lomax and Barbara (from the cruise). The pretty young woman was from an agency. Much as Lane had identified an agenda, so she had set out her own ambitions and they weren't so very much different from Lane's list on that piece of paper.

1/. Find John Lomax's money. Perhaps use Karen Lomax for this. Leanne saw no reason to spend the rest of her life in thrall to Lomax. He was certainly besotted with her, and treated her well, but she knew he did not really trust her, nor she him. She needed to be independent. She would use his ex, Karen, because she certainly had all manner of reasons for revenge.

2/. *Find a way to ensure Karen's silence; permanently.* Not such a shrinking violet.

Once Karen had served her purpose, Leanne intended to ensure her silence.

3/. *Find his fugitive wife, Judith. And then?* This item, for Leanne, meant *find Lane's fugitive wife.* That had proved remarkably simple and she had paid her a visit whilst she had been in Australia to see Billy. It had been an easy task to persuade her to return to England as part of her grand plan.

4/. *Find his son, Billy. And then?* Again, that had been easy. Billy had been a surprise, however, in that he had not completed the agreed task. Leanne had been forced to make alternative arrangements to deal with DCI Lane. It meant, therefore, that Billy could not be trusted and she would need to consider what to do about that. It made her uncomfortable because he was her son. Could she afford to leave him out of the plan and allow him to live his new life in Australia?

5/. *Deal with Barbara.* Barbara knew that Lomax had witnessed her murdering Margaret on the cruise, so she would have a very powerful reason for getting rid of Lomax. Barbara would want that loose end tied up.

7/. *Conclude matters with Lomax.* Did that have to mean his death? She had grown close to him, but wasn't sure whether what she felt was love. She didn't actually know what love is, but she told herself that very few people have ever solved that conundrum.

8/. *Settle Ray Quinn.* Leanne knew this would probably be the most difficult task. He was a man who was the best friend possible, but the worst enemy anybody could ever have. She would have to be very careful with him.

John Lomax looked at his friend Ray Quinn, and spoke in a hushed tone.

"We have a problem. I happen to know that Leanne has recently had a meeting with Judith Lane, Karen Lomax and Barbara. A representative from a certain agency was also there. I know this because I have been unsure about Leanne for a little while and arranged to have her watched. Please don't be offended, but I didn't ask you to do it, because some of the women concerned would have recognised you."

Quinn made no overt reaction, apart from a couple of nods of his head. He then replied, loudly enough for the young woman from the agency to hear, "I understand. Leave it with me. Perhaps it's time for me to have a little word."

He rose from his seat and walked towards the young woman, smiling at her. He whispered something in her ear, took her hand and they left the building together.

Lomax explained to Quinn's wife that he was dealing with some unexpected business and that he would take her home. Ray would be back before very long. He made sure Leanne heard his message, and noticed that she turned pale.

Judith Lane had to choose between following Quinn and the young woman and trying to speak to Leanne. She chose the wrong option.

"Please don't be alarmed," said Quinn to the young woman. "I just wanted to have a little chat outside in the fresh air. There are far too many people inside."

The young woman's initial relaxed demeanour changed as she became aware that she had been brought to a place where nobody could see them.

"I carry a spray!" she said, suddenly tense and alert.

"Please," soothed Quinn, "I mean you no harm. I just want a little chat and then I'll take you back inside or wherever else you would like to go." His voice was a mixture of melting honey and warm molasses, and it had the desired effect. "You seem to have taken rather an interest in my friend and I, and I'd just like to know why. We've never met, I don't know you and yet you only had eyes and ears for us back there."

"I don't know what you mean," she replied, trying to bluff her way out of the situation.

"Please don't insult my intelligence," Ray Quinn said firmly. "I know what I saw. You are not the police or you would have shown me a badge by now. Nor are you any form of official security, because we have no need to be followed. My friend and I have nothing to hide, but we don't like what you are up to. I'll ask you once, politely, to stop. Go back to whoever you are working for and say that there is nothing to report."

"I can't. She won't believe me," the young woman said all too hurriedly.

"I thought so," said Quinn. "Well, go back to Leanne and ask her what happened to a customer who once took too much interest in a certain jeweller's business. She won't know the details, but she will know the outcome. It will be enough to persuade you to walk away from whatever you are involved in. Believe me, she's not paying you anywhere near enough."

The young woman from a certain agency felt a terrible fear wash over her as she looked into his eyes and saw a steely menace the like of which she had never seen in her young life. She hoped never to see it again as Quinn hailed her a taxi and put her inside.

"Hello, Judith," he said, turning to the shadows. "I trust you heard all that. It beats me why people get themselves involved with things they shouldn't. I do hope that your return from Australia is purely social. I treated you well the only time we previously met, so I hope you remember that kindness. If you've run out of money, perhaps we could help, but apart from that I can't see why you're here."

There was no sound from the shadows as Judith held her breath and tried not to be there. Ray Quinn was far too good for that, however.

"Judith, Judith, Judith, what am I to do? You follow me outside, listen to a private conversation and then insult me by pretending to not even be there. You could have chosen to do anything, but you followed me here. That was the wrong choice. I don't like being followed and my patience is wearing thin, so, tell me, what's going on?"

Judith made no sound. Hers was not a world of subterfuge and danger, and she was, in truth, too afraid to move. Ray Quinn shot out his arm and clamped her wrist in a vice like grip. He dragged her from her hiding place with no apparent effort and held her arm tight. She let out an involuntary yelp, like a startled puppy, and found herself looking into the same steely eyes that had so frightened the young woman from a certain agency.

It took Ray Quinn a little under ten minutes to persuade Judith Lane to catch the next available flight back to Australia. He was even kind enough to accompany her to collect her belongings, help her pack and take her to the airport in a taxi. Along the way he arranged for a reasonable, but not exorbitant sum, to be electronically deposited in her bank account. She now had no reason to come to England again. He promised that he would give John Lomax her regards.

After he had seen her onto the plane and waited to watch it take off, he took out his mobile. He sent a simple text to his friend John:

Immediate problems resolved. Be alert. The female of the species is deadlier than the male.

He took another taxi home and apologised to his wife for his absence, who never questioned him about anything he did anyway.

-30-

"Hello," said Leanne.

"Leanne? It's Ray."

"Oh. Hello. Sorry I didn't recognise you for a minute. My mind was on something else. John's not here, he's at the shop if you want him."

I bet it was, thought Ray Quinn. "It's you I want, actually. I know he's at the shop. I think we need to talk, but not on the phone. How about lunch today? Say 12.30. I'll pick you up."

"I don't know," she stalled, trying to fathom what was happening. "I've got things I need to do."

"Do them later."

"Oh, that sounds ominous. Do I have a choice?"

"Not really."

"Will John be joining us?"

"No."

"Ray, you're scaring me. What's the matter? Has something bad happened?"

"Not on the phone. There's nothing to worry about. Pick you up at 12.30."

Leanne disconnected the phone and sat down. She had suddenly gone light-headed and began to perspire. She knew Ray's concept of *'nothing to worry about'* was not the same as that of other people. He didn't seem to worry about anything, he just dealt with things as they happened and she had never known him to be troubled by anybody or any situation. Usually, it was other people who had to do the worrying, as she was doing now.

"John? It's me. I've made the arrangement. I'll let you know when it's over. Don't worry, she won't be harmed, maybe frightened a little. It's just as we agreed; a lesson in the error of her ways and an indication of her best way forward."

"Ok, Ray. Thanks. I'll be here at the shop for the rest of the day, then I'll go home as normal." He disconnected.

John Lomax knew he could rely on his friend, but he also recognised that Ray Quinn was the master of the understatement. When Quinn said *'maybe frightened a little'* he knew it was akin to a doctor telling you that you'll only feel a little scratch as it feels like he has stabbed in the needle with all the force he can muster and then forced the plunger down to make sure you get the full dose. He remembered going to the doctor's once and being told that very thing and then, afterwards, the doctor telling him that he was afraid of needles himself He had believed ever since that to be a doctor you had to have a healthy mixture of sadism and masochism in your make up, tempered with a modicum of empathy of course.

The Biker knocked on Leanne's door at precisely 12.30. He had never got rid of the need for exactitude and punctuality that had been drummed into him when he was in the forces. Leanne opened the door and her eyes widened in disbelief. She was looking at Quinn dressed fully in his leathers, helmet in hand.

"Madam, your carriage awaits," he said with mock gallantry and stooped into an even more mocking bow. He had deliberately not told her that they would be riding his bike and was greatly satisfied and amused by her shocked reaction.

"But, I've never been on a bike."

"It's never too late to learn. It's good to have new experiences, they say."

"But....but. I'll have to go and change. I can't go on a bike in this skirt."

"I don't see why not," he replied. "Fresh air will do you good."

"No. I'll change," she said gathering her thoughts slowly. Il won't be long."

"I'll be outside on the bike," he said as the door was pushed closed in front of him.

It took her only ten minutes to change into something she thought more suitable for a bike ride. When she stepped through her front door, the leather clad figure handed her a helmet and gestured for her to sit behind him. She managed to sit, albeit with some difficultly, and circled her arms around his waist as the bike moved away. Her grip tightened as the bike accelerated up the road and she turned her head to lay it sideways on his back. She closed her eyes as the speed increased even more and prayed for the first time in her life. She was terrified.

She clung on for dear life as the bike leaned at horrific angles through blind bends and shot over bridges at hair-raising speeds. Leanne began to cry out for him to slow down or stop before she fell off, but he took no notice. She was so frightened that she actually wet herself and the tears ran down her cheeks in an ever increasing flood. Still he didn't slow down or stop. She reached a point where she no longer cared whether she lived or died. She prayed, whispering to herself as she had as a small girl and believed she would soon meet her maker.

The ride lasted over four eye popping, bone crushing hours. She was a quivering wreck long before the bike pulled back into the drive in front of the house. She hadn't met her maker, but she had been close. She couldn't move even after the bike had stopped. Her arms remained firmly locked in a deathly grip around his waist.

"Would you like to let go now?"

She didn't hear the words at first because they came from behind her, not from the man she was clinging to.

"Leanne, you're home. Did you enjoy the ride?"

She felt strong fingers prising her arms from around his waist and she was lifted from the seat. Ray Quinn bent to whisper softly in her ear as the helmet was removed. "Lovely scenery. I always enjoy that route. Shame I couldn't take you on it today, but I had other, more urgent, things to do. You might like to thank Frank here. He's a good rider, don't you think. Bit careless at times on bends, but he's still here, so I suppose he's got to be good."

Leanne fainted as she took in the words and realised what had happened.

"Thanks, Frank. Hope you had a good time. Not often you get a good looking woman clinging round your waist, eh?"

"Unfortunately not," agreed Frank, as he looked at the stricken female form on the floor. "I must be off. Hope that was what you wanted."

"Perfect," replied Ray Quinn. "I'll take it from here."

Quinn lifted Leanne gently as his friend shot into the road with a roar. He took her into the house, pushing the front door open with his foot, and then closed again behind him. It was not locked because he had spent the previous four hours there conducting a very thorough search. Lomax had agreed to the idea because it would prove once and for all whether Leanne could really be trusted.

"John? She's back. I think the ride took her breath away. She's sleeping at the moment. You will find no trace of me having been here. I'll leave her on the couch. I'm afraid she had a small toiletry accident, though, and she'll be embarrassed about it, but you can't make omelettes without breaking eggs. I'll see you at the shop tomorrow to go through what I've found. Be careful, my friend. Don't let anybody tell you the female is weaker than the male. Have you ever tried to get the duvet back during the night? Impossible."

Ray Quinn disconnected. He took a last look at the comatose Leanne and slipped out, pulling the front door locked behind him. He walked up the road a few hundred yards to retrieve his bike from its hiding place.

-31-

"I'm afraid you're going to have to face facts. This is going to get a great deal nastier before it gets any better. You won't get off this thing unless you hire me. I'm the best option you've got."

Billy Lane looked at the man and asked, "what are my options?"

"As I just said, I am your best option," replied the barrister named Anthony Warren, and he leaned back in the old oak chair and looked down at the arm, noticing the peeling varnish. "If you have ever been inclined to pray, I think it would be a good idea to start now."

The handcuffs rattled just a little as Billy Lane lifted his hands and rubbed his earlobe. Warren had met Billy only four hours earlier and he must have rubbed it at least a dozen times.

"I'm not religious," said Billy, "I don't pray."

"Well, you ought to start now and be thankful to God that I'm here. This is the end of the road."

"I've always got Mr Unwin," said Billy.

"Yes, you can stick with him if you want to end up doing more time than you may already be heading for. He has a nasty habit of getting his clients more prison time than they deserve." Warren looked down at his hand made Italian shoes and brushed a speck of dust from the lapel of his immaculate suit. "I don't mind, if that's what you want. I have plenty of work at the moment."

"It's just that he's been representing me since I was arrested, five months ago. He knows my case."

"Keep him then," responded Warren.

"Are you saying you're better than him? Is that what you're saying?" asked Billy. "How can I sack him? He's been good to me so far."

"Well, that's part of your problem. He's good to everybody no matter whose side they are on. He has a history of sitting on the fence rather than going all out to defend his clients. That's why you're in deep trouble."

Billy felt he was being pushed into a corner and did not like it, so he decided to fight back. "Just who says you are so good? Convince me."

Anthony Warren, Barrister, calmly regarded his potential client with the lasers that ordinary people call eyes. He pondered for a time, considering which of the long list of successful cases he should quote. He decided against getting into an auction. "There is no one better than me," he said, his sizzling gaze never wavering.

"But the trial begins tomorrow," said Billy Lane. Surely that's too short notice for you to prepare, apart from anything else."

"I am fully prepared already. I won't need to have a sleepless night going through it all. I've spent the last four days on it."

"Four days!" exclaimed Billy, again rubbing his earlobe and combining it this time with a confused blink. This was their first meeting, so why would Warren have spent the past four days studying the case? Warren didn't bother to explain. It was not his policy to explain anything to anybody unless it became absolutely necessary. In his experience life turned out better that way.

"I can't pay the sort of fees you charge, Mr Warren," Billy said. I can't even pay Mr Unwin's fees."

"I know," replied Anthony Warren. "I also know Mr Unwin is unaware of that at the moment, so he won't be happy when he finds out. Rest assured I do not ever work for free, Billy. Mr John Lomax is footing the bill. I believe you are familiar with him. I've had a meeting with him and his advisor, a Mr Raymond Quinn, and they both seem genuinely interested in making sure you get the best defence possible."

"But why would he do this for me?" Billy was struggling to make sense of it all.

"Because he thinks there is some hope for you; because he has helped you before, and you have responded in an appropriate way towards him; because you took his advice to start afresh in Australia, although I understand Mr Quinn also helped you make your decision about that."

"So, Billy, what are you going to do?"

Billy, young as he was, wanted to understand more." Why should I employ you, a barrister, as opposed to Mr Unwin, who is I believe a reputable solicitor and knows the case inside out?"

Anthony Warren let out a frustrated sigh and decided to break his usual habit and give a detailed explanation.

"A barrister, also called a Barrister-at-Law or Bar-at-Law, is a member of one of the two classes of lawyer found in many common jurisdictions with split legal professions. Barristers specialise in courtroom advocacy, drafting legal pleadings, and giving expert opinions. They can be contrasted with solicitors, who are the other class of lawyer in split professions and have more direct access to clients, and may do transactional type legal work. Barristers are rarely hired by clients directly but instead are retained or instructed by solicitors to act on behalf of clients. The historical difference between the two professions, and the only essential difference in England and Wales these days, is that solicitors are attorneys, which means they can act in the place of their client for legal purposed (as in signing contracts, for example) and may conduct litigation on their behalf by making applications to the court, writing letters in litigation to the client's opponent, and so on. A barrister is not an attorney and is normally forbidden from conducting litigation. This means that, whilst the barrister speaks on the client's behalf in court, he or she can only do so when instructed by a solicitor, or certain other qualified professional clients. There, aren't you glad you asked?"

Billy's eyes had glazed over after the first two sentences of Warren's explanation, but he was savvy enough to recover by the end. "So you would need to be instructed to act for me by my solicitor?"

"Exactly," said Warren. "You were listening after all." He could not resist the last patronising comment.

"Well, if we do this there's something you have to know, "said Billy, scraping his chair closer to Warren, who held up an admonishing finger.

"You're going to tell me a secret. Correct? You are innocent and did not have anything to do with the death of your father or your mother's part in it. Correct? It's all a big mistake. Correct?"

"No. I wasn't going to say any of that." Billy looked uneasily at Warren. "I was going to say that my father visited me in Australia and asked me to kill my mother and then my mother also came to Australia to ask me to kill my father. I had to make a choice. I chose to kill neither, but I made sure my father went to prison for his long list of evil crimes. I'm sure you're familiar with all this anyway. I'm also sure my mother arranged for my father to be killed in jail, but I had nothing to do with that. I was back in Australia by the time that happened. The other thing I'm sure about is that it's my mother who is behind me being arrested, brought here and charged with being an accessory to my father's murder. I didn't do what she wanted, so she's getting her own back. Hell has no fury and all that."

"Did you visit your father in prison on your short trip to England?"

"No," replied Billy. "I couldn't face it."

"Well, the prison records say that you did. They've got your signature."

"My mother must have done that. Perhaps she visited the prison and forged my signature."

Warren made no response to this conjecture. He contented himself with regarding Billy at great length, slowly dissecting his very soul piece by piece.

"What you couldn't face, Billy, was being seen as a failure by your mother. You arranged to return, set up your father's murder in prison, even visited him there, probably mentally saying goodbye for the last time. You also saw another prisoner whilst you were there and the instructions were given then."

"That's nonsense. I don't know who's been feeding you this rubbish."

"I'm taking the line that the prosecution will forward. We'll have to come up with something much better than saying it's nonsense and rubbish."

Billy rubbed his earlobe again.

"Listen, Billy. This case looks from the outside as a stone cold certainty. Everybody knows you did it and the evidence is pretty convincing. The prosecution are looking for a very long sentence. That's the future."

"I'll tell you what I think," said Billy, "I think you're the one who cannot lose out of all this. You get yourself hired for an expensive fee, do the trial and leave. If you get me off you'll be a celebrity for winning a hopeless case. If we lose, nobody worries because that's what is expected and I end up in jail. You get paid either way."

"Let's stop fencing, Billy. Mr Lomax and his advisor have hired me to help you at no little cost. They've helped you before, so you know you can trust them."

Billy had not had an upbringing to give him much experience of trust, so he had no benchmarks upon which to rely. He wished he could fall back on faith, but that had not featured either. He was totally at a loss as to what to do. In the end he made a decision based upon pure gut instinct. He had not particularly taken to the arrogance of this man, but finally reasoned that if Lomax and Quinn had pinned their colours to his mast, then so could he.

He rubbed his earlobe again and said "Ok, Mr Warren, but don't let me down. My life is in your hands."

Anthony Warren spent the remaining time before the beginning of Billy's trial learning everything he could about the judge who would be sitting, the prosecution team and, of course, the facts of the case. He viewed it all as a battle or a game of chess. Each person, each fact, every nuance of expression was an important part of the whole. He spent a good deal of time draining the solicitor, Mr Unwin, of every last drop of information. By the end of the session, Unwin felt utterly drained; emptied of all life. He had been forensically dissected by a superior mind and had not in any way enjoyed the experienced. Warren methodically and thoroughly went through police and prison reports, evidence from anybody who was likely to feature in the trial and a report from Ray Quinn, which gave much useful background detail to Billy's life and his relationships with his mother and father. He had also given Quinn another task, and looked forward to the result.

He had been ensconced in a rather expensive hotel in London, courtesy of Lomax of course. He had enjoyed a rather fine evening meal before going to his room to settle to work. He was enjoying himself and allowed a smile to pass his lips, while he called room service for fresh coffee. He let his mind wander through the labyrinth planning for battle, while Billy Lane lay fitfully on a hard bench in a cell unable to sleep, despite his exhaustion and worry, and Leanne Lane slept peacefully in the belief that she was about to delete another item from her list.

Warren arrived at court early, as he always did and sat, immaculately dressed as the court filled with witnesses, press and other interested parties. The public gallery was, he noted, crammed full. He was particularly pleased to note the presence of so many members of the press. He planned to manipulate them later. He turned his attention to Leanne Lane, who sat alongside John Lomax. He was slightly unnerved by the way she stared at him. It was the first time he had ever come across anybody who could make him uneasy in that way and it troubled him. John Lomax gave no sign of recognition as Leanne had not been told of the backing Billy was receiving from Lomax and Quinn. He was, however, pleased also to note that Ray Quinn was not present. He realised in those fleeting moments of eye contact that the whole thing was personal, and it made it far easier to do what he was about to do. He locked eyes with Leanne again, the electricity sparking between them.

A door opened and the clerk announced the arrival of the judge, making sure everybody rose in acknowledgement and respect. Warren had instructed Billy to avoid rubbing his earlobe, but it was the first thing that happened and it annoyed the barrister.

The prosecution barrister presented the forensic evidence surrounding DCI Sandy Lane's death first and Anthony Warren spent some time chipping away at it just for the sake of being seen to do something, rather than having spotted any flaws or weaknesses. Various prison officers were called and gave evidence, including the Governor, and then each and every police officer who had been involved in any capacity was questioned. It was a long and painstaking process and took several days. Warren made sure he asked each person at least one telling question as he wanted, needed, to sew doubt in the mind of each juror. Finally, Leanne Lane was called to the stand. She stood up, straightened her skirt and walked with a confidence she didn't feel. She subconsciously fiddled with her ring as she was guided by the prosecution's pedestrian questions to give an account of her relationship with her son, Billy. This was intended to portray a background that the jury could hang on to, with her coming across as a caring person and loving mother. As an example of this she recounted some information about a parent's evening at Billy's school. She always attended these as she believed it important to show support for her son. She pointed out that her ex husband, Billy's father, Sandy Lane, was always too busy to attend and Billy felt terribly let down by that. She therefore had a double reason for attendance as she wanted to make up for his lack of paternal support on such occasions.

At one particular such consultation, the Headmaster had addressed the assembled throng of parents and, amongst other things, made the point, very strongly, that it was crucial that students attend all lessons. When he had finished his speech, he asked if there were any questions. Leanne had put up her hand (which made her recall her schooldays!) and waited. The Headmaster pointed to her.

"Can you please tell us all again what you said about attending lessons?"

"Certainly," beamed the Headmaster, welcoming the chance to reiterate one of his main points. It was almost as if the good woman had been primed to help him. "I firmly believe that it is crucial for students to attend all lessons."

"Thank you, Headmaster," said Leanne, "and is it also important that your staff attend all lessons as well?"

There was an audible gasp from the assembled throng, and all eyes went from Leanne to the Headmaster. Recovering quickly, he said "absolutely, Mrs Lane, it's no good the students being there without anybody to teach and guide them, is it?" He knew he had left the door wide open, but he had no choice.

"In that case, Headmaster, may I have a word with you after this meeting, please? I've got no wish to embarrass you in public."

Leanne sat down and felt her cheeks flush, but she was pleased that she had made the point. It turned out that one of Billy's teachers had not stayed at his lessons for about six weeks. He had other, managerial duties, and these had taken over. He had got into the habit of appearing at the beginning of each lesson, setting work and then disappearing for the remainder of the time. She told the story in court not only to stress her commitment to her parental obligations, but also to demonstrate that she was prepared to do difficult things for him.

Warren could see that the jury were impressed, so he wanted to redress the balance. He rose, looked at the jury, unbuttoned his immaculate dark grey suit and ran a finger slowly over his hair. When he spoke it was to the jury as well as the witness.

"The death of a human being is a terrible thing, don't you agree?"

Leanne did not know what to say, but he deliberately did not wait for her reply.

"I am so sorry that you have to be in this situation, Mrs Lane, it must be very distressing." This time he waited for her to nod affirmation before going on. "I think it would be helpful if I could ask you to help us understand the situation. You see, the whole thing is obviously unusual and somewhat complicated and, being a simple man, I need to see the wood from the trees."

The prosecution team knew this tactic for what it was. They knew that Anthony Warren, Barrister-at-Law, was very far from being a simple man and that he was trying to set Leanne at her ease, so that she might drop her guard. They had warned her about this before the trial, but she was nevertheless taken aback.

"You may know, Mrs Lane, that both your team and our side will end proceedings with summaries of our respective cases and it is then up to the jury to make decisions, with guidance from the judge." He was being deliberately polite to Leanne and also gave a respectful nod of his head to the judge. "I don't normally make my summary until absolutely necessary, but I think in this case I may make an exception."

"May we get to the point, or even a question?" demanded the prosecution barrister, rising from his seat and looking at the judge.

"Mr Warren, please," admonished the judge.

"Of course, please forgive me. My points are these. My client, Billy Lane, stands accused of being an accessory to his father's murder and, indeed, of being the prime organiser of it. The prosecution have already set out their case and, on the surface, it seems somewhat compelling. My job is to establish this not be the case. I can do that by letting this court know that you visited the prison, and I have the documents to prove it." He asked the court to refer to the particular items in the evidence bundle, which had been circulated beforehand. They showed a record of a visit by a woman named Rita Webb, to an unnamed prisoner. He paused for effect. "This woman Rita Webb had never visited the prison before then, but prison staff had become suspicious about her application to visit, because that prisoner had not had any visitor of either sex before that day. Checks were made and her false identity discovered. It was decided that the visit would be allowed to proceed and that it should be secretly recorded. Before there are any objections, all necessary permissions were sought and given and these are in our bundles."

There was a discernible rustling of paper as pages were turned and the items found. There was also a low buzz of whispering from the public gallery.

"Mrs Lane, is it not the case that this Rita Webb was in fact you? May I remind you that you are under oath and you should consider your answer with great care."

Leanne did not bat an eyelid. She didn't even look at her legal team. "No sir; this Rita Webb was not me. I have never visited that prisoner. I don't even know him; have never heard of him until now. I wanted to avoid that place at all costs because my ex husband was in there. I was content that he was there and I had no need to visit anybody in there."

Leanne's legal team fidgeted in their seats. She had been warned not to give lengthy answers and to merely answer a question with yes or no if possible They had told her it was up to the other side to elicit detail from her and she must not give them more than they asked for in any question. They pleaded with their eyes for her to stop. The jury noticed, of course, and that was what Anthony Warren was after. He had sewn a seed.

Billy Lane thought the obvious next step was to have the recording of the prison visit played to the court so that it would be obvious Leanne was the woman visitor. Warren did not choose to that. He was saving that particular delicacy for the climax of his case.

"What do you do for a living, Mrs Lane?"

Lomax & The Biker – The Trilogy

The question caught her off guard. "Well I help my partner with his business, he owns a jewellery shop and I sometimes help out there."

"When was the last time you were in the shop?" Leanne noticed that her name did not accompany this question. The gloves were coming off.

"I can't remember exactly. We've had a holiday and John's been there most days since then."

"Well, help me please, was it last week, last month, yesterday?"

"Well, it obviously wasn't yesterday because I was here at the court. It may have been last month I think."

"It's a jewellery shop, you say?"

"Yes," she replied, seeming to recall her team's instructions.

"There must be valuable items there, so there must be a safe?"

"Of course," she replied, confused as to the direction or purpose of the questions; which was to establish that she was familiar with the workings of the premises.

"So, there must be CCTV there for security." It was not a question this time, but Leanne didn't notice the subtle change.

"Yes, there is."

"Good. I suppose it is positioned to identify all visitors to the shop as well as being aimed at the counter for transactions." Again, not a question.

"I've never had anything to with that side of things," replied Leanne. John looks after all that."

"So he does, Mrs Lane. He makes a very thorough job of it too. He has provided us with the recordings for the last six months. I had my investigator go through it all. He was very thorough and only completed the task this morning. The judge has kindly ruled that it may be used as evidence, despite objection from the prosecution side."

He smiled his thanks to the judge, who had given his consent before the morning's court proceedings at a tense session in private.

"May I ask who else is employed at the shop?"

"Well, there's John and myself and John's business partner, Ray Quinn."

"And nobody else?"

"No."

"I see. So, the three of you should appear on these records often over the past six months."

"Obviously," replied Leanne, becoming more worried now.

"And, of course, customers would appear as well." Another couple of statements, posed as if they were questions.

"Yes, obviously," she repeated with more than a trace of irritation.

"So, why is it, Mrs Lane that you do not feature on any of them? Six months is a long time and you have already told the court that you helped in the shop at least once in the last month alone. John Lomax and Ray Quinn appear every day, except when you were on holiday with Mr Lomax and Mr Quinn took a short break recently. Each customer is shown very clearly. Believe me, my investigator has gone through it with a fine toothed comb, and you most definitely do not appear."

"Objection! This side has not viewed this evidence. We only learned of it this morning and although it has been allowed to be used, we must be permitted to examine it."

"Quite so," ruled the judge. "We shall adjourn until first thing on Monday morning." He rose abruptly and the room scrambled to catch up, lifting from their seats at differing speeds. One or two didn't bother to try.

Lomax & The Biker – The Trilogy

-32-

The prosecution side examined the CCTV evidence throughout the weekend. It revealed no sign of their client having set foot in the jewellery shop during the six months in question. This was a major setback for them. The other major setback was that it clearly showed DCI Sandy Lane in the shop, with other officers, and a man named Bill Butler. The prosecution team recognised immediately that the man who had been visited in prison by the woman calling herself Rita Webb was that same man. They examined the CCTV evidence of the prison visit, but nothing leapt out at them from that. They realised, however, that their case was now untenable and sought instructions. The DPP gave instructions that the case be dropped and Billy Lane walked out onto the streets of London a free man. All he wanted was to return to Australia and get as far away from England and the madness it held for him as quickly as possible. He phoned John Lomax and Ray Quinn to express his heartfelt thanks and was told that his flight ticket and belongings were waiting for him at the airport. He couldn't wait. He hailed the nearest taxi and settled back, thanking his lucky stars for his good fortune.

As for Leanne Lane, the police had to begin all over again. They thought they now knew it was she who was complicit in the murder of DCI Lane in prison and they set out to build a new case.

Anthony Warren, Barrister-at Law, thanked the court usher as he was handed an envelope. It contained a large cheque to cover his fee and expenses. He was pleased that it had been paid so promptly, but he believed he had performed well and had been well worth the large sum.

He did not take much notice of the signatory to the cheque and phoned John Lomax to thank him.

"Mr Warren, I haven't paid you anything yet, but if you call in at the shop tomorrow we can settle up."

"Mr Lomax I have your cheque here in my hand and I am phoning to thank you for your prompt payment."

He looked down at the cheque and it was only at that moment that he noticed the name on the cheque. It had been signed by a woman named Rita Webb.

"I'm sorry, Mr Lomax. I was mistaken. I will drop in tomorrow as you suggest, say about ten in the morning?"

"That will be fine, Mr Warren, and thank you again for what you have done."

Anthony Warren was not usually a man easily confused, and his puzzlement was added to when his phone buzzed again.

"Hello, Mr Warren. I hope you've received my cheque. I did not want anybody else paying for the service you have provided. You see, you've been most helpful."

"Who is this?" snapped Warren, becoming angry as he regained his focus. "The sum is correct, but I have an agreement with another party in this matter and cannot accept your payment. If you'd like to let me know where to send it back to, I'll do so immediately."

"No, Mr Warren, you should accept the money. I couldn't possibly allow anybody else to pay. I am a great believer in family looking after its own."

"But I don't even know who you are or how you are connected to this matter. How can I possibly accept your money?"

"The real question is how can you refuse to accept my payment? As I just told you family should look after its own, and that's what is happening here. I can't say more than that, but you can surely put two and two together, even a simple man such as yourself."

The penny dropped.

"You hired the best because you wanted to be sure Billy was not found guilty. So for you it's money well spent. But why did you want Billy to get off?"

The penny dropped even further.

"Where is Billy? I'd like to talk to him, please."

"I'm sorry. That isn't possible. He's a little tied up at the moment." Rita Webb, otherwise known as Leanne Lane, pulled her lipstick coated lips into a thin smile and turned to view her son.

The taxi that Billy had hailed outside the court was not a genuine London black cab, but it certainly resembled one. Billy had been fooled, taken in just at the moment of his greatest success and therefore his greatest weakness. It contained two men who had easily restrained him and then delivered him to his current place of incarceration. He had narrowly escaped prison, but he would certainly have preferred to have been there at that moment. He was bruised and his head ached from the blow that had brought the black night. He was hooded and tied to a pillar in a warehouse. He gradually became aware of others close by. He could smell perfume, in spite of his scrambled senses. He was longing to relieve his screaming muscles, but did not want to move until he was sure of who was there. He remained immobile and concentrated on calming his breathing.

"Wake him up!"

A vicious kick to the stomach made him retch and he couldn't help groaning in agony.

"It's good of you to drop in, Billy," she said. "I think we need to have a little chat." She waited until there was another sign that he was listening, but none came, so she nodded to one of the kidnappers. Billy tensed his body in expectation of another kick to the abdomen, but it didn't arrive. Instead, Billy's hands were unbound, his right arm pulled straight and a strong grip clamped itself around his wrist on a hard surface.

"Do you remember the picture of you and Judith with your hands wrapped in a bandage, Billy?" Billy was by now far too frightened to say or do anything, so did not respond. "Surely you remember. Those pictures helped to get you and Judith to Australia. Of course, neither of you had come to any harm, but they looked very realistic."

Billy began to shake as he recalled his own hand, swathed in bandages. The photo was intended to show him having lost a finger and it was scarily real.

"I remember," he mumbled at last, not daring to imagine what was about to happen.

Leanne nodded once more to her accomplices. One of them took a pair of bolt-cutters from the bench and gently caressed Billy's fingers, one by one, with the tool. Billy shuddered and nearly lost control.

"Now Billy, you obviously know what that was, so let's not waste any more time. I have no wish to harm you. I am your mother, after all."

Leanne's mobile came to life. She cursed and looked at its screen to see a withheld number.

"Mrs Lane? It's Anthony Warren. Please listen to me, before anything ghastly happens. Whatever it is that has made you take this course of action, I beg you to reconsider. People are looking for you and Billy as we speak. The police have not yet been informed, but I will have to tell them what's happening soon or I will become complicit, and I can't afford that in my job. John Lomax and Ray Quinn are searching for you both as well. I hope I can come to an arrangement with you before the police have to be involved. More importantly, for your safety, I hope Ray Quinn is not the person who gets to you first. He's capable of anything and won't hesitate to make sure Billy lives. He will kill you if he thinks it necessary, and it won't be pretty."

Leanne listened impatiently.

"Where are Lomax and Quinn now?"

"I don't know, but they know what has happened and it won't take them long."

"They don't worry me, Mr Warren and neither do you. You called me Mrs Lane at the start of this call, so you obviously think Rita Webb is me. Please leave it at that for your own sake. I don't think you want to be involved any more than you already are. Cash the cheque, enjoy the money, you earned it, but don't try to find me or stop me. It isn't worth your while. If you insist on being honest burn the cheque if it maintains your self-respect."

"Let me talk to Billy, please."

"As I said before, that won't be possible, I'm afraid. His mind is on other matters at the moment. I'll have to go now, before the call can be traced. I hope we don't need to speak again."

Leanne returned her attention to Billy, who was still being held in the same position. Leanne nodded and the bolt-cutters snapped loudly close to his hooded face. The sinister sound made Billy convulse with fear and he whimpered.

"What do you want from me?" Billy croaked, his throat dry with fear.

"I want you to understand something," Leanne replied. "You really should have done as your mother asked. I came to see you because I had no choice, and you let me down."

"I didn't let you down! I couldn't kill my own father! I still made sure the next best thing happened." Billy was almost shouting through the hood, which went in and out around his mouth as he breathed and talked.

"Oh Billy," continued Leanne, "I was always there for you when your father let you down, and he did that a lot. What did I do to deserve your disloyalty?"

"Nothing," whispered Billy. "All I wanted was a normal teenage life and I didn't get it."

"I can understand that, but why shoplifting, Billy? It's demeaning."

Billy made no reply and Leanne waited. After a full minute, which is a long time when it's being counted in your head, Leanne nodded. The bolt-cutters were slammed down onto Billy's right hand. He had no warning, but was aware of the silence and it scared him. The red hot pain took a second or two to register, but when it did it shot through his hand and up his arm. He screamed in agony and his head fell in front of him as sweat began to gather inside the hood.

"Now Billy, please don't ignore me again. You still have all your fingers, after all. I don't like this any more than you do, so let's move along as quickly as we can, shall we?"

Leanne's mobile came to life again.

"Leanne? It's John. Where are you?"

Why do people ask that question every time they use a mobile? Leanne asked herself, annoyed by this second interruption.

"Hello, John. I was going to call you later. I've just got to do something first and then I'll be home. Thank you for offering to pay for Billy's defence, but I've done it. I really wanted to do it myself. You've done enough for him already and it's only right that his mother took the responsibility."

"Leanne, I've had a call from Anthony Warren. He's very worried and told me about your discussion. If what he says is true, I beg of you, don't go through with it. We can work this out. We can get Billy back to Australia unharmed and nobody can touch us. We'll make sure the police can't chase you for anything. There are ways I can get that done and you can't. Let me help. I can dig you out of this hole. If you go through with it, I won't be able to help you."

"I'm sorry, John. I love you, really I do. You've made me so happy, but it's all gone pear shaped now."

She was not fully in control of the words that were spilling from her mouth and tears were forming at the corner of each eye. She looked at the slumped form in front of her, which was moaning and groaning with the pain.

A sudden thought struck. "Where's Ray?" If there was one person of whom she was afraid, it was Ray Quinn.

"He's not here at the moment. His mind is on other matters," he said in a sinister echo of her earlier words. "I'll give him a call and let him know you wanted him."

"No!" she almost shouted into her phone. "Thanks, but I can manage without him at the moment. Quinn himself would have been pleased with the understatement. "Now, I must go. I'll see you later. Don't worry, John, I know what I'm doing and it will all be alright." She disconnected.

Lomax & The Biker – The Trilogy

John Lomax moved the phone away from his ear and looked at it as though it could actually conjure her to be there with him. If it had been a lamp he would have rubbed it to elicit a genie. Events were moving more quickly than he had planned for and were in danger of spiralling out of control. He tapped in the number for his friend. If ever he needed him, it was now.

Lomax & The Biker – The Trilogy

-33-

As these events were unfolding, Karen Lomax was having her own problems. John and Ray had made decisions as to how to deal with her and she was about to find out what those arrangements were. She still lived in their marital home and now John took steps to get his share of its value. Anthony Warren was engaged, in addition to his other brief, to take the necessary steps. John's options were to buy her out or force her to agree to sell and liberate his share. His preferred choice was the latter because he had already spent a good deal of the proceeds of the Anvex robbery, but Karen resisted. John thought the problem would be short lived and relatively easily solved. He was wrong. She proved to be the most intractable of their difficulties.

By means of thorough and judicious research they discovered her daily habits. It was necessary to do that because they found she had altered her lifestyle, and her habits, a good deal since John had departed. She had been a mouse-like housewife in her years of marriage to Lomax, but was certainly not that now. She had transformed her looks with good quality makeovers and her wardrobe was on the expensive and classy side. She had also purchased a computer and had taken to social networking and online dating. She knew the dangers, but loved the thrill of the unknown. Once Ray had found that out, the way to her demise was obvious. He did not need, however, to take any action at all.

Depression is a state of low mood and aversion to activity that may affect thought, behaviour, feelings and self esteem. Depressed people can have feelings of self pity, hopelessness, worry, helplessness, guilt, hurt and worthlessness. The worst cases may contemplate suicide. In Karen's case it was a reaction to the life changing event of her marriage breakdown. She had battled to overcome the problem and the changes she had made seemed to have helped, but they only made her difficulties worse. This was because her new life style could never be a replacement for what she had lost. Her depression deepened the more she tried to tackle it. Her doctor tried a variety of approaches, and was taking a long term view. He wasn't to know that he did not have the time to effect a significant improvement. She was found by a group of ramblers, in her car, in an overgrown copse. The post mortem pointed to an overdose. Nobody could have foreseen it, but it certainly helped John's problem. He actually arranged her funeral because there was nobody else to do so. She had made no will. Eventually the house was sold and John inherited the money. It wasn't his chosen method of obtaining the cash, but he felt he deserved a break, especially as he knew Karen had been plotting against him.

Lomax & The Biker – The Trilogy

-34-

Ray Quinn had taken the precaution of turning his mobile to silent. The last thing he needed now was a noisy interruption because he was concentrating on the CCTV from the prison. He had been doing so for a few hours and his eyes were becoming blurred. He was about to take a well earned break and get himself coffee, when he spotted something. He rewound two minutes' worth and pressed play.. There! There it was! He punched the air with a clenched fist in an uncharacteristic display of emotion. He had found Rita Webb deep in conversation with Bill Butler during her prison visit. He had turned the sound down to help him concentrate and that had worked. There before his aching eyes, Rita Webb was stroking a ring with a finger from the other hand and the ring was instantly recognisable. He had found the proof that Rita Webb was Leanne Lane.

He immediately phoned his old friend. After a few minutes they came to a conclusion.

"Ok, John, then that's what I'll do. I'll try to make sure she has a way out at the same time. Can I be frank with you?"

"You know you can, Ray. I'd be offended if you weren't."

"Well, John, my friend, I have to say that I can't see how we can save Billy, get him to Australia and end up with a situation in which you and Leanne can be together. She may have already gone too far. I can swing it with my contact at the Met to make sure she doesn't stand trial or go to jail, but I may not be able to do much more than that. There will also be some collateral damage, but I can't be sure about that until it happens."

"I don't care about anybody else. If you can keep her safe from arrest and get Billy away that will be a result. You know I love her, but it's really up to her now."

"I understand, John. I'll do whatever I can, but you are my priority, you know that. I'll always be in your debt."

"Thank you. I know you feel obligated, said Lomax, recalling the carnage of the 7/7 bombings in London and saving Quinn's life, "but I don't want you to be. Being firm friends is enough for me."

The conversation had been unusually long for the taciturn Quinn, who didn't like talking about emotional matters. He was much more comfortable being practical and taking action, which was what was about to happen. Ray Quinn kissed his wife gently before donning his helmet and gunning the bike's engine. She watched as he disappeared into the distance and wondered when he would return. He had always come back and always unscathed, even when in special forces. The only event that had troubled him was the London Bombings. It had changed his life. He had been badly injured and John Lomax had helped save his life. Since that day there had been an unbreakable bond between them. Since that day, Ray had taken life with a pinch of salt and nothing seemed able to worry him. He had taken up biking, loved the open road and was totally fearless. He had not yet encountered a situation he was unable to handle. He could be very persuasive and others had always come to see his point of view. Yet he was always gentle and loving with her.

She wistfully strolled back indoors, and her mind turned to happier times, but not before locking the door behind her. He had told her to do that long ago and she had maintained the habit. Locking the door seemed to jolt her mind away from happy thoughts and she sensed that there was something amiss this time. For a reason she couldn't put her finger on, Ray had been slightly different before he had departed and for the first time in her life she began to pray. Since she had married Ray he had not divulged any details of his service life to her, and she had never asked. She knew a good deal about his friendship with John Lomax, though, and the two couples had become firm friends, but she had never quite trusted Leanne. There had always been a reserve between them and somehow she knew in her heart that there was a serious problem that Ray had been asked to sort out. It troubled her and she prayed. She seemed to be doing quite a lot of praying of late and was getting comfort from it. She had never been particularly religious, but she felt something guiding her, something helping her cope with this new crisis. She also felt that Ray would be fine, but that John Lomax would not. She would have been far more worried if she had known the full extent of Leanne's treachery.

She was unaware of a woman called Barbara, whom John and Leanne had met on their cruise. She knew nothing of the fact that Barbara had committed murder on the cruise and John had witnessed it. She was also unaware of the fact that Ray knew all about that episode and had told John that Barbara was to be trusted. Had she known Ray Quinn was mistaken, she would have been even more troubled.

Quinn cut the engine, let his bike freewheel towards the gate and pulled to a halt. He put the bike on its stand to the right of the gate, where it couldn't be seen from the house. He did not remove his helmet as he strode towards the front door. He had already done his homework and knew the man of the house would be out for the rest of the day. Not that he intended to take that long.

Barbara answered her front door bell and was confronted by a biker in full leathers and a helmet. He stepped into the partially open doorway and his straight left arm pushed the door backwards with some force. Barbara had not put the safety chain on and so did not have time to react. The Biker had banked on the fact that Barbara had not engaged the safety chain, because he had timed his entrance for barely a minute after her husband's car had pulled out of the driveway. She had answered the doorbell assuming her husband had forgotten something. Barbara was flung across the hall and came to a halt with her back to a mirror. The Biker's image was reflected to make it appear as though there were two such figures in the hall. She saw a gloved forefinger raised upright in an instruction for her to be quiet, which silenced her inevitable scream. The finger then pointed towards the kitchen and the intruder's posture brooked no argument.

Lomax & The Biker – The Trilogy

Barbara was forced to sit on a stool at her breakfast bar. The Biker had still not spoken a word and Barbara opened her mouth to speak. This caused the Biker to clamp his hand over her mouth and the same forefinger to be raised again in the universal signal for quiet. The helmet shook to show that she must remain silent. Barbara was not a woman normally cowed by much, she had after all forced another human being to her death from a cruise ship, but the Biker certainly frightened her. There was just something intense and menacing about this figure, which was exactly what The Biker intended. He knew that people are frightened by what they don't understand and can't communicate with. The helmet and the full leathers were sinister enough, but the silence and aggressive demeanour doubled the effect.

The Biker pulled at a zip on his chest and produced an A4 sized envelope. It was sealed and had no writing or markings at all and was placed carefully on the work surface in front of Barbara. The Biker waited for her to pick it up. She looked at it, uncertain what she should do. After another silence she picked it up and, with trembling fingers, prised it open. She found photographs. Before taking them out, she looked at the figure which had now risen and was standing behind her looking over her shoulder.

He watched as she studied the images before her. They told a story of her life, from adolescence to the present day. They depicted all the things in her life that she would prefer to be kept secret. We all have things that we want to keep from everybody else and there are more of them as we progress with age. The only way to keep a secret, the only stone cold certain way, is to not tell a soul. Barbara saw before her, images of things she had never ever told a living soul about. She was shaken to her core. The final item was a sheet of paper upon which she saw some words.

Secrets and lies.

Yours to keep. Copies, I'm afraid. Originals are safe and won't be used unless......

You think you can keep secrets, so prove it. Never go anywhere near Lomax, Leanne or Quinn again. Never contact them, never even brush past them accidently.

You have finally found the love of your life. Don't make us make him disappear. It would have been very easy this morning, and will be easy at any time.

Don't be greedy. Keep what you've got.

Secrets and lies.

The Biker put his hand upon her shoulder and squeezed. In normal circumstances it would be a comforting gesture, but on this occasion it held menace. It was also asking a question. Barbara exhaled heavily. She knew there was no choice, so she nodded her compliance. The helmet nodded its satisfaction and the leather clad figure silently withdrew from the house. Barbara held the envelope close to her chest and closed her eyes. She had been planning to blackmail Lomax as he had witnessed Margaret's violent demise at sea, but she now realised that she would have to forget the idea. There comes a time in everybody's life when enough is enough. There had not been the need for even one word.

-35-

Leanne turned her attention back to the crumpled figure and smiled. Billy had made no sound for some time, so she decided to nod again. Her phone buzzed at exactly that moment and saved Billy from more pain.

"Hello, Leanne."

"Hello Ray." She was not in the mood for small talk and wanted to get him off the line as soon as possible, but she asked the inevitable question. "Where are you?"

"Oh I am so close." He wanted to gauge her reaction. There was silence between them and he knew she would have to speak next. He let the silence linger and do its work.

"Have you heard from John?" She was fishing now.

"Yes."

"So you'll know that everything is alright." She waited for a response to this hopeful statement. She desperately needed to make sure he did not interfere. She thought she could manipulate John, especially as he displayed all the signs of being besotted with her. She had made doubly sure of that on the cruise and he seemed putty in her hands. Quinn, however, was altogether another matter. She knew he was a good and loyal friend but a dangerous enemy. Still no response came from Ray Quinn and Leanne cracked first.

"Sorry, I thought you said something."

"No, I didn't." Quinn smiled to himself as he recognised the signs of her becoming more and more edgy.

"Look Ray," she finally volunteered, "I've spoken to John and I'll be with him later. Everything's Ok, so I honestly don't know what you want."

Ray smiled to himself again. He knew that people repeat things when they are trying be convincing and the use of the word "honestly" is always a giveaway. He decided to use his favourite phrase. "I'd like to have a word with you." So few words, so much meaning.

A low, desperate, distant moaning sounded through his phone.

"Oh-oh, I think I need to go," said Leanne. Can we talk later?"

"No, Leanne, we must talk now." Quinn showed no sign of having heard Billy's moan.

"I'm busy at the moment, Ray. I'm spending some time with Billy before he goes back to Australia."

"Quality time; that's good, Leanne," His words dripped with sarcasm. "Actually I need to see him as well before he goes. Just for ten minutes or so, I won't impose," he lied.

"Ray, please. Why don't you pick up Billy and take him to the airport? I'll come with you and we can have a chat on the way back."

There was silence as Ray made her sweat. He kept the line open, listening for any more moans or groans. He was not, however, doing nothing. The phone call was useful because it meant Leanne was not concentrating on Billy, so he was buying him some time. Also, it meant that she had to pay attention to whatever he said and he was deliberately being slow in making his responses. Finally, he was able to use time to his advantage as he worked his way into position.

He settled to await the outcome of the next few minutes. Before phoning Leanne he had made another call. This one was to his contact at the Met. He told him about Billy's abduction and, having followed Billy from the court and then followed the "taxi" anonymously, gave the location of Billy's current suffering.

He heard the approach of the police. Thankfully, they had decided upon a stealthy approach rather than a blue lights flashing, sirens screaming attack. He stayed in the shadows, not keen to be seen or identified by anybody.

Leanne disconnected the call and turned her attention once more to Billy.

"I'm not going to kill you, Billy. You are my son, and I couldn't do that. But you need to appreciate that I have to send out a message. It will be just one finger and then a photo with bandages. I'll make sure it's quick." She nodded again and Billy was given a sharp jab in the arm with a needle. "For the pain," she said. "We'll wait a moment or two to let it work."

Billy cried out, but the hood muffled the sound. That moment or two saved Billy's finger as a dozen armed police with dogs crashed in through the door. Leanne's two accomplices were rapidly pinned to the floor with a barking dog standing beside each. Each had been bitten and was bleeding heavily from an arm that the dogs had grabbed and held onto as they were wrestled to the floor. Leanne was face down on the floor, hands in cuffs behind her back in an instant. Billy was released and, wobbly and groggy, taken carefully to a waiting car. He was not in much pain, despite the dreadful blow he had taken to his hand, because the pain killing injection was now taking effect. He later returned to Australia and settled into life with the girl from the radio station.

Leanne Lane was convicted of abduction, GBH, and, most crucially, being responsible for the murder of DCI Sandy Lane. She was handed a life sentence. She did not have to be held in isolation as she was popular with fellow inmates, having killed a policeman. A few weeks into her sentence, Ray Quinn paid her a prison visit.

"I won't stay long," he said. I am just delivering a message for John. He asked me to read you this:

"Hell has no fury like a woman scorned, but about a wronged man you should be warned."

John Lomax had discovered that the only way to keep a secret is to never tell a living soul. It's the only real way to guarantee anything. But it has a price and that price is isolation, loneliness and silence. Isolation is frightening and loneliness is insidious. But silence is different. It encompasses isolation and loneliness. It is not quiet because it has a shattering noise all of its own and it gets into your very being.

He screamed his frustration and heartfelt agony. He knew then that he would be lonely for the rest of his life and that he probably deserved it. It was the price he would have to pay for

Karen's love turning to hatred and Leanne's love being scorned. He had tested the old quotation at least twice and felt the power of its truth for himself. He fervently hoped that DCI Sandy Lane had felt as lonely and desperate before he had passed on. It felt particularly strange to be so inextricably bonded to his greatest enemy, and to know that there was no escape from that tie for either of them, even in death. In his hands he held the ring that Ray Quinn had retrieved from Leanne before the police had taken her away and a mobile phone. He looked at both and considered the trouble they had caused. He heaved a heavy sigh and hurled them as far as his strength would allow, out from Westminster Bridge and into the murky water of the River Thames.

Lomax & The Biker – The Trilogy

Part 3 –
That's None of Your Business

Lomax & The Biker – The Trilogy

-1-

The mobile and the ring had hardly caused a splash as they were gobbled up by the river and the dark and murky waters mirrored his mood as he gazed down from the bridge. The current was fast and strong and he felt weak and helpless by comparison. He gazed down into the impenetrable night at those dark and gloomy waters and they mirrored his mood. The river had digested the mobile and the ring as if it were a living thing, without so much as a minor splash and it seemed to him that he might as well leap over the railing and follow them. John Lomax had never felt so alone.

He was totally unaware of anything or anybody around him as he gripped the rail, first with his left hand and then his right. He stood motionless and for him time stood still. The rain soaked his clothes but it didn't matter. His mind was crystal clear as he recalled the glorious hours he had spent making love with Leanne. He remembered the particular things they both enjoyed and the small murmurings of pleasure in his ear. Her perfumed smell was with him and filled his nostrils. He could actually feel her touch upon him as if it were real. They were such precious times, such wonderful moments. His heart broke and tears mingled with the rain upon his face. With an anguished cry he put his left foot on the railing and began to push upwards.

He was lifted up and he felt himself floating, but it wasn't the water that bore him. He became aware that he was airborne and being propelled backwards away from the parapet. His head thumped into something hard when he landed and he lost consciousness for a few seconds. When he opened his eyes his head hurt like hell and he was struggling to breath. He managed to sit up, but felt nauseous.

"Sit still, damn you. Don't struggle. You're safe; I've got you."

John Lomax stared up into the face of Ray Quinn, who just looked straight back at him with unblinking eyes and waited for his friend to recover his senses.

"Well, I guess we're even now," whispered The Biker. "I've got something for you which you need to hear. If you still want to jump after that I won't stop you. Listen and then decide. I'll throw this phone in after you if that's what you want, but at least listen."

John Lomax felt a mobile phone being held close to his right ear and heard the voice of Billy Lane.

"John, I am at a loss. I have lost my Father, but feel no regret. That part of my life will remain a dark and dangerous black hole and I must now seal it up. My Mother, however, is another matter. Although she is lost to me, she is at least alive and this gives me cause for hope. I don't know how I'll cope without being able to see her. You have been such a rock in my hours of need, so I turn to you. There is nobody else."

Quinn interrupted his reverie. "Now John, what do you want to do? I have to tell you there is more, but we need to get out of this rain and away from here. We don't want to attract any more attention than we already might have. Let's go."

Lomax & The Biker – The Trilogy

Lomax noticed that his friend had not given him time to answer his question and before he knew it he was being walked firmly off the bridge and into the darker recesses of a dingy London pub. Very soon after that an unnaturally large whisky sat invitingly before him on the sticky wooden table as he began to read.

<u>BILLY'S HOSPITAL RECOLLECTIONS SENT TO JOHN LOMAX FROM AUSTRALIA UPON HIS RETURN. THESE ARE NOT RAMBLINGS; THEY HAVE A POINT.</u>

At the tender age of ten I had to go into hospital in London. In those days children were often parked amongst adults and I ended up in a men's ward. My appendix was removed and so was some of my innocence. At the time we lived quite a way from the hospital, so visits were difficult, especially as I had a younger sister who wasn't allowed in. I remember being torn between thoughts of relief because I wouldn't have to tolerate her constant chatter and homesickness because I loved her and missed being at home. I didn't think it usual to be in such a place for something as mundane as an appendectomy, but I had had a heart problem from birth and thus it was deemed necessary to place me in a specialist hospital on a men's ward.

Not unnaturally my fellow patients all seemed ancient to me and loneliness gripped me very quickly. I felt small and vulnerable. That feeling was certainly not eased when I looked around the ward and took stock.

Lomax & The Biker – The Trilogy

Directly opposite was a grey haired individual who hawked, hacked and spat his way through my first day. Granted he used a receptacle, but I'd never seen nor heard anything like it in my life. On his left from my viewpoint was a thin bony skeleton which hardly seemed to move. His eyes, which were sunken into his completely bald skull, also never seemed to move. He had a sort of fixed, glazed stare. I did spot him move his arm once, but that was just to pick his nose.

To the right of the hacking man lay a grizzly bear. He was massive and had tubes and pipes appearing from every conceivable orifice and wires strapped everywhere else. I remember he moaned and groaned a lot, but nobody seemed to take any notice, so he just continued anyway. Looking back, I think he gained some relief just by doing that.

Beside me in the bed to my right there resided a most peculiar person. Or so it seemed to me. I couldn't keep looking at him because I was old enough to have learned not to stare for fear of giving offence or causing trouble. However, it is human nature to take in one's surroundings and I wanted to make sure I was safe! He was probably not very old and may have been a perfectly nice man, but he unsettled me by staring back. Surely, I thought, he must know it is rude to stare, but he just kept doing it. His eyes were a piercing blue; he had a mop of jet black hair on his head and much more of the same on his chest. He had no tubes or wires and so could move freely whenever the fancy took him, which it did quite often. I noticed that he visited every patient that I could see from my bed and talked in hushed tones to each. After such a visitation each bedbound recipient would be agitated and call for urgent assistance. Thankfully he never visited me, presumably because he thought it not so much of a challenge to upset a small boy, but I kept an eye on him.

Immediately to my left was a middle aged chatty man. He was quietly spoken, read his newspaper and his book and offered me sweets. I liked him.

The first night was very frightening and I tried not to sleep until I was sure everybody else was asleep first. I reasoned I would be safer that way. The plan didn't work. The hacking man did not sleep at all; he just carried on with his noisy, juicy expectorations and nobody came to check on him. The nurses had no need of a bedside alarm for him because they knew that if he went quiet they should come running. Skeleton Man, to his credit, moved even less at night. I think he was rehearsing for the time when he would close those staring eyes for the last time. However, he woke on my first morning, picked his nose as usual, and just lay there waiting patiently for the day to unfold. Grizzly actually slept all night, although I still don't know how. He snored and roared his way through the night, with his tubes and wires bouncing around and upon him. Again, the nurses paid him no heed, presumably employing the same principal as they did for Hacking Man. Old Blue Eyes was actually strapped to his bed at night. He had obviously made too many visitations and the nurses didn't want to be disturbed. Actually, I realise now that the way each patient was treated at night was individually tailored to ensure the nurses were not needed at all. Very clever, I thought. My chatty, book reading friend to my left was the man who discovered the real reason for this and shared his secret finding with me. He had, he told me before lights out, discovered that the doctors and nurses were playing a real life game of the same name during the wee small hours and made every possible arrangement not to be interrupted. Why my newly found friend should think a ten year old would be enriched by this knowledge I couldn't say, but it had a profound effect for years to come.

My operation took place on the second day of my stay. I don't remember much about it as I was asleep at the time. I was grateful for this because I had not slept at all on that first night. When I eventually awoke, I noticed an empty bed across the ward and asked my chatty friend about it. He looked at me morosely and said that Skeleton Man had picked his nose for the last time and was no more. I didn't respond, but remember thinking that I wouldn't like to be the next person to take up residence in that particular bed.

One incident that amused me happened on my fourth morning. By that time I had been allowed out of bed. Nowadays they boot you out of bed just a few hours after surgery, presumably because they don't want you getting used to the good life of doing nothing, eating their food and making a nuisance of yourself. On that morning the doctor, accompanied by the terrifying Matron, stopped at the hacking man's bed and in a voice loud enough for

Lomax & The Biker – The Trilogy

all to hear declared that cigarettes were the cause of his condition, it was not going to improve and would almost certainly kill him. He went on to advise anybody who was listening, which was everybody in the entire ward, if not the entire hospital, that smoking was sinful and he resented treating patients who ruined their own lives by practising such a filthy habit. Moreover, he railed, he would in future think twice about treating people who damaged themselves in that way. That was quite a radical thing to do in those days, but he has turned out to be quite a forward thinker. Anyway, when he and Matron had swept away in a cloud of disgruntlement, a few of us gathered on the balcony to get some much needed fresh air. The balcony overlooked the street and the front entrance to the hospital. On the opposite side of the road we could see a sweetshop, which obviously also sold newspapers, magazines and cigarettes. We watched with mild disinterest as people came and went, but our attention was caught by our eminent heart surgeon striding into the shop. He reappeared a few minutes later with a paper tucked under his arm and stopped on the pavement. He removed something from his pocket, put it to his mouth and lit it. With obvious satisfaction he drew a deep breath before exhaling a cloud of blue smoke. This drew a round of applause from our balcony and, after looking up at his cheering patients, he scuttled away in deep embarrassment. Skeleton Man would have smiled if he could.

Ironically the surgeon had been correct in his analysis and Hacking Man passed away that night. That meant that two of my fellow inmates had been taken by the grim reaper and it was only my fifth day. This set me thinking and I realised that if the attrition rate continued at the same pace, it wouldn't be long before my number was called. Unfortunately I had been told that I would not be due for release until at least ten days after my operation. I have to admit that I showed signs of panic. After all, I calculated, I therefore had to somehow survive for the best part of another week and there weren't that many patients left on the ward in front of me in the queue. Of course, I was relying on the fact that we would be taken in strict order of admittance, but I couldn't depend on that.

When my mother visited me that afternoon I managed to persuade her that I would be available for release within two days. She was doubtful, but between us we managed to cajole the surgeon and Matron to agree to the plan with the proviso that I could walk properly, that my eating and toiletry habits had been returned to normal and that I would return to have stitches removed on what would have been the tenth day of being an inmate. I was overjoyed, not least because it reduced the chances of my maker catching up with me in hospital. He may have had other plans for me elsewhere, but at least I was giving him a run for his money. My plan was further vindicated when I awoke the next morning to the news that Grizzly had been taken during the night. Apparently, even the plethora of tangled tubes, pipes and wires had not saved him. This worried me greatly because I realised that if all those accoutrements had not been able to save him, then what chance did I have with no attachments to protect me? I never did find out what his problem was.

So, six days and five nights had elapsed and three fellow patients had disappeared. Even my ten year old maths could work out that it was imperative my escape plan worked. When I awoke on my sixth morning I was staggered to learn that all of my previous day's companions were still present and correct. I reasoned that the odds had been tilted back in my favour a little. By this time I was able to walk reasonably well, although the stitches pulled uncomfortably. Toiletry habits were returning to normal, or as normal as possible given the awful hospital food with which we were provided. I had discussed my plan with Chatty Man and he ventured that I was being very sensible because if the law of averages in the ward didn't get you then the food would. He admitted that he had noticed the mortality rate and was very worried because he was next in line.

As it turned out he was wrong. Chatty Man and I had noticed that my neighbour with the blue eyes, who was strapped to his bed each night, had not had his bindings removed that day and was very still indeed. As there were no monitors with tell tale beeps that hover over each patient as is the norm nowadays, nobody could tell whether he had just decided to continue sleeping in order to avoid the perils of breakfast or something more sinister had happened. It was mid morning by the time a diligent nurse took some notice and discovered his unblinking blue eyes gazing up at the ceiling. Curtains were hastily drawn around his bed, which, apart from cutting off my view, was also rather unfriendly, and several other nurses and Matron scuttled into that sanctum. A senior looking doctor appeared and I heard him make an authoritative pronouncement to the assembled crowd. I didn't catch what he actually said, but the meaning was clear from his low rumbling tone. Curtains were then drawn around everybody's beds, which annoyed us all as the developing drama had become the highlight of the day and we wanted to see what happened next. As if by magic, when our curtains were removed, Strapped Down Man had disappeared and a freshly made bed stood there, inviting its next victim with its crisp white sheets, neatly turned down to resemble a toothless maw topped by a perfectly laundered pillowed headstone.

Being only ten years old I didn't know where hospitals put dead bodies, so I imagined another ward which was gradually being filled by my erstwhile companions. I confided to my chatty friend that I thought they wouldn't take much looking after and that at least they were avoiding the hospital food, but he didn't seem to find that funny and returned to his newspaper for quite some time. There wasn't much time for anything else to happen because I was let out the next day. The most long lasting memory of that hospital stay is something that didn't happen, rather than anything that did. My father did not visit once. I still resent it. Mum said he was extremely busy with his police work, but I became increasingly aware of his lack of parental interest and we gradually grew apart. I never forgave him for that, not even when he died. The other memory is that my parents split up during my stay and my father had moved out by the time I arrived home. I have bitter memories about these things."

"John, I have bitter memories about so many things. I have learned much more about dead bodies and people's motivations in life. I know too much about these things and I have nightmares. Help me to at least have better thoughts and peaceful nights. I know Mother and you had some happy times and no doubt some fond memories. Please help me to have some of my own."

Lomax & The Biker – The Trilogy

-2-

Ray Quinn studied his friend as he read Billy's entreaty. He knew instinctively how much pain Lomax was feeling and did not interrupt. He knew what it was like to be so utterly low, so profoundly without hope. He had experienced it in the aftermath of the London bombings. He remembered how John Lomax had come to his rescue and helped him recover both physically and psychologically. They had been firm and steadfast friends since that dreadful day and he shared his angst.

For his part John Lomax's eyes welled with the tears of loneliness and despair and he turned his head to the wall to hide his weakness. All he wanted at that moment was to sleep and never wake up. It was all too much to bear.

He pictured Billy, totally alone, on the other side of the world. He imagined the horror of his nightmares and the grinding treadmill of his days. He wondered how long Billy would survive without hope; without so much as a sliver of a chance of seeing his mother and living with the knowledge of what a monster his father had been and the ignominy of his death. It was as if Billy had become the son he'd never had. His shoulders slumped as he attempted to wipe his eyes without being seen.

Ray Quinn placed another large whisky on the sticky wooden table and watched his friend closely as he struggled with Billy's demons as well as his own. He allowed Lomax time. He waited for him to fill the space. Eventually Lomax turned his head from the wall, ran his trembling hands through his hair and raised his damp and misty eyes to meet those of The Biker. Quinn saw that they were devoid of light and there was no life behind them. He recognised the unmistakeable plea they carried; the despairing, deep pain. The Thames had taken more than just the mobile and the ring.

He had waited long enough and Lomax had not filled the space.

"John, my friend, we need to do something. I don't mean you; I mean us, both of us. We are not going back to the bridge. I've got you this far and you're not going back. Don't try or I swear I will stop you and you won't like how I do it. Take one step at a time. We'll get you out of those wet clothes and find somewhere to eat. Then we'll sort this mess out."

The Biker had deliberately taken control and Lomax was grateful beyond words.

Quinn phoned his wife while Lomax showered and changed into dry clothes. It was not a long conversation, but she indicated her understanding and agreement. He had completed the call before his friend came back into the room.

"I've got one or two ideas, John. Let's eat and we'll talk."

-3-

Billy's mother, Leanne Lane was serving a life sentence for the murder of her estranged husband DCI Sandy Lane. She was both respected and popular amongst inmates. Her popularity stemmed from the fact that she had got rid of a hated policeman, and their respect was founded upon the knowledge that having killed once she was obviously capable of doing so again. She had never showed any sign of that, but nobody was brave enough to upset her. Leanne, for her part, was content with the state of affairs and her time in prison passed on its slow, inexorable way without many hitches. Her prison guards also showed her similar leniency because they believed she would never repeat her crime. It had been, they reasoned, a "one-off", purely aimed at DCI Sandy Lane whom they knew she hated. From an early stage she had never given them any trouble at all and, because they also all knew Sandy Lane's history and resented the ignominy he had brought to "the authorities," they were content to let routine take its peaceful course. In their eyes justice had been served, albeit of the roughest kind. She was therefore deemed trustworthy enough to spend time in the prison garden and, with the help of other inmates, was making a good job of growing vegetables for the kitchen on an almost industrial scale. This saved the prison a good deal of money and pleased the Governor immensely.

On one particularly gloomy morning Leanne was to be found as normal in the vegetable garden. It had rained steadily throughout the previous night and it was slippery underfoot.

Leanne slipped on a steep slope and cried in agony as her ankle broke with a sharp crack. She lay in the mud, waiting for help to arrive, clutching her rapidly swelling leg and gritting her teeth to combat the pain.

The prison did not have the facilities to deal with such injuries, so Leanne was taken to the local hospital several miles away.

The Governor reasoned that she was most unlikely to attempt escape with such a serious injury and in any case she could not walk unaided. So it was that Leanne Lane came to be in a trauma ward in the local hospital, due to reside there for three weeks. The doctors couldn't do anything until the swelling had gone down and only then were they able to scan the injury. She had broken her ankle in two places. Eventually they operated and set the ankle as required, but she was forced to remain in bed for two weeks. No handcuffs were used as she obviously couldn't move and the doctors had insisted that they be removed for the duration of her stay. She had no visitors. She was of course accompanied, but only by one guard, a female prison officer named Ruth, because she was not thought to be a danger. For Ruth the assignment was a welcome break from the drudgery of her normal routine; a welcome relief from being inside the prison and she relaxed noticeably as the days passed.

Leanne noticed that Ruth had caught the eye of a ward clerk who made a point of being close to her as often as possible. It was obvious to Leanne that Ruth was attracted to him, not least because of his tight jeans which helped display his best features, but also because when he was close enough he never missed the opportunity to display his tactile nature. To Ruth and her newly found suitor Leanne became almost invisible and that suited her.

Ostensibly, Leanne spent her time concentrating on reading the books she had borrowed from the touring hospital library trolley, but, being female, she was able to multi-task and her brain was working overtime. Ruth's distraction and less than attentive attitude were easy to spot and the kernel of an escape plan was born. Leanne realised that she could use her accident to its best advantage, along with Ruth's new love interest. She had noticed that afternoon visiting was when staff took the opportunity to have a little downtime and made themselves as scarce as they could. This often resulted in an increased level of controlled chaos.

On one particular Tuesday afternoon the ward was more than usually frenetic.

The woman opposite Leanne was 91 years old; in fact all the women patients were older than Leanne. They were therefore by dint of their very age much more demanding and difficult.

The woman refused to wear her hearing aids and thus couldn't communicate with her fellow patients other than by smiling and waving at every opportunity. She had regular visitors with whom she communicated in the same way and visiting time was often reduced to farcical levels of hand waving, smiling and other gestures. She also had an inordinate number of phone calls, which were an absolute waste of time for all concerned. Whenever she thought she was not being heard, either on the phone or in person, she resorted to shouting and repeating the same thing over and over again. "I didn't expect to be here you see. I simply came in to see the doctor as I couldn't stand without my knee giving way and they said to me 'you will be having an operation.' I was most surprised. You see I always said that after the age of 90, no more operations and here I am at the age of 91 and they are talking about another operation." That entire story was the sum total of her verbal communication and was repeated ad infinitum to anybody and everybody.

Another woman called for a commode just after the tea lady had done her rounds. This resulted in patients and visitors, who were enjoying refreshments and biscuits with their loved ones, being treated to most unfortunate noises and an all-pervading foul smell.

One woman had just been admitted with a broken hip and was due for her surgery the next morning. She was therefore a nil by mouth patient by the time of afternoon visiting. She had loudly refused to remove her bracelets and wedding ring as her husband had given them to her, so all her jewellery was covered with sticky tape. She also thought the doctors would steal the items and loudly shared her thoughts with all within earshot. She said she had been married for 59 years to the most wonderful man on earth. She described him as an Adonis. Almost as soon as that description had flown from her lips the most unattractive pipsqueak imaginable settled into a chair at her bedside.

Lomax & The Biker – The Trilogy

Another of the ward's residents was a rather confused old lady. She had oxygen fed to her through a tube inserted into her nose which she found difficult and uncomfortable. She repositioned it constantly, so that it was often at the top of her nose which meant the oxygen blew into her eyes. She was therefore constantly blinking. She would talk to the other patients, explaining that "Joan is dead, and I'm finishing the sewing for her." She went through the motions of sewing with a needle and thread, gradually sewing all round the edge of the top cover of her bed. As she made progress with her sewing she slowly gathered more and more of the cover up her body, piling it up on her lap. She stopped occasionally to thread the imaginary needle and managed the whole process with her eyes shut, presumably due to the oxygen blowing into her eyes. Eventually the nurses came to her aid as she had no underwear. She was totally exposed but at least she had finished Joan's sewing.

There is little dignity in being ill and even less when a person is elderly and in hospital.

Meanwhile Ruth had taken the opportunity to disappear with her Ward Clerk to a convenient nearby office. They had drawn the blinds in order to get to know each other better. Before leaving Leanne's bedside, presumably in preparation for her tryst, Ruth had visited the toilet and that was when she made her mistake. Her mobile phone sat on her chair. Leanne seized the opportunity. She removed the SIM card, inserted her own and tapped in the number. By the time Ruth returned Leanne had re-inserted the

Lomax & The Biker – The Trilogy

original card, replaced the phone on the chair and was peacefully reading a book. Leanne noticed that Ruth took her phone with her when she got up to meet the Ward Clerk and smiled to herself.

Lomax & The Biker – The Trilogy

-4-

Billy was surrounded by lions. He was walking alone along a flat, grassy path which ran down the middle of some open and overgrown countryside. The path was narrow and the bushes dense on each side. He had neither seen nor heard the pride stalking him, and the hungry cats had stealthily worked themselves into position. He stood no chance. The lions gradually closed the trap until Billy froze with fear as he spotted the lead female ahead of him on the path. She stared at him with eyes that became narrow slits as she laid her ears back. He heard rustling on each side, but didn't dare to take his eyes off the spectre of death a few steps ahead. He was aware that he was sweating profusely and shaking uncontrollably. There was a single tree ahead of him. He knew it was too far away, but he had no choice but to try. Taking a deep breath he launched himself into a sprint and lunged upward at the lowest branch. He thought he had made it but, in an echo of John Lomax being pulled back in mid air from going over the bridge, he felt himself being grabbed from behind.

He was drenched in sweat and shaking with fear as he jolted awake at the insistent trill of his mobile phone.

"Hello Billy."

Billy looked at the caller's details on the screen. He ran his hand through his hair and licked his lips to try to get enough moisture to speak. He was pulling away from the terror of the nightmare as he tried to clear his head and regain his senses. He was certain he was bleeding from a wound to his thigh, but discovered it must have been the last act of the horror and was only sweat running down his leg.

"Hello, Mum."

He was beginning to emerge from that halfway stage between waking and nightmares.

"Billy, Listen. I can't talk for long, so please just listen. I'm in hospital..."

Leanne briefly explained her situation and finished by saying, "we can sort this out. You need to get in touch with you know who. He can help."

The call was disconnected, but Billy had understood perfectly. He had ended the call by telling his mother that he would let her know, but inwardly he knew he was at a loss as to how he could help her. He could simply ignore her plea and let her stay where she was; he could visit her and reassure her that she would be better off accepting her situation, even though it would entail another round the world trip, or he could contact Ray Quinn or John Lomax. He wasn't even sure he wanted to do anything. At the end he had been firm with her in order to demonstrate that there might be nothing he could do, but he had heard her whimper in the distance as he had removed the phone from his ear and it wrenched at his heart.

He became aware that he was still shaking violently and had locked his grip on the phone so tightly so that he couldn't put it down on the table. His head swam and he felt nauseous. In an unwitting pastiche of John Lomax, he poured himself a large whisky and lost himself in his thoughts. Eventually, emotionally drained, he fell asleep in his chair and the glass gently slipped from his fingers and fell softly to the carpet, spotting it with the remaining drops. As the spillage dried on the carpet so the nightmare was upon him again.

Lomax & The Biker – The Trilogy

-5-

The day following Leanne's covert phone call to her son, she was sitting in her hospital bed chatting amiably to her guard, Ruth. They had become quite friendly, or as friendly as the situation allowed. For her part, Ruth was appreciating the break from prison routine and was enjoying her liaison with the Ward Clerk. Leanne had promised not to betray her to her employers and there was an implicit understanding between them. Ruth would slip away for opportunistic meetings with her newly found lover, whilst Leanne would press the alarm bell at her bedside if she needed to warn Ruth to return quickly. In this way Ruth had become more indebted to Leanne as the days passed.

Ruth had been gone for about ten minutes when a visitor appeared at the foot of Leanne's bed. She was an elderly woman who introduced herself as being from the hospital's befriending service. This, she explained, involved going into wards and seeing if any patients were in need of "counselling" or, indeed, just somebody with whom to chat and relieve the unending tedium. The woman was frail in bearing and gentle of manner. Leanne recognised strength shining through her steely blue eyes, but there was also a sadness which could not be hidden and Leanne understood that she needed to talk as much as she wanted to offer a service. Although not keen on her afternoon being interrupted, she decided not to be dismissive because Ruth would come back soon enough and send the old woman on to her next helpless patient.

"Hello, my name's Molly," she said as she held out her hand in greeting. "Would you like someone to talk to? You look quite lonely all on your own, just laying there."

Leanne looked at her uninvited visitor and reluctantly returned her handshake.

"Actually, I'm perfectly happy by myself. I've got books and papers to read and things to listen to, but if you want to sit awhile I don't mind."

In the coded language of the hospital befriending service that was as loud a plea for company as is ever heard.

"Thank you; I am a little weary. These corridors are endless and I'm not as nimble as I used to be," said Molly. "I'll stay for as long as you want. Just tell me to leave when you're ready and I won't be offended."

"Ok," said Leanne.

"Is there anything you want to talk about?" Molly continued. "Any moans and groans that I could pass on to make things better for future patients? If not, then perhaps you'd like to tell me what happened to you or a little about yourself?"

Leanne stared intently into the blue eyes and said, "I think perhaps you might have much more interesting things to tell me. You wouldn't be interested in my boring life, but I think you have much to tell." Leanne was not going to divulge the details of her life, especially not the latest few chapters.

Lomax & The Biker – The Trilogy

"Well," said Molly," we are trained not to intrude and to be discreet, so I'll tell you about my own life. I have nothing to hide, you see."

Those last few words seemed to indicate that Molly already knew a good deal about her and Leanne shifted uncomfortably in the bed. Molly reacted by moving from perching on the upright bedside chair to settling herself at Leanne's side on the bed. She seemed to take an age to compose herself before she began her tale. She had already removed her coat, which was draped around the chair, and she placed her old person's handbag on the bed between them.

"My story begins when, at the age of two, I was abandoned by my mother along with my brother, Harry, who was three. Our mother was young, Jewish, and struggling to find employment in 1932. In the end she must have snapped and, in desperation, left us at the roadside. Thankfully we were found and taken to an orphanage in London. Life at the orphanage was no picnic for Harry and me. The regime was strict and children were forced to conform. Breaking any rules always met with punishment. For example, one day young Harry was caught playing with matches. In order to teach him not to do it again, a match was lit and used to burn the centre of his hand. When I refused to sleep, I was often isolated from the other children. The one thing both of us craved was love, but no one in the orphanage showed us real love or tenderness. I have never forgotten what that was like."

Leanne's concentration began to wander and she searched with her eyes for the return of Ruth. Molly, though apparently elderly, was sharp and picked this up.

"I imagine prisoners are punished for breaking rules in strict regimes, even these days," ventured Molly, looking straight at Leanne with her clear blue eyes.

The parallel was not lost on Leanne and neither was the thought that Molly may even know something of her situation. But what was the woman trying to impart? Was there a message that she wasn't seeing? Her attention became focussed again and she motioned with her hand for Molly to continue.

"Being young children we were heartbroken at losing our mother. We longed for her to come and rescue us; but our hope was in vain. I'd like to think that any child, no matter what age, could be rescued by his or her mother, no matter what the circumstances. Oddly enough the reverse has happened to me as my own son has saved me a few times from various difficulties. You have a son, don't you Leanne?"

The question stunned Leanne, who realised that the old woman was not asking a question but was making an assertion.

"Well, um. ......yes I do. He's in Australia and I miss him badly."

Leanne did not know what had come over her to allow this private information to pass to the other woman. There was just something about her that seemed to say 'trust me, I can help.'

Molly, for her part, saw the realisation seep into Leanne's eyes and took her hand.

"I understand your pain Leanne, and Billy's."

Leanne was startled. She had not given Molly her son's name and yet she had just heard her clearly say it. Her hand tensed inside that of Molly.

"Please, go on. You can't stop there. I....I need to know the rest."

Listen carefully, Leanne and you may be helped. Ruth won't be back while I'm here. She's with her Ward Clerk."

"But..." protested Leanne, "she might and I want to hear the rest of your story."

"She won't be back," insisted Molly, leaving Leanne in no doubt. "So...to continue. Some years later I discovered that when our mother tried to visit us, the orphanage forbade it. Mother was only allowed to visit on a Sunday, but no visits were allowed on the Sabbath Day, so we never saw her again. Do you know the pain of that loneliness, Leanne? I think you do. Can you imagine the desperation of a child who is destined never to see his mother again? I think you can, Leanne. What about you? How do you feel about not seeing your son again? I know how I would feel if I could never see my son again. The pain works both ways. It's unrelenting and the sting gets sharper by the day.

But let's press on. At the age of fifteen I left school without being able to read or write, but managed to find employment as a servant girl in a large house. I told my employer, a disabled lady, that I would love to be able to read and write, but the lady showed no interest in helping me. Life was tough as a servant. I had to rise very early each morning to light the fire, and work until late in the evening. One night, filled with despair, I thought about taking my own life. Have you ever reached such depths, Leanne? I think perhaps you may have.

After a few years I decided to go back to the orphanage where I had grown up, and work there as a house-parent looking after the younger children. I fell in love with a young lad, and became engaged. We married and we were blessed with a son. He was, and still is, the centre of my universe. He is the reason I live. Can you say the same, Leanne? Is Billy the centre of your universe? Is he the reason you live? I think the answer to both questions is yes.

Sadly my dreams of future happiness were dashed when my husband died in a road accident. He loved riding his motorbike and in the end it killed him. I've hated bikes ever since.

I struggled for years to bring my son up on my own. Rather than giving up in despair I trained as a State Enrolled Nurse in Winchester, and qualified after two years. The thought then came into my head that perhaps I could try to become a State Registered Nurse. I travelled to a hospital in Hertfordshire for an interview with the matron in charge of training nurses. I told the matron that I did not have the same education as the other girls, but the matron still accepted me for the course. She advised me to spend one hour each evening, learning what I had been taught during the day. I had never worked as hard in my life. Learning, nursing, providing for my son; just holding things together was all I could manage."

Leanne had the beginnings of cramp and struggled to change position in bed.

"I can't imagine how hard it must have been," offered Leanne, "but, please don't take offence. I admire you for what you have achieved in your life and you have my utmost respect, but how is it relevant to me?"

"Patience!" snapped Molly, showing her steel. "Let me go on. I'm on your side. Please believe me, all will be well if you just listen and then do as I say."

Leanne was both quieted and disquieted. This old woman whom she had never seen before had suddenly appeared at her bed in the hospital and related something of her life and had the effrontery to tell her do as she was told! Why should she? What right did she have? What did she know that would turn the tide for Leanne?

Her face must have shown all her emotions because Molly gave her the sort of look that only a senior citizen can give.

"Right! No more interruptions! We haven't got much time now," Molly said. "I took the matron's advice and studied conscientiously. I would lay each text book on the bed and paw over them until my eyes bled and I fell asleep. When the results were released and pinned up on the wall, I scanned down the list of names and to my dismay could not find my name anywhere. Due to my poor education I was used to always seeing my name at the bottom of the list. Nervously I went back up the list again and to my amazement, found my name was at the top of the list with a pass of 92.5%. I couldn't believe it. I was so excited that I moved on to midwifery training in a hospital in Cornwall. After completing that I applied for a nursing job in the Accident and Emergency Department of this very hospital. I worked here until I retired in the 1980's. That's how I can move about this place so easily.

There are so many tales I could tell about my time in nursing, but we haven't the time for all that now. Perhaps another time," said Molly. "There is one I must tell you, though. There was one occasion that I had to minister to a young man who had been involved in a motorbike accident. It's strange how things go round in circles in life. They say that what goes around comes around, and, for me this was it. He was in a lot of pain due to fractures, much like yourself I imagine. Several years later I was walking in the High Street when a smartly dressed young man called out to me. It was the motor bike accident victim, but I did not recognise him due to the transformation in his appearance. Instead of long greasy hair, his hair was cut short and neat. He had replaced his dirty leather jacket with a clean suit. The young man called out to her "My little staff nurse – you saved me!" He now had a new purpose in life as he had joined the army. My son was in the army as well, you know, but that didn't save his life."

"Please excuse me, but I must pay a visit. I'll be back in a minute." Molly lifted herself from Leanne's bed and walked, bent and stiff, underneath the exit sign. Leanne just sat. There was so much to take in, with so much meaning. What on earth was going on?

Her dazed thoughts were interrupted by the Ward Clerk.

"Ok," he said, "let's get you moving."

"Where's Ruth?" asked Leanne.

"She's OK. She'll be along soon," he replied. "Make sure you bring all the things you need," he advised, as he drew the curtain screen completely around the bed and instructed Leanne to change into the clothes he had tossed onto the bed.

"Why? Where am I going?"

"Out of here," was the reply.

"How?" asked Leanne, now fearing for her future.

"By bike," was the reply.

"I hate bikes," said Leanne. "I can't even bend my leg; it's in a cast. The last time I was on a bike I was damn near killed and I wet myself."

"It's the only way," insisted the Ward Clerk, as he swept her into his surprisingly strong arms and hurried off the ward.

He paused only to cast a meaningful glance at Ruth, the prison guard. He was again struck by her resemblance to Leanne. It was if they were sisters. He held her attention for a few moments, savouring the memory of their time together. Ruth disappeared behind the curtain screen and hurriedly arranged the bed and dummy, which bore a remarkable resemblance to Leanne. She then slipped out from behind the curtains and made her way via staff corridors out of the hospital. The time that the Ward Clerk and Ruth had been together had not been spent in amorous entwining, much to the disappointment of both parties, but had been spent in manufacturing the dummy using clothes that Leanne had not noticed had been extricated from her locker. Even her watch had been pressed into use.

Leanne was so dumbfounded by the turn of events that she could only just manage to gather herself sufficiently to pose two questions.

"Who was that was the old woman?"

Her name is Molly Quinn," replied the Ward Clerk. "You might know her son, Ray."

"What about my watch? asked Leanne.

"Oh, I think John Lomax might be able to find you a replacement, don't you?" was the reply.

Lomax & The Biker – The Trilogy

-6-

The Ward Clerk did not carry Leanne for her entire journey out of the hospital as it would have drawn too much attention. Immediately after leaving the ward he set her down in a wheelchair, which had been carefully placed just by the door and arranged a blanket over her lap so as to hide anything in her lap. He made sure she bent her legs at the knees so that even her plaster cast was covered. To all intents and purposes she appeared to be just another woman in a wheelchair being pushed along endless corridors from one hospital department to another. He added one clever addition to the disguise when he gave Leanne a large folder to carry above the blanket, which was a genuine x-ray folder that patients take from A&E to the X-Ray Department. He also made sure that their exit route took them back to A&E from X-Ray, so that nobody would have any reason to hinder their progress. It was an easy exit for them and she was pushed into a private ambulance which was waiting outside with its engine running. Hospital CCTV, of course, had recorded the entire internal wheelchair journey, its exit from A&E and their entry into the ambulance.

The ambulance drove for about ten minutes until it arrived safely at a pre-arranged secluded spot for its rendezvous with the bike. There was no CCTV to record Leanne, by then suitably clothed in leathers, being transferred to the passenger seat behind The Biker, who was waiting with his helmet already on. The Ward

Lomax & The Biker – The Trilogy

Clerk lifted her gently onto the seat, pushed a helmet onto on her head and patted the driver on the shoulder to signal his departure.

"Hold on tight," advised the Ward Clerk. He was wasting his breathe because Leanne had previously experienced the back seat of a bike and was already holding on for dear life.

The Ward Clerk watched as the powerful machine drove away and disappeared rapidly into the distance. He turned and climbed into the front passenger seat of the private ambulance. Ruth, The Ward Clerk and Molly Quinn exchanged smiles and the vehicle moved silently into the anonymity of the countryside.

No phone calls were made from the ambulance as they could have been traced. John Lomax therefore had no idea as to the success or failure of the escape attempt. Similarly, Billy, far away in Australia, was ignorant of progress. Both paced up and down in their respective homes and neither would settle until it was over.

The plan had been the result of Billy contacting Lomax after having received his mother's call from her hospital bed. He actually need not have bothered because John Lomax had already concluded that loneliness was not a future he could contemplate. He had lost the one true love of his life, and whatever she had done could be forgiven. He had already been thinking of ways to liberate Leanne from captivity and had shared his thoughts with the only person in the world whom he could completely trust: Ray Quinn.

It was decided that Billy should not return to England as it would be far too obvious to the authorities. It was also decided that John Lomax should not be overtly involved for the same reason. It was Ray Quinn who had drawn up the operation and masterminded its execution. His mother's involvement was a nice touch, because she was helping her son to help another mother and her son respectively. She thought it a wonderful connection. The story she had told Leanne in hospital was a complete fabrication devised by Ray's mother herself and she played her part to perfection. She had thoroughly enjoyed herself and had carried it all off with aplomb and style. She was inwardly very pleased with herself at the part she had played and secretly hoped further adventures might follow. She knew the risks, but didn't care. At her age, she reasoned, there was not much time left for this kind of fun.

The Ward Clerk was found by Ray Quinn. He had been in the forces with him before having become, along with many compatriots, victims of government cost cutting measures. He had drifted from one unsatisfactory job to another, never really settling into civilian life. He had jumped at the opportunity to help his old friend Ray Quinn. Indeed, it was he who had made the suggestion to involve Ruth, with whom he had developed a relationship.

Ruth had experienced what is known euphemistically as workplace harassment from one or two of her colleagues at the prison. She had been told it was very much part and parcel of working in such an environment and she should accept such practices without complaint. The final straw had been when the Assistant Governor had locked her in his office and made it very clear what was expected of her. She had only escaped the inevitable by sheer good fortune when the prison alarm sounded as a fight had broken out in the dining room of her wing. Ruth had bottled the incident up for a while, but had quietly resolved to exact revenge. She had been delighted to become involved with Leanne's escape, seeing it as her chance to hit back at the corrupt regime and the loathsome treatment she had received. She had managed to get herself attached to Leanne as her guard in hospital and her partner had inveigled himself into the role of Ward Clerk. Together they taken their real relationship and used it in the hospital as part of building a believable cover story. Ruth had even left her mobile phone on the bedside chair on one occasion and Leanne had seen it as slackness and taken the opportunity of contacting Billy. It was vital to the plot that Leanne did not understand what was happening, so that her actions were at all times real.

The authorities never chased Ruth and her Ward Clerk because the government department concerned received an anonymous document containing photographic evidence of terrible abuse in the prison, both by and of prisoners and guards, particularly involving senior staff. There were even a few examples of such activity proving political involvement. For publicity purposes the police were shown in the press as trying very hard to find Ruth, The Ward Clerk and Leanne but behind the scenes and over a period of time it became old news and the public turned its attention elsewhere as it always does when the currency of a story runs out.

-7-

Leanne was sleeping like a baby. She was more calm and peaceful than she had been for a long while and a prolonged period of restorative slumber was precisely what she needed. John Lomax sat at her bedside, keeping vigil, ensuring that the one true love of his life was not disturbed. He remained there, unmoving, for many hours recalling and reliving the path of their extraordinary relationship. He remembered with wonder when she had walked into his life and stayed for a week. Neither had managed much sleep, but oh what happiness and joy she had brought with her! He had never known anything like it and just being with her after all the heartache and painful vicissitudes of his life, brought the ecstasy flooding back again.

Ray Quinn slipped into the room unnoticed. "Penny for your thoughts," he whispered, as he laid a calming hand on his friend's shoulder.

John Lomax smiled and, without looking away from his beloved Leanne, said "you may be my friend, but that's none of your business."

Quinn smiled, reflecting that almost everything that had happened to Lomax was actually very much his business, but he took no offence at the remark. Their friendship was deeply rooted and had been tried and tested on many occasions. They were completely at ease with each other and their bond was firm. He allowed his hand to rest on Lomax's shoulder, giving reassurance and succour. He was pleased to have been able to bring Leanne back to his friend. The moment stretched and there was peace in the room.

Eventually Quinn gently broke the silence. "We should talk, John. It's time to make some decisions."

The brevity of his friend's words, and the manner of their delivery, moved John Lomax. His friend had always had the knack of precision and the ability to summarise a situation rapidly, which had been nurtured by his time in the forces. It was part of what made him such a wonderful friend as well as a terrifying enemy.

Spiriting Leanne away from the hospital had taken a good deal of planning, as well as a not inconsiderable sum of money. Quinn had also called in a favour or two from the people who had so convincingly played the parts of Ruth and The Ward Clerk. He had deliberately made sure John Lomax had not been actively involved in order to preserve his innocence if ever events took a turn for the worse. All Lomax had known was that he had been taken to a remote house on Exmoor and Leanne was already there and asleep when he arrived.

Lomax stroked Leanne's cheek tenderly with the tips of the fingers of his right hand until she stirred. Her long-lashed eyes flickered into life and she turned to meet his gaze.

"It's alright, my love; you're safe. I'm here," he said.

"Mmm," was all she could manage as she slowly emerged from the depths of deep sleep and an even deeper duvet. She held his hand to her cheek. "Where am I?"

"It doesn't matter, Leanne," said Lomax. "You're safe and we're together. You won't be going back to that awful place."

"What's happening?" she asked. "How?...."

"Quiet now," he whispered as he bent forward to kiss her. "You need to sleep."

"I was asleep," she said, "but you woke me up."

"I know. You need to take this," said Lomax as he showed her the pill resting in the palm of his hand. "It will help you sleep some more."

"But I don't understand. Why wake me up to give me a pill to make me sleep some more."

"Because we need you to get as much rest as you can. We have a lot to do tomorrow."

"You said 'we'. Who else is here?"

"Ray," replied John Lomax.

"That's all right then," she said, before swallowing the tablet with a sip of water.

She settled back into the bed and was soundly asleep within thirty seconds. John Lomax wondered to himself how the mere mention of Ray Quinn's name always produced the desired effect whatever the situation. Lomax had never doubted his friend's talents, but he now realised that his legend and mystique was spreading. Lomax left the room noiselessly, even though it would have taken a herd of elephants to rouse Leanne.

Just outside the bedroom door Quinn was using his mobile phone. "Don't talk, please just listen. Everything is going to plan.

Lomax & The Biker – The Trilogy

She's out and safe. No details; you only need to know what effects you. Everything else is none of your business. We'll be in touch soon."

On the other side of the world Billy Lane clamped a mobile phone to his ear and listened intently to the tinny voice. Ray Quinn disconnected the call and Billy, realising he had been holding his breath in the tension of the moment, let out a huge sigh of relief. Ray Quinn removed the sim- card from the phone, dropped it to the floor and crushed it beneath his biker's heavy boot heel. He would scatter the fragments from the bike as he swept through the countryside. The chances of them being found and put together again were close to nil. On the other side of the world Billy Lane understood perfectly the need to mirror these actions, so that to all intents and purposes their brief conversation had never taken place. It would have taken the facilities of GCHQ to identify it, but they would never become involved. Billy also understood the subtext of Quinn's call and would wait for twelve hours before moving, as previously directed and agreed, at the same time as his mother and John were due to commence their own journey.

"How is she?" asked Quinn.

"Sleeping like a baby," replied John Lomax. "She'll be ok. We've got about twelve hours to get things sorted out."

They spent half an hour putting the final touches to their plan before concluding their business.

"It'll be tight," said Ray Quinn, understating as ever. He knew the scheme would need a modicum of luck but was quietly confident. He had already donned his leathers. "I'll be off then," he said. "Don't worry, it will be fine. Don't forget to get some rest yourself; you'll need all your energy later.

The two friends shared a firm handshake and looked with complete trust into each other's eyes. The Biker had disappeared round the first corner by the time Lomax returned to keep his vigil at Leanne's bedside.

Billy was overjoyed that his mother, Leanne, was no longer incarcerated and desperately wanted her to be part of young Raymond John's life. He could not, however, fathom how that could be brought about. All he did know with absolute certainly was that if there was anybody who could make it happen it was Quinn. He had many reasons to be grateful to John Lomax, and was fairly sure that he would look after his mother, but he did not have the absolute certainty, the total unquestioning belief in Lomax that he had in Ray Quinn. That man was in a different league; a class of his own.

Lomax & The Biker – The Trilogy

-8-

By the time Billy received the call from The Biker, he had made a life for himself in Australia, living with the reporter who had knocked on his front door when his mother had secretly visited him asking for his help. They had gradually fallen in love and had been blessed with a son. They named him Raymond John in honour of the two men, Ray Quinn and John Lomax, who had been most influential and instrumental in Billy being able to survive his traumatic history and the ravages of a fractured and torn family background. Billy was relieved when he saw that his son bore no likeness to his own father, Sandy Lane, who had died so ignominiously in prison. He idolised the little boy and was determined that he would have the upbringing that he had missed.

There was one physical feature that Billy had inherited from his father; namely a nose that was not straight and which had, over a period of time, gradually grown more out of line. It caused him breathing problems and gave him debilitating headaches. The fact that hospitals had played such a prominent part in the lives of himself and his mother was not lost on him. He had been mentally scarred by his own childhood experience of hospital and was fearful of what he might encounter again. However, surgery became inevitable as his breathing difficulties and headaches increased and he was also determined to expunge the paternally inherited feature.

After the operation, Billy left hospital with sutures, inside his nose, firmly ensuring the splints on either side of his septum were held in place. The operation to straighten his nose and clear his nasal passages had been declared a success by the surgeon, but he had been warned that the problem could well recur. For his part Billy was pleased with the outcome, especially as it meant he no longer bore that resemblance to his father. In fact, he had also seriously considered changing his surname in order to complete the process of distancing himself from his heritage. In the end he decided to keep the Lane surname and use it as a constant reminder of everything he should avoid in life as well as a motive to cleanse the family name. He was determined not to view it as a millstone.

Billy was instructed to return to outpatients a week later to have the splints and stitches removed. He was delighted to be home and his two year old son was equally pleased to have him back. He sat on his father's knee and giggled mischievously. The youngster celebrated his father's return by grabbing the ends of each splint, which protruded temptingly from each nostril, between his forefinger and thumb. It is surprising how strong even a child as young as that can be and his strength was matched by his speed. He yelled with glee as he yanked at the prize he had captured. Billy also yelled, but not with glee. His yell was accompanied by an eye-watering, red hot searing pain as his son held up his newly captured prizes and expected praise for his efforts. The boy's laughter turned to tears as blood poured from his father's nose and he was dropped unceremoniously onto the unforgiving floor.

Lomax & The Biker – The Trilogy

Billy's partner, Charlene, was every inch an Australian young woman. She loved the outdoor life and was determined that their son would enjoy the same lifestyle. She had grown up in a cricket loving family surrounded by two brothers and parents who talked of little else. At the first sign of good weather the barbeque would be set up and an impromptu game of cricket sprung into action. These games were highly competitive, as is the Australian way, and no concession was given to the fact that Charlene was a girl. She sported many bruises as she grew, but never complained. She became an avid cricket fan and was no mean performer with bat and ball. Nothing pleased her more than inflicting defeat upon family members or, if that wasn't achieved, she regularly left her siblings with cuts and bruises as the price they had to pay for their victories.

Her fondest memory was when, at the age of seven, she had asked her twelve year old brother to explain the intricacies of cricket. They were both sitting on the lawn in the back garden. He thought for a moment and, recognising the opportunity to display his teenage importance, he launched into the most confusing explanation he could think of.

"You have two sides, one out in the field and one in. Each man that's in the side that's in goes out, and when he's out he comes in and the next man goes in until he's out. When they are all out, the side that's out comes in and the side that's been in goes out and tries to get those coming in, out. Sometimes you get men still in and not out. When a man goes out to go in, the men who are out try to get him out, and when he is out he goes in and the next man in goes out and goes in. There are two men called umpires who stay out all the time and they decide when the men who are in are out. When both sides have been in and all the men have been out, and both sides have been out twice after all the men have been in, including those who are not out, that is the end of the game."

It was the same deliberately confusing nonsense that he had been told by his older brother, so he felt he was passing down family wisdom.

Charlene recognised pretentious rubbish when she heard it and, in common with most seven year olds, preferred a much more straightforward approach to life. She stood up, looked at her brother, told him he was stupid, picked up her bat and whacked him with all her not inconsiderable strength. She left him with a multi coloured bruise on his knee that took quite a few weeks to heal. Charlene was pleased with herself, even though her mother gave her the worst scolding she had yet experienced in her young life. Charlene noted that it seemed to cure his arrogance, so felt it had been worthwhile. For his part, her brother learned his salutary lesson and thereafter afforded his sister the respect she had earned.

Billy had also taken to their lifestyle and was happier than he had ever been at any time in his life. It was a far cry from the shredded remnants of his upbringing with parents who were constantly at war and afforded him little attention. He often thought that the manner of his father's demise had been inevitable and that his mother deserved all that had happened to her. He had, of course, told Charlene everything. He felt it important for them to be completely open and honest with each other and for that to become the central tenet of Raymond John's childhood.

It was against this idyllic background that Billy had listened to Ray Quinn's phone call. He had understood the message but had no inkling of the subsequent ramifications. He feared his life was about to take another turn for the worse and long buried feelings of helplessness returned. The nightmares came back again that night as well. He woke with a start, sweating profusely just as the lions were closing in. Charlene stroked his matted hair and caressed his face with a concern she had not had to feel before. She knew that whatever it was that had so frightened Billy would also affect her, and she was deeply troubled.

She could not have known how far reaching it was all going to be.

The next morning Billy told Charlene that he would have to respond to Ray Quinn whenever he was next contacted. He explained their options.

"We could stay here and carry on as we are," he began, "but if we do that my mother will never see her grandson or any other children we have. She won't be allowed into Australia, even to visit, because the authorities here are reluctant to grant entry to a convicted criminal, even though the British are not actively pursuing her. Ray has contacts and has put out feelers, but the feedback is negative. Another option is for us to go to England and live there. I'd be able to work in John's jewellery shop and we would be well looked after. John has even said I would take it over when the time came. If we did that my mother would see Raymond John regularly and I know she would be very happy about that. One bonus would be that Ray Quinn would always be readily available if we ever needed help of any sort. That's more difficult if we are here in Australia, though not impossible. He is a resourceful man and a wonderful friend. Another thought is for us, together with John and mother, to move to somewhere else. Again, that is not really on the cards due to the problem of Mum's status, unless we choose a country that isn't too fussy about who it lets in. We have been told that if we did that, Britain would not seek Mum's extradition. It would be a case of out of sight out of mind, I think."

Billy paused in order to discern Charlene's reaction, but she was giving nothing away.

"Of course, I realise that you have your family here and you are all close. If we went away your parents would not see their grandchildren." Billy stopped again. This time he waited patiently for Charlene to say something.

"Oh Billy," she whispered, "I don't want to leave. I can't leave my family and I love Australia, but I know you have a chance to build bridges with your mother. This is so difficult."

As with all families considering such moves, emotional and practical attachments, preferences and conflicts were almost impossible to reconcile. They calculated that they would be financially better off moving to England, as the jewellery business was thriving and had real prospects. They would become part of its success and expansion and Raymond John would have a guaranteed future. Billy would be able to repay Lomax and Quinn for all they had done for him and Ray Quinn would be available should problems arise. It was a ready- made head start. On the other hand would it be better to stay in Australia and fend for themselves, with Charlene's family close as well?

Neither Billy nor Charlene said very much that morning. There is a difference between a comfortable quiet and uneasy one, and it was the latter that had insinuated itself between them. Each was worried about the other and both were concerned to make the right decision for their young son. Billy knew the phone would ring before long and it would be Ray Quinn wanting an answer, so he needed to resolve the impasse more urgently than Charlene. As far as she was concerned, they could take their time, so she was in no hurry.

When the call came the ringtone meant different things to each. For Billy it carried an urgency and an implied threat. He knew a decision was wanted immediately if John, Leanne and Ray were to have the time to make their plan work even though he had not been told very much. Ray had told him 'that's none of your business," when Billy had tried to elicit further details about the plan, and he steeled himself to be more determined to get the answers he needed. As far as Charlene was concerned it carried no such urgency or threat, it even sounded softer to her as it represented an opportunity to find out more and have further discussion. She was perfectly prepared to talk to Quinn and Lomax if necessary and she wanted time to sound out her own parents. It boiled down to the difference between action and prevarication.

"Hello Billy," said Quinn. He waited for a reply.

"Hello," said Billy. He said nothing else as he waited for The Biker to move the conversation forward.

"Please listen, Billy. Things have changed. I need you here as soon as you can. Don't bring anybody else. I need your help. There is a ticket for you at the airport in Sydney; the plane leaves in three hours. This is serious."

Billy was stunned. Ray Quinn was not a character easily rattled, but something had obviously happened to unsettle him and now he was asking for Billy's help. He could not envisage any situation in which he could help Ray; it had always been quite the reverse, so something must indeed be serious.

Lomax & The Biker – The Trilogy

-9-

Billy joined the moving mass of arriving passengers at Heathrow as each collected luggage from the various carousels. He had fought for and won a prized trolley, successfully fending off competition from other tired and aggressive travellers, and hefted his luggage aboard. He did not know who to look for or what the next few hours and days held for him and was surprised to find Ray Quinn himself waiting behind the barrier. Things must indeed be serious, Billy thought to himself.

The two men shook hands but no words were spoken until they were safely inside the car, which Billy did not recognise. He asked no questions as he awaited news.

"I hope the flight was OK," said The Biker.

"Not bad," replied Billy. "As long and boring as ever, but made much better for being in First Class. Thank you for that."

"No problem," said Quinn. "Charlene and the boy OK?" He asked.

"Yes thanks. He's growing so quickly, it's hard to keep up. So much energy. Charlene sends her regards and is looking forward to meeting you and John," said Billy.

"That will have to wait," Quinn responded sharply.

Billy looked across at him as he drove and tried to discern what was happening, but Ray Quinn's face was a mask.

"I have things to tell you, Billy," said Quinn.

Lomax & The Biker – The Trilogy

Billy said nothing; preferring to wait for whatever was coming. Quinn noted the young man's silence, taking it as a sign of growing maturity.

"John's in trouble and we need to sort it out," Quinn began. "Your mother and John are now happily together and safe, so that's not the issue, but it's been difficult to get them to that point. Like most things in life the problem revolves around money. The jewellery shop is thriving, but it's not producing sufficient for our purposes. John's solution was to become involved with the local drugs business, but he failed to discuss the matter with me beforehand. The result is that he got in deeper than he could handle. I only found out when things went pear shaped. I discovered him at home with a needle hanging from a vein in his arm. He had been left for dead and it was meant to look like suicide, but I got there just in time. To cut a long story short, he owes money to some very nasty characters. I have made some enquiries through my contacts and by myself, but progress is slow. These people are well hidden, well protected and not particular about who they hurt. I cannot sort this out on my own, which is why I called you. Between us, and with your mother's help, I think there's a way to settle the matter and come through it in the clear. Before we do anything, though, you need to rest. I'm taking you to a hotel. I want you to sleep off the jet lag and then call me. Sorry to insist, but I need you alert and flying from the other side of the world, however much you slept on the plane, isn't good preparation for what we have to do."

Lomax & The Biker – The Trilogy

Quinn drew up outside the hotel and accompanied Billy to reception. He made sure Billy was safely ensconced in his room before returning to reception. He found the Duty Manager waiting for him.

"Thanks for this," Quinn said. "Let me know immediately if Billy or Leanne or John leave their rooms and if they make any phone calls."

"Certainly sir," replied the Duty Manager, with a twinkle in his eye. "Your wish is my etc.," he said as he bowed to his former commanding officer and smiled knowingly. He wasn't about to seek information as to what was going on. The less he knew the better it would be for him if things went wrong. It was, after all, none of his business.

Ray Quinn had put Billy in a room two floors below John and Leanne. He had arranged for all meals to be taken in their rooms and for their landline and mobile calls to be monitored. He did not want them to get together until he was ready. He was using them as bait. He found himself a dark corner in the lounge bar and waited. He hoped nothing would happen, but he had a nasty feeling, a premonition, that this night would be significant.

And so it proved.

Quinn's senses were on full alert. He glanced at his watch again and noted that it was still only eight fifteen. He was a patient man; something learned from his time in the forces and he was quite prepared to wait for as long as it took. He sipped his coffee and blended into the scenery. Nobody paid him any heed, which was exactly as he wished. He knew he would have to make his coffee last and that he may have to order quite a few more, as he snapped open his newspaper and began to attack the crossword. There were doubts in his mind, which was unusual for him. He hoped he would be proved wrong and that his three "captives" would remain in their rooms for the entire evening and throughout the night.

He was so engrossed in his deliberations that he almost missed Billy walking into the room and sitting at the only available stool in front of the bar. Billy looked around nervously, but failed to spot Quinn. The Biker hoped Billy was only doing what so many lonely hotel guests had done for time immemorial: seeking solace at the bar and, perhaps, the chance of an opportune meeting. Quinn looked around the room and was struck by something odd. The couples around him, and there were a few, seemed ill-matched. The comfortably anonymous mix of blond wood, brushed steel and pale blue leather upholstery made the bar of the hotel perfect for any assignation: business or pleasure or a combination of the two. Also, he noted, there were no groups of people and he would have expected at least one or two company gatherings or birthday celebrations.

"Billy?" The girl who approached was slim and attractive with thick, chestnut hair and eyes the colour of dark chocolate pools. Quinn was luckily positioned such that he could hear conversation at the bar whilst remaining unnoticed.

"Yes," he heard Billy reply.

Lomax & The Biker – The Trilogy

Quinn was on full alert and he had to make a real effort to appear to concentrate on the crossword. He had no doubts that she was what is euphemistically labelled "escort." Quinn felt a deep sense of disappointment in Billy. With a brief smile that left her eyes untouched she tottered on ludicrously high heels to take a seat on one of the squashy blue sofas, crossing her long tanned legs and waited for Billy to join her. For a moment Quinn half wished he was Billy. It would be so much more simple. Quinn scanned the room, not allowing his eyes to rest on anyone for too long. His attention was rapidly drawn back as the brunette had risen to her feet and was engaged in animated discussion with another man. This man was a rough diamond, unshaven with collar-length dark hair, in jeans and a well-worn leather jacket, the Harley-Davidson logo stretched across his broad back. The body language was pure agitation, and he seemed to be giving her a hard time about something. At one point he grabbed her arm but she wriggled free. Even though he suspected she was capable of looking after herself the old fashioned values that he held dear rose to the surface and he was sorely tempted to cross the room and offer her assistance. It was only the current circumstances that prevented him from doing so. As he continued to observe the developing scene her resistance seemed to crumble before his eyes and, with a last cursory glance around the room, she slung her bag over her shoulder and reluctantly walked back towards Billy.

The whole exchange made Quinn uneasy. He was feeling angry that Billy was letting himself down as he discreetly followed the pair out of the hotel and watched them climb into a taxi. More importantly he was endangering their plans and that could not be allowed. He had trusted Billy and was disappointed that his judgement was awry. He made a mental note to be more dispassionate in future. He also made a mental note of the name of the taxi company and was deciding upon his next move when he spotted the leather jacketed man again, further down the street. Quinn was puzzled and he couldn't decide whether he was perceiving trouble where there was none. He had learned long ago to trust his own judgement and it was telling him to follow the man, but couldn't because he was on foot. That would have to wait as he wanted to catch up with Billy. He walked back into the hotel and, using the Duty Manager's office phone, persuaded the taxi firm's despatcher to tell him where Billy and his newly found lady friend were planning to consummate their brief acquaintance. He made sure the Duty Manager was keeping a watchful eye on Lomax and Leanne and set out in pursuit. As he was driving the car he had borrowed from the ever accommodating Duty Manager his mind was racing. The presence of another woman was a complication he could do without and Leanne and John would not be best pleased. If Billy was stupid enough to jeopardise their plans then he would have to be brought back into line quickly. Quinn threaded a path through the snarled traffic and quietly drew to a halt in an unlit side road close to a seedy looking building. Paint was peeling from the facade and two of the neon letters of its name had refused to light up.

Lomax & The Biker – The Trilogy

Quinn walked to what passed for a reception and spotted a man behind a desk.

"I need a word," said Ray Quinn, almost in a whisper.

Less than one minute later he exited the front door, armed with the knowledge he required, whilst the badly shaken and ashen faced clerk sat and stared rigidly at the back of the disappearing figure.

Quinn crossed the road and found himself a seat at a table. It suited him that the pub was dark and the bar rowdy and nobody seemed to take any notice of the new arrival. He set his glass down in front of him. He would have preferred something non-alcoholic given the situation, but had bought a pint of Guinness as anything else would have been out of place. He was quietly grateful for the forces training that had taught the finer points of blending in. He had hardly settled into what he hoped would be a short wait for Billy to emerge when his attention was caught by the unmistakable sight of a Harley Davidson jacket disappearing into the building opposite. He hadn't heard the characteristic burble of the engine due to the noise in the pub. The hairs on the back of his neck stood on end and he recognised the signal. He knew trouble was in the air and did not hesitate. Moving quickly he ran across the road and, like a shadow, found his way into the building via the rear entrance that he had earlier stored in his memory. The door was slightly ajar, as it was the same route used by his quarry. Quinn heard the babble of a distant TV as he advanced cautiously along a bare, parquet-floored hallway, alert to any possibility. He silently climbed to the first floor and, controlling his breathing, listened intently.

He eased open the door in front of him and steadied himself for what was to come. He was already imagining the scene. Would he find Billy alive or dead? What of the brunette? What about the mystery man? He visualised the brunette cowering in a corner, her face bruised and bloodied, with Billy standing over her, absolutely rigid with fear. In the event there was no blood, only a sterile and unnatural calm. He scanned the room and his eyes settled on Billy. He motioned with a finger to his lips, ordering Billy to stay silent as he continued to search the room. The brunette sat hunched in a chair, clad only in her underwear, her entire body shaking uncontrollably. Drug paraphanalia was scattered everywhere.

Quinn stood motionless, listening intently for any approaching footfall. There was none and he made his decision. He eased the door shut and moved towards Billy, who quaked before him.

By the time Quinn and Billy left, again by the rear exit and totally unnoticed, the Harley Davidson man lay sprawled on the floor, his eyes glazed and staring, his complexion waxy. The right sleeve of his leather jacket was pulled up to above the elbow and a hypodermic syringe dangled grotesquely from his inner arm, its needle still tugging at the vein. The brunette still sat motionless hunched in the chair, her entire body shaking uncontrollably as her overdose took hold. Quinn offered a silent prayer of thanks that the seedy rent a room that masqueraded as a hotel had no CCTV and was situated in a dark and lonely street.

"I need a word," he whispered in Billy's ear as he propelled him along, gripping his arm tightly. Billy understood the meaning of those words and was more afraid than he had ever been in his entire life.

-10-

Quinn drove back to the hotel in silence. Billy knew better than to say anything. Words would be said soon enough, he knew.

Billy was spirited back to his room and the door was locked. Quinn checked with the Duty Manager, as he returned his car keys, who confirmed that John Lomax and Leanne had remained in their room all evening and had made no phone calls.

Ray Quinn slid the room key card down the groove in the lock and the door clicked open. Despite the late hour, he found Billy wide awake. He had decided it was time to bring Billy to heel, so he told him to sit down and listen.

"I don't know what the hell that was all about tonight," he began," but I didn't bring you back from the other side of the world just so you could play away from home. You have a two year old son and a loving woman and you risk losing them because you can't keep it in your trousers. I brought you back to help John. You owe him. You bloody well owe him! He saved you when you were going off the rails...."

"Actually, he used me for his own ends, if you remember," said Billy.

"Don't interrupt, you ungrateful little shit. How dare you? You stole a watch and John saved you. Yes, he saw an opportunity to get at your father, but he deserved it, didn't he? Lomax loves your mother and she loves him. She's out of prison thanks to us and they're together now, but they still need help. Our help. That means you need to grow up."

"I came, didn't I?" Billy began again.

Ray Quinn was standing over Billy now. "You came because I gave you no choice. I would have fetched you myself if necessary. I told you earlier that John Lomax owes money to some nasty people; drugs people. They don't mess about, Billy. I was afraid they had found out you were in England and I was right."

"You mean you set me up? Used me? Put me out there, knowing what might happen?" exclaimed Billy, incredulous that his supposed protector could do such a thing.

"It was the only way I could bring them out into the open and it worked. I knew they were aware that you'd come back to England. I even knew they had found out you are here in this hotel. I used an escort agency to get the brunette for you, knowing they would recognise the opportunity it gave them to get at you. The man in the leather jacket was sent to kill you, Billy. The brunette didn't know him, but she was promised more money than she could earn in a whole year to lure you to that place. They were banking on the fact that you were away from home, lonely and uncertain. They were right. Your weakness almost got you killed. No matter; I now know what we face, who we are dealing with. Nobody's going to help your mother and John, Billy. They've only got us. The police aren't interested. I have contacts and they'll let me deal with it all provided it doesn't get too messy. From their point of view your mother isn't a threat to anybody and they know she did time wrongly. She's out but they won't spend valuable resources looking for her unless she does something stupid. Also, they'll let us clean up this drugs mess because they know I've got a better chance of success than they have. They can't lose either way. It's win, win for them." It was almost the longest speech Quinn had made in his life.

"You saw how we left that man tonight?" continued Quinn. "That was exactly how I found John Lomax and that was what they intended for you as well. The only difference is that I managed to save John, but that won't stop others coming after him or your mother or you. The only way to end this is to pay them off along with enough of a warning, but Lomax hasn't got the kind of money they're after and neither have I."

Billy was stunned into a prolonged silence. Eventually he asked "but what would have happened if I had 'kept it in my trousers' as you so delightfully put it?"

The sarcasm was not lost on Quinn, and it tested his patience and control, but he remained calm. "They would have tried something else," he replied.

Billy sat and squirmed. He knew he had been weak, had been found wanting and had let Ray Quinn down, but ironically the outcome was exactly what Quinn had wanted. He eventually came to the realisation that Quinn was a very clever man indeed and, rather belatedly, he also came to the realisation that he knew which side his bread was buttered.

"So what happens now?" asked Billy.

"For you, nothing. I want you to stay in your room and wait for me to contact you. If you decide to plough your own furrow again, I won't be responsible for the outcome. Stay here, relax, use room service for your meals, watch TV, recharge your batteries and don't use the phone or your mobile. You may find it boring and lonely, but it's better than the alternative. Believe me, I will know if you do anything other than follow these instructions. I have things to do and I don't need to be distracted by having to rescue you again. You have my mobile number but only use it in a dire emergency."

"I hear you, but I don't understand what's happening," said Billy. " I know I can trust you, but please don't leave me here for too long. It's the isolation that gets to me."

"I'll be back as soon as I can," replied Quinn. He deliberately avoided giving him any idea of time scale because he wanted Billy to be constantly unsure of when he would return. He hoped that ploy would ensure Billy's compliance.

Ray Quinn closed the door to Billy's hotel room as he left and nodded to the man sitting in a chair just down the corridor. The man, who had been positioned there by the Duty Manager, looked up from his reading, and returned the silent acknowledgement. Both knew that Billy's door had been set to lock automatically and could now only be opened from the outside.

Quinn took the stairs and headed for the room containing John Lomax and Leanne. They had used their forced incarceration much more positively and, when he quietly knocked and entered, he found them fast asleep in each other's arms on a bed which had obviously witnessed much activity and was completely dishevelled.

Lomax & The Biker – The Trilogy

He coughed politely and waited. When there was no response he coughed a little more loudly. Leanne was the first to stir. She lifted her head and raised her arms to run fingers through her hair. In doing so, the covers slipped away to reveal her nakedness. She blushed, smiled and unashamedly sat upright, enjoying his attention. She gazed into his eyes and held them. He returned her gaze for what seemed like an eternity, until he deliberately and slowly let his eyes move from her face to take in the rest of her body. He eventually returned to her eyes and then did not look away, not wishing to spoil the moment. His entire being was taken over by what he was seeing. He was beginning to comprehend some of the reasons for his friend's attraction to her.

Neither of them moved when John Lomax opened his eyes to witness his best friend and his beloved Leanne staring at each other. He gradually took in the scene before coughing politely to break the moment.

"I need a shower," said Leanne. She didn't bother with covering up as she rose from the bed and padded across the room, preferring to revel in the admiring eyes that she knew were following her progress, before disappearing into the bathroom.

Quinn forced himself to concentrate. "Billy has helped us today," he said, "and we need to move quickly."

John Lomax was appreciative that his friend had not referred to the scene they had just witnessed. Both knew that complications would follow and it would have to wait.

"Somebody made an attempt on Billy's life today," said Quinn, "but I've managed to make sure he won't try again. I'm going to take you there now because I want you to understand fully what we are up against. Leanne will have to stay here until we get back."

The Biker failed to mention that it was he who had used Billy as bait and set him up, or that Lomax and Leanne were being used in the same way. If he had told Lomax that, then it would be very difficult to make sure he carried on co-operating, much as he might trust and rely on Quinn.

They waited for Leanne to reappear. This time, much to the disappointment of both men, she was wearing a hotel bathrobe.

"So what happens now?" she asked. She couldn't know that Billy had asked the same question only minutes before.

Ray Quinn answered her with an echo of his reply to Billy, omitting only a few phrases.

"For you, nothing. I want you to stay in your room and wait for me to contact you. Stay here, relax, use room service for your meals, watch TV, recharge your batteries and don't use the phone or your mobile. You may find it boring and lonely, but it's better than the alternative. Believe me, I will know if you do anything other than follow these instructions. I have things to do and I don't need to be distracted. You have my mobile number but only use it in a dire emergency."

Leanne was taken aback by his change in tone and attitude.

"I don't understand what's happening," she said, "I know I can trust you, but please don't leave me here for too long. It's the isolation that gets to me." Another echo.

Like mother, like son reflected Quinn.

"I'll be back as soon as I can," he said. Again he deliberately avoided giving any idea of time scale because he wanted her to be constantly unsure of when he would return. He hoped that ploy would ensure Leanne's compliance.

Leanne noticed that he had not referred to both of them returning, but decided not to pursue the point.

Ray Quinn closed the door to the hotel room as he and Lomax left and nodded to the man sitting in a chair just down the corridor. The man, who had been positioned there by the Duty Manager, looked up from his reading, and returned the silent acknowledgement. Both knew that Leanne's door had been set to lock automatically and could now only be opened from the outside.

Lomax & The Biker – The Trilogy

-11-

"Do you know him?" asked Lomax, as he and Quinn stared down at the inert body of the man in the Harley Davidson leather jacket.

"Not exactly," replied Quinn. He then went on to recount the events of the previous few hours, finishing the story with himself entering the hotel room occupied by Leanne and John Lomax. Again, he stopped short of dealing with the embarrassing detail of Leanne's performance. "What does this look like to you, John?" he asked.

Lomax thought for a while and considered the scene. They were in a seedy room in a run-down hotel in a dubious part of town, a man's body, a needle hanging from a vein, drug equipment, and a stoned young woman, clad in only her underwear, totally oblivious of all around her.

"It looks like they were here for obvious reasons, which also included drugs. He's dead, probably from an overdose. I can't tell whether he injected himself or she did, or perhaps he injected them both. So it's accidental, misadventure, murder or suicide. Whatever, the result is the same. An overdose for both; one fatal and one will possibly prove lethal," said Lomax.

"Ok," said Quinn, "does it look like anybody else was here, before, during or since?"

"Oh, come on Ray," said Lomax, "I'm not a detective."

"Try," said Quinn.

"I can't see anything that points to that. If anybody was here, it could have been the clerk from downstairs. Perhaps he wanted some of the action and it all went wrong. No doubt fingerprints and DNA will sort it out," said Lomax.

"Indeed they will," replied Quinn, wondering whether his friend had been astute enough to realise that the only man wearing gloves was Quinn himself.

Lomax hadn't spotted the gloves issue but he was wondering why his friend had endangered them both by coming back there.

"Billy was here," said Quinn. "The Harley man followed him after he had picked up the brunette in your hotel bar. I followed them all. The girl is an escort that Billy found and she brought him here. I'm very disappointed by him, by the way, and I should imagine Leanne will be as well. Not to mention his Australian love. Ironically, it helped. The Harley man is interesting. You know you owe money to an unsavoury gentleman? Well, this is his muscle. He was sent here to eliminate Billy as a means of warning you of the dangers of not paying up. Now you really understand what you've got into. Sorry, but this was the most effective way of showing you."

John Lomax was deeply shocked. He had suddenly realised that Quinn had obviously set Billy up in order to flush out the enemy and that both he and Leanne were also being used in the same way.

"Remind me to stay on your side," said Lomax.

Quinn took that as a compliment and smiled.

"So, what now?" asked Lomax.

"Well that depends on you," said Ray Quinn. "We need to look at the options, but I don't think we should hang around her much longer."

They departed via the rear exit and found a suitable pub. It was full of workers, lingering before catching trains home, and others with different reasons for their presence, all filling the place to listen to the stand up comics who were hoping to climb the greasy pole to stardom. They found a table, moving in rapidly to stake their claim as two young men rose and departed, hand in hand, for pastures new. They settled themselves and assessed their surroundings, Lomax noticing that his friend was being particularly cautious and alert, which indicated that the situation was serious.

Having satisfied himself, Ray Quinn was about to begin when the characteristic high pitched screeching sound of electrical feedback assailed the crowd from the small stage near the bar. It had the effect of stopping all conversation as people, some wincing in pain, pressed hands to ears and turned to find the cause of the assault. It stopped as quickly as it had begun, and Quinn waited for the buzz of chatter to resume. He wanted to explore the situation with his friend and explain his thoughts about what actions they should now take. He tried to begin again, but the voice of the landlord, amplified to an excruciating level, beat him to it.

Lomax & The Biker – The Trilogy

"Good evening and welcome once again to our weekly charity night. I know you will give them all a fair crack and show your appreciation in the usual way. Don't forget there's a bucket at the bar for your donations as we raise as much as we can for the local charities. Tonight's charity will be chosen by the winner of the raffle at about 10.30. Please remember to only put money in the bucket; we found some condoms in there last week and I don't want to explain it again to the wife. She's easily offended you know."

"She's tougher than you think," shouted a wag from the rear of the room, "she put them in there herself. She told me you only use the small ones!"

"Speaking of tough old birds, here's one now. Please put your hands together for our very own Annie Hall." The landlord was pleased to hustle from the stage.

This drew a roar of approval and a round of applause, and the tone was set for the evening. The microphone was handed to Annie, who was in her seventies if she was a day. She was dressed to kill, and wearing as much war paint as a native red Indian.

"I went to the doctor's with my old man Jack the other day," she began.

"Did you leave him there?" shouted a heckler.

"Shut up and listen; you might learn something," Annie replied quickly. "You were born with one mouth and two ears. There's a reason for that."

Lomax & The Biker – The Trilogy

"Anyway, as I was saying, before I was so rudely interrupted, I went to the doctor's with my old man. The doctor examined him all over and told him he was in good health. He asked my Jack if he had any questions. Jack said he did and told the doc that after we have sex…"

"At your age? That's disgusting!" The crowd was warming to its task now.

"I'm still young enough to teach you things you've only ever dreamed about," replied Annie, "see me after if you're up to it; which by the look of you, you're not!"

The heckler leaned against the bar and went back to sipping his pint.

"So, Jack's told the doc that after we have sex he feels cold and chilly. He then says after the second time (this drew a prolonged ooooh from the room) he feels hot and sweaty. The doc called me in and gave me the once over. He told me I was in good condition for my age (another drawn out oooh from the crowd) and asked what Jack could mean. I said it was obvious. He's cold and chilly the first time because it's January, and hot and sweaty the second time because it's July."

She waited for the laughter to subside before launching into another tale.

"So," Ray Quinn began, "let's sort this out."

He was conscious of the fact that they may be overheard and had lowered his voice almost to a whisper. Lomax had to move closer and strain to hear. Annie Hall was in full flow now and their conversation was interrupted by bursts of laughter and clapping.

"Billy is safe and being watched, so I don't think we need worry about him for a few hours. I've also made sure Leanne is safe. She's also being watched. Again, provided she does as I asked before we left, she will be ok," stated Quinn.

"Was that really necessary? I can understand you being careful about Billy, especially in view of how he has behaved since arriving, but Leanne was with me all the time," Lomax was hurt by his friend's treatment of his beloved.

"Yes, it was," replied Quinn. "I know she's been with you all the time; that much was obvious! However, she could easily try to contact anybody when you're not there with her. I particularly don't want her to speak to Billy. They'd only put two and two together and come up with who knows what number. No, we need to deal with this together; just you and me. What we get up to is none of their business, but you know it will be in their best interests. Besides once this is all over I want you and Leanne to live happily ever after and Billy to be able to return to his own utopia down under."

"Don't patronise me, Ray," said Lomax.

"I'm not; really I'm not. I'm just making sure all our ducks are in a row. Believe me, we are not up against amateurs. These people mean business," Quinn was in business mode himself.

"So, what's the plan?" asked Lomax.

"In short, you haven't got the money they're chasing you for. The amount will increase with every passing day because they see it as loss of face. They'd prefer to have the money, but will get rid of you, or worse, as an example to others if necessary. They inhabit a murky world and reputation means everything to them. If they can't get to you, they will go after the people closest to you. You made the biggest mistake of your life when you got involved with drugs. You don't understand how it works and you're not equipped to cope with it. It's vital you follow my instructions to the letter." Quinn ended his speech by holding his friend's gaze with an unyielding stare.

"My plan involves raising enough money to get them off our backs and then giving them a warning of our own so that they leave you alone for ever. After all, I do have my reputation to think of as well," Ray Quinn smiled at Lomax. "One day, when this is all over and peace has broken out, I'll let you into a secret. It will help you understand everything that has passed between us since the day we met when you saved my life."

Lomax was about to ask but Quinn cut him short. "Not now. Not until it's all over."

Lomax studied his friend's face and knew better than to pursue the matter. The silence between them was short and the moment was filled with electricity.

Quinn broke it. "I intend to pay them using their own money," he said.

"Surely that's a dangerous game," Lomax put in.

"Yes it could be," answered Quinn, "but it has a certain irony and the message will not be lost. There's no other way, my friend."

Ray Quinn extricated a phone from his pocket and dabbed his finger onto the screen before holding it to his ear.

"It's all set," he said, "I need you to give us about an hour in there before you arrive. Usual arrangement. I'll call when I'm done and out."

Lomax thought it strange that Quinn had made the call in public, or, more significantly, in front of him. He couldn't hear any reply from within the phone. It wouldn't have mattered if he had because the only response to Lomax had been "ok, no problem."

"Right," said Quinn, "let's go."

"Where?" asked Lomax.

"Back to that lovely room," replied Quinn.

Lomax hoped he meant the hotel room in which Leanne was now residing at her leisure, but he realised that wasn't what was meant when they approached a familiarly seedy building and entered via the same rear entrance through which they had exited a short while ago.

"Don't touch anything," ordered Quinn, "just stand in the middle of the room and let me know if you spot anything which seems odd or out of place. Nobody will disturb us."

Lomax knew better than to ask how he expected them to remain undisturbed. He would have understood more if he had seen the desk clerk slumped and tied in a dark cupboard apparently sleeping like a baby, with a needle dangling from a vein in his right arm.

As they entered the building Quinn caught a whiff of something; an unwashed smell. He was about to open his mouth to warn Lomax when he noticed the grimy rim around the collar of a man's white shirt.

"How long have you been on duty?" Quinn asked the shadowy figure.

"This is my third straight shift," came the reply. "My wife has locked me out so I had to sleep in the car. I've been waiting for you for a long time. I'll get a shower after this is over."

"Good idea," said Quinn with feeling, making an effort at shallow breathing.

Taking the hint, the figure moved away, further into the shadows. "I'll check out the rest of the place," he said. "Oh, you'll need these," he added. Throwing Quinn a small polythene packet he left the room, speaking into his lapel radio as he went.

Quinn opened the packet and squeezed his hands into the tight latex gloves, grateful that he was not a vet.

The shadowy man reappeared. "We're on our own," he confirmed, tactfully keeping his distance. "No sign of life, and we've got one hour."

"Good," said Quinn.

Taking care not to disturb the syringe, he slid his hand into the inside pocket of the Harley jacket and retrieved a soft leather wallet. It contained a hundred and thirty pounds in notes, along with a variety of credit and debit cards and a photograph of Billy Lane. Turning it over he saw a phone number. He'd been right, the man had been after Billy. Quinn was in no doubt the cards were in false names, so there was no means of identifying him. That did not worry Quinn because he now had the phone number he needed. He rummaged around in the man's jacket and trouser pockets and found what he was looking for.

He looked at the phone's screen and saw that a message had been received. It said, "all done?" The sender's number matched that which was written on the back of the photograph. Ray Quinn knew the question was asking whether Billy had been dealt with, along with the brunette.

Quinn thought for a moment and entered, "all done. No problems." He wanted to let the anonymous texter know that Billy and his brunette escort had indeed been dealt with. He did not anticipate any further message and was thus surprised when the phone lit up again.

"Ok, move on. The next one's tomorrow. You know what to do."

Quinn thought for a few seconds before typing "Ok. Time?" He waited, hoping that he hadn't blown the chance of making progress.

"Midday," the text read, "let you know where tomorrow."

Ray Quinn smiled a satisfied smile and pocketed the phone. He now knew that Lomax and Leanne were safe for a few more hours. It gave him leeway; time to plan.

-12-

"I bet this is a prime area for burglaries," said Lomax, his hands firmly planted in his pockets to prevent him inadvertently touching anything.

"Definitely," said Quinn, "and we'll use that. Plus this place is used by escorts to entertain their punters. Up market, it most certainly is not," he added grimly. "You see that camera up there in the corner? I'll bet you a pound to a penny it's used to record the action and blackmail the poor punter. That desk clerk confirmed as much before he decided to inject himself into oblivion."

If Billy is on the recording, we'll need to get hold of it before it links him to matey's demise," suggested Lomax.

"You're right, of course," said Ray Quinn, but it's going to save us a hell of a lot of trouble as well." He left that thought hanging in the air and turned his attention to the wallet, in which he had now found a folded page recently torn from a newspaper. Flattened out, Quinn recognised it as the column for 'Personal Services', well-thumbed and with several of the numbers emphatically ringed in black ink. He wondered if one of them was for the brunette.

Something stale invaded Quinn's nostrils again. The shadowy figure was back peering over his shoulder. "See," he added helpfully, "what kind of sad so and so gets his sex out of the paper?"

"The kind that is there before you," said Quinn, keen to link the Harley jacketed man to the brunette and this seedy room and thus distance Billy from any connection.

"You might be right," came the reply, but it was not convincing.

"Look," said Ray Quinn, " I don't mean to be difficult, but aren't you supposed to be watching out so that we are not disturbed? We'd be happier if you left us to it. This is not your business, and the less you know the better it will be for you."

Suitably chastened, the shadowy man returned to being shadowy and Lomax and Quinn were grateful that the stale smell left the room with him. Quinn made sure he had gone, before taking a silver wrapper from his pocket and partially hiding it between cushions on the sofa.

"That should help convince them," he muttered.

"Just one wrap?" queried Lomax. "Not much of a party."

"It'll be enough for our purposes," replied Quinn, as he moved across the room and turned on the TV. It provided a distraction to the bleak silence of death.

Satisfied that he had arranged the scene in sufficient detail he motioned to Lomax and they slipped away from the building as silently and unobtrusively as they had entered it. The shadowy figure watched them leave and settled down for another long and tedious wait.

His sojourn was interrupted by a knock echoing at the door, followed rapidly by the entrance of the police surgeon. He was carelessly dressed and bleary- eyed. The shadowy watcher, recognised him from other cases, and wondered enviously whose bed he had just vacated. Why was it that when your own love life was on hold everyone else seemed to have it on tap?

"She's young enough to be my granddaughter," he said.

It was said so quietly that the shadowy watcher thought he must have misheard. He hoped that the thud of his jaw hitting the ground wasn't audible.

"Granddaughter? he asked."

"That's right," the unkempt surgeon turned to face him, a wicked grin spreading out across his face.

"I never had you down as a granddad," said the watcher truthfully.

"Neither did I," the surgeon replied evenly. "But some things are out of our hands, aren't they?" and with a minimal lift of his eyebrows continued his work. Subject closed.

After a suspiciously quick and cursory examination of the Harley man's body, as well as that of the by now deceased brunette, he announced that overdoses had done for them both. Satisfied with his pronouncement, he snapped his case shut and strode away, presumably to restart whatever activity had been so rudely interrupted.

By the time the surgeon had left, Lomax and Quinn were seated at the same table in the pub as they had vacated when Annie Hall was holding court. Quinn had arranged for two of his friends, dressed like himself and Lomax, to take their seats immediately they had left. Their drinks, two pints, were even drunk to the same level in their glasses. The CCTV picked up neither their leaving nor their return. It was badly positioned anyway, and there were many standing bodies between it and the two men. Even if it had picked them up, the room was so dark, with the main light shining on the stage throwing shadows around the room, that recognition would have been impossible.

"Ok," said Ray Quinn, "that's Billy's first problem sorted out. The phone number and text messages are a real bonus."

He made two quick phone calls; one to each of the Door Manager's men standing watch in the corridors outside the rooms occupied by Leanne and Billy. Both confirmed that neither of their charges had ventured out or made any calls. In fact neither had even ordered any food or drinks. All seemed quiet on the western front.

Ray turned his attention back to his friend. The bar was still a frenzy of raucous laughter and good natured banter between stage and audience. Annie Hall had been replaced by a man in his mid thirties who engaged in attempting to educate the crowd.

"I want to tell you about some little known facts. Did you know, for example, that in the 1400's a law was passed in England that a man was allowed to beat his wife with a stick no thicker than his thumb. That's how we get 'the rule of thumb'.

"I've got a better measure!" shouted a man from the back of the bar, the announcement laced with innuendo.

"That's what you think!" retorted the woman standing beside him as she smashed him over the head with her rolled up umbrella. "My rule's much more use 'cos it keeps me 'ead dry an' all."

This was greeted with a huge round of applause as the chastened man blotted blood from his scalp with a bar towel.

"Did you also know," persisted the man on the stage, "that if a statue in the park of a person on a horse has both front legs in the air, the person died in battle. If the horse has one front leg in the air, the person died because of wounds received in battle. If the horse has all four legs on the ground, the person died of natural causes. Next time you're wandering around London, have a look."

"My wife's often got both legs in the air!" yelled somebody from the crowd.

"That's because you're about to die in battle, mate." The retort was quick and drew another round of applause.

Ray Quinn allowed himself a smile before bringing them both back to reality.

"Before our Harley jacketed friend decided to move to another realm I had a quiet word with him. He kindly agreed to pass me some helpful information," he said.

Once more, John Lomax knew better than ask for details.

"He told me the name of the man who is chasing you for money and threatening your life. He seemed relieved to be unburdened. By the time our conversation had finished he seemed to want a rest and he nodded off to sleep. As you saw, he decided not to wake up. Such a shame; he might have been useful, but I think we had gone as far as we were going."

"Do I know this man?" asked Lomax.

"I doubt it," responded Quinn, "but you may know of him. His name's Jack Noble. He has a reputation for certain unsavoury activities, which I'm sure is well earned. He sent our late lamented friend to deal with Billy. It was supposed to be set up to appear that Billy and his brunette had indulged in vigorous activity followed by an over indulgence in the old white powder. It would have worked if I hadn't followed him and altered his plans slightly."

"That's an understatement," reflected Lomax.

"True," replied Quinn," but that's life sometimes." He let this last philosophy linger, before continuing. "Anyway, he's gone to Scotland for the weekend, so I think we should toddle off and take a look around his place. I'm told it's quite an eye-opener."

The house was in darkness when they arrived. It didn't take Quinn long to disarm the disappointingly inadequate alarm system and close down the CCTV. The motion sensors in each room were also disabled rapidly. Of the four first-floor rooms the most promising appeared to be a small back bedroom that had been converted into a working office complete with computer, printer, scanner and other electronic devices. This room was by far the untidiest and therefore the one that mattered. Papers were scattered haphazardly over every horizontal surface and drawers were pulled open to varying degrees, spilling out diverse contents.

"Somebody's been here already," said Lomax, aware that he was stating the obvious.

"Yes," said Quinn. "It's almost as if he was looking for something, too," he added sarcastically, surprised by Lomax's statement of the obvious. If he had any sense he'd have been looking for an anti-virus program. Look at that,"

Lomax tracked Quinn's gaze to the computer screen. The machine was already booted-up and, as Quinn nudged the mouse, the screensaver cleared to reveal a scene of technological devastation. Rows of data merged and tumbled from the screen, dancing and swirling before their eyes before mutating into giant insects that scuttled off the screen, cackling nastily. Although functionally competent, Lomax's interest in computers pretty well ended there. This was the first time he had witnessed a virus in action, but even he understood the implications. "'Can you stop it?' he asked.

From the doubtful expression on his friend's face he guessed the answer. As he sat down on the swivel chair he wondered to himself why they had found it already turned on and why it had now taken to destroying the data it held. Suspending these questions for a moment he cleared a space to the left of the keyboard and moved the mouse and mouse mat over to it. He tried valiantly to halt the progress of the virus but was fighting a losing battle. Eventually he shrugged his shoulders and began to explore the contents of Jack Noble's desk, looking for any personal papers to help them build a picture of the man.

"Eureka!" exclaimed Lomax, triumphantly holding aloft a single suspension file which had been squeezed between others in the bottom drawer and was labelled 'current'. In it were bank statements and credit card invoices, some going as far back as a year. There were other files in the desk, which contained correspondence and newspaper cuttings. Closing the drawer, Quinn straightened, and as he did so, noticed a filofax that had fallen on the floor, down the side of the filing cabinet. He picked it up and tossed it to Lomax.

"We'll take this as well," he said. "Have a flick through will you while I have a look round the rest of the house. There might be some useful names and addresses."

Unsurprisingly, the remaining four rooms lacked the hi-tech input and were furnished more in keeping with the age and style of the house. Old-fashioned, Quinn would have called them, though the lingering smell of paint hinted at recent decoration. Only one, the master bedroom, was obviously inhabited, although a single bed in the spare room was also made up. Quinn opened drawers and cupboards, but there was no trace of any female apparel, ruling out the brunette as wife or partner, but several wardrobes, including those in the spare room, were full of men's clothes and shoes. There were a couple of suits and some formal shirts but mainly it was casual wear: Next, Gap, fashionable off-the-peg stuff. Reasonable quality but like the leather jacket, most of it well worn. This wasn't a man who lived extravagantly. Some of the sizes fluctuated slightly too, making Quinn wonder if Jack Noble was a man battling with his weight. In any event there seemed far more clothing here than one man could reasonably wear. Quinn picked up the book on the nightstand: the selected poems of T S Eliot.

"'So what was he into?' asked Lomax, appearing in the doorway.

"Eliot," Quinn replied.

"Not a bad choice,' approved Lomax. Leanne likes Eliot and she's told me a bit about his work.

"I didn't know you liked poetry," said Quinn, teasing his friend whilst at the same time acidly implying that a liking of poetry was connected to cross dressing.

"Why would you? said Lomax, ignoring the tacit insult. "Anyway, I don't particularly. This was an 'A' level set book when I was at school. Before putting it back Quinn turned to a page that had been book-marked. He read quietly and was lost in thought. "We'll take this with us as well," he announced. "I think it might be significant."

He gave the book to Lomax and moved on, eventually arriving at the medicine cabinet. He was surprised to find it had a lock on its door, which he thought was unusual for a normal household medicine cabinet in the bathroom, especially as there was no sign of children living there. He quickly dealt with the flimsy lock. Inside, amongst the normal run of the mill cold remedies, he found six white plastic syringes. Quinn thought that was definitely not the normal contents of a family medicine cabinet. Even a diabetic had equipment different to that.

"It's strange," mused Quinn aloud.

Lomax & The Biker – The Trilogy

"What is?" asked Lomax.

"Well, we haven't found much preparation debris, either here or in that seedy room where Harley man died," observed Quinn. "Granted we found some there, but I would have expected more."

"Unless he buys it pre-packed; the ultimate in convenience shopping, eh" said Lomax.

Something was bothering Quinn. Something didn't sit right and he couldn't pin it down, but he kept his thoughts to himself for now. He disliked the unexplained; it indicated a lack of complete control and he was not used to that. He parked his disquiet somewhere in the back of his mind and consoled himself with the promising information they had collected.

"What's that? Quinn asked suddenly.

"What? I can't hear…"asked Lomax listening hard.

"Sshh!!" hissed Quinn.

He pointed to a low door under the stairs, from which a barely discernible, but very definite, high-pitched keening sound could be heard. Lomax moved towards the door and opened the lock. He turned the handle and was about to peer inside when a battering ram hammered flush into his nose.

-13-

After Quinn and Lomax had left the hotel room, Leanne had gone back to the king-sized bed. Now she stretched lazily and, although the hollow remained where John Lomax's head had been on the pillow, the other side was cooling fast. In the darkness she imagined she saw his shadowy figure as he hastily pulled on his clothes and she wished he was there with her. She remembered him, fully dressed, leaning over and kissing her on the forehead. His unshaven face scratched her skin. Leanne wished he'd shave more often, but lately he had taken a liking to the modern fad of designer stubble. She resolved to talk to him about it at the next opportunity.

She had enjoyed her display in front of Lomax and Ray Quinn, and had not missed the latter's involuntary reaction. She eschewed the hotel's towel robe, preferring to slide into her Japanese silk kimono, John's latest gift. Leanne opened the blinds and relished the view. As part of the city's new and prestigious canal development, the hotel guests enjoyed looking out over freshly painted black and white bridges, magically hovering over the canal that snaked darkly on its journey out of town. She took in the backdrop provided by the pale blocks and tinted glass of the International Convention Centre, today rendered sharp by a burst of February sunshine. She drew herself away from the window and glided into the bathroom. She took a long time choosing gel, shampoo, exfoliating cream and body lotion from rows of bottles and sachets which sat invitingly on a glass shelf. She ran herself a deep, steaming hot bath and gingerly lowered herself inch by inch into its relaxing clutches. If she must wait in that room, she reasoned to herself, then she may as well make the most of it. She sank further into the bath and, resting her head and closing her eyes, she drifted to sleep.

The bathroom door was partially closed, so she neither saw the handle of the hotel door turn nor heard its click as it was carefully pushed open. The Duty Manager's watcher, supposedly stationed in the corridor outside the room and put there to protect her, peered round the door. He had heard the bathwater running and knew his chance had come. After answering Quinn's earlier phone call and confirming that all was well, he had patiently awaited just such an opportunity. He crept toward the bathroom door and was able to see Leanne's slumbering recumbent figure.

He felt in his pocket for the syringe. His gloved fingers wrapped themselves around the implement and he held it out in front of him, preparing to slide its sharp needle into whichever part of her body best presented itself. He knew he should do it quickly. Jack Noble had told him that Quinn and Lomax were on their way, so time was of the essence. He needed to get on with it, but couldn't help himself. He was transfixed by the beauty of the glistening wet body before him and just stood there, gazing and wishing.

Ray Quinn bundled John Lomax into a taxi and left the cabbie in no doubt of the need to hurry. The driver cursed them roundly, saying that his cab was not a bloody hospital, but he nevertheless recognised the chance to make a fast buck. Lomax's nose was pouring blood and was a frightening sight. Quinn had never been phased by the sight of blood; not even when he had been caught in the horror of the 7/7 London bombings. He had found then, and in his time spent in theatre with the forces, that he could deal dispassionately with gore and injury. He knew his friend's nose was broken, but couldn't be sure there was no other damage. The cabby drove across the river Thames, from north to South.

Quinn leaned forward so that his face was visible to the driver through the sliding glass partition. "Now listen," he said, without a trace of annoyance, "I know London, and I know the quickest way to our hotel from where you picked us up, so please don't cross the river when you don't have to. The fare should be £7.50. I'll give you £10 and you can keep the change, but please don't take me for a tourist or a fool. And don't talk about road works or diversions."

The shaken cabbie eventually dropped them at the entrance to the hotel and Quinn pushed a note into his hand, telling him to keep the change. He also told him that he had taken his licence number, his name and other details and would be in touch. His exact parting words were, "I'll need a word with you later." The puzzled cabbie watched them disappear through the hotel entrance, innocently oblivious of the ominous meaning carried by those words.

Ray Quinn helped his friend John Lomax up the stairs and along the corridor. Lomax was concentrating on catching the blood which was still pouring from his nose and had ruined at least three man sized linen handkerchiefs. Despite his efforts, the hotel carpet was still suffering. Quinn looked up and caught the ominous sight of Leanne's hotel room door. It was ajar, rather than being noticeably open, but he had spotted it.

The Biker was fully alert. He recognised the danger. Gently setting Lomax down on the chair which should have been occupied by the Duty Manager's trusted employee, he made a mental note to discuss the question of trust. He moved quickly on the balls of his feet and glided silently into the hotel room. All his training and experience rose to the surface. His ears strained for any noise and his eyes took in every little detail.

It was too easy. The man's back was towards Quinn and he was totally concentrated upon whatever was in the bathroom. Quinn guessed what held the man's attention so completely. Having seen her beauty for himself, he couldn't blame the man. He was two feet behind him when he saw the needle. Without so much as a heartbeat's hesitation he struck. The man in front of him slumped and he caught him before he could hit the floor. He never knew what hit him, but when he awoke no amount of effort could free his bonds.

For a reason beyond his comprehension his jacket seemed to be stuck to the wooden arms of the chair and the same was true of the seat of his trousers.

"Hello," said Ray Quinn from behind the chair. "I'm sorry to cause you such inconvenience, but you need to explain yourself. Don't bother to fidget; the glue is strong and you can't get up.

Have you ever read "Red Dragon?" Perhaps when this is over you should get a copy from your library."

The captive man breathed heavily and his nostrils flared with fear. He had indeed read the novel to which Quinn had referred and the thought terrified him. In that story, the captive hadn't been glued to chair by his clothing; he had been stuck fast by the skin of his naked body. He also remembered that man's fate and he squirmed with sheer panic.

The effect was all Quinn had intended and it didn't take long for him to ascertain all the information he required.

Leanne had heard nothing of the disturbance and her eyes widened in alarm when she saw Quinn standing over the captive figure in the chair. Her kimono slipped from her body and Quinn couldn't help looking. She coolly took her time to retrieve the fallen garment, knowing very well the effect of her movements.

"I'm sorry to have disturbed you, Leanne," said Quinn, trying but failing to avert his gaze. "It seems our friend here decided to change his allegiance and work for the ungodly. There's enough in that syringe to have done you no good at all. He cannot harm you now, but I'm afraid I need to ask him a question or two and you may not wish to witness at first hand the method I shall use. So, please, go back to the bathroom, shut the door behind you and relax. I'll come and fetch you."

"I'd rather stay here," she replied. "I feel safer when you're around. Besides, my imagination will only run wild and I'm sure the real thing won't be as bad."

The captive in the chair heard the exchange, as he was meant to, and his own imagination was working overtime. His eyes widened with fear and he bounced up and down, struggling for freedom.

"Very well, "said Quinn, "but I must ask you not interrupt or interfere. I shall be as quick as possible, but you never know how long these things take. Everyone's different and you can't tell at the beginning."

He turned to the man in the chair and, having placed the syringe just out of his reach on a table, he stood directly in front of him and began his address.

Quinn knew that most people can withstand some degree of pain. Simple everyday dealings with the doctor or dentist bear witness to that truth. There are also some who can resist more severe levels of discomfort, albeit for short periods. The history of warfare and interrogation confirms that. There are also individuals who are at either end of this spectrum, being able to withstand either chronic pain or no pain at all. But Quinn understood the psychology of fear. He knew what the anticipation of pain can do; especially if it involved the expectation of the captive being subjected to the very treatment he had intended to use on another just a few brief minutes ago.

The shattering completeness of the role reversal was not lost on the man in the chair. That man also knew that Quinn could be a most unforgiving man. His head bowed in submission as his resistance crumbled before it had even begun.

"Now, we'll keep it civilised, shall we? I shall be polite to you and I hope you'll return the courtesy. Look at me, please. I only want to have a word with you. I'm sure you have the answers to the questions I am about to ask and I'm equally certain you'll assist me in any way you can."

The formality of the language Quinn was using and the politeness he employed increased the effect of the message. That effect was not lost on the captive. Quinn was conveying to his prisoner that violence was the last thing he wanted to employ, but he most certainly would if necessary. The anticipation of pain.

"Who sent you?" asked Quinn.

"Jack Noble," replied the captive.

"What were you supposed to do?"

"Use the syringe on her," he said, nodding in Leanne's direction.

"Would it have killed her?" asked Quinn.

"I don't know. I was given it just as it is."

"That's not good enough," said Quinn sharply, moving his hand towards the needle. "Perhaps we'll jog your memory."

The prisoner's eyes couldn't help but follow his movement.

Leanne was spellbound. The power exuded by this man Ray Quinn, combined with its controlled understatement, excited her. She was surprised by her own reaction and became acutely aware that it was almost sexual. She couldn't take her eyes off The Biker. Such calm; such power; such total control! She would have done anything he asked at that moment.

"I don't normally repeat myself, but I'll make an exception just this once. I'll ask you again. Would it have killed her?"

"I think so," replied the man in the chair, looking at his captor with red running eyes. "I honestly don't know, but I think there would be no point in Noble sending me otherwise."

"What was Noble going to do then?" asked Quinn.

"He didn't tell me," said the man, desperate lest his answer was inadequate. "But he told me not to leave. He said to stay in the room and make sure nobody else got in."

"Did he tell you to contact him once you had done it?"

"Yes."

"I see," said Quinn, his mind working at breakneck speed. "So he won't expect to see anybody outside in the corridor standing guard."

"I suppose so," said the captive, utterly spent now.

"Then we'll make sure he gets his wish," said Quinn decisively.

Ray Quinn opened the door and called to John Lomax, who was sitting in a similar chair to that occupied by the captive inside the hotel room, nursing his battered nose. It had stopped bleeding, but a livid maroon bruise was starting to swell beneath his right eye socket. The cause of Lomax's discomfort was a terrified woman, who had been shut in the cupboard below stairs. She had seen her chance to escape and exited her prison with all the force of a runaway train. Ray Quinn had not even seen her and Lomax had tried to cling on to her, but had failed. She had not been seen since. Quinn was unhappy about that particular loose end, and had promised himself to resolve the matter in due course.

Unfortunately for Quinn something else had taken place which he could not have foreseen. Before Billy left Charlene in Australia she insisted on knowing where precisely he could be contacted in case of emergency. Billy had argued that he really didn't know, but trusted Ray Quinn. The row was only settled, albeit uncomfortably, after she had reminded Billy of the actual wording of Quinn's text message, which read:

"Please listen, Billy. Things have changed. I need you here as soon as you can. Don't bring anybody else. I need your help. There is a ticket for you at the airport in Sydney; the plane leaves in three hours. This is serious."

Billy had to promise to get the details before Charlene relented. Neither Quinn nor Billy could know that Charlene had persuaded her parents to look after their two year old grandchild in Australia and had travelled to England. She had told her parents that she wanted to be with Billy so that they could assess their options and decide their future. Her parents were sceptical to say the least because they did not wish their daughter and their only grandchild to move so far away. They only agreed to look after the boy on the proviso that they would bring him to England in six weeks time and all the family could enjoy a once in a lifetime holiday together.

Charlene had not contacted Billy before travelling as she was determined to surprise him. As soon as Billy kept his side of the arrangement and texted his whereabouts to Charlene, she jumped on the next plane to London. She entered the foyer of his hotel at the same time as Billy was meeting the brunette. She was so stunned that she stopped in her tracks. Quinn was paying such rapt attention to Billy and the brunette that he had set him up with that he failed to spot anything else. As Quinn and Charlene had never met, they naturally could not recognise each other. The scene was a moment frozen in time; Charlene, rooted to the spot, aghast at what she was seeing and noticing nothing else and Quinn, concentrating on the tableau, failing to notice the change to the normal rhythm of the hotel reception.

The moment was broken as Billy and the brunette left the hotel. They were followed closely by Charlene. Quinn failed to see her because his attention had by then been caught by the appearance of the leather jacketed man. The outcome was a procession which finished in a run- down building which called itself a hotel and which rented rooms by the hour. Billy and the brunette thought they were the first to enter the room, but were interrupted before making any progress by the presence of the leather jacketed man. He had already solved the unexpected problem posed by the arrival of Charlene, by shoving her unceremoniously into a low under stair cupboard, which he duly locked. He could not have known the effect that being in a confined space had upon Charlene. As a young girl she had experienced the same thing and been forced to undergo therapy for over a year afterwards. Thus, when the door to the cupboard closed and entombed her, it had all come flooding back. She was reduced to a quivering wreck in a matter of seconds. She heard muffled voices through the door, but could discern nothing apart from those same voices being raised in an argument. The Harley man had calmly awaited the arrival of the amorous couple and surprised them as they entered the room. He was following instructions given to him by Jack Noble and had been forced to extemporise by the unexpected appearance of a feisty young Australian woman. Charlene made no sound until she entered the keening phase of her desperation. Thinking on his feet he drew a knife, threatened Billy and moved to the brunette to inject her with a lethal dose of heroin. He was about to start on Billy when Quinn entered the arena and finally settled matters.

Billy had not seen Charlene because she had already been locked in the cupboard by the time he entered the room. Also, as she was silent none of the participants were aware of her presence. It was only when Quinn took Lomax back to the scene, after having returned Billy to his guarded hotel room, that her plaintive keening was heard. When Lomax opened the cupboard door it was Charlene who came charging out, like an enraged bull, head down. She was totally out of control when she smashed into Lomax, broke his nose, and careered out of the room, easily brushing aside his feeble attempt to stop her.

She was thus now one loose end that Quinn needed to resolve.

Lomax & The Biker – The Trilogy

-14-

Not normally susceptible to self-doubt, Ray Quinn reviewed matters. Apart from the immediate situation in the room in which he had a terrified captive glued to the hotel chair, an extremely shaken John Lomax with a broken nose, a doe-eyed Leanne waiting upon his every word and the very real prospect of Jack Noble appearing at any moment, there was the question of Billy. He was still in another room waiting for Ray, being guarded by another of the Duty Manager's men. Had that man also swapped his allegiance? Was Billy, even now, in difficulty up there? Quinn thought that unlikely because he had used the text message to tell him that Billy had been dealt with at his seedy assignation with the brunette. The question was whether Jack Noble had checked on that? If he had, he would have found his leather jacketed man and the brunette there, both deceased and, more significantly for him, no Billy. Noble would have recognised the scene for what Quinn intended it to be: a warning. Quinn knew it wouldn't stop Noble. In fact he knew it would have the opposite effect. Noble would view it as a challenge that could not be allowed to go unremarked. In an ideal world Quinn needed to keep Billy apart from Leanne and Lomax so that Noble's targets were not in one place. He also needed time to deal with them in accordance with his original plan, but the situation had taken a turn for the worse. Then there was the potential complication posed by the desperate figure from the cupboard. Quinn felt sure it was female, despite not having seen her, but who was she and why was she there in the first place?

Who had shut her in that cupboard? Where had she gone and how could he find her now? Leanne also preyed on his mind. She had blatantly flirted with him in front of Lomax and seemed to be giving him a message. He obviously recognised it for what it was, but it was a dangerous game. He wondered if it really was just a game or whether she meant anything more concrete and would see it through. He admitted to himself that the thought wasn't without its appeal, but knew he would resist the temptation. He had a wife, after all, whom he loved. Besides that, he was caught up in a rapidly developing and increasingly serious situation.

He told himself that, just as he always had when out on a mission, he must concentrate totally on the job in hand. He must focus on the desired outcome and ignore side issues. He must be ruthless. He knew he was proficient in that regard.

Sometimes in life one had to adjust, think rapidly and be decisive, he concluded. Perhaps it was time for reunion. Perhaps the lure of just one target would prove too much for Noble to resist. Quinn began to admit that the idea had its merits. He held the initiative, which was an advantage. He was no longer merely reacting to change; he was driving it.

He picked up the phone and entered Billy's room number.

"Hello Billy?" he said. "Have you eaten?"

"No," came the reply. "I've been just sitting here watching TV waiting for you. I was getting worried. The isolation gets to me and time drags. I can't stand it."

Lomax & The Biker – The Trilogy

Quinn recognised the signs of panic and knew it wouldn't be long before Billy did something silly again. Quinn had specifically instructed him to sit tight, but Quinn knew that if he was left to his own devices he wouldn't be able to resist the temptation for too long.

"That's ok," said Quinn, "the waiting's over. I need a word with you, so let's talk over a good meal. I'll meet you in hotel restaurant in five minutes."

He had deliberately neglected to let Billy know that Lomax and Leanne would be joining them because he wanted to assess his reaction when he saw them sitting at the table waiting for him. Quinn punched another number into the phone and spoke in hushed tones to the Duty Manager. He then turned to address the room.

"So, dinner anyone?" he asked as he replaced the handset. "Oh, I'm sorry," he said to the chair bound captive, "I nearly forgot. You can't, can you. Never mind, we'll try to bring a doggy bag back for you. Meanwhile, why don't you enjoy the view?"

Quinn moved the captive, still glued to the chair, so that he was facing the bedroom window with his back to the door. Having satisfied himself that the gag he had just tied around the man's mouth was tight enough to prevent him calling out, but only just loose enough to allow breathing, he led Lomax and Leanne out into the corridor.

The Biker, Ray Quinn, his senses on full alert, saw it first. The lift was on the move and heading their way. He hustled his charges towards the stairs and told them to wait at the first turn. He climbed back up the twelve steps and carefully positioned himself so that he couldn't be seen. He heard the soft 'ching' of the bell announce its arrival. The only passenger in the lift stepped out. Quinn saw in him an assured confidence, a man who was used to being in control. He was carrying something that was partially hidden to Quinn. The man moved down the corridor and knocked on the door from which Quinn had only moments earlier emerged. There was, of course, no reply from within and the man rapped more loudly and urgently. He became impatient and opened the door quietly.

"Hey, it's me; Noble. Is it all done?

As Quinn could not see into the room he could only guess at what happened next.

"Don't just sit there, answer me!" ordered Noble.

The captive could only wriggle, stamp his feet and twist his head in a vain attempt to communicate with the man who had sent him there.

"What the hell....?" shouted Noble as he saw the plight of his hired muscle.

The glued man was desperate and the chair keeled over as he pushed and pulled in different directions to no avail. He grunted, his nostrils flaring as he hit the floor. He lifted his head in time to see Jack Noble flick his lighter and hold it against the rag which had been stuffed into a glass bottle. Noble tossed the flaming bottle toward the stricken chair-bound man and calmly walked from the room, closing the door quietly behind him.

Quinn saw the flash and heard the 'wumph' as Jack Noble, unhurried and in control, returned to the lift. He watched Noble re-enter the lift but had no time to find out whether it was going up or down. He could only hope that Billy had already left his room and was either in or on his way to the restaurant. He bounded down the stairs towards Lomax and Leanne and told them to stay exactly where they were as he rushed passed them. He slowed to compose himself before entering the restaurant and his eyes sought the table he had booked. To say he was relieved to see Billy sitting there reading a menu would be an understatement. He turned on his heels and found Leanne and Lomax impatiently waiting for him exactly where they had been left. Although he had planned for Billy to be the last to arrive because he wanted to assess his reaction, he was pleased that he now had all three of them safe in one place.

The hotel's fire alarm sounded just as Lomax, Leanne and Quinn sat down, almost as if it had been triggered by pressure pads in their chairs. The evacuation was for the most part an orderly affair. The car park was used as the gathering point and hotel staff checked names against lists of residents. The last people to vacate the building and be checked against the list of residents were an elderly couple, dressed in full wet weather clothing, who emerged from the hotel's entrance foyer carrying their suitcases. The Fire Brigade had arrived within a couple of minutes of the alarm sounding and the Officer in Charge could be seen giving them a piece of his mind. He had, after all, risked his men's lives by searching for them whilst the fire was taking hold. For their part, they seemed totally oblivious to the danger they had caused and were more concerned as to when they could return to the restaurant to finish their meal. This annoyed the officer even further because it showed that they had left the restaurant when the alarm sounded, returned to their room, packed their cases and donned their outdoor clothing before sauntering from the building. Other residents had evacuated immediately, some even in their nightwear. Thus the delay caused by the couple was doubly annoying because it was cold and raining.

Once the fire had been extinguished people were gathered into public areas in the hotel, but not into the bedroom section in which the fire was located. The damping down process was in full swing, but the room occupied by Lomax and Leanne, now reduced to a smouldering hollow, was being treated as a potential murder scene because the body of a man in a chair had been found.

Quinn overheard the Fire Officer confirm that only one room had been involved, so it seemed that Noble had not torched Billy's room. Quinn had made sure his three charges stayed close to him throughout. The checking of names in such situations is designed to ascertain whether anybody is unaccounted for rather than discovering extra people and therefore it did not reveal the additional figure in the car park. Jack Noble had calmly joined the gathering assembly and, placing himself as close to his four targets as possible without being discovered, watched proceedings with an eagle and predatory eye. Ray Quinn spotted him, but made no mention of it to the others. Quinn had also taken note of the presence of the man designated by The Duty Manager to guard Billy's room. He was standing behind Jack Noble and was whispering into his ear.

"Billy," said Ray Quinn, "was there anybody outside your room when I called you down to the restaurant?"

"No," replied Billy. "There was just an empty chair along the corridor."

"Are you sure?" pressed Quinn.

"Yes, I'm certain," answered Billy.

"Ok," said Quinn.

His mind was racing and it did not take long for him to make a decision.

"I think we should go back to the restaurant. We are not in any immediate danger and I don't know when we'll be able to eat again."

Leanne, Lomax and Billy each looked at their protector with a plethora of questions forming in their minds. Their faces reflected their puzzlement, but Quinn was in no mood for his group to remain standing in the open in deep discussion. He ushered them back to their table. An overly attentive waiter appeared and took their drinks order. Quinn insisted they each decide upon their meal before he would contemplate anything else.

Lomax & The Biker – The Trilogy

The waiter returned with their drinks and carefully took their food orders. When he departed, Ray Quinn raised both hands in front of him, palms outwards, resting on the table just above the wrists.

"Now," he began, as his three fellow diners stifled their own questions in response to the body language, "let's take stock. How you each came to be here tonight is not important. We'll discuss that another time. It's obvious that this Jack Noble, to whom you owe money John, knows we are here and is upset with you."

"That's an understatement," interjected Lomax, "he's just tried to murder Leanne!"

"And failed," Quinn reminded him. "But he won't accept failure. He need not have torched that room tonight. He could have released his man and perhaps got information about us from him. He chose not to do that. He preferred to torch the room and let the man die an horrific death. He even stood in the crowd outside and made sure we knew he was there. He was giving us a warning. Of equal importance is that he was issuing a warning to everybody else, his own staff included, that failure is not an option. It also lets us know that he will stop at nothing. It's not about money any more, John, it's about respect and loss of face."

Quinn looked at each in turn, studying their eyes. He took his time. He was seeking confirmation of their commitment, but he was also asking for affirmation of their trust. As his gaze fell upon Leanne, she returned his look with a barely perceptible blush and lowered her eyelids in submission.

"Now that we're all together," he continued, "I think you should remain so. There is strength in numbers. I realise it gives Noble just the one target, but he won't be able to pick you off one at a time. Let's enjoy our meal, as much as we can, and restore some sanity here."

"But Ray," queried Billy, "why were you keeping us separated? You asked me to come to London alone as a matter of urgency to help John. You've no idea what trouble that caused, by the way. No sooner do I get here than I'm set up to be killed. On top of that I don't understand my mother's part in all this."

"We've already had that discussion, Billy," Quinn flared. "As I said at the time, there are things that are none of your business." Quinn was now all business, irked by what he saw as Billy's selfishness. "Suffice it to say that we are where we are. We have flushed out John's enemy, given him a bloody nose (if you'll pardon the obvious irony there) and effectively taken charge of the pace and direction of events. He is on the back foot. We are no longer having to react to him; he is now forced to be on the defensive. It's a stance he won't like, so we need to be alert."

There was an authority, recognised by Lomax and Leanne, that brooked no argument.

"Talking of bloody noses, what happened to you?" asked Billy, looking at John Lomax, whose face was growing a multitude of interesting colours, but keeping a wary eye on Quinn's reaction.

"I walked into the edge of a door," said John Lomax, infusing his answer with as much sarcasm as he could muster.

Lomax & The Biker – The Trilogy

"Actually, I'm glad you've brought that up," said Quinn, looking directly at Billy again. "Obviously, John didn't actually walk into the edge of a door. He's not that daft. There was a door involved, but what lay behind it caused the injury. We heard crying noises from behind a door under the stairs and as soon as John opened it somebody hurtled from the dark depths and smashed into his nose. John tried to grab whoever it was, but he or she escaped. I was looking the other way at the time and so didn't see anything except a fleeing figure. I'm pretty sure it was female. Whoever it was will certainly have a headache by now. We do have one clue though. I found an earring on the floor not far away. I haven't mentioned it to John before, because there's been no chance. Does anybody recognise this?" he asked, fishing in his trouser pocket and producing a droplet shaped pierced earring which boasted a not inconsiderable diamond at its centre.

The earring was passed from Quinn to Lomax.

"That's a very nice piece," said Lomax; "quite expensive." His jewellery shop experience was showing. "Perhaps we'll keep it and I can have a second one made for Leanne when this is all over. What do think, my love?" he asked as he passed it to Leanne.

"Well," she said, "it's a lovely thought, but whoever it belongs to will certainly want it back. It's beautiful."

She placed it carefully in Billy's palm and let go reluctantly. He looked at it and slowly closed his fingers around the gem. He closed his eyes to hide his tears.

"That belongs to Charlene," he whispered. "I gave them to her when our son was born. But I don't understand. How did it get onto the floor in that room?"

Ray Quinn was on the verge of losing what little patience he had left with Billy.

"When will you ever learn?" Quinn asked through gritted teeth. "I asked you to come over to help John and I specifically told you not to bring anybody with you."

"But I didn't!" exclaimed Billy.

"Then how did she know where to look for you?" asked Quinn.

"I sent her a text, but I didn't for one moment think she'd come all the way here. She must have left the boy with her parents," responded Billy, his face reddening with shame.

"For heaven's sake, Billy! It's hard enough helping your mother and John without having to be a babysitter for you as well. Now we've got to find her. You better pray Jack Noble doesn't get to her before we do."

"So what do we do now? asked Billy.

"You need to be very quiet while I think. Don't even consider interrupting. Don't even breath loudly. Can I trust you to do that? I need John with me and I need Leanne to start playing her part. But you? What do I do with you? Unfortunately, you're the only one of us who will recognise Charlene, so you'll need to be with us. Were it not for that fact, I'd put you away in a place so remote that nobody would ever find you. So just tread very carefully, Billy."

Lomax & The Biker – The Trilogy

It was as clear a warning as Ray Quinn had ever issued to anybody. Normally he used understatement as a means of stressing the import of his message, but he was at the end of his tether with him.

Lomax & The Biker – The Trilogy

-15-

Some situations demand radical solutions and The Biker considered this was one of them. He had detailed his plan to the others, who had agreed with varying degrees of enthusiasm. The main reason Leanne was keen to play the part given to her was that it would give her the opportunity to spend more time in Quinn's company. She had noticed his reaction to her lately and was also drawn to the power he radiated. John Lomax was grateful that it would mean the end of his present difficulties, a future with his beloved Leanne with sufficient money to support them. Billy's agreement took the form of silent, resentful acquiescence. He just wanted to find Charlene and live happily ever after with their son. For Ray Quinn, it had become a matter of honour and, besides that, he was enjoying himself.

And so it was that he was sitting on a bench by a table outside a pub in Hertfordshire. Dressed in his full leathers with his helmet resting within reach on the table, he had chosen the location carefully, so that he had plenty of escape routes. It had been an easy task to find Jack Noble and arrange the meeting. The latter had responded as he knew he would. Noble was a confident man, not used to failure, and that made him predictable. He would neither refuse the opportunity of making money nor resist the chance to settle a score. Ray Quinn had simply sent him a voice mail with enough of a temptation for him to take the bait. It said:

"We must stop playing games. I have something you need. We can do each other some good, so I need a word." He then gave his proposed location and time.

Jack Noble was intrigued as well as angry. He was determined that whoever this upstart was would soon be put in his place. It shouldn't take long; it was a simple matter of teaching the stranger to have some respect. After all, who was this who was treating him like an errant schoolboy?

He had, however, never been treated to The Biker's "I need a word" invitation, so could not understand its full meaning.

Noble swept into the car park and brought his BMW to a gravel crunching halt in the only available space, which was just out of sight from Quinn's position. He strode towards Quinn with purpose; a man on a mission.

"Hello," Quinn said wearing a relaxed grin, purposely not proffering his hand. "It's good of you to come."

"Let's not play games, whoever you are. I saw you after the fire in the hotel car park, with the man who owes me money. I hope you've got it with you, for his sake," said Noble through tight lips.

"Let's not rush," said Quinn. "Take a seat, have a drink. The least we can do is to be civil to each other."

"Why should I waste time?" responded Noble, becoming visibly agitated. "It's a simple matter. You've either got the money or you haven't."

"How much was it again?" asked Ray Quinn, smiling again at his adversary.

"You've got some nerve!" Noble hissed. "You sit here as if butter wouldn't melt and you think you can haggle with me. Well think again. Who do you think you are?"

"I am the man who can save you from yourself," said Quinn brightly. "I've got the money, but I've also got a proposition. If you accept then I can guarantee you'll make more money than you've ever dreamed of. If you don't then I can guarantee you end up rotting in some cell or perhaps even worse. Now be a good boy, settle down, and listen. You're making a spectacle of yourself."

Noble fought the temptation to throttle this stranger who had the effrontery to treat him like a child and smile whilst doing so. He was struggling with his demons when another car crunched across the gravel. It drove straight into a space that had been vacated only a few seconds previously, not ten yards from the two men. The driver's door opened and a woman alighted. Quinn was struck by her poise and assured calm whilst Jack Noble was struck by her other obvious attributes as she walked towards them, her breasts upon the offbeat. She sat beside Quinn and smiled at him before turning her gaze towards Noble.

"I am sorry to disturb you, but I have an important document that needs your signature," said the woman.

"No problem," said Ray Quinn, studying the paperwork for a brief moment before using the pen offered by the woman. "I am sorry. Excuse my rudeness, let me introduce you. Leanne Lane, meet Jack Noble."

"Pleased to meet you, Mr Noble," said Leanne, "I've heard so much about you," she continued, treating him to her best breathless huskiness.

Jack Noble was speechless. He had recognised her immediately as the woman who had been in the hotel car park after the fire, with John Lomax and the man who now sat in front of him. His brain was working overtime. There was obviously something suspicious going on, but he couldn't work out what it was.

"Is there something the matter?" asked Quinn kindly. A waiter was close by and he asked him to bring a glass of water for his friend who was by now coughing and spluttering. "Perhaps this will help," said Quinn as he handed Noble a plastic shopping bag. Jack Noble wiped his eyes and peered warily inside the bag. He discovered several neatly tied bundles of notes.

"There's half the money John Lomax owes you," said Ray Quinn. Please don't insult me by counting it; that would cause me great offence. I am a man of my word. You will receive the other half in due course. However, if you take the opportunity of joining our little venture this will be as nothing."

"Why should I trust you?" asked an incredulous Noble.

"Several reasons, actually," replied Quinn. Firstly, I invited you to meet here and you are not in any danger. In fact you are safer with me than you'll ever know. Next, I've brought you some money as a sign of good faith. I need not have done that. Then I have obviously kept my word and come alone, showing trust in you that you will not endanger me. Finally, I've introduced you to Leanne. That's a risk on my part because she is John Lomax's partner. I trust you will show her the same courtesy as you have me, because if you don't then the rules change. So as you can see, I've come here in a spirit of peace and goodwill."

Jack Noble took a while to compose himself before asking a question.

"My man in the chair...did you do that?"

"I am afraid so. Most regrettable, but he was a loose end. Call him collateral damage if you like," replied Quinn, with a disarming smile.

"I'm not sure I can view it like that," responded Noble, "but we'll let that slide for a minute."

"No," said Quinn, "we won't let it slide. You don't control this. He worked for you, so he deserved what happened to him. He's gone; so forget him. Oh, and while we're on this subject the other one outside Billy's room at the hotel has decided not to work for you anymore. He's asked me to let you know. Don't bother to look for him; he's far away and not coming back."

Noble sat there with his mouth open in stunned amazement. Who was this man who had come into his life and rearranged it so dramatically? Who did he think he was? Whoever he was he was certainly sure of himself, thought Noble.

Quinn pressed ahead, not wanting to allow Noble any thinking time. He had him off balance and was not going to let him settle. He nodded imperceptibly at Leanne who reacted on cue.

Lomax & The Biker – The Trilogy

"The first draft of the contract for London is ready on your desk for your approval, and I've confirmed your flights for next week. Mr Lane has booked a table for eight thirty this evening at your usual restaurant," said Leanne, playing her part wonderfully.

"Perfect," Quinn said, nodding his approval. The charade was meant to convince Noble that he was not dealing with lightweights. The use of 'Mr Lane' was intended to catch Noble's attention. He would know that DCI Sandy Lane was no longer of this world, so the only 'Mr Lane' would be his son, Billy. The hook worked. The fact that Leanne had made such an obvious physical impression as well was a bonus and Quinn made a mental note to use that advantage again.

Leanne crossed her legs, making sure Noble saw just enough of her charms, and flirted with her eyes for good measure. It was like taking candy from a baby, reflected Quinn. They had found Noble's weakness.

"So, what's the plan?" asked Noble, without taking his gaze from Leanne. "You've given me half the money your man Lomax owes, but haven't told me how or when I'll get the rest. He'll regret it if he thinks he can con me. People have died for less."

"I am fully aware of that," responded Ray Quinn. "He is not treating the matter lightly and neither am I. You may be assured you'll receive the rest of your money within seven days from today. I do not intend to let you have the details of our further plans until then. We need you to show some good faith as well. I think our meeting is at an end. We'll meet here at the same time on the same day next week."

The money that had just been given to Noble had been raised by Lomax selling some of his jewellery stock at a reduced price. It was, after all, an emergency. The other half of the cash that Noble was expecting had already been similarly raised, but neither Quinn nor Lomax intended to hand that over despite the promise they had just given.

Ray Quinn rose from his seat and motioned for Leanne to follow. If Noble spoke to Leanne next he would know they had their man.

"Will you be here as well?" asked Jack Noble.

It was the same principle as somebody looking backwards over a shoulder to indicate interest after having passed by and The Biker smiled to himself.

Jack Noble watched them leave and waited for his observers to break cover and follow. If Ray Quinn thought things would be easy he would be made to think again. He would let his followers lead him to Billy and correct the mistake. Billy would pay the originally intended price. He took his time leaving. There was no need to hurry because he trusted his followers to ensure Quinn and Leanne Lane did not realise they were being watched. Others had underestimated him before and regretted it and those two would go the same way. He thought it a shame that Leanne could not be saved, but he could not afford the luxury of pity. This was going to be interesting, he told himself, as he climbed into the driving seat of his BMW and buckled on his seatbelt. His mobile buzzed.

"Did you catch it all?" Noble asked.

"Yes, Jack. We've got the lot. Arrangements have been made, as you'll soon see."

He had only been driving for a few minutes when he rounded a bend to see Leanne Lane's car in a lay-by, having been stopped by a police patrol car. He was tempted to stop and offer assistance, but he thought better of it. Now was not the time to derail his plans by becoming involved in a trivial incident. It was probably just a speeding offence or a routine check, he told himself. He slowed to match the speed limit and drove past, hoping not to have drawn attention to himself.

"Hello Jack. Did you see them?" asked the disembodied voice via his Bluetooth.

"Yes. I saw them. That was quick, though. It will give them something to think about. Thanks. See you when I get back." Noble smirked as he drew away, glancing in the rear view mirror as he did so.

As he was looking backwards Leanne was being asked a question.

"Is this your car, madam?" asked the officer.

"Yes," she replied.

"Do you have your driving licence with you?" the officer persisted.

"I'm afraid not," she replied.

"And your name is..?"

"Leanne Lane," she said.

The second officer spoke into his radio, asking for a check on her details. Confirmation came within seconds.

Leanne couldn't help herself. She was still tense from the meeting at the pub, so she began her carefully rehearsed delivery. Talking herself out of difficult situations was one of her specialities, but in the half-minute or so she'd had, she'd already decided to come clean. They must at least have her licence-plate number and had probably filmed her in the act of defying the diversions with closed circuit cameras, although she was staggered that such a petty traffic offence should result in her being pulled over at the roadside.

'I'm really sorry,' she began, apologetic but coolly professional just the same. 'I know I shouldn't keep ignoring the signs, but I forget and before I know it, I'm just way past..."

The traffic officer just looked at her.

"Sorry?" Leanne helped him out. "The diversion signs, I should follow them, I know."

"This isn't about driving, madam." The officer was suddenly floundering, but held up a photo. Leanne glanced at it and was confronted by a face with an obviously broken nose and swollen, multicoloured cheeks.

"Well, I don't remember assaulting a police officer" she began, instantly regretting the flippancy.

Lomax & The Biker – The Trilogy

"It's nothing you've done, Miss Lane," the policeman persisted, with a touch of irritation. "You may want to sit down," the officer indicated the back seat of his car and more from surprise than anything else, she did as she was told. "This man was found dead a couple of hours ago."

He may as well have punched her in the stomach, and for several seconds her whole world seemed to sway.

"No!" Leanne blurted uncontrollably. "No, he can't be."

A sudden vision flashed through her mind of another occasion many years ago when, as a young teenager, she had got home from a party to find police in the house and her mother crying uncontrollably. Her father had been killed in a road accident.

"When, how?"

She was so sure that this couldn't be right.

The second officer had taken out a small, black notebook. "We'd like you to help us identify him. Would you like one of us to be in the car with you?"

"No, thank you. I'll be fine. I'll follow you."

She felt the first creeping chill of apprehension as she allowed herself to consider the seriousness of what she'd been asked to do.

"'Right," she said, "let's get this over with."

As soon as she got back into her car she used her hands free set to call Ray Quinn.

"Hello Ray. You were right; Noble cannot be trusted. I've just been pulled over by a couple posing as police officers. They showed me a photo of a man with a broken nose and swollen cheeks. It looked like John, but I don't think it was. I'm supposed to be following them to the station to identify him, but I don't think they intend to take me there."

Quinn listened intently.

"Can you see this through?" he asked.

"Do I have a choice?" she asked.

"Not really," replied Quinn, trying to sound reassuring, but not certain he was succeeding. "Ok. You'll be fine. They won't hurt you. Stick with it. I've got Mr Noble with me and I need a little time to have a word with him."

-16-

Ray Quinn disconnected the phone and turned to Jack Noble. He smiled pleasantly at him, but his eyes betrayed his true feelings. He was still fully clad in his leathers, but had removed his helmet.

"I'm sorry I've not had time to dress properly for the occasion," he began, but events have moved on apace. It's unfortunate," he continued, "that we seem to have come to such a situation. It appears your people have Leanne whilst I have you. I am prepared to wager the entire sum of money contained in that plastic bag I gave you, that your BMW had brake trouble and you couldn't stop running into that tree after our meeting at the pub. I'd chase your garage if I were you; BMW's are not supposed to have such faults. They're not cheap, after all. I hope the car's not too badly damaged; trees can be so unforgiving. I really didn't want to ruin the car, I only wanted a word with you, but time was against me, so it had to be a sledgehammer to crack a nut, so to speak. Such a shame you had to park it out of sight at the pub, you just can't trust anybody these days, can you? I'm sorry it has come to this, but I had to take precautions, you must understand that."

Quinn was leaning comfortably against a chair directly in front of his adversary, who was having trouble clearing his aching head and getting his eyes to focus. "No need to get up and shake hands," continued Quinn. "Try and relax," he said, "it will all become clear in a few minutes. Please don't waste your energy trying."

Lomax & The Biker – The Trilogy

Jack Noble's senses were indeed returning and his situation shocked him. He was stuck fast to a chair, in exactly the same way as his man in the hotel room before he had torched it. In addition this man Ray Quinn was mocking him, taunting him. Nobody had ever had the effrontery, much less the courage or stupidity, to do that before. He was quite literally puce with rage but no amount of struggling made any difference. Quinn watched patiently until his fury ebbed away.

"May I welcome you to our humble abode?" he asked, the mockery increasing. "It's not much, but it will suffice for now. After all, we haven't got much spare cash now that you seem intent on bleeding us dry. I need to talk to you about that. In fact I need to chat about a few things. We might as well begin with money."

Noble's body shook with anger and his eyes blazed. He couldn't speak as his mouth was full of one of his own rolled up socks. He therefore had one foot fully clad in sock and shoe whilst the other was bare. His eyes took in this detail.

"I'm sorry about that, "apologised Quinn, "but I need to make sure we don't disturb the neighbours. Just a nod or shake of the head will be enough. Do you understand?"

Noble stared fixedly at The Biker without moving. He knew this was a test, to make sure his resistance had been broken. He neither nodded nor shook his head.

"Now that's not very polite," said Quinn as he moved a bowlful of water close to Noble's bare foot. "I'm sorry the water's a touch cold, but we haven't sorted out the hot water system yet. Never mind, it will serve to make sure we don't stain the carpet, won't it?" He produced a pair of bolt cutters from beneath Noble's chair. "The state of your nails! You really should look after yourself better, you know. Perhaps there will be no need shortly. Shall we try again? I don't normally repeat myself, but it seems I've had to do so a fair bit lately. It's a bad habit; I really must stop it. Now, do you understand? A nod for yes and a shake for no will do."

Quinn's hand moved slowly toward the bolt cutters and Jack Noble felt an unmistakable stirring within his lower abdomen as resistance flowed from him like water rushing down a drain. His head nodded furiously.

"That's better, Mr Noble. You'll notice I'm still being polite even though you don't deserve it. I always think that manners maketh man. Decorum at all times. Don't you agree?"

Noble had come to the conclusion that he was being held by a madman, and his head nodded furiously. His feeling was confirmed when Quinn rolled up a rag and stuffed one end into a bottle so that it was just soaked with the liquid contained therein. The bottle was carefully placed upright on the table beside him.

"Do you recognise that?" asked The Biker.

Noble nodded.

"Thought you might," said Quinn. "I thought at the time it was a touch clumsy; not precise enough. Why ruin a perfectly good hotel room? I'll try to resist that temptation, though it's quite appealing at this present moment. As I said, welcome to our humble abode. We haven't been here long and we don't intend to stay once our little misunderstanding has been cleared up. Now where was I? Oh yes; money."

Raving lunatic, thought Noble, trying not to show his thoughts.

"I gave you half the money my friend John Lomax owes you. He is a man of his word as am I. I told you the other half would follow in seven days' time, but you didn't appear to understand the message. That promise still holds. However, the rules have changed somewhat. Mr Lomax is not at all happy that your people appear to have kidnapped his beloved Leanne. Notice the words I use, please. They indicate the depth of feeling he has for her and reflect the lengths to which he will go to obtain her freedom. It goes without saying, of course, that she must be unharmed. Not so much a hair must be touched or a scratch be inflicted, even accidently. Both Mr Lomax and myself are quite clear on that. May I take it that we can agree upon her immediate release, in exchange for your good self, obviously?"

Jack Noble knew he had no option and nodded wearily.

"Good," said Ray Quinn. "That wasn't so hard, was it? I'm pleased we haven't had to lower ourselves to unpleasantness."

The necessary arrangements for Leanne's release were agreed. She was brought to the flat, apparently none the worse for her ordeal and Jack Noble was given his freedom. It had been a deliberate act on Quinn's part to allow Leanne's captors to bring her to the flat because he wanted them to know where to find her. He wanted Noble to trust him. He would test that trust later.

Lomax & The Biker – The Trilogy

After Noble and his two men had departed, Quinn looked at Leanne with questioning eyes.

"I'm ok," she said. "Not a scratch. I really did think they were policemen for a while, though."

There was a disturbing silence between them and Ray Quinn began to feel uncomfortable in her presence. He was worried she might refer back to their significant moments of eye contact and was relieved when John Lomax and Billy walked through the door.

"Thank God that's over," breathed Lomax as he hugged Leanne tightly.

Quinn, Lomax, Leanne and Billy spent the whole of the next day at the flat finalising plans. They agreed on the following:

1/. The need to find Charlene.

2? The need to raise money.

3/. The need to settle with Jack Noble.

4/. The need to return Billy and Charlene to Australia in one piece.

5/. The need to arrive at a situation that would mean Lomax and Leanne could live undisturbed.

"So that's it then," said Quinn smiling at his own understatement. It's all very easy really. It shouldn't take much doing. Let's have a meal, drink some wine and relax. Get as much sleep as possible tonight and the fun will start in the morning." The Biker's eyes were sparkling.

They laughed nervously. Experience had taught them that whenever Ray Quinn was in this mood significant events were about to occur. They were all tired and nobody had any trouble getting to sleep, after their meal and wine. They closed their eyes, each knowing that others ought to be restless that night.

-17-

Billy was the last to make his appearance at the breakfast table. He looked exhausted.

"You look awful," said Leanne.

Billy nodded and smiled weakly.

"He ought to be tired," Quinn put in, with a smirk.

"Is there something you want to share with us?" asked Lomax.

"Cross out point number one on your lists," said Quinn. "Even as we speak Charlene is sleeping peacefully. She managed to text Billy last night and we fetched her. She's a little embarrassed about your nose, John, by the way."

"So she should be," said Lomax, gently rubbing his soreness.

"I think it's improved your looks, actually," ribbed Quinn.

"Hmph," was all Lomax could muster.

"I'm glad she's with us now," continued Quinn. We're all together and that makes it easier to control."

"It also makes us an easier target," put in Billy.

"Yes it does," said Ray Quinn, so we'll have to be that much more careful. Now, let's move on to the other items on our list. I think we can deal with point number three with Charlene's help. Leanne, take Charlene to the library this morning. We need information about Jack Noble from its archives. Anything you can dig up might provide vital clues as to how to deal with him. I intend to use whatever you find against him. We need to reduce his power and influence in the city; to show others that they too could stand against him; to undermine his standing. Apart from that, Charlene needs to be given something useful to do; something to get her out. She's already showing signs of rebellion at being cooped up indoors. Being shut in the dark under stair cupboard has traumatised her and I can't have her being fragile. Being a careful man, Quinn insisted that Charlene and Leanne used a transmitter and tracking device so that Charlene would always be located. While you're doing that John, Billy and I are going to deal with the money side of things. Jack Noble hasn't learned his lesson yet, but by the time we're finished he'll be looking forward to early retirement.

    Charlene proved an imaginative and insightful researcher. She found a good deal of information about Jack Noble, including newspaper cuttings, local authority searches, microfiche records of criminal activity and court papers, financial details and some tax records. Leanne settled at a desk to examine what Charlene had brought to her. She was so engrossed that she didn't notice time passing quickly. When she eventually realised that Charlene had not been to her desk for quite some time, she placed her hand on the paperwork to keep her place and raised her head to look around. Charlene was nowhere to be seen, so Leanne rose to her feet and scanned the entire room. There still no sign of her. She was annoyed and wondered to herself why both her son Billy and now his betrothed shared a propensity to disappear at difficult moments.

    Leanne's initial calm began to accelerate into concern and towards mild panic as she realised that Charlene wasn't within sight. Leanne had not considered the possibility that she would ever really walk off without her, but now she'd done it. Why the hell hadn't she insisted on her wearing the tracking device? The transmitter button was burning a hole in her pocket when it should have been buried somewhere within Charlene's clothing. Leanne swept her eyes up and down the library, desperately seeking out Charlene's familiar clothing. At one point she thought she saw her flapping coat tail, but it was only a middle-aged man scratching himself in concentration. She'd covered the whole of the fourth floor of the library but Charlene wasn't in evidence. The escalators were tucked into one corner of the building and Leanne felt sure she wouldn't have had the time to get that far, but now she had to consider the possibility that she must have. The problem was, had she gone up or down? It would be impossible to search the whole six-floor library herself, so she approached the library desk.

"I'm sorry to disturb you," she said, trying to keep the tremor from her voice," but I need some help. I've lost my daughter."

"Oh, I see," said the woman from behind the desk. With a minimal hand signal she beckoned to a uniformed security guard. "This lady has lost her little girl, can we do a search?"

"No," Leanne interrupted. "She's not a child, she's a grown woman, but she's a bit upset at the moment and is a stranger to this country. I have to find her."

"Don't worry, madam, this happens all the time. We'll soon find her." The guard was reassuring. He activated a button on his walkie-talkie. "Put out a missing person, please," he said and relayed the description Leanne provided.

Meanwhile Leanne went shakily to the main library reception area from where, she had been told, the search would be coordinated and to where Charlene would be taken when she was found. She waited for an agonising fifteen minutes, at the end of which the original guard came back to her shaking his head.

"We've looked everywhere. She's not in the building. Would you like us to call the police?' Leanne was at a loss. Why would Charlene suddenly wander away when she had been warned that she must stay with Leanne. She didn't know what to do and was about to phone Lomax when, by the main doors, she caught sight of something sparkling on the floor. Trying to maintain her composure she scurried across and picked up the teardrop shaped earring. It had an expensive looking diamond at its centre. Leanne recognised it at once. She felt as if someone had walked over her grave.

"Are you alright, madam?" asked the guard who had by now appeared at her shoulder. Would you like me to call the police?"

"No," she blurted forcefully. Realising the guard had baulked at her reaction, she tried to calm herself and said, "no, thank you, "it's kind, but I'll do it. I know who to speak to."

Outside the library, and away from the guard's hearing, she took out her mobile phone to call Ray Quinn. Before the call was connected she realised that she should be phoning John Lomax and entered his number instead. Was she becoming infatuated with Quinn? she asked herself.

"Hello. John. Thank God you're there! I'm at the library. We found a lot of good stuff, but I've lost Charlene. I've searched all over, but...." Leanne's words tumbled out in a garbled rush.

There was a deafening hiss and Lomax's voice was drowned out by a wave of interference. Leanne waited for the static to clear. It didn't and there was no other option but to terminate the call. She would have to move to somewhere else and try again. But before she could, her phone rang again.

"Thanks for ringing back," she began.

There was some more interference.

"Is that Leanne Lane?" The unfamiliar male voice was sharp and cutting.

"Yes?" she said.

"Let me reassure you your daughter in law is safe and well."

"What? Who is this?" Leanne grappled for understanding. What was going on?

"Don't worry," the man reassured her. "As I said, she is perfectly safe, but she's going to stay with us now, because you have something that we want."

"What do you mean?"

"Why don't you just listen for a moment, and I'll tell you how you can ensure her safe return." Leanne tried to place the accent. She thought she detected a trace of Welsh, but wasn't sure.

Lomax & The Biker – The Trilogy

"It's very simple," the voice went on. "As soon as we have finished this conversation, I want you to take your phone and drop it in the black rubbish bin five yards to your right, just so that you won't be tempted to use it again to dial 999."

Leanne looked across to her right. About five yards away was an ornate, cast-iron bin. Whoever he was had her in his sights. He was right there with her. She scanned the crowd of people around the square. Everyone seemed to be hurrying to the shops, back to the office, in and out of the nearby museum. She could see no-one talking into a phone.

"All right,' she said, trying hard to keep her voice steady. "What do you want me to do?"

"I want you to go back to the library and gather up all the material you have been working on relating to Jack Noble. Then go to your bank and withdraw the amount of money that John Lomax still owes Mr Noble. I know the bank will say they cannot release that amount without at least 24 hours notice, but you will just have to be persuasive. We know you have the money in an instant withdrawal savings account, so don't let them fob you off."

"But what's going on? asked Leanne.

"That's none of your business," came the reply, "and if you know what's good for you you'll make it stay that way. Make sure you don't leave anything behind in the library. I know what should be there."

"Then what?" asked Leanne, fully focussed now.

Lomax & The Biker – The Trilogy

"Go to the Conference Centre. Sign in as a delegate. There's only one presentation there today. The receptionist will give you a pack. Ask her for a spare, because you have a friend who can't attend and you've promised to pick up any materials. Go into the hall, sit two rows from the back. Empty one pack and put the materials under your seat out of sight. Put the library stuff and the money into the empty pack. Stay for ten minutes and then leave. Make sure you leave the pack on your seat. Go to the coffee shop on the corner and sit down. Order a coffee and wait for my call. When we're satisfied that we have everything we need, I'll call to let you know where you can find Charlene. Don't make any attempt to contact your friends or involve the police. If you do I won't be able to guarantee her safety. The same will be true if you try to evade us or do anything to draw attention to yourself. You are being watched. Do you understand?" The caller's voice was barely a whisper. "I hope you appreciate how serious I am."

"How do I know you'll do what you say?" asked Leanne.

"I don't think you have a choice, do you?" the chilling voice replied, before the line went dead.

She had been through a great deal in her life, but could not remember feeling as alone as she did at that moment. Charlene had not wandered off, she'd been abducted. She had to do as she was told. Sick with fear she gathered up the materials from the library and hurried towards the bank, dodging other pedestrians as she forged her way through. Someone was observing her, following her, but she dared not look back. Leanne had to resist the urge to grab someone, another woman perhaps, and plead with them to call Lomax or Quinn. She kept an unnatural distance from everyone she encountered.

At the bank there seemed to be an unusually large number of people queuing to carry out their business. The line moved agonisingly slowly and Leanne had to overcome the urge to shout "hurry up!" or barge her way to the front.

Ray Quinn shifted uncomfortably in his seat. He made a mental note not to buy that particular make or model when the time came for him to own a car. He had hired the vehicle to help maintain anonymity because he had driven a hundred miles each way to sell the drugs to a well known dealer. He had made sure the car was the same make and model as that owned by Jack Noble, and had also taken the precaution of using forged licence plates. To anybody casually looking it was Jack Noble who had made his regular journey on the usual day at his normal time. He hadn't actually met the dealer because he always used a different runner as a precaution. The drugs he had sold had been stolen earlier from one of Noble's own runners. The overall outcome pleased Quinn. Jack Noble had been deprived of a significant amount of gear which had been sold to his usual contact for the normal price. Quinn was therefore in possession of much more money than they needed to pay Noble the last half of what Lomax owed. Quinn would keep his word by paying Noble with money raised from the sale of his own drugs. There would be a great deal left over, which they would use to put back the cash that Lomax had earlier raised by the sale of some of his jewellery stock and make sure Lomax and Leanne were able to live without financial worry for the foreseeable future. It was also sufficient to return Billy and Charlene to their domestic bliss in Australia and still leave a tidy sum for himself. It was a very neat arrangement, thought Quinn. Very neat. He felt even more relaxed about the situation because he knew, from high up inside police sources, that a decision had been taken to turn a blind eye whilst he solved the Jack Noble problem for them. They were happy as long as he was careful. He smiled as a motorway patrol car passed in the opposite direction and flashed its lights. The automatic number plate recognition would have pinged, but they officers had obviously been told to ignore it.

Traffic on the motorway had been light, but had built up as he approached the city on his return journey. It was moving at an uneven, caterpillar pace and he was beginning to develop cramp in his right leg. He also needed to pay a visit to the nearest facilities, so he pulled in at the next services. He calculated that Leanne and Charlene would be back at the flat so he made the call. John Lomax and Billy had been left there to hold the fort and keep a wary eye out for any sign of Jack Noble or his workforce. His call was answered almost before it had rung at the other end.

"It's John. I think we've got a problem, Ray. Leanne tried to phone me, but she was cut off. I recorded what she said. Listen. Leanne's alarmed voice sounded in Quinn's ear as he heard her exact words.

'Hello. John. Thank God you're there!" "I'm at the library. We found a lot of good stuff, but I've lost Charlene. I've searched all over, but..'

"She was cut off by interference before she could say anymore," said Lomax.

"And she didn't call back?' asked Quinn.

"No, Ray."

"And she was definitely on a mobile?"

"Definitely. The number came up as hers," confirmed Lomax.

"Ok. You two stay there in case anybody comes back. I'm not far away now. Phone me if either of them returns or anybody arrives. Also, let me know if there is any phone contact from anybody at all." Quinn finished issuing instructions and disconnected.

He eased himself back into the driving seat, waited for the Bluetooth to connect and moved off into the traffic. He tapped in Leanne's mobile number. It worried him that it was obviously switched off. As soon as he disconnected, the hands free rang loudly in the car. He was surprised by its volume and, momentarily distracted, he veered out into the adjacent lane of traffic, causing the car coming up alongside to stand on his brakes. The driver hooted and gestured angrily.

If only you knew, thought Quinn. "Yes?' he shouted at the unit set into the dashboard.

He recognised the voice immediately as that of one of his most trusted biker friends. It was Frank, the same man who had treated

Leanne to the ride of her life for four hours on the back of his bike and frightened her to death. "I'm outside the library, Ray. I can see Leanne, but she's on her own. She was on the phone for a little while and is obviously agitated about something. I've never seen the other woman before so I wouldn't recognise her. Do you want me to keep an eye on Leanne?

"Definitely, Frank. Stick to her like glue. She won't recognise you because you were in biking gear when you last met. Be careful, I don't want anybody to know you're interested in her."

"No problem," replied Frank, "but I might need support if this Charlene or the opposition turn up."

"Good man," said Quinn. "I'm not far away now."

He disconnected the call and drove on, deep in thought, whilst not many miles away Frank continued his surveillance. He saw Leanne return to the desk she had been using in the library, gather up a good deal of paper and other material, put it into a bag and walk out as nonchalantly as she could. He followed her at a discreet distance to the bank and, having ensured she was in the queue, retreated to a shaded shop doorway across the road. He swept the area looking for anybody or anything out of the ordinary, but saw only normality.

Leanne left the bank a worried woman, not only because of her situation, but also because she was carrying a great deal of cash. She looked both left and right before seeming to make a decision and heading for the nearby Conference Centre.

Quinn was parking the car when Frank called again.

"She's at the Conference Centre. She's carrying the stuff from the library and she's been to the bank, so I bet there's money in there as well."

"Get in there and see if you can see what's happening," said Quinn. "Let me know as soon as you can. I'll be outside."

Frank watched Leanne as she walked to the front desk and spoke to a receptionist who turned an open file round for her. Leanne picked up a pen and wrote something on the page. She was then given a pack and the receptionist pointed with her finger, obviously giving Leanne directions. Leanne was about to walk away as directed but stopped and said something to the woman behind the desk, who leaned across her desk to hand Leanne a second pack. Frank waited until she was out of site and strode up to the desk. The receptionist began her rehearsed dialogue.

"Welcome to the conference, Sir. If you could sign in please." She turned the open file towards him and he saw Leanne's nervously scribbled name. He signed himself in as Billy Rubin and smiled inwardly. He wondered if anybody would work out the meaning of the name. "You'll need this pack, Mr. Rubin," the woman continued with her intonation. Frank wondered why she had been placed as the first person that delegates would see upon entry. She certainly wouldn't win any prizes for her enthusiasm. She raised her finger, as she had done for Leanne, to point the way.

"Do I need a second pack?" enquired Frank.

"No, Sir. There's everything you need in the one I've given you." She dismissed him by looking over his shoulder for her next customer.

Quinn had arrived just in time to see Frank's back enter the Conference Centre. He settled himself on a wooden bench and awaited developments.

Inside the Conference Hall itself seats were filling quickly. Frank watched as Leanne, following instructions to the letter, sat two rows from the back. She carried out the bag exchange as directed and settled into her seat. He managed to find a seat not far away. Now that he was close he could see her discomfort. Surreptitiously she glanced around to seek out anyone who could be the one watching and waiting. She obviously needed help, but he couldn't risk using his phone to seek instructions from Ray Quinn. He made a decision and the noise attracted her attention. She saw a balding man in a black leather jacket spill the contents of his delegate's pack and kneel to retrieve them. He looked up and his eyes met hers. He gave her what he hoped was an imperceptible but reassuring nod, before gathering his papers and moving off.

Leanne's heart pounded. Who was that man? Why had he attracted her attention? Was it the end of the matter? Should she still do as she had been instructed? She looked around, desperately seeking familiar faces, but she knew she was alone. Her desperation was interrupted by the duo of presenters introducing themselves. Leanne hoped it wouldn't be one of those events where the delegates were asked to introduce themselves as well. "Hello, my name's Leanne and I'm being blackmailed." Now that would cause a stir.

The passage of time seemed interminable as she looked at the clock on the wall ahead of her, but, finally the minute hand hit two and she quickly got to her feet. She left the bag on her seat and walked out of the hall. She half expected someone to hurry after her to point out that she had forgotten the bag, but they didn't. The door closed behind her and she walked across the now almost deserted foyer towards the entrance, her footsteps echoing unnaturally loudly on the marble floor. No one had followed. With relief, Leanne forced her legs to keep moving. She was telling herself that the ordeal was nearly over. Once they had what they wanted they'd let Charlene go. She didn't know whether to be pleased or disappointed not to be greeted by the sight of police surrounding the building. Why is there never a policeman around when you need one? She asked herself the age old question. There was no reason to expect police to be there, but it is a natural instinct to rely on them when all seems lost. Unfortunately, everything seemed oddly normal and the world was going about its business.

Then she caught sight of Ray Quinn sitting on a bench not fifty yards away, seemingly without a care in the world, soaking up the sunshine.

Lomax & The Biker – The Trilogy

-18-

Leanne's heart leapt at the sight of her saviour and she almost broke into a run across the square. She didn't understand how Quinn came to be there just when she needed him most, but her only thought was to run to him, melt into his arms and feel his strong protection around her. She knew he had seen her but was puzzled by his lack of movement. Then she remembered the instructions she had been given. The caller had been definite and threatening, and she knew she must resist temptation.

She forced herself to concentrate and looked for the coffee shop on the corner. She had to search hard because it was partly hidden by the awning of its neighbouring hardware outlet and a newly erected bus stop. She tried to maintain her composure as she walked towards the inviting aroma of freshly made coffee, but inside confusion, rage and turmoil were winning the day. She imagined hundreds of pairs of eyes burning into her from every conceivable angle, seeking and discovering her innermost secrets.

The last few steps were made on shaking and wobbly legs and she grabbed the nearest chair with the desperation of a late night drunk taking his final fall. A waitress approached and her bored voice began to recite the litany of coffee options. It was the last thing she needed and she switched off, waiting for the girl to finish before asking for something normal. She fished her phone from her pocket and placed it directly in front of her, desperate for it to burst into life. She looked at her watch, but couldn't focus at all.

Lomax & The Biker – The Trilogy

She gazed across the square trying to locate her nemesis as well as searching for Ray Quinn. She found neither.

She forced herself to sip from the foamy brown and white mess resting on the top of the oversized bowl of a cup and winced at the bitterness. I could swim in there, she thought. Her mobile phone buzzed and bounced on the table in the throes of its vibration, before bursting into noisy life. Startled from her self-pity, Leanne grabbed it with both hands, anxious to prevent it crashing to the floor. With fear fumbling fingers she managed to press it to her ear.

"Not bad for an amateur," mocked the voice. "You've done well so far. Sit tight and wait."

From the comfort of the bench, and with the benefit of the low sun dazzling anybody looking directly at him from the coffee shop, Ray Quinn saw Leanne Lane emerge from the Conference Centre. Against the immense building she looked more vulnerable than ever and he was surprised by a rising urge to run over and gather her up safely. He saw her lunge at her phone and listen intently. He saw her puzzlement when she put it back on the table and sit back in her seat.

Minutes beforehand Frank had managed to find an empty seat along from the one recently vacated by Leanne. He'd been puzzled by her actions, but catching the bag she'd left behind, he suddenly realised what was going on. He stayed for the rest of the lecture, which was greeted at the end with tumultuous applause. As the clapping died away, people began gathering their belongings to leave. While appearing to scan the course brochure, Frank kept his eyes riveted on his target. As it was, he nearly missed the pick-up when it happened. A man shuffling along behind the row, a quick lean over the back of the seat and it was gone, but Frank had him: medium build, red hair, charcoal suit and a bag identical to at least fifty per cent of the other people in the room. Frank knew it was going to be tricky as two hundred delegates surged simultaneously towards the exits.

"Excuse me, excuse me," he repeated to anybody blocking his way, as he stumbled and skipped sideways between aisles to keep up. His quarry had moved off at a pace, but Frank stayed with him, ducking and diving his way through the crowd. Outside the lecture hall the task was much easier. Frank had expected him to make for the main entrance and the pick-up bays, to a waiting car, so he was surprised when he seemed to be heading in the opposite direction. He was making for the rear exit of the Conference Centre, going toward The Festival Hall and the canal, away from where Quinn was waiting. As he ran Frank put a call through to Quinn waiting outside.

"I've got him. Male, thirty-ish, five-eight, short, stocky, ginger hair, wearing a grey suit and white shirt."

"He's not coming my way," said Ray Quinn, "so where the hell is he off to?"

"I think he's going out the back way," said Frank, "towards the canal."

"Where the hell is he going?" shouted Ray Quinn at the phone, uncharacteristically agitated.

"The flat?" asked Frank.

It was certainly a possibility. They began moving to the other side of the building. But as Quinn ran, Frank's voice broke in again.

"We're going over the bridge towards the canal. Oh shit! You'd best get round here!"

"What?" asked Quinn.

Frank couldn't believe his eyes. Approaching the canal side, the man had suddenly broken into a run, at about the same time as Frank became aware of the background revving of a high-powered motor. It was over in no time as the man jumped into a motor-driven inflatable dinghy moored to the side of the canal. It roared away as the pursuers realised the hopelessness of their situation.

"Come on, I know where they're going," Quinn affirmed. "The canal doesn't go on forever. It gets close to the motorway, so they'll head north from there."

Quinn, in his hired car, and Frank, on his bike, gave chase. They swore in equal measure, but in the dense traffic Frank was able to take more risks and closed the gap sufficiently to spot a blue transit van parked on a side street. It was as close to the canal as any road could get and was about fifty yards from the motorway junction. It was the ideal spot. Weaving through the heavy traffic, progress was still painfully slow for Quinn and he had to rely on Frank to keep a close watch on the van.

Ray Quinn was painfully aware that he had left Leanne unguarded, but there was nothing he could do. He called and she told him everything. He took it all in quickly and told her to stay put, trying to transmit confidence and calm. He also told her not to worry, but he knew that had no effect. He was also mindful of Lomax and Billy, so he checked their status and was hugely relieved to find them untroubled. He asked whether they had seen Charlene and was not surprised by their negative response, because he was certain she was in the back of the transit van. He guessed they were either going to drop her unharmed at a motorway services or dump her suffering from a severe shortage of breath.

"She must be in the back of that van," said Quinn, talking to Frank on his mobile and sounding more confident than he really was.

"You think they'll keep her?" asked Frank.

"Or dump her off at a motorway services somewhere. What could be more natural? They can make it look as if they're dropping off a hitch-hiker, then blend back into the traffic."

They closed the gap as they talked. Just as the blue transit came into view Frank drove past it, round the corner and out of sight, made a three point turn, doubled back and pulled into a gap at the kerb-side. He called Quinn and confirmed his position. The driver of the Transit may have seen them, but Quinn doubted it. He was too busy watching for someone else.

With surprise on their side it should have been easy. Like many traumatic events things seemed to happen in slow motion. The getaway craft drew to a halt and, scrambling up the slipway, they made a run for the van. As the rear door was pulled to a close it began to pull away. Quinn's car screeched to a stop blocking the van. Frank was already on foot and had pinned two men to the floor. He was whispering in their ears, explaining reasons why they should remain perfectly still. One man didn't believe him, but was immediately convinced by the sight of his compatriot gasping for breath as Frank knelt on his windpipe, gradually exerting more pressure. Frank had indeed learned a great deal from his friend and mentor.

It was left to Ray Quinn to pursue the other escapee. He gave chase to the driver of the Transit, running along the towpath past soaring concrete pillars that shored up thousands of continuously flowing motorway vehicles. He sprinted into a dark and dank no-man's-land of concrete and scrubby wasteland that echoed to the deafening thunder of overhead traffic. The Transit driver ran behind a concrete pillar and sprinted into a tunnel. Quinn pursued him, his lungs burning, splatting through puddles that soaked his socks, pursuing his quarry into and out of the walkways that crossed and re-crossed the tarmac bound road maze as HGVs trundled along high bridges like a procession of lethargic snails.

Lomax & The Biker – The Trilogy

For a while it looked as if Quinn would lose the runaway in the complex mass of tunnels and bridges, but following under a low, dark flyover he emerged to be confronted by a sheer forty-foot wall, the only way out via crudely hewn steps leading up to a slip road high above. Undeterred by the dead end, the driver was heaving himself upward already twenty feet from the ground. But this was Quinn's territory and launching himself at the wall, he ascended quickly and began to gain ground. He made a lunge for the man's ankle, but simultaneously the driver kicked out viciously, causing Quinn to momentarily lose his footing. For several seconds he flailed in mid-air while he struggled to regain a hold, before slithering down again over the jagged concrete, landing hard on the dirt at the bottom. The driver gave a triumphant leer back over his shoulder before vaulting over the crash barrier to freedom. Almost instantaneously, there came a prolonged, chilling screech followed by the smallest muffled thud and a cloud of bluish smoke billowed into the air. It was freedom short-lived. Quinn halted his pursuit before he could be seen and, gasping for breath, smiled. He turned up his collar, gathered himself and calmly walked away.

He returned to the Transit van, but Frank was waiting with more disappointment. All that had been found in the back of the van were some bags, clothing and empty fast-food cartons. Charlene wasn't there. Quinn asked about the two men who had succumbed to Frank's non too gentle questioning, but there was nothing to be gained from them.

"'What happened to the package?" asked Quinn, looking at Frank's two captives.

There was no response. This was largely because one of Frank's captives could not speak as his throat had been crushed beneath Frank's knee, and his partner seemed unwilling to part with any information.

"Oh please," said Ray Quinn. "Why am I having to repeat myself so much today? I won't ask again."

"You'd be well advised to answer his question," said Frank to the reluctant one, "my friend doesn't share my unending patience and forgiving nature, if you follow my meaning."

Realising the futility of silence he pointed at the grill of a storm drain in the gutter. "It's down there."

Ray Quinn rolled his eyes heavenwards and walked over to the drain. He peered down into a black abyss and his nasal passages were assaulted by the stench of sewage. He turned to the two captives and pointed to the man who had been so helpful.

"Your friend has suffered enough, I think. If we put him down there he'll only go and get an infection in his throat on top of his other troubles. It's down to you, I'm afraid. Be a good chap and retrieve our belongings, would you?"

The man stared at Quinn in stunned disbelief and remained rooted to the spot. Quinn lifted the drain cover with ease and moved swiftly across to him. He held the drain cover in one hand and gently laced the man's fingers through the grill bars, pinning them tightly with his other hand. His strength astonished his adversary.

"Now," said Quinn, "it's getting late and it's nearly time for my supper. I am a man of regular habits, and will have a meal in the next thirty minutes whatever happens. Either you'll be in that drain with the grill safely back in place while my friend and I enjoy our meal, or you will have found our items and possibly, just possibly, you could be breathing fresh air. It's really up to you. Don't forget though, you're making a decision for two people. It's called teamwork."

There was a husky intake of breath from the man with the damaged throat. He tried to free himself from Frank's grasp, but the attempt only brought more pain. Ray Quinn didn't wait for an answer. He pulled the man to the drain opening and swept his legs from under him. He was prostrate on the ground with his head over the hole before he knew what was happening.

"Oops," said Quinn, "that was clumsy. I apologise. Still, now you're there you may as well give it a go."

He unlocked his grip on the man's hand and pushed the grill away. "You can't get in carrying that, can you?" he said.

With one swift movement he tipped his quarry upside down and, holding him only by his ankles, lowered him headfirst downwards.

"I think you'll have to use your hands; you surely can't see anything can you?" asked Quinn, lowering the man a touch further so that the top of his head was washed by the foul waters. "Don't worry, I've got you. You can rely on me."

The unfortunate man stretched out his arms and began to search frantically for the bag that he himself had thrown there.

"You know," mused Quinn to Frank, "I'll have a bet with you that it was my friend down there who is the litterbug. It's only fair that he should pick up his own rubbish, don't you think?"

The man being held by Frank nodded vigorously, hoping his agreement would spare him. Frank merely smiled at Quinn's dark humour, knowing what the outcome would be. They were interrupted by the upside down man wriggling madly, trying to bend backwards to pass his find up to Quinn. Letting go with one hand, Quinn grabbed the bag and peered inside. He smiled when he saw the findings from the library and, equally important, the cash bundled neatly in its bank bindings. Remarkably everything was dry, thanks to having been carefully wrapped in plastic bags and tied tightly.

"That's it. Well done that man!" he said. "It must have got snagged on something, otherwise it would be miles away by now. Are you sure that's everything?"

The man waved his arms to indicate there was no more to be found.

"Perhaps you should make sure. I'd hate for you have to do it all over again," said Quinn as he released his grip and the man plunged out of sight. He said nothing as he calmly picked up the grill and stamped it back into place over the hole. He looked at the remaining captive. "You will notice that you've escaped the same fate as your friend. I didn't think you'd quite fit through the hole, so you'll have to accept our hospitality for a while longer."

The man made no sound as he collapsed in Frank's arms.

"Take him back to the flat," said Quinn to Frank. "Clean him up, give him something to eat and drink. Show him we're not animals. He needs to be convinced that working for Jack Noble is not a good lifestyle choice. I'll leave that bit to you. You'll have to take the car and I'll use your bike. Oh, by the way. There's something in the boot that needs special care. I'd like you to take personal charge of it until I get there. I'd better get a move on and retrieve Leanne. Hopefully, she'll still be sitting in the coffee shop awaiting instructions."

Lomax & The Biker – The Trilogy

-19-

Leanne finished her third cup and was awash with coffee. She needed to deal with its effects, but was afraid to leave her seat in case that would be the very time something happened. It's well known that women can resist the urge to empty their bladders for far longer than men, but just as she decided to give up the unequal fight Ray Quinn walked into view. He had returned to his bench across the square and waited there for a full fifteen minutes, making sure that nobody else was taking an interest in Leanne. He watched as she gazed at an information system which was on a loop around the top of a building rather like the Stock Exchange issuing the latest share prices and news. He glanced at it from time to time and was vaguely amused. It had become well known for its out of the ordinary content. Today someone with a sense of humour had placed oddball definitions to spread smiles across the square and both Quinn and Leanne followed the moving text from their separate positions.

'ADULT: a person who has stopped growing at both ends and is now growing in the middle......CHICKENS: the only animals you eat before they are born and after they are dead...COMMITTEE: a body that keeps minutes and wastes hours.....DUST: mud with the juice squeezed out........EGOTIST: someone who is usually me-deep in conversation.....HANDKERCHIEF: cold storage..........INFLATION......cutting money in half without damaging the paper......RAISIN: a grape with sunburn......SECRET: something you tell to one person at a time......SKELETON.....a bunch of bones with the person scraped off......TOOTHACHE: the pain that drives you to extraction.......TOMORROW: one of the greatest labour saving devices of today.....YAWN: an honest opinion openly expressed.....WRINKLES: something other people have, similar to my character lines.'

The loop was on its umpteenth repetition, before he made his approach.

"Is this seat taken?" he asked politely for the benefit of other ears.

"No, please feel free," replied Leanne matching his courtesy.

Quinn sat opposite Leanne Lane, placed his hands together on the table and gave her his best winning smile. Anybody watching the performance would assume they were meeting for the first time, having been matched by an online dating agency, and would be going for a meal somewhere in town.

"Coffee?" enquired Quinn.

"No thanks," she replied. "I've had more than enough already. In fact I really have to pay a visit. I've been stuck here in case I missed something or somebody. They told me to wait here and not to move."

"They won't be contacting you," Quinn assured her. "Things have moved on a bit. I'll wait here while you do what comes naturally."

Leanne breathed a sigh of relief and hurried away into the depths of the coffee shop. Quinn watched her all the way until she disappeared through the appropriate door. His eyes made another sweep looking out for any sign of interest in Leanne or himself. He dug into his trouser pocket and extricated a scrap of paper upon which he had written the number of a taxi company and a driver's licence number. He used his mobile to request that driver in particular. He was told it would take ten minutes for him to get there, but Quinn insisted he wanted that driver and said he was happy to wait. He looked around again and, satisfied that all was well, he stood up as Leanne returned. He didn't want her to sit again.

"We need to get back to the flat," he said. "Unfortunately, I came here by bike and I haven't got a spare helmet, so you'll have to use a taxi. He's on his way now. Don't worry, I'll be right behind. Nothing will happen."

Leanne instantly remembered an earlier bike ride and was thankful not to have to repeat it. Quinn spotted her relief. He laughed and she couldn't help laughing too. The taxi appeared and Quinn ushered Leanne inside. As she was in the process of settling into taking her seat, Quinn arrived behind her. Puzzled, she gave him a quizzical look. He responded by putting his forefinger to his lips. He slid the vanity glass across and addressed the driver.

"Hello," he said," you may not remember me, but you made an impression on me the last time we met." He put his face closer to the opening to allow the driver a closer look. "Remember now? I thought so," he said as the driver's eyes betrayed him. "I asked for you specifically as I thought I'd give you the opportunity to make amends. I need you to take me to the train station, so that I may collect my bike. Then we need to get this good lady home. I'll follow on the bike. Seeing as you tried to overcharge me before, and today's journey is not all that far, let's agree that there will be no charge. If all goes well, that will be the end of the matter. I'm sure you wouldn't want any further complications, would you?" Quinn treated the man to a meaningful smile and the one-sided debate was over.

Ray Quinn helped Leanne exit the taxi. He turned his attention to the driver, who was badly shaken by the constant looming presence of the bike and the impenetrable helmet in his rear view mirror.

"Thank you," he said pleasantly. "Now I'll be able to recommend you to my friends. Don't worry they pay better than me!"

Leanne and Quinn watched as the driver scuttled away as quickly as his cab and its diesel engine's tapping rattle, would allow.

They walked into the flat to be greeted with handshakes and hugs by Lomax and Billy. Frank was standing in the corner of the living room, close to a window.

"Where's our throaty friend?" enquired Quinn.

"Resting," replied Frank. "He's had a rather traumatic time, I'm afraid. He only wanted to sleep when we got back here, but you asked me to talk to him about his lifestyle. I'm afraid he was somewhat reticent at first but I believe he now sees the error of his ways."

John Lomax giggled quietly.

"Why is it," he asked his friend Ray Quinn," that anybody who is in your company for a period of time becomes almost a clone?"

"No idea," answered Quinn with a grin, "it must be a gift."

"I'm hungry," moaned Billy, "anybody fancy ordering a Chinese?"

"Good idea," said Lomax and wrote down everyone's wishes. "What about our resting friend?"

"Leave him, "said Frank. "I don't think he's hungry right now. Anyway, we'll only have to blitz it and feed him through a straw. Too much trouble for my liking."

Nobody disagreed and Billy phoned the order through. They then turned their attention to analysis and planning.

"So," Quinn began, "we've now got plenty of money. You have still got it Frank," he asked.

"Of course," replied Frank with a smile. "Why doubt it?"

"I gave my word to Noble that he'd get his other half within seven days," said Quinn. I don't want to break my promise so if we have to pay John's debt to Jack Noble we'll do so using his own cash. At least we haven't lost anything. In fact we're very much in profit. I asked Billy to come here to help get money for John and we've done that. I did not bank on Charlene becoming involved."

Lomax & The Biker – The Trilogy

The last comment was a direct reference to his directive that Billy should come alone. Billy reddened at the overt criticism, but Quinn ignored his discomfort and continued.

"I didn't want that and hadn't planned for it, but we now have no choice. It was the first item on our list when we last went through all this and now it's become top priority. We must find her as soon as possible. The longer she's out there, the more danger she's in. Apart from that, all the other things we identified have still to be covered. To reiterate: Apart from finding Charlene, we need to settle Jack Noble, return Billy and Charlene to Australia and we need to sort out John and Leanne's situation."

Ray Quinn did not mention that his own future was inextricably linked to the whole issue, but he had already started thinking about it. The intercom buzzed as the food arrived. Billy collected it at the entrance. Once it had been set out on the table plates were put in front of each of them.

"I can't remember what I ordered," said Leanne.

"Doesn't matter," said Lomax, "let's all just dig in and share. It's no time for niceties."

Silence descended as five hungry people made short work of their tasty food. Five brains worked overtime as they ate, but nobody seemed to want to be first to speak. Eventually, as the last of the meal was consumed, Quinn posed the question.

"Any ideas? I know what I think we should do, but I'd like to hear what you all have to say."

Nobody spoke. There was a tangible reluctance to appear stupid.

"I think I can help," offered Frank, looking at the expectant faces around the table. "Our resting friend was keen to share his burden, so I know where we can find Charlene. Obviously there is a chance that he may have told me lies, but I really don't think so. By the end of our conversation he was thankful to have been able to clear his conscience. I thanked him for his assistance, but made no promises as to his future."

"How did you manage it?" asked Billy.

"You should know better than to ask," Frank reprimanded him, "but if you must know I used my very limited artistic skills to draw a simple sketch of a drain cover being held by a matchstick man and another man looking down into a hole in the ground. I think he got the message."

"Inventive," said an impressed Ray Quinn. His friend Frank was showing promise.

"What on earth is that all about?" asked Leanne at the same time as Billy asked "what does that mean?

"None of your business," said Ray Quinn with authority.

Lomax & The Biker – The Trilogy

-20-

Apart from an ominous creaking and whirring of the lift mechanism, the trio descended to the basement floor in silence while Quinn gave Leanne and Billy time and space to assimilate what they'd been told. Frank was exercising some discretion too. He had wanted to accompany them, but had finally agreed to remain at the flat and look after John Lomax and keep the resting man under control.

Frank had passed on the information that Charlene had been left by some of Jack Noble's accomplices in a room in the basement of the apartment building. He told Quinn that she had apparently been drugged to the extent that, to an untrained eye, she appeared dead and it had been made to look like suicide. Quinn decided not to pass the information to the others because he knew suicide threw up all kinds of powerful and often unwanted emotions. He also reasoned that they would act more effectively if their reactions were genuine. Quinn was the first to think of the solution and the others helped complete the minor details. It was entirely possible that they were walking into a trap, but Frank had been adamant that he believed there would be no opposition.

The first thing they noticed as they entered the room was that it was icily cold. The other details made themselves apparent thereafter. It reminded Ray Quinn of the room from which he had rescued Billy after his assignation with the brunette and Quinn realised that it was meant to. They were being given a highly personal message. There was a woman, curled into the foetal position, with unblinking staring eyes and there was an unmoving man on the floor with a needle hanging from his forearm. There were also newspaper cuttings with highlighted advertisements for personal escort services. A pro would have cleaned up, but whoever had set up this tableau knew what he wanted them to find. Quinn knew it was becoming increasingly commonplace for some higher class call girls to supply, and if that was the case it would explain why everything had been left just so. Quinn was unsure of the identity of the unblinking woman, but Billy knew as soon as he set eyes upon her. He was completely overcome with guilt and fear and was rooted to the spot. Quinn looked at Leanne, who was taking in the scene and hiding her reaction very well. Quinn knew better than to make any comments at that stage, because death is much like life in that everybody handles it in his or her own unique way. Shock can do funny things to people and Quinn bided his time. He wanted Billy to be gradually overtaken by thoughts of atonement and then revenge. The more genuine those feelings were, the better it would be.

"Are you alright?" he asked Leanne. She was clearly shocked, as Quinn would have expected, but still far from being distressed. Instead, she appeared more puzzled and detached as if presented with a conundrum.

"Are you all right?" he repeated.

"Yes." With a brief nod of thanks, she awkwardly moved close, as if seeking reassurance. I just can't believe it."

Lomax & The Biker – The Trilogy

Ray Quinn looked at her and her eyes looked directly into his, steady and unblinking. There was no avoidance, but no trace of any tears either.

She read his thoughts. "You must think I'm hard." It wasn't an apology and Quinn only shrugged.

"Everyone reacts differently in these situations," he said. "You'll probably cry your eyes out when we get back."

Leanne smiled weakly. "That's tactful of you,' she said. "But I don't think so. If I do, it will be for Billy," she whispered softly, hoping her son hadn't heard the exchange.

"I don't understand," Billy's voice was shaky and uncertain. "Charlene.....she's never used drugs. What's happening?"

"People change," said Leanne showing little compassion. "Sometimes pretty dramatically."

"Not in these few days!" said Billy, his eyes welling with tears.

"It can happen," continued Leanne, choosing to ignore the growing rift between mother and son which was becoming increasingly painful for both of them.

"'No!" The anger flared from Billy as he turned to face his mother, adopting a threatening posture.

The silence stretched to breaking point as each stood their ground.

Quinn spoke sharply, "we haven't got time for this! You can sort it out later. We need to get Charlene away from here now."

His words cut into each of them

"Is she going to be alright?" asked Billy, gazing with love and tenderness at her small and fragile body.

"I don't know," replied Quinn, "but we can't deal with it here. She's alive but she needs all sorts of help, and I don't just mean the medical variety."

"What on earth do you mean?" Billy reacted swiftly in her defence. "She's a perfectly normal, beautiful woman."

"And head butting people is a normal part of her behaviour, is it?" Quinn persisted. "We found her hiding in a cupboard under the stairs and when we let her out, she went crazy and John's nose got in her way."

Billy shook his head in disbelief at Ray Quinn's lack of understanding.

"Look," continued Quinn patiently, "I've had plenty of experience with users, you don't have to pretend to me and Frank's also had first- hand experience of it; he can straighten her out. I'd trust him with my life and you can too. He'll get her off the stuff, but it won't be easy. First, though we need to move. Don't touch anything if you can help it."

"She is not a user," Billy persisted, "she was just frightened. She's terrified of the dark and enclosed spaces. When that door was opened she just panicked and came flying out. Check her over for yourself; you won't find any tracks on her arms, I promise you."

Ray Quinn was unused to being proved wrong and didn't quite know how to react. "I'm sorry," he whispered, "it appears I jumped to the wrong conclusion. Let's get her back to the flat, there's nothing we can do here."

"What about the newspaper cuttings" asked Leanne.

"Oh, I think we'll leave those here. I don't think Charlene needs to see them, do you Billy?" said Quinn.

Billy nodded his head in agreement and smiled his silent thanks to Ray Quinn. He bent down and tenderly gathered Charlene, still in her foetal position, into his arms. He straightened his back and turned to follow Leanne. Ray Quinn watched and saw the love in the young man's eyes as he looked at Charlene's pale face.

The mood for their reunion at the flat was not celebratory and an uneasy quiet prevailed. Charlene had not woken from her drug induced stupor and Billy was at the bedside, desperately worried. She was breathing, but it was shallow, rapid and uneven and he noticed that she was sweating profusely. Leanne sat beside Lomax in the living room, holding his hand as they whispered in tones too soft for the others to hear. Frank and Quinn parked themselves in the kitchen, hands gripped around mugs of coffee, recognising that people needed space and time to recover. The resting man was still resting and would do so for quite some time to come. Frank had put him through an ordeal the like of which he had never before experienced or witnessed. It had been the only way to extract the vital information required to affect Charlene's rescue.

"He'll survive, I expect," said Frank, although Quinn noted that he didn't sound entirely convinced.

"It doesn't matter either way," responded Quinn. "He's no more use to us." His voice trailed off as he lapsed into thoughtful silence. "On the other hand, we could send him back to Noble as a message."

"That's risky, Ray," said Frank. "He'll lead Noble here."

Their deliberations were interrupted by Billy as he walked slowly into the kitchen.

"How is she?" asked Frank.

"Asleep," replied Billy, despair etched into his face.

"She's not asleep, she's unconscious," said Frank. "It looks like she's been given cocaine. Do you know much about it?"

"No!" Billy was startled at the mere suggestion.

"I didn't mean have you taken it, Billy, I meant do you know much about the drug itself and what it can do?"

"The answer's still no," replied Billy, trying to settle his inner turmoil.

"Then sit down and I'll educate you. Cocaine is a stimulant manufactured from leaves taken off the coca plant. There are specific cocaine overdose symptoms that should be watched for to recognize an overdose at its earliest stage. By catching the overdose as early as possible and getting immediate treatment, the user has a better chance of avoiding serious injury. When ingested, it increases alertness, causes euphoria and leads to general feelings of well-being. We haven't seen that in Charlene, though. Actual use and overdose can have different signs. Have you noticed dilated pupils, high energy levels, greatly increased activity, excitability or enthusiastic speech? The time these things last depends on how the cocaine has been taken. Obviously smoking or injecting makes it happen faster so the effects last for a shorter time. It can be difficult to spot. Perhaps you can think of times when she's been like that." Frank paused to allow Billy the opportunity to think and reply.

"I haven't seen any of the things you've described," said Billy.

"I have," said John Lomax, who had come into the kitchen unnoticed. "She was very excitable when I opened that cupboard door and she smashed me on the nose." He ran his fingers lightly over his misshapen nose and heavily bruised cheeks.

"I've explained that," countered Billy. "She's scared to death of closed in spaces and the dark. It was no wonder she bolted."

"It suits you," grinned Ray Quinn, trying to lease the tension. "It's given your face character, don't you think, Leanne?"

"Wonderful improvement," she said with all the sarcasm she could muster.

"So, let's move on," said Frank. "An overdose from cocaine use can have significant effects. The symptoms are easily recognizable. The normal side effects of the drug's use include a rise in the user's body temperature, heart rate and blood pressure. While these effects are rarely in the dangerous range for those in good health, they can be dangerous to those who have previous conditions, such as high blood pressure or a heart condition. For those people, an overdose can lead to abdominal pain and nausea, seizures, heart attack, stroke or respiratory failure. Cocaine overdose symptoms are both physical and psychological. They include nausea, vomiting, tremors, irregular breathing, increased temperature and heart rate, chest pains seizures, anxiety, agitation, paranoia, panic, hallucination, and delirium. Is that enough education for one day?" he asked with a smile.

"Ok, so you know what to look for in a user and how to recognise an overdose, though I hate to imagine where you came by all this information," said Leanne.

Ray Quinn and Frank exchanged a rapid and meaningful glance.

"That doesn't matter, does it? said Frank. "The important thing for us now, and of course Charlene, is what to do about it all." He didn't wait for a response. "Normally, she should be taken to hospital straight away, but I don't suppose that's an option, so we'll have to treat her as a doctor would and the sooner the better. A doctor would treat cocaine overdose as a poisoning, but unlike some poisons, there is no antidote. She must be constantly monitored. As she's unconscious she needs ventilation and she might need saline for hydration. If she's burning hot, we might have to sedate her and put her in an ice bath. There is a risk her heart may stop, but we'll deal with that then. With luck she should gradually return to normal. It really all depends on how much of an overdose she has been given. And there, children, endeth the lesson."

The kitchen was silent as each digested the information.

"Can you deal with all that?" asked Billy, fearful now.

"Yes," replied Frank, "but I'll need your help. John, I've made a list of things I need. Would you slip out and get them from the nearest chemist?"

"Of course," said Lomax, pleased to be given something practical to do.

"I'll come with you," said Leanne.

"No," Quinn said sharply. "I don't want more than one person out at a time. Look how difficult it's been to get us all together here. Be careful, John."

"Remember what your mother told you; don't stop and talk to strangers." Leanne's sarcasm had not abated.

"Right," said Quinn, "John, you fetch the stuff that Frank and Billy need, and I'll deal with our resident resting man. I may need some help with that, so I'll wait until you get back, John, and then the three of us can sort it out. Oh, and I'm going to have to talk to Charlene."

"I'm sorry to have to disappoint you, Ray, but she won't be making any sense for a quite a while," said Frank.

"I'll still need to talk to her as soon as possible," said Quinn with authority.

Leanne watched Lomax leave and returned her attention to Quinn.

"You haven't told us what you intend to do with our resting friend," said Leanne.

"That's because I hadn't decided until now. I believe we should hide him away. Jack Noble will be missing him," mused

Quinn. "Come on Leanne, you can help me. We might as well make use of the time until John gets back."

The resting man was bundled up and shoved unceremoniously onto the back seat of the BMW. He didn't respond in any way because he was so heavily drugged that he was lucky to be alive. They drove for over half an hour through darkening lanes until they reached the electric gates of an expensive looking property on the outskirts of the city. The plaque on the gate post bore the legend 'Priory Place – No cold callers.' Ray Quinn smiled at the irony.

"How do you know this is the right place?" enquired Leanne.

"Because Frank told me. It seems our friend on the back seat was very keen to help as much as he could and Frank promised him home comforts in return. This will be his home for a while. He won't remember anything, though, after what Frank's given him."

He stopped the car and switched off the engine. He quietly opened the door and stepped out onto the tarmac surface. He had made sure they had halted just out of the range of motion sensor lights or cameras, but nevertheless told Leanne to stay in the car and keep watch. He dragged the inert body out and placed the resting man sitting upright, leaning on a fence. He made sure he was still breathing and slipped back behind the wheel. Satisfied, he eased the car away and accelerated only when they were a good distance from the gates. Leanne did not notice Quinn slip an envelope into the man's pocket, nor did she notice the resting man being lifted by two members of staff and taken inside.

-21-

"She's awake!" shouted Billy, unable to hide his relief.

Frank leapt up and sprinted to Charlene. "Don't leave her alone," he shouted as he went past Billy. "This is going to be difficult for her."

Nobody knew how accurate those words were going to be. Frank and Billy tended to her every need for many days, but, although she was recovering in the physical sense, her mental state proved an intractable problem. Eventually, after much soul searching, it was agreed that she needed specialist care. Charlene's health was the key for all of them. Billy couldn't be settled without her; their two year old son needed her; Leanne and John could not be free to live the rest of their lives unless Billy and Charlene were sorted out as well as Jack Noble. For Quinn and Frank it all represented unfinished business.

It was decided that Charlene should be nursed at Priory Place. It was a convenient arrangement because they could also keep a watchful eye on the resting man at the same time. Quinn left strict instructions that the two new inmates must never meet nor even set eyes on each other.

Over the course of the next month a pattern of visiting became established. Leanne, Lomax and Billy visited Charlene individually and occasionally in pairs, whilst Quinn and Frank went to see the resting man. The pattern changed occasionally and so it was that Quinn and Leanne came to be on visiting duty together.

Lomax & The Biker – The Trilogy

Priory Place was Monday morning busy when a security guard let Quinn and Leanne in with a smile and a pleasantry.

"That resting man isn't resting anymore," said the guard." He's been creating havoc."

"Doing what?" asked Leanne.

"Trying to crack his head open on the walls, mainly. We've put him in a safety room for now. Through here."

Moving swiftly on he led the way through a maze of brightly lit corridors, until they reached a door, which he pushed open, standing aside to allow them in. The room itself was empty but the entire width of the end wall was panelled with glass and on the other side was the Resting Man.

"We really must find him a name," said Quinn, as much to himself as to Leanne or the guard. "We'll come back to him later," he said. "We'd like to see Charlene now."

The sight of Charlene shocked them both. Clad in a dressing gown, she paced restlessly around the perimeter of the room, stopping now and then at some random spot to spread the fingers of both hands on the wall, laying her cheek in between, as if listening for something on the other side. Her wild, agitated appearance emphasised her distressed state, but even so Quinn was struck by underlying fragility and beauty. The guard eased back to allow a doctor to step alongside them.

"She's in the agitated phase," he announced.

"How long will it last?" asked Leanne.

"We can't tell," said the doctor gently. "It varies from case to case. Thankfully, I think we can say there should be no long term damage."

"Billy will be pleased," reflected Leanne.

"I think it would help speed her recovery if she could be surrounded by people and things she loves," offered the doctor.

"That sounds the right kind of thing,' Leanne agreed. "We'll bring some stuff in tomorrow."

"She keeps asking for Billy," said the doctor.

"He'll be in tomorrow as well," said Quinn, "I'll make sure he comes."

"You do know that she's here voluntarily," the doctor said. "Nobody can legally stop her leaving, although we would try to dissuade her obviously."

"Yes, we know," replied Leanne.

"Do you think it could help if Billy took her out for a while?" he asked. He was getting the impression that the doctor was subtly suggesting a change.

"I don't think it will do any harm," Mr Quinn.

"Good, then that's what we'll do. Billy and I will pick her up tomorrow morning, say about ten?"

"That will be fine," replied the doctor, obviously pleased that he was dealing with a man who recognised and appreciated his subtlety. He was also pleased with the fact that he had not been asked to give his name.

Billy was overjoyed by the news that it was time to take Charlene out, if only for a little while, but Quinn tempered his joy with words of caution when they reached the car.

"Listen, Billy, I know you'll be glad to have Charlene back with you, but I'm not doing this just for that reason. You do realise that the only way to sort out this whole sorry mess is to use her to get to Jack Noble, don't you? He won't let it go, Billy. We, no you actually, owe John Lomax for everything he's done. Come to think of it you also owe me, but I'm not going to worry about that. Also, your mother wants to see you settled and happy and she knows Charlene's the one for you. You cannot afford to make a mess of this, Billy."

"I know," replied Billy, finding it difficult to look Ray Quinn in the eye.

"How well do you know me?" asked Quinn.

"Enough to know I can trust you," replied Billy.

"How well do you know John Lomax?"

"Enough to know I can trust him as well," said Billy, puzzled by the questioning.

"Last question; how well do you know your mother?" asked Quinn.

"I love her," said Billy.

"That's not what I asked," said Quinn quietly.

"I know," replied Billy, but I don't think I can answer your question.

"Good. That's an honest answer. I can work with that."

"Can you really sort all this out, Ray?" asked Billy.

"I can't," said Quinn, but we can. That's what I'm getting at. We must all trust each other. It's going to get worse before it gets better. There will be times in the next few days when we'll all be tested to the limit, and doubts will creep in. I'm not going to be very pleasant, but remember it's for a reason. You'll see me do things and say things that may repulse you. I'll push each one of you to the edge, including Charlene, and success depends on how you deal with it. If you don't think you can do this, you'd better say so now."

"I don't understand," said Billy.

"You don't need to know all the details," said Quinn. "The most important thing you will need to hang onto is the fact that Charlene loves you. She followed you all the way from Australia and is in a real mess now. If you let her down now, you'll never see your little boy again and she may never recover either."

"What about mother?" asked Billy. "What do I do about her?"

"Nothing. You don't need to do anything. What will be, will be. She will be sorted out as things progress. You'll have to use up some of your trust in me with that one."

"Have you had this conversation with the others?" asked Billy.

Ray Quinn smiled. "No, and before you ask, I have my reasons. Suffice it to say that they'll understand eventually."

When they returned the following morning Charlene was dressed and ready to go. She flung her arms round Billy's neck and wouldn't let go until he eventually prised her fingers free one by one. He smiled and laughed with her, as he took her by the hand and they hurried out of Priory Place.

Ray Quinn watched it all with a warm glow, but did not let it continue for long. He had already decided that the action would begin today.

"Be careful, Billy" he said, "remember John Lomax's re-arranged nose." He was deliberately beginning to apply pressure to them both, because he wanted to test their reactions.

Billy shot him an appalled look, but Charlene didn't even seem to notice.

"I think we should take her back to the house?" said Quinn.

"Not the flat?" asked Billy.

"No. I said the house. You know, the one that rents rooms by the hour. I think it might be worth a try," continued Quinn.

Quinn drove while Billy and Charlene sat in the back. He had already taken the precaution of setting the child locks to the rear doors. There was no conversation as he drove, but he kept glancing in the rear view mirror and was pleased to note that they were holding hands. He was taking them back to the room in which Charlene had been locked in an under stair cupboard. He was keen to asses her reaction. He hoped they would learn something.

As he drew up in front of the building Charlene became agitated. She withdrew her hand from Billy's grip and reached towards the window. She tested the door handle and began to panic when it wouldn't work.

"She thinks we're going to shut her in the cupboard again. We've brought her back here too soon. This is too frightening for her," said Billy.

"Shut up, Billy," rasped Quinn.

He was pleased to see that Charlene immediately cupped her hands protectively around Billy's face as the shock of Quinn's reprimand hit him.

"Terrific," commented Quinn, pondering on his next move. He didn't want to upset Charlene further and he decided to leave. He took a last look around and spotted the front door of the adjacent house open. A woman emerged, carrying a small fluffy canine, and stepped delicately around the piles of sand and bricks.

"Hold on." Seeing an opportunity Quinn jumped out of the car and introduced himself over the low hedge. The woman squinted at him through bottle-end glasses, trying to look over his shoulder towards the car.

"Have you got Charlene in there? I thought so."

"And you are ... ?" he asked.

"I live next door," she replied evasively.

Quinn decided not to pursue that point. Her name wasn't important and she no doubt had her reasons. Perhaps in return she wouldn't ask his name.

She shook her head sadly. "I can't believe a thing like that could happen round here."

Quinn thought to himself that news certainly travelled fast. "Did you notice anything out of the ordinary?" he asked.

"No . .I've had the workmen here working on the drive. This job should have been finished in three days, but you know what it's like. They start one thing and then there's a problem. Five days it's been going on and it's still not done."

"Did you know the man or the woman?" Quinn cut in.

"Not really, no. We only moved in two years ago in February. The man seemed to live there all the time, but we hardly ever saw him. He had lots of girls visit him, though. We were out here when that one came. I told her we lived next door and asked her name. That's how I know she's called Charlene. She seemed different to the others; you know, nicer, if you know what I mean."

"I understand perfectly," said Ray Quinn, smiling at her.

"I assumed it was just another girl, but I hoped for his sake it was more than that," the woman continued. "You don't like to be nosy, do you?"

Quinn thought that took a stretch of his imagination.

"'We were just pleased to see that he had found a nicer young lady. The others had skirts up to their embarrassment, but she was different."

Quinn was surprised by her clever use of language.

She went on. "He seemed such a decent man."

Quinn thought that even more of a stretch of the imagination, but he decided not to disillusion the woman. He also decided not to ask questions about the man. He already knew enough about him.

"But if I can be of any more help, officer.." the woman was still talking as he turned to leave.

After what he'd just heard, he doubted that she could, but he politely nodded thanks anyway, deciding not to inform her he was not from the police. He went back to the car, mulling over the new information.

"Don't worry, Charlene," he said as he sat down, "you don't need to go back in there."

Charlene broke down and wept bitterly. She clung on to Billy for all she was worth and her stuttering and muffled words came through her tears, as she pressed her face into Billy's chest.

"Thank you, thank you, thank you."

-22-

"Now we need to find Jack Noble," announced Ray Quinn the following morning over breakfast. We've rattled his cage, but he doesn't seem to want to put in an appearance. Wherever he is, we need to find him. I'll need to go back to our resting friend at Priory Place and see if he can help."

Ray Quinn also had other plans. He decided that it was time for Billy to step up to the mark. If Billy and Charlene were to have a future, then Billy would have to fight for it. He was not going to lay it on a plate for him. He had also decided to keep a much closer eye on Leanne. Her flirtatious behaviour had not gone unnoticed and he needed to nip it in the bud. John Lomax was owed that at the very least. He was ensuring he maintained the momentum. He wanted all concerned, friend and foe, to be off balance. He had not discussed his intentions with Frank, but he knew he would realise what was happening and react accordingly. He hoped Lomax would also understand.

"I think the best thing is to go back to the flat and pick up your mother, Billy. Charlene needs a woman with her at the moment and I need you to do something for me."

He drove back to the flat with the car in silence. Charlene was hanging on to Billy, who was at a loss as to what Ray Quinn was up to now. He brought the car to a halt, but kept the engine running.

"Say your goodbyes, Billy, then go inside and fetch your mother. Tell her to bring her overnight bag. Don't worry Charlene, I'll look after you, I just need Billy to do something for me."

"But, I don't understand. Charlene needs me with her. What's going on?" pleaded Billy.

"Don't ask questions, we haven't the time," asserted Quinn, turning to face Billy in the rear seat.

Billy kissed Charlene tenderly, gave her a reassuring hug and walked into the flat. He had been given no choice; no leeway. Ray Quinn in this mood was not a man it was worthwhile challenging. He just had to trust him.

Leanne appeared a short while later, carrying a small bag. She opened the front passenger side door.

"No, you sit in the back with Charlene," said Quinn. "She needs you now."

Leanne slammed the door with more than the necessary force and Charlene jumped with shock. Quinn looked in the rear view mirror and noted that Leanne was sitting as far apart from Charlene as possible and sulking like an adolescent schoolgirl. She had obviously been fooled into thinking the need for her overnight bag was the result of her advances to Quinn. She had fallen at the first fence and she would have to prove herself more and more as time went on if Ray Quinn was to be able to leave his friend John Lomax in her tender care. It amused him to think that she would be tested to the limit before long.

"All buckled up?" he asked.

"Yes," replied Charlene. Leanne did not respond.

Quinn drove without hurry to Priory Place. When they arrived he courteously opened the back doors for the two women to slide out. Leanne's bag remained in the foot well of the front seat, but she didn't notice the only bag he was carrying was Charlene's. They spent a good hour settling Charlene back into her room at Priory Place and, although Quinn was anxious to move on, he knew it was time well spent. His resources were stretched and he needed Charlene to feel safe so that he did not have to keep worrying about her as he drove things forward.

"It's time we went," announced Quinn, "Leanne and I need to chase something up. You'll be fine here, Charlene. I'll ask the doctor to look in on you shortly."

He gave her a hug in what was, for him, an unusual display of affection. Leanne merely smiled at her and raised her hand in half-hearted farewell.

"I need to look in on our resting man," announced Quinn.

With Leanne in tow, he sought and found the doctor.

"How's our resting man?" asked Quinn.

"Much the same," the doctor replied. "He's asleep at the moment and I'd like him to stay that way, if you don't mind. If you need to talk to him, perhaps you could come back tomorrow."

"That's fine." Quinn was in no hurry; tomorrow would do.

Leanne trailed behind like an obedient puppy.

"Am I allowed in the front now?" she asked, the question dripping with sarcasm.

"Naturally," he said, "why not?" He replied, ignoring the acid.

"What now?" she asked.

It was obvious to Quinn what she wanted and, smiling inwardly, he restricted himself to a sigh. He looked at the front of Priory Place and noticed that it was already in darkness. The only illumination was provided by the lights of the drive.

The doctor turned out the light and watched them leave, peeping round the edge of drawn curtains. He smiled, turned and made his way to the room where the resting man was far from asleep.

-23-

"I need a drink," said Quinn. "You?"

Oh yes," she said.

They found themselves a quiet corner in a nearby bar and after fifteen minutes of meaningless chatter, their drinks sat untouched on the table in front of them.

"Ray, I am sorry," Leanne finally got to the point. "It's just that there is a magnetism about you that I can't ignore. You must have noticed women being attracted to you."

"I can't say I have," replied Quinn, inwardly pleased by the news. "But, I can't let this go any further. John is my friend and I just couldn't do it to him. More importantly, I'm married and intend to stay that way."

"She's a very lucky woman," commented Leanne. "If I were her, I wouldn't let you out of my sight."

"She knows she can trust me," Quinn responded. "If I were John Lomax I wouldn't let you out of my sight either, because he obviously shouldn't trust you."

"I'll behave, don't worry. I know he loves me and I'd have too much to lose."

Ray Quinn decided to leave it there. If Leanne let herself and Lomax down again, she would only have herself to blame. Nevertheless, he promised himself that he would discuss the matter with his friend at the earliest opportunity.

"I'm hungry. Shall we eat here? It seems as good a place as any."

"Fine," she replied, "it will do us good to do something normal."

They ate and chatted for a good half an hour and the atmosphere between them became less charged as Quinn worked to put Leanne back into a happier place. They had just begun coffee when Quinn's mobile announced itself.

"What now?" he asked. "For two pins I'd throw this thing in the river. They've taken over our lives. Hello," he barked irritably.

"Ray, sorry to disturb you. It's Frank."

"Trouble?" asked Quinn, glancing at Leanne simultaneously. "Hang on, I'll turn the volume up. Whatever it is, Leanne should hear it as well."

"Are you sure?" asked Frank.

"Definitely," asserted Quinn.

Frank understood perfectly. "I'm at the flat with John. Billy's disappeared. We've looked all over but he's vanished into thin air. I was getting some sleep when John burst in and told me Billy is nowhere to be seen. Is he with you?"

Quinn gave Leanne a meaningful glance and her heart pumped. "No," he said. "I specifically told him to stay there until I got back. Why on earth does he insist on disappearing? It's getting an annoying habit."

"Hang on Ray, John's just found a note. It's not Billy's writing. I'll read it to you. Oh, it's hard to read, the writing's terrible."

Leanne's curiosity knew no bounds as she took it all in.

"Don't bother, Frank. Just send it to my phone now. Is John alright?"

"Yes, he's fine. I'm sending it now. I'll hang on here in case Billy comes back."

"Good. Yes, I've got it. Thanks. Wait a minute." Quinn's lips moved as he read silently from his phone. "Frank, you need to batten down the hatches. Lock all doors, shut every window. Neither of you must leave the flat. Be with John all the time. Do not let him out of your sight. Sleep in the same room if you have to. The resting man's out of Priory Place and he's gone after Billy. I don't give much for his chances without help. Jack Noble's behind this, I bet. He's splitting our resources, Frank. I'll keep Leanne with me. If he really means business, he'll also have Charlene by now. You must stay there with John, do you hear?"

"Of course," replied Frank. "Ray, be careful. This Noble character is either very brave or incredibly stupid. Whichever it is, it makes him dangerous. Good luck."

"Yes, and you too," replied Quinn. "I'll be in touch."

"Damn," said Quinn. "I didn't see that one coming. Drink up, we're off."

The accelerator of the BMW stayed pressed hard to the floor for the few minutes it took to get back to Priory Place. It was still in darkness, save for the lights on the driveway. Quinn bolted from the car and hammered on the front door. He was surprised to find it unlocked, but was grateful nevertheless. He sprinted the short distance to Charlene's room and was hugely relieved to see her looking up at him with an inquisitive frown. He saw that she had not yet got ready for bed. He breathed out heavily, and held out his arms to her. She came to him and they remained in a mutually enriching hug for what seemed an eternity. He was fast becoming a father figure to a vulnerable young woman who was very much out of her depth.

"Come on," he whispered, "let's get out of here."

Charlene allowed him to guide her to the car and slid onto the back seat. Quinn noticed that Leanne had moved into the back to be with Charlene and was pleased when she took her hand. He smiled his gratitude; at last she was thinking.

They drove in silence as Quinn's mind worked overtime. He did not return to the flat. If Noble wanted them divided it was better to let him believe he had succeeded. He would have to rely on Frank to look after John Lomax. He returned to the seedy run-down building that rented rooms by the hour. The nosy neighbour appeared right on cue, as if by magic.

"Hello again," she called. "We didn't expect to see you this quickly."

"What do you mean?" asked Quinn.

"Well, we saw the young man go in there," she said, "and he looked upset."

"Which young man would that be?" Quinn asked, his patience being tested.

"The same one as before. The one who went in with the brunette with hardly any skirt and tons of make up. Here, what's going on? That brunette never came out, did she? Is she still in there? Is that why the young man came back? I don't know what's going on, but it's all very fishy to me. I don't know what the world's coming to." She was building up a fine head of steam and looked to be heading for a long rant. Quinn didn't have the time.

"Thank you," he cut in, "you've been most helpful."

"You said that last time," she recalled, and her ample bosom expanded as she took in a huge gulp of air, ready to begin again.

"Yes, I know," Quinn continued, "and I meant it. Now, will you do me a favour? Keep a careful eye out and write down details of anyone who comes and goes from here. You know, dates, times, what they look like, what they're wearing, who they're with. Anything at all, in fact. You'd be doing me a huge favour. Don't tell anybody; it'll be our secret. I'll come back in a few days and see what you've got."

"How can I get hold of you?" she asked, swelling with pride at being asked to do such important civic duty.

"You can't," said Quinn, "as I said, I'll be back in a few days and call on you. In the meantime, don't say anything to anybody, not even the police. This is bigger than the local lot, and I've got to make sure security is maintained." He had adopted an imposing, official manner and the woman positively squirmed with delight at being the chosen one.

"You can rely on me," she affirmed with due seriousness.

"I'm sure I can," purred Quinn. "Now, excuse me, I must get on."

"Of course," she whispered.

Ray Quinn turned on his heel and strode into the building, aware of the woman's gaze on his back. Once out of her sight, he slowed to a halt. There was nobody around. He did not intend going anywhere; he was just killing time. He wanted Leanne and Charlene to wait long enough to believe he had been doing something. If he took enough time, he knew he'd be able to tell them anything when he returned to the car and they would believe him. They would have no reason for doubt. Although he didn't intend to go anywhere in the building, he couldn't resist stepping into the room in which Charlene had been incarcerated. The same room that Billy had been in with the brunette, she of hardly any skirt and tons of make up. The same room that Quinn had entered and dealt with the Harley jacketed man. The clean up team had been thorough. There was no trace of anything at all. The room was pristine. Actually, that wasn't true; the room was in a condition befitting the building in which it was located. It was ready for the next hour's rental.

"Bad news, I'm afraid," Quinn reported as he got back into the car. "It's obvious Billy's been here. There's some blood on the floor and a smear on the wall. I'm afraid something nasty has happened. He's obviously hurt, unless the blood belongs to somebody else, but I doubt that. You'd better be prepared not to see him again."

Ray Quinn looked into the back of the car to assess their reactions to the harshness of his delivery. Leanne looked away from Charlene and gazed out of the window, whilst Charlene took a sharp intake of breath and began to sob. He had been deliberately short and sharp. He was testing them both.

He allowed them an extended silence. Charlene was the first to find her voice.

"When? How?" she whispered.

"Recently, obviously," he replied. "I'm not sure of the circumstances just yet. I need to talk to Frank before we jump to any conclusions. If our not so resting man has taken Billy to Jack Noble, then he's in for a very uncomfortable time. He's tough though, isn't he Leanne?"

Quinn was referring to the episode in which Leanne had subjected her own son to some extremely nasty treatment in the not too distant past. Leanne's eyes widened in a plea for Quinn to go no further. He took pity and changed the subject for Charlene's sake, not for that of Leanne.

"We're going to have to follow the trail, wherever it takes us, ladies. Notice I said 'we.'"

"It's not that simple," Leanne said. "I must be with John. He needs me more than ever now."

Whilst Quinn thought the sentiment admirable, he saw it for what it was. Leanne was petrified. She was unsure that she could cope with it all. She didn't want to be seen as weak, but knew she was. In her short sentence, Quinn could hear the desperate desire for her life to be normal, as it had been before the whole terrible nightmare had shockingly disrupted it, a need to step out of this surreal sequence of events. She hadn't yet recognised and admitted her part in it either. It was a common enough feeling for anyone following traumatic blows, and one with which he was all too familiar.

Lomax & The Biker – The Trilogy

-24-

Ray Quinn selected The City Post because it boasted a huge circulation for a local newspaper. It focussed on the sensational and didn't pay much attention to the accuracy of its content. It reflected the approach of its editor, Ken Harvey, so he was also selected. It was living proof that sensation sells and it was housed in one of the city's newest and most impressive buildings. One of the triumphs of the building was the complete lack of parking space, so Quinn was forced to resort to using a taxi. He hoped he would meet his favourite cabbie again, but that wasn't to be. Once inside a vast open-plan lobby, Quinn hardly merited a glance from a whole bank of receptionists.

'I'd like to have a word with Ken Harvey,' he said, having selected one of the faces.

He was directed to a glass-sided lift, which would transport him up to the eighteenth floor, a ride that afforded a spectacular panoramic view over the city's sprawling urban skyline. It gave him a yearning for wide open spaces. It was a longing that had been growing within him for quite some time, and he knew it would lead to the heart of Exmoor, hopefully on a permanent basis. He had become disillusioned with city living, with its noise, dirt and dreadful anonymity. He had already promised himself and, more importantly, his wife that they would make the most significant move of their lives as soon as the current affair had been settled.

Ken Harvey greeted him at the door to his office. Despite the smoking ban in offices, and almost everywhere else, he still managed to carry the signs and smells of his addiction to tobacco. The effects of his forty-a-day habit, along with burning the midnight oil to meet ever tightening deadlines, were imprinted in his coarse complexion. Add to the picture his several chins and lank, thinning hair, and he did not present a physically attractive role model.

Quinn declined the offer of tea, coffee or mineral water on the grounds that they would all taste the same and thus best avoided..

Ken Harvey smiled and said, "I don't blame you. What can I do for you?" he asked as he squeezed himself behind an enormous mahogany desk, which was as scarred by life's battles as its owner.

"I'd like to talk to you about Jack Noble," said Ray Quinn.

Sizing up Quinn, Harvey broke into a broad nicotine-stained grin. "Oh yes. What's he done now?"

"He's running a vendetta at the moment," answered Quinn, "and he seems to have kidnapped a friend of mine."

That took the wind out of Harvey's sails. In fact, judging from the blanching effect on his face, it had scuttled the whole boat.

"Jesus Christ," he wheezed, "are you sure?"

Quinn nodded. "That's certainly how it looks."

"Jesus Christ," Harvey repeated. "I knew things were going on, but I didn't know the details."

"You must know him pretty well then." Quinn was alert now.

"We aren't what you'd call friends. I've run stories about him in the past, but I'd be wary now. He's not a man to be trifled with." Ken Harvey was also alert. "My pet theory is that he wants to become a national figure. He's already got most of this city in his pocket. I have heard, though, that there is somebody at the moment who is challenging him."

Quinn smiled at the newspaperman.

"Jesus Christ," he completed the hat trick. "You're either very brave or very stupid."

"I can assure you, Mr Harvey, I am certainly not stupid. Ask around," said Ray Quinn as he treated the man on the other side of the desk to one of his significant looks. "How would you like to have the sole rights to this story?"

Ken Harvey's baser instincts kicked in immediately. He saw the opportunity of national, as well as local, stardom.

"I'm not sure I follow," he lied.

"I intend to make sure my friend is recovered in rude health and this Jack Noble understands the error of his ways."

Ken Harvey was incredulous. "How on earth do you imagine you are going to do that?"

"Oh, that's simple. Your paper is going to report that my friend, his name is Billy Lane by the way, has been kidnapped and killed and the word on the street is that a local drug baron is involved." Quinn detailed his plan in matter of fact terms.

Ken Harvey was dumbfounded.

"Why should I do that?" he asked in amazement.

"Because you don't have a choice." Said Ray Quinn, smiling innocently.

"I think you need to explain yourself before I have you thrown out!" Harvey exploded. "You wander into my office without so much as a by your leave and tell me what I must do! I don't even know you. I've never seen you before. Who the hell do you think you are?" he was puce by the end of his outburst and breathless enough to have to sit down quickly.

"Please, Mr Harvey, take care. I've no wish to upset you. I'm here to give you a story the like of which you've only ever dreamed of. You'll be able to retire a rich man. Let me explain while you gather yourself. A few years ago a company called Anvex was robbed of well over £300,000. Although that's not a huge sum nowadays, it was worth more then. The thieves were never caught. You do remember it?"

"Of course I do," wheezed Harvey. "It led to a senior copper's death didn't it. DCI Sandy Lane, as I recall."

The penny dropped.

"This friend of yours, Billy Lane, wouldn't happen to be related, would he?" asked Harvey.

"Yes, he's DCI Lane's son."

"Wasn't there also something about a Leanne Lane as well," asked Harvey, becoming interested in where this was leading.

"Right again," said Quinn. What a fine memory you have. She was convicted of the copper's murder and ended up in prison. She's out now, of course, but I expect you also knew that."

"I remember," Harvey confirmed, "but what has this got to do with Jack Noble?"

Lomax & The Biker – The Trilogy

"Patience, my friend."

The next part of the story laid out by Ray Quinn was a total lie, but the aim was to hook the newspaperman. "What you don't know is that there were two other people involved in the Anvex raid. They have fallen out since. One of them was Jack Noble. I represent the interests of the other. Jack Noble stole the proceeds from my client to set himself up in the drug business. He has now kidnapped Billy Lane as well. He also tried to kill my client with a drug overdose. My client wants to, how shall I put it?....rectify the situation. Oh, by the way, the police are not interested in any of this. They just want it cleaned up. They have promised to allow me to do just that. Between you and I, if certain people happen to fall by the wayside during my intervention, and that unfortunately could now include your good self, the blindest of blind eyes will be turned. I shall present you with the complete story, with full and binding permission to publish in your newspaper or even a book should you wish. Your part will simply be to publish exactly what I tell you at exactly the time I choose. It's a shame you now know all this. It means you are now part of the story, so you cannot refuse my offer. Your choice is between the chance any editor only ever dreams about, along with the income that will bring, and refusal. Actually, refusal is not really an option, because you know too much. Both my client and Mr Noble would agree on that point, and they aren't in agreement about much at the moment."

Lomax & The Biker – The Trilogy

"I'm still worried. I need to check up on a few things." Ken Harvey was thinking about Jack Noble. He had contacts in that direction.

"Feel free, Mr Harvey." Quinn's confidence told Ken Harvey all he needed to know, so he began to set out what he knew about Noble.

"You will probably find him behind all sorts of things in this city, from the low level to the far more serious," Harvey ventured. "He has a talent for being involved in nefarious activity. Once he starts something he doesn't let it go. He is known to be persuasive, if you follow my drift, and is very good at getting people to go along with him. He is normally in a hurry to get results, but he has been known to bide his time. In other words, Mr Quinn, he knows how to get what he wants."

"He's sounds a formidable foe," offered Quinn.

"Exactly," replied Harvey, "I wouldn't want to cross him or be in his debt. Rumour has it that he hates being owed money more than anything else. Local legend has it that there are several bodies buried in concrete, holding up new buildings and motorway bridges."

"Nice man," commented Quinn. "Has there been any indication lately that things are getting too much for him?"

It took Harvey several seconds to meet Quinn's eye.

"The man thinks he's a pro. He views his work as others treat their careers.

"Has he any particular friends?" asked Quinn.

"I'm not sure that he has any what you'd call close friends. He gets along with anybody who serves the purpose of the day. In truth, he's a loner, and a dangerous one at that."

"Does he have a woman in his life?" Quinn pursued.

Harvey shook his head. "I never got the impression that there is anyone, but I suppose there could be."

"Do you know a girl called Sally?" asked Quinn.

"No, can't say I do." Harvey's reply was tellingly quick and Quinn spotted it.

"I know where I can find Jack Noble whenever I need," said Quinn, "but I've always found a little research never does any harm."

"Where is all this coming from? Where is it going?" Harvey was now more than worried. He fidgeted, played with his pen and couldn't hold Quinn's steady, probing gaze.

"Do I frighten you?" asked Quinn.

"No, of course not," Harvey replied. "I admit you've unsettled me, but scare me? No. Jack Noble frightens me, though."

"Let me give you a piece of advice, Mr Harvey. You've got it the wrong way round. You need to re-assess your perception. The status quo is changing around here and you'd be well advised to take notice and change accordingly."

The interview had run its course. "Well, thanks for your time Mr Harvey."

"No problem. Anything I can do," said Ken Harvey."

Quinn stood up but he saw that something was bothering Harvey.

"We can run this as a story?" he asked.

"It's news, isn't it?" said Quinn, drily.

"So what can we print?" Harvey was brightening now.

"Let's go for novelty. How about the facts?"

His sarcasm went unremarked.

"Which are?" asked Harvey.

"That Billy Lane was discovered dead late last night. Police are not currently looking for anyone else in connection with his death, but would like to speak to a woman who may have been at the scene, and a man who made the emergency call. Between you and I, Ken, I can call you Ken, I presume, I'm certain Noble is involved and I will make sure he will meet his maker, but you'd better not print that last bit, eh?" Quinn was at his sinister best.

"I'm sorry about Billy," said Harvey, making a valiant attempt at complete sincerity.

Quinn was impressed; a press man with a conscience was a new phenomenon. He thought about what he had learned. Although he had never personally dealt with the man on a one to one basis, Jack Noble was the name you heard everywhere around the city and it was always connected with just about anything criminal you could shake a stick at. Drugs, gambling, prostitution, Noble was up to his neck in it. Life was becoming rather interesting.

Lomax & The Biker – The Trilogy

If Harvey printed what he'd been told, Jack Noble would either read it or know about it. It may even get to him from Harvey personally before being published. Quinn didn't care how it got to him as long as it did. He also knew Jack Noble would find out the origin of the story. He would surely find that the story came from Ray Quinn, which was what Quinn intended. He was flushing him out. He was intrigued as to how long it would take. The speed would be a measure of the man in his surroundings. A measure of his support or, equally likely, the fear he engendered.

Lomax & The Biker – The Trilogy

-25-

Ray Quinn was tired of being in the field. When in the forces, especially when on operations, life had an edge; adrenalin coursed through his veins. The London 7/7 bombings had changed his life completely. John Lomax had saved his life and they had become firm and steadfast friends. He viewed life through different eyes. He had been retired on medical grounds and now his life had a changed meaning. He loved the freedom of the open road and his powerful bike. He did what he wanted whenever he wanted, with no exceptions. The first was his obligation to his saviour, John Lomax. He viewed it as a lifelong commitment and would walk to the ends of the earth for him. The second was his wife. Without her, he was nothing; his life would not be worth living. Now, he was at a crossroads. He needed to rid John Lomax of the spectre of Jack Noble and then withdraw to the quiet contentment of a settled retirement. His wife deserved it. She never pushed, but he knew it was time and he longed to be back with her now. She was patiently waiting for him.

Eschewing the inflated prices charged for the exotic beverages of the Chain Locker, Quinn deferred having a drink until he was closer to the flat. Being the centre of attention was becoming wearisome, but some ten minutes later he pulled into the car park of the Oak Tree Inn. His vehicle brought the total number to five, mainly because most of the Oak Tree's regulars were beyond the age when it was safe for them to drive. Lacking the dubious attractions of piped disco music, slot machines or wide-screen satellite TV, the pub was on borrowed time, ripe to be snapped up by one of the larger brewery chains and turned into one of the 'fun pubs' that, in Quinn's view, were too much of an assault on the senses to be anything like fun. He had heard it called an old man's pub, and not as a compliment.

He had been deliberately frequenting the pub on a nightly basis and Jack Noble would certainly know of his whereabouts by now. The only sounds to greet his ears in the Oak Tree were the clatter of dominoes that underpinned the low buzz from four elderly gents playing fives-and one at the end of the lounge bar. He went to the bar and ordered a pint of Guinness.

"I'll leave the car," he told the barmaid.

"Right you are, darlin."

It was something Quinn had been doing regularly; using the car as bait. In fact it meant he was also putting himself out there as he walked the 100 or so yards back to the flat. The others at the flat knew of his attempt to lure Noble to him and were worried. He had made Frank their guardian and nobody dared to challenge the arrangement.

His pint didn't last long.

The rain had stopped and, though it was mild for February, a fresh breeze blew as Quinn wound his way along the sixties-built cul-de-sac that was to the one side of the pub, and into the small service road that few people even knew existed. Ominously, a silver Ford Focus was parked just down from the flat. There was movement within, but no light.

Lomax & The Biker – The Trilogy

His routine continued for several evenings. On each walk home, the silver Ford Focus was in the same place, as if it had not moved at all during the day. Quinn knew it had because the ground underneath it was wet. Nevertheless, it's vigil continued. The untrained eye would not have seen the movement inside its dark interior, but Quinn was very far from untrained. He spotted the dark shape that sat in the back seat and pretended not to look at him.

On the fifth evening the silver Ford Focus was in its usual place. Quinn knew something was odd. The car's interior light was on. Quinn's interest was piqued. He carefully checked his periphery, and then did a 360 degree circle rapidly, but he caught nothing. Not even a slinking cat.

Staying in as much darkness as possible he worked his way to the near side rear door of the car by the kerbside and peered inside. There, laid on the back seat was a prone figure. Quinn recognised him instantly. His training took over and he backed away carefully. He had seen too many of his comrades blown apart in dusty foreign places by just such a ruse. He inspected his surroundings again, but could see nobody. He knew he had to find out.

Inch by painstaking inch he crawled his way, laid out flat, using his elbows and toes to propel himself, until he drew level with the rear door. He knew he must open it, and that would be the time of greatest danger. With a last intake of breath, he pulled himself up and eased the door open. It was not locked. He did not open it fully. Bitter experience had taught him to open it as slowly and marginally as possible. It required a steady hand and an extraordinary courage. He had both.

He expected a wire that would trip an explosion if he opened the door too far, but there was none. He found out why. He was meant to find the body in one piece. As he moved it gently, its right forearm was exposed, with a needle hanging from a vein. It was a trademark that told Quinn everything.

Billy Lane's demise was faithfully reported in the City Post the next day.

'A body was discovered late last night. It is believed to be that of Billy Lane, son of the late DCI Sandy Lane and escaped murderess Leanne Lane. Police are not currently looking for anyone else in connection with his death as a self inflicted drug overdose is suspected, but would like to speak to a woman who may have been at the scene, and a man who made the emergency call. Our editor is personally taking charge of the reporting of this story and will have more tomorrow on Billy Lane and his life history.'

Ray Quinn reflected that Ken Harvey had gone beyond the brief he had been given and he would need to talk to him about that. He was also reminded of a line from a Kenny Rogers song, 'The Gambler.'

'The best that you can hope for is to die in your sleep.'

He promised himself, and Billy, that Jack Noble would not be afforded that luxury.

Lomax & The Biker – The Trilogy

The flat was deep in shock that night and everybody went to bed much later than usual, almost as if sleep would bring unimaginable horrors. Leanne was inconsolable and John Lomax was bereft, but had to show stoicism for her. Charlene's reaction was unexpected. The only sentiment she expressed was a burning desire to go home to Australia and then she simply locked herself in her room. She was shutting out the world, lest it harm her any more. Frank took the opportunity of Quinn's presence to get some much needed sleep.

After everybody had gone to bed Quinn sat on his own a while longer with the window wide open despite the drizzle and the lights turned out. He breathed in the cool air and listened to the low, distant rumble of the city, punctuated incongruously by the occasional croon of nocturnal wood pigeons. The chirping of the phone jolted him back to the here and now and he scrambled to get it. He picked up the phone.

"Ray, it's me." said the voice from the other end.

'Me' was an old friend of Quinn's, who had steadily risen through the ranks of his macabre profession and was now a pathologist. Technically, he was not supposed to be talking to Ray Quinn, as an outsider, but Quinn was calling in favours from every direction.

"You're working late," commented Quinn.

"I know," replied the pathologist, "but all hell's broken loose here. Suddenly, all sorts of high up busy bodies have come out of

Lomax & The Biker – The Trilogy

It felt like only minutes after closing her eyes that a crash startled Leanne awake, and she looked up to see Charlene flash by her bedroom door. Naked? Naked. In the bedroom her underwear lay on the floor in a soggy heap and there was a funny unidentifiable smell. She'd wet the bed. Ripping off the sheets, Leanne bundled them into a heap and took them into the kitchen, stuffing them furiously into the washing machine. The TV blared out from the living room but Leanne tracked Charlene to the bathroom where she was busily working her way along her row of toiletries, sniffing at each container of moisturiser, shampoo and talcum powder before pouring its contents into a congealed sticky mess on the floor.

"Charlene!" Leanne struggled to hold back her anger. Charlene just ignored her and kept on emptying. Her fury erupted.

"Stop!" she yelled.

Charlene stopped what she was doing and calmly walked over to her. She took Leanne's hand and pulled it towards the shower. Leanne thought she was asking, so she turned on the shower and tried to persuade her under the jet of water. Charlene wouldn't go, so she ran a bath and Charlene slipped into the water. She lay there happily, so happily that twenty minutes later when the water was tepid, she wouldn't get out. Help was needed, but there wasn't another female in the flat. In desperation Leanne grabbed the TV remote control and, dangling it in front of her as bait, pulled out the plug. It gurgled loudly and Charlene leapt out of the bath, snatching the remote and running through to the lounge, still dripping wet. Leanne gathered up what remained wearable of Charlene's collection of clothes. She dried her and then started to dress her. Charlene had other ideas and Leanne found herself physically manipulating her into every garment while she sat with his eyes glued to the TV screen. By the time Charlene was dressed Leanne was exhausted and they both looked as if they'd spent a night on the streets.

The commotion disturbed the rest of the occupants of the flat, and, no doubt, many neighbours as well. Nobody came to assist Leanne, however, and she felt completely helpless. She knew Charlene needed help, but did not understand what steps to take. She resorted to staying in the living room with her charge, whilst they both watched the TV.

Leanne had an idea. She would call the doctor. Charlene obviously needed medical help.

'I'm sorry," declared the irritatingly cheery reply, "there is no one here to take your call, if you would like to leave......." Leanne slammed down the phone in frustration.

She returned to Charlene and sat beside her once again, waiting for the rest of the flat to rouse themselves and rescue her.

Eventually, after what to Leanne seemed an eternity, first John Lomax and then Frank emerged. Ray Quinn was a little later. He was normally an early riser, having formed the habit earlier in his life, but nobody begrudged him the extra half an hour he had taken.

"Good morning, one and all," he chirped as he entered the kitchen. "I smell coffee; any for me?"

Lomax poured him a cup. Quinn took his time taking the first careful sips of the hot liquid, looking around his assembled troops through the curling, rising steam. He knew they were waiting for him to announce the day's activities. Eventually, just before he judged one of them was about to speak, he began.

"I heard the commotion last night. Is Charlene ok, Leanne?"

Leanne noted that he had spoken as if Charlene wasn't there. Perhaps he knew she had shut everything out.

"It's ok now," Leanne replied, "but it needs sorting out. We can't go on like this. Charlene needs proper medical help and counselling as well. I can't cope with her, especially straight after Billy..." she burst into tears and sobbed loudly. Lomax put his arm around her again.

"I agree," said Quinn. "We must get Charlene some help, and then we can concentrate on everything else."

"What do you suggest?" John Lomax asked.

"I've been thinking," replied Quinn. "Charlene's been to Priory Place before, but we had to get her out. But the picture is different now. I don't trust the doctor there, but at least he's a known quantity. If we get Charlene to go back there and leave Frank there as her guardian, there's no way the doctor can harm her. It would leave the rest of us to get on with what we have to do."

"How can you be sure she'll be safe?" asked Leanne, showing concern for a fellow member of the sisterhood.

"Because I would trust Frank with my life," he answered. "Believe me, there's nobody else to touch him. He scares me at times."

"That's good enough for me," put in Lomax, who was trying to distance himself from any responsibility for Charlene. He had been thinking overnight and come to the conclusion that she was not his kith and kin and was not even related by blood to Leanne, so why should he take any responsibility for her? All he wanted to do was to sort out this Jack Noble business and then settle into a quiet life with Leanne. It was a shame about Billy, but he had been weak too many times. Charlene's present state was Billy's fault completely.

Leanne had been listening intently, despite her sobs, and had come to a decision.

"I can't put her back in there," she pronounced. "It would be the end of her."

"What's the problem," persisted Lomax, "look at her; she's not exactly flourishing is she? Besides, Frank will be with her, and if Ray trusts him as much as he says he does, then she couldn't be in safer hands."

Leanne shivered as Lomax watched her efforts to come to terms with the situation.

"It's funny,' she said eventually, but went no further. Her eyes glazed over as she momentarily drifted off into her own thoughts, and Quinn could only guess at the images crowding her head. It was the stuff of nightmares. He began to wonder if she could cope, but in a matter of minutes she seemed to come round again.

"So what happens now?" she asked at last. She obviously assumed that her decision was binding upon them all.

"That's easy," replied Quinn. "I think we all need a break. We'll have a night out together. A few drinks, something to eat and some laughs. I know just the place."

-26-

Ray Quinn arranged a table at the pub for stand-up night. He remembered the last time he was there and knew it would serve his purpose. He had told them it was a night out; a break, to release pressure. He also said it may be just what Charlene needed. He had a private discussion with Frank to let him know the true purpose of the exercise.

"What do you think?" Quinn asked Frank.

"That you're a devious bastard. Remind me to stay on your side."

The Biker laughed with his friend. They shook hands as Frank set out from the flat to play his part.

"OK, ladies and gentlemen, let's go. We'll take a taxi. Frank's had to go out for a few minutes and has got the car. He'll join us there later."

Frank watched from a distance as they piled into Quinn's favourite taxi and rattled into the distance. He then drove the car back to the flat and left it there. He took another taxi and headed for the City Post offices.

Ray Quinn, John Lomax, Leanne Lane and Charlene sat at their table with drinks in front of them. Lomax noticed six chairs, but didn't comment. Perhaps Frank had gone to fetch someone else to join them. He didn't realise how right he was.

The familiar screech of feedback assailed their ears as the landlord took to the tiny stage at the front of the bar. There was a packed crowd as usual. Word had spread about the stand up nights.

"Where's your old lady?" came a cry from the back. "she still checking you've got the right size condoms?"

"Nah," shouted another wag, "they don't make 'em that tiny!"

"Now settle down, please, ladies and gentlemen. Let's have the usual warm welcome for out old favourite Annie Hall."

The crowd burst into applause as their favourite act levered herself up to the stage. She gripped the microphone in a very unfeminine fist and squeezed hard.

"Ohh, makes your eyes water. Glad she's not my old lady!" the crowd were in fine form.

"Now, now boys. Settle down, let's have some decorum," she instructed as her full face make up began to give the unequal struggle under the lights.

"I went to my golf club the other day," she began.

"Did you score?" came a cry.

"Nobody's that stupid," came a loud shout from the back.

"As I was saying before I was so rudely interrupted," she grinned through sticky bright red lipstick, a reporter was creeping to the pro yesterday. You're amazing, he said. You really know your way round the course. What's your secret? Easy, the pro replied the holes are numbered."

The crowd groaned in unison. It was reminiscent of old time music hall, and obviously very popular, as more and more people squeezed into the bar.

Annie Hall ploughed on.

"I remember when my old man and me got married. He had his golf clubs and all his kit with him at the church. I asked him what he'd got it for. He said, well this ain't going to take all day is it?"

"I would have 'it 'im with one of 'em," advised an inebriated voice from the crowd.

"I did," said Annie, quick as a flash. "He was a bloody mess. The police asked 'ow many times I'd 'it 'im. I said put me down for a five."

"Now 'ere's one for the gents. There are four most important things that you must 'ave in a wife. A pint for anyone who gets any of 'em."

The landlord shouted his agreement and the crowd cheered loudly.

"Any offers, then?" Annie called.

"She' as to be a good cook," came a call from the front.

"A pint for that man," yelled Annie and the crowd applauded,

"She ' as to make you laugh," offered another wag.

"A pint for that man," yelled Annie and the crowd roared its agreement.

"You 'ave to be able to trust 'er," another man shouted.

"A pint for that man," yelled Annie, giving away the landlord's profits with impunity and thoroughly enjoying it.

"She's got to be good in bed," and the crowd roared its loudest approval.

Lomax & The Biker – The Trilogy

"A pint for that man," yelled Annie.

"Actually," she said, "there is another most important rule."

"We give up," bayed the crowd.

"You must make sure that the first four women never meet each other!" Annie landed the punchline.

"A pint for Annie!" screamed the crowd.

The mayhem continued around them and the group gradually relaxed and began to smile and eventually laugh. Quinn's constant supply of drinks helped eased the situation as well. Annie Hall finished her stint and departed to huge and raucous approval and the landlord announced a short break for people to replenish their glasses. He had to make up for the free drinks he had given away, after all.

"I wonder what's keeping Frank," said Leanne.

"He'll be here before long," promised Quinn.

-27-

Frank Quinn's taxi dropped him outside the City Post's magnificent building. It was way past normal working time, but various lights burned in random offices on several floors. Receptionists had been replaced by a single security guard in the entrance foyer. Frank waited for him to be occupied by a visitor and slipped past the lifts to reach the stairs. He pressed the lift button on his way past as a distraction.

Ken Harvey was not in his office and had his back to the stairs when Frank saw him. He only became aware of Frank's presence when he felt the prick of a sharp knife under his chin.

"It would not be advisable to move, my friend," said Frank, understating Harvey's predicament. "This is very sharp and my hand is not steady." The second part was a lie.

Ken Harvey froze.

"Who are you? What do you want?"

"All in good time," answered Frank. "You and I need a little chat. We should leave now, so walk calmly in front of me and be very careful; you've only got eight pints in your body, so you can't afford to lose much."

He walked the ashen and shaking Ken Harvey out of the building via the fire exit.

"Where are we going?" asked the newspaperman.

"I want to show you something," replied Frank, and he walked his man all the way to a certain drain, covered by a metal grill. "Lift it up." He commanded.

Harvey bent down and strained to remove the object. He succeeded and stood up.

"No, stay there," ordered Frank. "Tell me what you see."

Harvey stared into the black abyss as others had done before him, and just like the others before him he was very afraid.

"Anticipation is a powerful force, don't you think?" asked Frank. "Can you see anybody down there? Perhaps if I turned you upside down it would help."

He swept Harvey's legs from under him and in one swift and dextrous movement had his opponent hanging over the drain, held only by his ankles. Harvey's bladder gave up the fight.

"Oh dear, it's lucky you're over a drain. Now, Mr Harvey, you made an agreement with a friend of mine about what you would print in your rag. What was it exactly? Word for word, if you please."

"That Billy Lane was discovered dead late last night. Police are not currently looking for anyone else in connection with his death, but would like to speak to a woman who may have been at the scene, and a man who made the emergency call", whispered Harvey.

"You are very fortunate that is exactly the correct answer. Now please tell me what exactly you did print? Word for word again, if you please.

"A body was discovered late last night. It is believed to be that of Billy Lane, son of the late DCI Sandy Lane and escaped murderess Leanne Lane. Police are not currently looking for anyone else in connection with his death as a self inflicted drug overdose is suspected, but would like to speak to a woman who may have been at the scene, and a man who made the emergency call. Our editor is personally taking charge of the reporting of this story and will have more tomorrow on Billy Lane and his life history." Harvey was in severe danger of his bowels copying his bladder.

"Well done, Mr Harvey. What an excellent memory you have. Now, my arms are getting tired and I may not be able to hold you much longer. I'm afraid it's happened before. Not very professional, eh? I really must get round to doing more weight training. I don't know whether they've found him yet. Obviously not, or your paper would have known, eh?"

Harvey wriggled in desperation.

"Settle down, Mr Harvey, please. Now, let's make an agreement you WILL keep. I have written down what your paper will print tomorrow. No ifs or buts. I'll put you down now, beside the drain and you will phone it through. Word for word, if you please."

He eased Harvey onto the ground and knelt over him as the call was made. Harvey turned over and was sick into the drain.

Frank leaned over so that he was whispering into the man's ear.

"Thank you, Mr Harvey, you've been most helpful. I'm sure the entire community will be grateful. I know Mr Quinn will also be almost satisfied. I don't think Mr Noble will be pleased with your latest literary effort, though. You are in a most difficult situation. On one hand you have an unhappy Jack Noble and on the other you have an unhappy Ray Quinn. A rock and a hard place if ever I saw one. I know which way I would choose, but, hey, I'm not in your position am I?"

Ken Harvey's eyes closed in abject fear as he heard Frank's words. They bulged open again as he disappeared into the black hole and was engulfed by the rushing foul black water.

Frank calmly replaced the drain cover and stood up.

"Most unfortunate," he said to himself, "just as we were beginning to get along."

He brushed himself down and strolled to the pub to join the others. No cabbie to give evidence later. As he entered he caught Quinn's eye, and shrugged his shoulders with his palms outwards in the age old gesture.

"Welcome stranger," mocked Ray Quinn. Won't you join us? There's a pint there on the table for you."

Frank noted that there was only one pint, but two chairs.

"Is your friend not coming along?" asked Quinn, with an innocent look.

"I'm afraid he had a prior engagement," answered Frank." He's had to pop along to interview some bigwig from the water company. He did ask me to give you this, though Ray. He said it would be on the front page tomorrow."

Lomax & The Biker – The Trilogy

He passed Quinn the statement that was due to be published the next morning. Quinn scanned it and smiled his quiet smile. Jack Noble would not be pleased, he mused, which made him smile all the more.

Quinn suggested the group return to the flat as he had some news. When they were all sitting comfortably he read the statement.

"The City Post's front page tomorrow will carry the following in bold print.

"A body was discovered late last night. It is believed to be that of Billy Lane, son of the late DCI Sandy Lane and Leanne Lane. Police wish to speak to well known local businessman Jack Noble (pictured) in order to eliminate him from their enquiries. The public is warned not to approach him. Readers are asked to contact the police if they see him."

Quinn looked at each of his group in turn. He paid particular attention to Charlene.

"That's it. From now on, it's up to us. I will catch up with him, I promise, and he will pay."

Both Frank and John Lomax drew breath as one. They, more than anybody, knew what such a Ray Quinn promise meant.

"I suggest we all turn in for the night. It's been an eventful day and I think tomorrow will be even more, how shall I put it, interesting," said Quinn in a tone that nobody challenged.

-28-

By eleven o'clock, most of them had taken themselves to bed for the night, but Quinn remained in the living room going back over the details of the situation again and again, trying to find something, anything, that would prove a link to Jack Noble.

Frank appeared in the doorway.

"Bugger off," said Quinn, only half joking. "I'm trying to think."

Frank ignored him. "You might want to hear this," he said. "The women's refuge just phoned. They've had a woman show up there in a bit of a state. They don't think she's on booze or drugs, but the description fits Charlene. I asked them to keep her there. Here's a strange thing though. Those places don't normally allow men on the premises, but when I gave them your name their attitude changed. They said you could go in provided you brought a woman with you."

"It's a long story Frank, and I can't tell you about it because I swore to the people concerned that I wouldn't. You know how it is; if you need to keep a secret, don't tell another living soul. I'll have to go and Leanne will have to come with me. You stay here in case anything else comes up."

Quinn swept from the room and banged loudly on John and Leanne's door. "Leanne, I need you. I need you now. Stop whatever you're doing and hurry up. We have to go out."

Quinn was in a rush and had no time for niceties. Leanne poked her head round the door and looked at him questioningly.

"You choose your moments, don't you?" she said.

"Never mind about that," he barked. Get dressed and come with me. You've got one minute and no more."

She rushed from the bedroom five seconds after her deadline.

"Now, what on earth is so important?" she demanded.

"I'll tell you on the way," said Quinn as he pushed her out of the door and towards the car. "Get in; come on, hurry up."

He started the engine and began to move almost before she had settled into her seat.

"The women's refuge has phoned. They think they may have Charlene down there. I need a woman with me or they won't let me in. You've been elected."

"Does the fact that I'm the only female around have anything to do with it?" she asked tartly.

"I like your company," responded Quinn, meaning exactly the opposite.

He made sure he didn't attract any unwanted attention from roaming police vehicles, but still drove very quickly. They arrived at the refuge and Leanne pressed the intercom.

"Ray Quinn and Leanne Lane to see the manageress," she announced, putting her lips close to the microphone set into the wall.

There was a buzz and the heavily reinforced door, having decided to let them in, opened slowly. Waiting at the desk in the entrance hall with the manageress was a loudly protesting Charlene. She was filthy and her clothes stank, but Quinn wanted to hug her.

He walked straight up to her and, placing a firm, comforting hand on each shoulder looked directly into her eyes. He made sure she was looking at him before saying, "Billy is exhausted, so we left him asleep. He's Ok though. I had to bring Leanne with me because the people here insist on a woman being with you."

Leanne's lower lip trembled at the dishevelled and desperate state of the mother of her grandchild. "Hi Charlene," was all she could manage.

Quinn could see she was holding back tears. "She needs a doctor," he said.

"If you can wait a few minutes, we can get our on call GP to give her the once over," the manageress offered.

"No," Leanne said with unnecessary rudeness. "Her own doctor will do that. Come on, Charlene, let's go."

The manageress watched them leave the refuge and was puzzled by Leanne's curtness. She was, however, pleased with the outcome. There would be one less troubled woman in her care that night. She put her hands in her pockets, ready to prepare for the long night ahead. Her right hand found something and she rushed to the door in pursuit of the leavers. Ray Quinn turned round at the sound of her approach and took a couple of steps towards her. It was enough to take him out of the earshot of the others.

"I almost forgot," said the manageress," I found this in Charlene's coat pocket."

She handed him a mobile phone. He closed his hand round it and touched her fingers at the same time. She couldn't help herself as she self-consciously blushed.

"Thank you," he said, pressing her hand in return. "I mean thank you for what you've done for her," he said. I'm glad it was you who called."

"No problem, she replied. "I'm glad it was you who came. It's good to see you again. Sorry about having to bring a woman, but it would have looked very strange if we had ignored the usual protocol."

"I understand," he replied. "Keep in touch."

"I will," she whispered as he turned to take his leave.

"You make an impression wherever you go," said Leanne acidly.

"It's a gift," he replied, "or a curse. It depends."

Leanne chose not to pursue the topic.

"You said we've got our own GP," said Quinn. "Who do you have in mind?"

"Well," she offered, "I thought that doctor at Priory Place seemed sympathetic and helpful, but I think we should clean her up first."

Charlene and Leanne fell asleep in the back of the car even though it was a short journey and they had to be woken when Quinn stopped outside the flat. Charlene was so groggy that she didn't even protest when Leanne put her under the shower, and afterwards she munched her way slowly through almost a whole pizza while Leanne put a call through to the doctor. Inevitably, all she got was the after- hours answering service, but moments later the doctor himself called her back. With some difficulty, Leanne explained what had happened. The doctor was typically unfazed and full of sympathy.

"And how are you," he asked solicitously.

Leanne was struck by the thought that when a patient enters a doctor's surgery she is often greeted with the words "how are you today?" She had always thought that a stupid question because if the patient was well, she would have no need to attend the surgery in the first place. She had often been tempted to reply "I'm well, but I thought I'd drop in and ask about you." It would be far better for the doctor to ask "what can I do for you today?" In fact, she mused that would be a good name for a doctor's quiz team. She was somewhat taken aback by his kindness, but was pleased as well.

She restricted herself to "Fine thank you. A little tired, but nothing too bad. It's Charlene I'm called about. We've just been called to pick her up from the women's refuge and she's a mess. We wondered if you'd take a look at her."

"Bring her to Priory Place and I'll meet you there," he replied. "I'll let them know you're on your way."

"I appreciate that," said Leanne, thank you."

She put the phone down and looked at Quinn, who had heard everything. She knew she had been pretty unpleasant to him and her anxiety about Billy and Charlene had compounded the feeling, but he didn't really deserve to be treated badly. After all he done for Lomax and the rest of them, she felt very guilty about her own responses to him. She must apologise and resolved to do it later when Charlene was settled.

"Frank will take you," instructed Quinn. "I have something I must attend to here."

Leanne wondered whether he was stepping back to give her time with Charlene. She also thought he may be giving her the space to formulate a proper apology. In fact his reason was much more down to earth. He had been thinking of the encounter with the manageress at the refuge. She had been trying to tell him something without using the words and he needed to find out what it was. He had a feeling, a gut feeling, that he was being told something about Leanne. He always trusted his gut feelings and he saw no reason to change its tried and tested success rate.

Quinn took Frank aside into the kitchen. "I think it would be a good idea if you let Leanne take the lead with this," Quinn said to Frank. "It might be better coming from a woman, and besides, I want you to take careful note of her throughout. There's something wrong here. We'll talk when you get back."

"No problems," replied Frank. He knew that when Ray Quinn had instincts about something he was invariably correct.

"Is everything ok here?"

"Fine."

Leanne sat in the back with Charlene on the way to Priory Place. Nothing was said at all, but the silence was comfortable.

They were let in almost immediately after Frank had pressed the buzzer by the doctor in person.

"So, how's the patient?"

"Ok, we think," she replied, "but very quiet. Silent in fact."

"Do you recognise the doctor?" asked Leanne.

Charlene had already seen who it was and was suddenly animated again. In fact Frank saw sheer abject terror on her face.

"No! No! No! No!" she shouted, backing away from the doctor hastily.

Leanne was stunned. Charlene was obviously more traumatised than she'd realised.

"Charlene! It's all right. It's Dr Boyle, Charlene. He's your friend." She tried to reassure her, casting the doctor an apologetic smile. "I told you. She's all over the place." After a few minutes, she managed to calm Charlene by fetching her a drink.

Dr Boyle dismissed Charlene's reaction with his customary understanding. "She's been through a lot. It's not at all surprising that she should be reminded of the ordeal. It might help if I prescribe you something to help her sleep, just for a few nights, until she's back into normal routine again."

Sitting down at a table in the hallway, he took out his prescription pad and pen and scribbled down something. "Now, let's go and have a look at her." This time Charlene remained passive while Leanne helped the doctor listen to her chest.

Leanne's mobile buzzed into life. "I'll take it in the hallway," she said, to minimise disruption. It was Ray Quinn.

"Hello, how's it going?" he enquired.

"All right, thanks." Now that he was on the line, Leanne didn't know quite what to say to him. "Look, I wanted to.." but as she spoke something caught her eye. Something embossed in gold on the leather case of Dr Boyle's prescription pad: JAN, the capital letters all interlinked. That was interesting. Leanne's mind raced, as she grappled to achieve some kind of coherency to the invading thoughts.

"Are you all right, Leanne?" Quinn asked from the other end of the line.

"Yes," Leanne said, immediately distracted by further unease in her brain. Why was the doctor so helpful, so solicitous? He was only a duty doctor after all. Granted he was attached to Priory Place, but it was above and beyond the call of duty to come out here at night at such short notice, wasn't it? Why had Charlene reacted so strongly when she saw him? Leanne shivered violently as understanding took shape.

"I've got to go," she said suddenly. "The doctor is examining Charlene."

"Okay," said Quinn, uncertainly. "We'll keep in touch."

She could sense his confusion at the other end of the line but she had to give herself time to think this through. There would be a reasonable, rational explanation for everything. All she had to do was ask.

"Dr Boyle," Leanne walked back into the lounge, but unexpectedly the doctor and Charlene weren't there. She went through to the bathroom. "Charlene, Dr Boyle," she called out, bewildered. She returned to the examination room and, finding it empty, she rushed back out into the hallway. What the hell was happening? Then she noticed that the door to the stairwell was slightly ajar. She was lucky to have seen it, because it normally banged closed as it was pulled shut by its spring. Struggling to quell a rising panic, Leanne rushed through the closing door and sprinted up the stairs, her fears beginning to crystalise. This late at night everything was deathly quiet and there was no one around. Her blood ran cold.

"No," she gasped out loud. Charlene!"

Leanne burst through the front door onto the roof to see Charlene and Dr Boyle standing by the waist height railings, like a couple of old friends admiring the view. The doctor turned towards her.

"Leanne," he said, mildly, stretching out a beckoning hand, "why don't you join us?"

Leanne walked slowly towards them.

"What's going on? What are you doing?" she asked, hoarsely, her voice barely audible even to her own ears as she struggled to regain her breathing.

"Surely you must have already worked that out, Leanne, "the doctor smiled. "I'm protecting myself. I have to make sure that no one will ever know."

She was chilled to the marrow. Her misgivings were right.

"I can help you," she said, realising how feeble it sounded.

-29-

As weird phone calls went, that one was off the scale, thought Quinn. Leanne hadn't completed her sentence when she was interrupted by something. He had the feeling she was about to apologise for something, but couldn't. Then there was the manageress at the refuge. She had definitely been trying to tell him something. Perhaps he was wrong. Perhaps his gut instinct had let him down for the first time or were these disparate and seemingly unlinked pieces of a jigsaw coming together? The last few days had been a hell of a strain on them all. He was exhausted. He couldn't do this anymore. He needed a drink and to sleep for a very long time.

His mobile prevented any of that.

"Frank?" said Quinn.

"Get here now!" barked Frank.

He knew his ally well enough. Grabbing his helmet, forgoing his leathers, Ray Quinn roared into the black night.

At the same time the doctor was talking to Leanne.

"I don't want your help. I only want to square my account with John Lomax. It's unfortunate that you're here, but I can't get to him except through you. In fact, to hell with it; all of you deserve what's coming. You're all the same."

In the white glow cast by the floodlights his face took on the grotesque appearance of a gargoyle.

"'What can you hope to do?" Leanne said, finding sudden strength. "I'm not here alone, you know that. The man with me won't let you get away with it and Ray Quinn's on his way. You know what he can do, don't you? If anything happens to us I would not want to be in your shoes."

The doctor smiled grotesquely. "It will be an accident. They'll understand. It's the kind of thing that could have occurred at any time, especially now, when Charlene is so traumatised."

"What accident? What are you talking about?"

But even as she spoke, Leanne knew.

"How far would you go, Leanne? How far would you really go for Charlene? Or John Lomax? Or the little boy? Charlene's not blood is she, Leanne? Billy was but she'll get the little boy, so you won't see much of your grandchild anyway. The child needs his mother. You need to make the sacrifice for his sake. That would be a noble thing, Leanne, wouldn't it?" he coaxed her by using her name over and over again, as he took a step nearer to the edge.

Ray Quinn's mind was racing' at a speed that was equal to his bike.

'Christ, I can't believe I didn't see it before. It's been there all the time, staring us right in the face!' The streets were steady with traffic even at this time in the evening, but with enough slack for the machine to make rapid progress. He dreaded what he would find. "Please God, let me not be too late," he murmured under his breath.

He roared into the drive and sprayed gravel and grit everywhere as he slammed on the brakes. His eyes searched for clues. He forced himself to rely on his training, his experience. He saw the BMW and noticed the car beside it.

"And there it is," he said to himself.

There was even a 'Doctor on call' sign resting audaciously on the dashboard.

"On the roof, Ray," called Frank, but Quinn only partially heard him as he ran.

"Don't let anyone out of this building until I say you can," Quinn shouted back over his shoulder.

He used the run up the stairs as thinking time. It had been quite a while since he had experienced any action such as this and he forced himself to think clearly. The doctor's car was the clue. He had seen it before, but where?

The roof garden was beautiful. An effort had been made to create a soothing green oasis away from the stress of city living. But in the light of the horror unfolding before her it had become monstrous and ugly. Leanne was exhausted and part of her just wanted this over. She wanted to close her eyes and for this to end. But she had to keep Dr Boyle talking. If he let go of Charlene now, it would be disastrous. But she needn't have worried. The last couple of days had reaped one advantage at least, and Charlene was clinging to the doctor like a leech.

The doctor was still cajoling, coaxing. "Believe me, I don't want to hurt you or Charlene. It's Lomax I want. He owes me money and nobody gets away with that. I can't get to him, so it has to be like this."

He was sickening. Leanne couldn't imagine now how she'd even liked the man. Beads of sweat had broken out on the doctor's upper lip. Leanne was close enough now to see them glistening in the light.

"How many have died?" she asked. "How many have died at your hands? You may not have killed them yourself, but the drugs you put on the streets did. You're sick! No, you're repulsive."

Charlene moaned and wriggled at his side.

"She's getting bored," he said. "We should get this over with."

Leanne wouldn't let it go. Why should she make it easy for him?

"It's simple," she heard him say. "It's your decision. Charlene or you? I'm going, but who with?"

"How do I know that you won't let Charlene fall anyway? Why should I trust anything you say?"

"That's your choice, of course. But you're her only chance, Leanne." The doctor relinquished his grasp slightly and Charlene struggled to wrench herself free.

"Wait!" Leanne blurted, desperately. "I'll do it. You don't have to hurt her. She won't give you away. Look, I'll do it."

Feeling suddenly weightless with fear, her legs shaking almost uncontrollably, Leanne stepped up on to the first and then second rung of the railings. The doctor watched, urging her on with his eyes. She glanced below to where the city streets swayed and blurred. So this was how her life would end, in ultimate, futile sacrifice.

"Leanne, stop!" Another voice rang out over the roof and with overwhelming relief she recognised it as Quinn's. "You don't have to,' he said. "It's over. Walk away from the edge, doctor, and bring Charlene with you."

Everyone on the rooftop froze.

"It's the only sensible thing, doctor," Quinn continued, persuasively. "You can't win this. We know what you've done. We've just heard your confession. You have nothing to gain by this now. There's nowhere else to go."

For what seemed an eternity nothing happened as the doctor hesitated, weighing up his situation. Leanne halted, poised on the precipice. Seconds ticked by, everything deathly silent, but for the background hum of an ignorant city amplified by the light rain that had begun to fall. Then miraculously the doctor began, inch by inch, to move back across the roof towards Ray Quinn. For a moment it looked as if he would comply, until suddenly, as Leanne's foot touched back down on the roof, he shoved Charlene to one side, turned and lunged for the railings.

Frank had disobeyed his friend's instructions and was by now also on the roof. Quinn yelled at him to stay put as Charlene, panicked by the sudden activity started running towards the outer edge of the roof.

"No! Leanne screamed. Quinn took a flying leap at Charlene, bringing them both crashing heavily onto the concrete, but for the doctor it was too late. Frank, trained by Ray Quinn in the forces, obeyed the command instantly and without question. He watched with detachment as the doctor hurled himself over the edge to certain death.

Retaining a tight hold on Charlene's clothes, Quinn got to his feet and walked over to where Leanne stood, dazed and shaking. By the time he reached her, Frank had put a protective arm around her.

"Come on," suggested Quinn, "let's get off here."

The men shielded the women's eyes as they skirted around the mutilated body of the doctor. Frank loaded his precious human cargo into the BMW whilst Quinn prepared to mount his bike. They returned to the flat in convoy. When they arrived John Lomax was there to hug and kiss his loved one and Charlene. He had ordered yet another Chinese takeaway and it didn't last long even though nobody professed to being hungry. It was the shared experience of a communal meal that was important.

"What made you come back tonight?' Leanne asked. "Was it my phone call?"

Quinn was tired and sore. "Don't flatter yourself," he answered. "Your call certainly got me wondering. But when we picked Charlene up from the refuge, the manageress gave me a mobile phone she found in her clothing. I traced the calls on it. One of the names that featured on it regularly was a Dr Boyle. Two plus two make four.

"Not bad for a beginner. Thanks for showing up," she said, unable to prevent sarcasm spilling out.

Quinn put a hand to his heart and mocked her. "Ouch," he said.

"I was trying to say I'm sorry, I've been a bitch."

"Well, the last few days haven't been much fun, for you have they? Although I must say, I've enjoyed myself. But if you want to make it up to me you could spend the rest of your days keeping out of trouble and looking after John. I want a quiet life from now on and I want to spend time with my wife." Quinn announced.

Leanne smiled her agreement, but couldn't stop herself from making one last comment.

"That shirt's a mistake by the way, she said, grinning from ear to ear. "I'm not sure that the bloodstain effect really works."

Quinn glanced down at where blood had seeped through the fabric. "My wife's going to love that," he said, "but she knows I've no eye for fashion."

The following morning their final arrangements were settled. Lomax and Quinn had already had a long discussion which resulted in the arrangements that were now outlined to everybody. John Lomax and Leanne returned home to run the jewellery shop, the business buoyed by a substantial boost. Charlene, her small son and her parents were put on a cruise ship at Southampton to take the slow route back to Australia. There was no way she could face being trapped in a flying tube. Her bank account had been injected with sufficient funds to open a jewellery shop, as part of the growing family empire. The business partnership would ensure they all got together as regularly as possible, but not enough to fall out. Nobody dare argue with any of it. The last detail was that Frank agreed to take over Quinn's role as protector of one and all. He knew he would be kept busy for the foreseeable future.

They stood together in the living room before Quinn was due to leave. He was already dressed in his full leather biking gear and held his helmet in his left hand. There was a prolonged silence as each didn't know quite what to say.

"I'm curious," John Lomax eventually broke the embarrassment, "we've got all this money, we've split it up and you don't seem bothered about Jack Noble. In fact you've not mentioned him since we got back last night. How can we be sure it's all over?"

"Where do I start?" teased Quinn. Firstly, the prescription pad bore the initials JAN. They stand for John Anthony Noble. Secondly, the other car at Priory Place had a 'doctor on call' notice in the windscreen. Two and two make four. Finally, I knew he was Jack Noble anyway."

"But how? Lomax asked.

"That's none of your business," replied Ray Quinn enigmatically, as he turned and strode out through the door. They had shaken hands firmly earlier and their mutual friendship had been recognised. It would remain unchanged. He hated goodbyes, anyway.

Outside, the rain had turned into a steady downpour. Frank turned up his collar ineffectually against the torrent and walked into town to flag a taxi. He also hated goodbyes. Ray Quinn, still

Lomax & The Biker – The Trilogy

sore from his cuts and abrasions, sat astride his bike and gingerly coaxed it out into the traffic.

-30-

Ray Quinn drove with skill and care. He was enjoying the warming sun which was pouring though the car's panoramic window. His wife sat beside him and let the scenery unroll before her.

"Do you remember the last time we went to Exmoor?" she asked, looking across at her newly reclaimed husband.

"Of course, my love. It's gorgeous there," he replied, wondering what was coming next.

"I think I'm going to buy a horse and go for long rides," she said wistfully.

"Well don't expect me to come with you. Damn things are evil. I prefer to be in control of what I sit on, thank you very much. I'm not going anywhere near something that's got four legs, has a mind of its own, has sharp metal on the end of its legs and is that big. I'll stick to my bike. Oh, by the way, you did pack that copy of T.S Eliot didn't you? I'm going to become intellectual," he grinned.

"Of course I did."

Quinn hoped she would consider the subject closed and concentrated on driving the car.

Silence prevailed for many miles as the car carried the happy couple towards their new beginning.

"Raymond," she said, after a suitably long silence.

Quinn was immediately alert. She only ever used his full name when there was a problem. His mother used to do a similar thing just before telling him off. She never lost the habit, even when he had fully grown into adulthood. There's something about mothers, he thought.

"Raymond," she repeated, "this is all very nice and I know we are going to have a peaceful time living on Exmoor, but is this really the end of it all?"

"What do you mean," he asked warily.

"I mean what I said. Have you really retired? Is this the end of you solving the world's problems by yourself? Can you actually switch off now?" she continued.

"Which question would you like me to answer first?" he teased.

"Don't be obtuse," she replied rather sharply. "Have I got you all to myself from now on or not?"

Ray Quinn let silence fill the car again. The passing breeze was barely discernible and he caressed the steering wheel as he guided the car round a bend. A pheasant wandered across the road in front of him and seemed unconcerned by the possibility of imminent death.

"Stupid things, pheasants," said Quinn, pleased that he had avoided the meandering bird. He had also avoided giving his wife an answer and he knew she had noticed.